John Masters was born in Calcutta in 1914.
Educated at Wellington and Sandhurst, he
returned to India in 1934 to join the 4th Prince
of Wales' Own Gurkha Rifles. In 1944 he
commanded a brigade of General Wingate's
Chindits in Burma, and later fought with the 19th
Indian Division at the capture of Mandalay.

Masters retired from the army in 1948 as a
lieutenant colonel with the DSO and OBE. He
went to America and turned to writing. Several
short stories were succeeded by *Nightrunners of
Bengal*, the first of an outstanding series of novels
set in British India. His most recent books are
*Now, God Be Thanked, Heart of War, By the
Green of the Spring*, a highly-acclaimed trilogy of
the Great War, and *Man of War*, all available
from Sphere Books.

John Masters died in 1983 in New Mexico.

The Venus of Konpara

JOHN MASTERS

SPHERE BOOKS LIMITED
London and Sydney

First published in Great Britain by
Michael Joseph Ltd 1960
Copyright © 1960 by Bengal-Rockland Inc
Published by Sphere Books Ltd 1985
30–32 Gray's Inn Road, London WC1X 8JL

**TRADE
MARK**

This book is sold subject to the condition that it shall not, by
way of trade or otherwise, be lent, re-sold, hired out or
otherwise circulated without the publisher's prior consent in
any form of binding or cover other than that in which it is
published and without a similar condition including this
condition being imposed on the subsequent purchaser.

Set in 9/9½ pt English Compugraphic

Printed and bound in Great Britain by
Collins, Glasgow

UPPER PLATEA

KONPARA CLIFFS

Rainbow
Falls

Buddha
Tumulus

Tiger
Pool
Bund

Inlet

Tiger
Pool

KONPARA RIDGE

Rest House

Southdo

Underground
Conduit

DOBEHARI RIDGE

Cheltona

INDRA'S ROCK

Outlet

Sc

Indra's Rock
Tumulus

THE PIT CLIFFS

THI

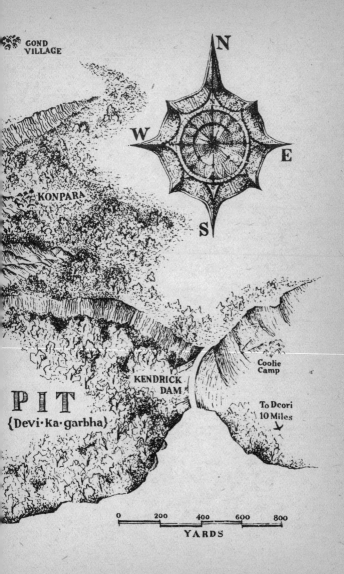

Sulvala-Gita

Chapter One

Coming up out of the south on the wings of a hawk, we see the land rising below. A long rocky slope runs away to the right. Here it is split by a narrow chasm, the only exit from a vast, irregular pit. Cliffs of reddish rock ring the pit on all sides, and beyond them the land is folded into a long ridge, and another, and so up to the rolling highlands in the north.

There is jungle everywhere but the trees are not tall, nor are they densely spaced, for it is a dry country and a rocky soil. Some water there is – small lakes on the upland, and from them a river winding among the rock and the bamboo, here brilliant under the sun, here dim and green under trees. Before it reaches the pit the river plunges over a steep place and seems to vanish, for the forested ridges hide it.

The heat of the sun, burning away the thin vapours of the night, creates a steady south wind. The wind blows over the jungle, up the ridges, and up the steep, against the falling water. The river curves over the red stone lip in a full sensuous curve, and meets the wind. Immediately it begins to waver, to lose shape and substance, to evanesce, almost to vanish behind a wide curtain of mist. The sun shines on the mist and from it creates the second of the two signs that mark this place as immediately different from any others that pass under the hawk's wings: a vivid rainbow spans the sky above the fall as long as the wind blows and the sun shines. The rainbow and the pit, and a barren rock upstanding on the edge of the pit, define this place, more than any name.

There are men on the land. One collection of their dwelling-places crouches on a ridge below the fall, near the rainbow's end; another on the upland, around a reed-rimmed lake. The men know whether the lower village has yet been named Konpara, but the hawk does not, nor does the pair of sarus cranes dancing among the reeds. Here, what is not known to all creation is not of importance; nor does time have any real existence or definition, and five thousand years are not to be understood as different from the rainbow. Like it, they come and go; but remain.

1

In other parts of the earth, even in other parts of this sub-continent called India, one element is clearly the master, the others its servants. There are deserts where rock and sand luxuriate without effort, but plants and animals use their whole force merely to exist. There are plains where the animals have taken possession and roam free in huge herds; but no vegetation lives except that which the animals need, and man is an intruder whose planted fields the elephants destroy and the bison trample upon. There are valleys where it is man, and man alone, who belongs; all is his, the stacked corn, the channelled stream, and the pollarded willows, the beaten paths and the tamed beasts that follow them, uncalled, to the milking byre.

Here, by the pit and the rock and the rainbow, there is no master and no servant but a unique harmony where man, animal, plant, and rock are parts of a single entity. The relationships between them overlap and intertwine, so that there is a closer bond between the tiger and the man than between the man and another man from another place. There are carvings on rock here. They show man and woman, and the curved neck and soft eyes of the bull between them, a garland round his neck and the woman's hand resting on his horns; the monkey watching from the twisted bough above and the leopard watching from the denser forest behind. No house exists, or was made, as a device to separate man from rock, air, and tree, but rather to fuse them closer to his needs. The creepers twine alike up the rock wall that man builds and the rock wall that was standing there when he came.

It is a harmony of change, of creation, preservation, and destruction – not of peace. A child lies dead outside the ruined shrine, and the cobra watches from a crevice while the mother mourns. The rock falls from the cliff, split by the sun and rain of a million years, and the bull (Is he yet sacred? He does not know) dies under it. Fear is an element of the harmony of this place; but not fear of the unknown, for everything is known – the mark of cholera, the way of a falling rock, the nature of a tiger, and the exact appearance of evil (sometimes in animal shape, sometimes human, but well known, and feared).

This is Konpara, seen out of time.

Chapter Two

Near five o'clock in the afternoon of March 31, 1890, a young man walked slowly along a path near the rim of the pit. He was tall, slender, and large of eye, the mouth voluptuous but not weak, the hair shiny black and long, the skin a golden-brown wheat colour. He wore white flannel trousers and a striped red and white blazer and carried, rolled up in his hand, a towel and a small 'triangle,' such as young Englishmen wore to go swimming when no ladies would be present. He walked slowly, head down, with a vaguely oppressed hunch to his shoulders, swinging the rolled towel like a club.

Something caught his eye ahead, among the trees. He saw an easel, a folding canvas stool beside it. He made out, also, the pale lilac of a woman's skirt arranged in the shade, beside the easel.

Barbara Kendrick. She had not been here when he went to the pool an hour and a half ago. He began to creep away to the left, meaning to pass her before she became aware of his presence.

He stopped. Perhaps she was hurt. Perhaps the sun had affected her. In any case, he could not avoid her for ever. He walked directly towards her, the dried teak leaves crackling under his shoes.

The skirt moved, and the woman rose quickly to her feet. She was about thirty, tall and boyish in figure, the lips surprisingly full and generous in the long face. Her eyes were pale blue, her hair thick and brown – usually in disarray, as now. Her complexion had been good, but the Indian sun had affected it. The hands she raised to adjust her hair were strong and square.

'Oh,' she said, 'Mohan. It's you. How nice to see you again.'

'It's only a week,' he said, attempting a light tone. He looked at the painting on the easel. A water-colour of the pit which yawned below them. Quite pretty, though she had somehow managed to turn the lowering red cliffs of the opposite wall into a gentler slope, and soften the rolling jungle into a sweep of English woodland.

She said, 'I spent all morning getting Southdown ready for the hot weather. I'm always glad to get out of Deori. Aren't you? Mr

Kendrick went over into the Betwa Hills. Something to do with a deer the Gonds have reported.' She began to unpin the painting from the easel. 'But he's back now . . . We must continue the sittings for your portrait. You look even more handsome out here than you do in Deori. You must give me plenty of your time.'

She kept her eyes on the easel and the slow business of unpinning the water-colour. The forwardness of English women had astonished and at first shocked Mohan, especially when he reached Sandhurst after the monastic atmosphere of his public school. But those tall girls in the great London drawing-rooms, those youngish married ladies in the salons of Belgravia, had spoken such sentences with an insolent assurance that left you to guess whether or not their words had any ulterior motive. Barbara Kendrick's manner was not insolent. It was pleading, and carried a message of availability that no one but a fool could miss.

It had begun as soon as he returned from England, just before Christmas, after seven years in England. And this was Mr Kendrick's wife. The wife of the man who had been more a father to him than his own father. Mr Kendrick was more than a father. He was a friend.

To change the subject he said, 'Whatever happened to that portrait of Mr Kendrick you were doing when I came back from Sandhurst? That was . . . well, it was so different from anything else you've ever done.'

'Oh,' she said in a flat voice, 'that got lost.' She went on quickly, 'Tomorrow, about ten o'clock, at Southdown? Good!'

She was gone, without giving him an opportunity to speak. He walked slowly on along the edge of the pit towards Cheltondale. The portrait he had mentioned was both terrible and wonderful, and he had an idea that if Mr Kendrick knew about it he would hate it. It did not look at all like him, yet it did; or, it looked like a nightmare someone might have had about him. Once seen, you could never forget it. How could it have got lost?

The path rose gradually now towards the foursquare bungalow. Mr Kendrick had had it built last year for him – for the Rajah of Deori, he corrected himself quickly. He himself had named it 'Cheltondale' on his return from England. The name seemed wrong now, and strangely defiant, like Mr Kendrick's own 'Southdown.' But after all Mr Kendrick was English.

On his left here, fifty yards from the bungalow, the earth was raw and all the trees and bushes had been cut down over a space of about forty yards by twenty. The contours were in the process of being flattened by digging into the upper slope and filling in the lower. The labourers had finished work for the day and returned to Konpara, leaving the usual mess of earth-carrying baskets, frayed rope, broken tools, betel-juice stains, and the rank smell of bidi cigarettes. This was going to be his cricket pitch – not a complete field, just the length of a pitch, round which there would be a net. Here he could practise his bowling. No one ever became good at anything except by hard practice, as Mr Kendrick had often told him, not to mention the masters at Cheltenham and the instructors at Sandhurst.

He went on up the path, crossed the lawn and entered the bungalow.

A little after five. He felt restless. Nothing to do . . . yes, there was. Mr Kendrick had asked him to prepare a paper on the reorganisation of the Deori army. All thirty men. He had worked two hours on that last night, and then it became ridiculous. Thirty men, for the army of the Suvala, who could trace his line back to the God Indra . . . Thirty men, for a potty little Indian principality which not more than five of his Sandhurst fellow cadets had ever heard of.

He might send for the dishwasher, whom he'd been teaching cricket, and spend half an hour at the slip-catching cradle. But it wasn't here. One of the lathes was broken and had not yet been repaired. That was India, everywhere the same, ramshackle, nothing ever finished, nothing maintained or looked after when it was! The great dam down there, across the narrow mouth of the pit, now near completion, would suffer the same fate. So Mr Kendrick believed, in his heart of hearts.

Standing in the window of the big drawing-room Mohan saw a portly old gentleman in traditional Rajput costume riding eastward along the path below the unfinished cricket pitch. It was the City Warden of Deori, a distant connection of his family's. He must have been reporting to Mr Kendrick, and was now starting on the ten-mile ride back to Deori. Yes, there were a couple of liveried servants riding a respectful distance behind him.

Mohan hurried across the room, ran down the verandah steps, and then slowed to a stroll. Now the old man could hardly pass without speaking.

The City Warden came past, saw Mohan, and at once began to slide off his horse. One of the servants trotted forward to take the reins. The old man stooped to touch Mohan's knee with his right hand. 'My lord,' he said submissively, 'are you well?'

'I am well,' Mohan said. The Hindi came more easily now, as easily as when he was a child. For the first two months after his return from England he had spoken as badly as a mem-sahib; and the language itself had seemed barbarous and awkward to his tongue.

'I have been making a routine report to the Honourable Resident and Administrator,' the old man said.

Mohan waited. The other knew well that he wanted to know the substance of the report.

The City Warden said, 'Your uncle, the noble Prithwi Narain Suvala, returned yesterday from Calcutta, where he had the honour of seeing the Viceroy.'

Mohan waited. Eastern diplomacy, oriental deviousness . . . Before he went to England the obliqueness of the old man's method would have seemed quite natural. Prithwi was a younger brother of his father.

The City Warden said, 'It is known from another source that the Viceroy told your noble uncle that he would decide the case here on its merits, as reported to him by his Agent. Who will decide as reported to him by Mr Kendrick.'

'Prithwi's finished then,' Mohan said slowly. 'That was his last card.'

The old man nodded. 'The last he held . . . but the sun rises each day, my lord, and each day the Almighty deals a new hand. Your noble uncle will search the more desperately for an opportunity to prove that you are unfitted to rule. If he does not find one, he will try to create one. You are young . . .'

'Twenty,' Mohan snapped. 'And don't keep saying that. Mr Kendrick does; everybody does. I'm tired of it.'

The old man was contrite. 'I apologise most humbly . . . I mean only that your uncle will hope that some impetuousness, some violence in your lordship's hot-blooded nature, can be used to create the situation he seeks. But I think he will fail. You are up here. He is down there. The city and the state are calm. Mr Kendrick has, I am sure, made up his own mind in your lordship's favour.'

'If Prithwi succeeds,' Mohan said, 'he will not appoint Mr Kendrick as Prime Minister.'

The old man said smoothly, 'Nor, in that case, would Mr Kendrick resign from the Indian Civil Service. He would remain here – as Resident. . . . I do not think your lordship needs to worry, merely preserve watchfulness and – ah – decorum . . . The invitation to the Deputy Commissioner of Saugor was sent off by registered post today.'

'Good,' Mohan said absently. He had determined to make Deori famous as a cricket centre. When he succeeded to the gaddi, the cushion which was the Indian symbol of rule, Deori would have three or four cricket festivals a season. Club teams would come, regimental teams, pick-up teams such as the one he was inviting now, from the Gentlemen of Saugor.

The City Warden was humbly begging his permission to proceed on his way. 'Go, in peace,' Mohan said.

Soon he was alone. The land sloped down from the limit of the rough lawn to the edge of the pit. The low sun slanted a yellow and pink light across the farther cliffs, but the new dam was out of sight to the left. To the right, Indra's Rock stood bleak on the cliff edge. Farther right again, the Deori River fell down the Konpara Cliffs but the wind had died with the sinking sun and there was no rainbow. The bats were coming out and the men going home, the villagers from their little fields, the aboriginal Gonds from their hunting of snakes and lizards. The wild animals would be stretching and yawning, ready to step out into the evening.

All settled, then. On his twenty-first birthday her Majesty the Queen-Empress would announce her assent. Mr Kendrick, with permission, would resign from the Indian Civil Service and become his Prime Minister. Deori would prosper. There would be better roads, new schools, the dam down there finished, another one started the other side of the state. The cricket festivals would begin. Deori would look and feel like Cheltenham.

And that was what he wanted?

Yes, of course! The sanitation in the state was appalling, the poverty terrible. Mr Kendrick was the best man for the job. But he must have failed in Gwalior, or he wouldn't have been sent to finish his service in a little place like Deori.

It was a lie! In Gwalior, Mr Kendrick had been betrayed. Then why did he himself not repel Barbara Kendrick's advances? It could only lead to one end. A terrible scandal, and Kendrick leaving. He thought of her long legs. The flatness of her stomach. The hidden mysteries. Her white skin.

He jumped up and went to the desk in the corner, unlocked a drawer, and drew out a packet of postcards. A man had sold them to him outside the Gare de Lyon in Paris on his way back to India. He studied them. A fat woman wearing corsets, high-buttoned boots, and nothing else lounged over a high-backed chair. A man in long underwear, with a walrus moustache, approached her. The series showed the two in poses of lust, and finally coupling. It was all grotesquely ugly – the people, the costumes, the attitudes. But these were the attitudes of the temple carvings. As a boy he had thought nothing of them. He had been to the temple only a week ago. There the stone lovers moved gracefully, their nakedness of desire expressed joy, there was beauty in the expansive generosity of the bodies.

He put the postcards away and strode rapidly up and down the room. He would have to get married. He was years late already,

7

according to the ideas of his own religion. The City Warden had an idea that might be sound – to marry his Uncle Prithwi's daughter. His first cousin. A dynastic marriage. Why not?

But love, the Western love, the romantic love he had come to understand though not yet to experience – he must have that. And the Indian love, the totality of the carvings, where spiritual and physical love became one, he must know that, too.

The major-domo knocked on the door and entered, carrying a lighted lamp which he placed carefully on a table in the corner. Other servants followed with other lamps and soon the big room glowed. The major-domo drew the curtains. At the door he turned, 'Lord, the headman of Konpara is here.'

Mohan asked, 'What does he want? Why doesn't he go to Mr Kendrick? What can *I* do for him?' The major-domo said nothing, and Mohan grunted, 'Let him approach.'

He sat down and picked up a book. An hour to dinner and then – nothing. Nothing, until his twenty-first birthday. If then.

The major-domo came back. 'The headman of Konpara.'

The man bowing low in the doorway was slight, dark, and grizzled, the skin of his face lightly pitted with the scars of a childhood smallpox. (Vaccination, Mohan thought; Mr Kendrick will have everyone vaccinated.) As he raised his palm to his forehead Mohan noted again that the man had no thumb on his left hand – a hereditary defect, he said.

'Well, Huttoo Lall, what is it?' he asked.

The headman stood erect. His eyes were deep set, and though he observed the rules of behaviour with great care – almost obsequiousness – Mohan thought, not for the first time, that he did not really give an impression of humility. Yet he was a low-caste fellow, of no wealth and no position beyond the hereditary headship of the little village on the next ridge.

The headman said, 'For the past week a troupe of entertainers has been giving shows for the coolies working on the dam. Yesterday they performed at Konpara.'

Mohan remembered that he had seen them rehearsing one afternoon when he rode through the coolie camp on his way back from Deori. And last night he had thought of walking across to Konpara to see the show, in his boredom.

'They are nothing,' the headman said apologetically. 'A juggler, a singer, a magician, a drummer, a flutist, and a female dancer . . . but they wish to give a performance here.'

'Here?' Mohan said. 'Who for?'

The headman threw him an odd, surprised look. 'For the Suvala.'

Mohan tapped his fingers uneasily on his knee. Of course, he was in India now, where performances for a single man were nothing rare; and he was the Suvala. But Mr Kendrick would not approve. That was the kind of irresponsible 'oriental potentate' behaviour which he did not like at all.

The headman said, 'We of Konpara can recommend the troupe to your lordship.'

Mohan felt the subtle pressure, and understood completely. The troupe had given the performance to the village free, in return for the headman's assurance that they should perform before the Suvala. When he paid them tonight he would be paying for both performances. So he should. The villagers of Konpara were poor, they were his subjects, and he was the Suvala – whatever the Viceroy decided.

'Very well,' he said. 'Ten o'clock.'

'Very good, lord,' the headman said, bowing deeply. He backed out of the room.

Mohan looked at the book in his hand. Vilely printed at a cheap press in Allahabad, it was written in the most high-flown type of Hindi, almost unadulterated Sanskrit, and he found it hard to understand. It was a history of the Suvala family and the State of Deori – the two phrases meant the same thing – and had been written ten years ago by the State Archivist. What a jumble of superstition and fairy tale and legend it was! What strange, lurid people his ancestors had been!

Where had he got to? Twelve hundred and fifty B.C. He read on, and read till his bath was announced. He took the book in to dinner with him, and was still reading when the major-domo announced that all was prepared for the show. Then he walked out on to the front lawn.

He expected to find that the servants had placed the biggest armchair, from the living-room, near the foot of the verandah steps. They had not. Instead, in that place they had piled five or six of his thickest cushions. He paused, flushing. That was a gaddi, the royal seat.

He should order them to bring out the chair. Or he should change into Rajput clothes. The major-domo was at his elbow. 'The dancer ordered it so,' he muttered.

'*Ordered?*' Mohan said in astonishment.

The major-domo looked nonplussed, as though he, too, could not understand why he had used the word. 'She said it was important for the performance. I am sorry, lord, if . . .'

'Let it be,' Mohan said, and sank down on the cushions, his legs crossed beneath him. It was hard to sit like this in a dinner jacket and trousers.

Lamps from the dining-room stood on the lawn, and the

young dishwasher was tying hurricane lanterns to the trees at the edge of the cut grass. The troupe were dim shapes in the far gloom. From there came the tentative thud of the drum, several rapid beats, then a pause, then the drum again, pitched higher. The drummer was tuning his drum. The flutist blew a long quavering note.

Mohan remembered that Southdown was only a quarter of a mile away across the shallow valley. Mr Kendrick would hear the music, perhaps even seen the lights. Perhaps he'd come over, and find him sitting on a makeshift gaddi – like Prince Hal trying on his father's crown before he was dead.

Too late now. The major-domo had placed a low table at his elbow, with a bottle of brandy and a glass and soda beside it, in ice. He became aware of a larger, unseen audience. The bungalow was behind him, the thatched roof full of mysterious creaks and murmurs, but those were bats, or perhaps the rats that lived above the ceiling cloths. The servants' quarters and stables were invisible behind the bungalow and to the left as he sat; but the servants were here, grooms and dishwashers and sweepers and water carriers and gardeners, and their women. The cricket pitch was to the right, down the slope of the ridge there. Ahead, the darkness of the pit, and behind, a sinking half moon.

The drum picked up a complicated rhythm, the flute told the tune, and the entertainment began. The music ran alone for a minute or two, then the dancer glided out of the shadows on to the centre of the lawn, three rows of bangles chinking heavily on her right ankle. She was not a very good dancer, Mohan thought, or she was not interested. She gyrated there twenty feet from him, performing the simple steps of a nautch. She wore a short red skirt that came half-way down her calves, and a bodice, and carried a scarf in her hands. Her face was pretty enough. She never looked at him as she went through her steps and stylised attitudes. He wondered whether she was venereally diseased. Anyway, she was low caste. Why had she 'ordered' the preparation of a gaddi? And why had his pompous major-domo obeyed her?

At the end, he clapped politely. The echo came back very loud from the trees and the bungalow. Why did not the others clap, the servants concealed at the edges of the light? Of course, they must pretend they were not here. The show was for him alone.

A man came out and sang, interminably, with gestures. Something about his – Suvala's – ancestors; about Indra riding the heavens and hurling thunderbolts upon the black heathen.

The juggler followed. Mohan's interest quickened. The fellow was a pale Punjabi, very stocky. He threw up small wooden balls until he had a dozen of them in the air at once. By Jove, Mohan thought, that fellow would make a first-class cricketer, if he was taught. He toyed with the idea of giving him a job in Deori, and teaching him . . . Now it was plates . . . Now he was standing on his head and juggling nine-pins on his feet. Marvellous! Mohan applauded enthusiastically and with an instinctive gesture reached in his pocket and threw the man a silver rupee.

The singer walked out again, palms joined. Mohan poured himself a brandy and tried to maintain his look of regal pleasure. When he became Rajah, this would be his lot for the rest of his life. *Noblesse oblige*, Mr Kendrick said.

The conjurer, or worker of magic, came. He cut ropes in two and made them whole. He caused objects to disappear. He spouted flames from his mouth – and this time Mohan heard the involuntary gasp and the woman's stifled shriek from the shadows to the left. He isolated the walls of his stomach, and moved any piece of skin, as Mohan ordered, at will. He swallowed a long sword and pushed a needle through his hand. Mohan leaned forward, absorbed. Where was the trick? There'd got to be a trick somewhere. There was a trick in all this Indian magic.

A snake charmer now. Ah, it was the singer. The girl had a pretty easy time. Probably just a prostitute whom the men took along to save them paying others in the cities. Then why was it she who spoke to the major-domo? The singer was not very good as a snake charmer, either. The cobras rose out of the basket, swayed, and subsided.

More singing and Mohan glanced surreptitiously at his new wrist-watch. More juggling. More singing. Nearly midnight.

The music stopped. The girl glided towards him across the lawn, stooped low with joined palms, and said in a low, hoarse voice, her Hindi better accented than his own, 'That is the end of our programme, Mohan Singh Suvala.'

'Very good,' he said, and began to fumble in his pocket. Five rupees? Ten? He handed her ten rupees. She passed them to the juggler, who had appeared at her elbow, very humble.

She straightened. Her hands were no longer submissively joined, but held at her sides, the palms a little towards him. Her neck was erect, and he saw that her breasts were full and firm, her waist very small.

She said in a slow, inquiring voice, 'Art thou *the* Suvala . . . Eldest Son of Indra, Beloved of the Gods?'

It was silent in the garden. The bungalow behind him made no sound and the people in the darkness were silent. The last moonlight shone on the farther wall of the pit.

What was he to say? That he was the Suvala, but his uncle was

11

trying to protest his legitimacy, and the British Government would have to decide?

'I am the Suvala,' he said.

She said, 'You have spoken truly. Your people believe you are the Suvala, but they doubt – for you yourself have not been sure. It is here that we know who we are.' She touched her bare navel. She stared at him, and spoke with sternness, an authority, that he realised was amazing: yet it did not amaze him. She said, 'I have watched you, every day, for seven days, Suvala. *You are the Suvala* . . . I shall dance for you. A Bharata Natya of love and pride. For you, the king, for you alone. Only the king may see the queen dance as I dance now.'

She turned, raised her hands, and spread them wider. Addressing the unseen audience, she said, 'Go to your own places. Let none stay. I dance for the Suvala.'

Now she's a queen, Mohan thought. No wonder the major-domo obeyed her, and the servants. He heard the sounds of movement in the darkness and knew that the people were going away.

She had gone, too, and the drummer was beating a different rhythm. Damned cheek, she had. He poured out another brandy and soda. Bad for training, but he felt unsettled and nervous. The jungle seemed to stand closer to the edge of the lawn than it did by day, and the pit was bigger, and the moon had set.

The girl came out of the opposite trees, her legs gliding forward to the slow chink chink of silver bangles. She wore only two now, on her right ankle, and much lighter than the heavy ones she had worn for the first dance. A small ruby gleamed on the outside of her left nostril. Instead of the scarf she carried a snake. Apart from the bangles, the ruby, and the snake, she was naked.

Mr Kendrick, Mohan thought wildly. Suppose Mr Kendrick . . .

She advanced steadily, not writhing as before, but with a stately motion, her head high, the snake curving gently across her body as she held it, her hands moving.

The old way, this is the old way, he thought – I remember the statues, I remember someone telling me, this was the way it used to be, the women, even the queens, naked and unashamed, sometimes carrying a snake in the dance . . . He began to feel bigger. It was a sexual arousing, and sexually sited; but the expansion spread all over the body. The dancer could achieve no more than the audience, the man for whom she danced, would give. He must become as great a man, as strong, as tenderly proud, as she was a woman. She was precisely formed in the ancient manner, a little over five feet high, narrow-waisted, her breasts high and full and mathematically round, the hips springing out to strong slender thighs, a wide space between, where the smooth-shaved delta curved down broad and fat and firmly cleft. Her neck was long and her head small, her mouth wide and firm, and her eyes enormous, the lids very heavy.

The brandy stood untouched on the low table. The glass and the bottle and the gaddi itself became immaterial and soon ceased to exist. The woman – she was not a girl, though she was about his own age – could not be held in place or time. She belonged to a place where there was no knowledge of time, and so no knowledge of the customs and beliefs which time brings and time changes. Naked, the breasts firm when she moved, the muscles holding her stomach firm though her legs trembled in the dance – it was possible to see her as clothed. As her thighs spread and stretched the sign they disclosed was not of sexuality, but of creation.

Now her eyes never left his and he tried with all his might to read the message she gave him. She could not speak, that he knew. It had to come from the soul, through the body. Physical ecstasy, she was saying, and love . . . but there was more behind and as yet he could not understand it. He heard himself groan and shook his head angrily. If she heard she would think it was a groan of lust, but it was not. It was a cry of failure, of striving.

She had danced ten, fifteen minutes and sweat gleamed on her body. She opened her hands and poured the snake to the ground. It was a young cobra and, as she released it, it rose again, spread its hood, and swayed beside her, the small eyes fixed on her.

Her hands swept out and touched Mohan. He rose, and she sank, bowing her head to the ground between his feet. Without looking at her he walked up the steps and into the bungalow, full of an enormous strength and certainty. He knew she followed at his heels. The cobra swayed alone in the centre of the lawn, and one by one the lamps went out.

Chapter Three

'But how do you know so much, Rukmini? Where did you learn it all?' Mohan cried, laughing, and embarrassed that a stranger, and a woman, should know more of history, and of Deori, than he himself did. She had been talking about the *Suvala-Gita*, a collection of rhymed couplets which told the history of his family from two thousand years back.

She did not smile, or turn to him. They were sitting on the bare summit of Indra's Rock, looking down the pit towards the dam and the ant-like figures that crawled and scurried over it. She wore a pale blue sari of the finest South Indian cotton, and thin sandals, and her toenails were painted light blue. She said, 'About the past, and the world – my mother had me taught.'

'So much, in so short a time? You're only twenty-one now.'

'I was learning the *Bhagavad-Gita* at five,' she said.

'At five?' he exclaimed. 'But why? Surely it must have cost a lot of money.'

'To fit me to be a queen,' Rukmini said quietly. 'When I was a baby my mother saw that I would be beautiful enough to become anything I was fitted for. When I was old enough to understand, she told me I would be what many of our ancestors had been – a queen. The money . . . she became a prostitute in order that I might not have to. Besides, a prostitute is the only sort of woman in your Brahmins' India who has freedom to govern her own life. As for the *Suvala-Gita*, I came to Deori the day after you returned from England. Ever since, I have been studying this land, these people. And you.'

'Me?' he said softly, pressing her hand. Every time she looked at him, every time she spoke to him, every time their skins touched, he felt a helpless pang of love. 'You mean you loved me even then?'

She said, 'No. I came to Deori in search of myself, and of love. When I saw you, I *thought* you were my love, but before I danced I had to be sure that you were worthy and that you were the king of my dreams.'

Mohan stretched playfully and pressed his head against her

14

slender neck and, when she leaned back against him, bit softly at her skin.

The troupe of entertainers had vanished during that first night. This was the seventh day afterward. He remembered that night's feeling of vast power, and of forward motion from a high place, as though he were sliding down the front of a huge wave, and the wave racing fast towards an unseen shore. The feeling had not been a fantasy of the moment, but a continuing reality. The sexual experience, his first, came in a series of such waves, each bigger than the last, each timeless; but the hands of the clock had moved when the wave passed on; and between the waves, the swelling calm of such moments as this on the rock, or at the Tiger Pool below the Rainbow Fall, or walking through the jungle hand in hand, or studying the books by lamplight. All the while the rest of humanity had been no more than shadow forms which placed food before him and hovered, smiling, about house and garden and forest.

'Who are you?' he asked suddenly, sitting up.

'That is for me to find out, my lord,' she said. 'And for you to decide.'

'I don't understand,' he said humbly.

She pointed along the edge of the pit, where two dark shapes stood at the rim of the cliff, staring across at them. They were small, very black men, carrying bows and arrows and wearing nothing but loin-cloths. As soon as Rukmini raised her hand they disappeared. 'Who are those?' she said.

'Gonds,' Mohan said. 'They are black savages, and eat snakes and lizards and ants, and use poisoned arrows. We have quite a lot of them in Deori. But you know what the Gonds are!'

'Black savages,' she repeated. 'True. And also the oldest inhabitants of your country, and a part of it, like the trees. Perhaps they always were hunters. Perhaps the next who came drove them into the jungles. In any case, they are your landlords, Suvala, like the tigers and the deer. You should pay them an annual quit-rent – a handful of understanding. And who are those?'

She jerked her head backwards in a graceful gesture. Mohan knew, without turning, that she was indicating the area where a dozen men from Konpara worked at the shaft which allowed inspection of the conduit that would carry the waters of Tiger Pool through to the pit.

'Villagers,' he said. 'Peasants from Konpara.'

She nodded. 'Yes. Also, priests and kings.'

'Priests!' he exclaimed. 'There isn't a Brahmin or Kshatriya among them, nor even a Vaisya. They are all Sudras – those that are not outcaste.'

15

She said energetically, 'You see, Suvala, it is not so easy to know who anyone is. But you cannot be king unless you do know, and are a part of each one of them, just as each is part of you. Listen.'

She faced him, sitting up like a teacher in the school. 'First were the small dark people – the Gonds. Then, thousands of years ago – six or seven thousand years – new invaders drove the small dark people into the deepest jungles.' Her sweeping hand embraced the ridge, the pit, the valley, and the upper plateau. 'Those first invaders were the Dravidians. They flourished all over India until 1500 B.C. Those were my mother's people. In 1500 B.C. the second invaders came, out of the Central Asian steppe. They were the Aryans – your people. They fought the Dravidians, took their land from them, and drove them south, or into the jungles to join the Gonds. Gradually the Aryans spread over the whole of India. In the far south they lived with the Dravidians, as rulers, rather than destroying them. And they established the caste system, for their own selfish convenience.'

'But . . .' Mohan began unhappily, 'we are Hindus. Caste is part of our religion. If we try to do away with it . . .'

He could not finish the sentence. Caste could not be justified or explained. It was.

'There would still be the continuing soul,' Rukmini said quietly. 'The belief that successive lives on earth are given to us to purify our souls until finally they can join with the Infinite. Have you ever been given memory of a past life?'

'No,' he said, 'I can't say I have, really.' The memory of Cheltenham embarrassed him. There, one did not ask such questions.

'Few are,' she said. 'I have. I think I was a fish once. Water feels strange on me sometimes, as though it were my element. When I was six I was nearly drowned that way. There was no pain, though. And I know I have danced, naked, holding a cobra. In more lives than one.'

Mohan sat, his hands clasped round his knees, staring out across the pit. It was only a week since he had felt that he had nothing to do, no responsibility, no place; only a week since he had sat in his room looking at a future of cricket matches, as a figurehead nodding assent to the decisions of Mr Kendrick, who would rule his people for their own good. Now Rukmini had thrown a powerful and unsettling light on to his position, even as her body had carried him into strange territories of the senses. All that had happened before this week had lost substance and meaning.

He said, 'Rukmini, stay with me.'

'For how long?' she said.

'For ever.'

'As what?'

He hesitated. 'As . . . I love you, Rukmini.' He mumbled the words in despair.

She said gently, 'I know. I love you. But between thee and me there is only one relation which can last through this life and beyond.'

He cried, 'I can't marry you, Rukmini! I am a Kshatriya. You . . .'

'My mother was a Tamil, a low-caste Sudra Tamil from the south,' she said. 'My father – my mother would not tell me.'

He looked at her. Her father might have been a Northern Brahmin. Or an Englishman. Certainly someone paler skinned than a black Tamil. But it was the female line, the Dravidian, of which she counted herself.

He said, 'What you have been telling me about the past . . . I'm sure it's all true, Rukmini, but it's not the rule now. If I married you, I'd never become the Suvala. You don't understand how orthodox the people are here. And the British more so. If they don't go out of their way to uphold caste, everyone will say they're planning to destroy Hinduism. Mr Kendrick has often explained it to me.'

She stood and he followed her example. She was looking up at him, her dark eyes wet. 'You are saying that with me you will never become the Suvala. I am saying that without me you will never *be* the Suvala. I will stay with you, Mohan, as your concubine and lover. But remember what I said – as between thee and me, there is no true relation, except marriage. Remember, when thou art angry.'

'But what can I do?' he cried. 'You've just said it's impossible.'

'I did not say that,' she said; and then, with sudden passion, 'Why do you think I am here unless I believe the gods can unite us?'

She turned and walked down the slope of the rock, on the east side. Mohan followed ten feet behind her, so uneasy and unhappy that it did not strike him as out of place that he should be walking behind her instead of the other way round, the universal rule in India.

'Someone is coming across the valley,' she said in a conversational voice. 'Two Englishmen. One of them is Mr Kendrick.'

Mohan looked to his left. With a shock he saw the two men striding across the intermediate valley, on a path that would in a few moments join this one. Then the trees hid them.

The situation which he had known must come, but had refused to allow to the surface of his thoughts or even his dreams, was now upon him. He had not seen the Resident, or spoken to him, or sent word to him, for seven days. He had not gone to South--down for his portrait sitting. Mr Kendrick must have heard about Rukmini. Soon he'd be sent for. There'd be an interview. He felt as he had before his first prefects' beating at Cheltenham.

He might hide, with Rukmini, and pray they would not turn back this way along the Dobehari Ridge when they reached the crest. He might leave her here and go on alone . . .

Rukmini glided on ahead of him. He gritted his teeth and hurried up level with her. She looked into his eyes, a long, warm, approving look. He said, 'Don't be afraid.'

'Why should I be afraid?' she said, laughing. 'I have seen him many times, riding through Deori. From the way he looks at women, I think it is he who will be afraid. Who is the other man?'

'I don't know,' Mohan muttered. Then they came to the place where the tracks met, and the two Englishmen were walking up fast among the trees on the left, no more than ten paces away. Mohan stopped.

'Hello, sir,' he said, and tried to find a smile. Rukmini should be turning away, the end of her sari drawn across that side of her face presented to the strangers. Then they would pretend she did not exist. That was the custom.

The sari end hung over her smooth head in a graceful curve, but she had not turned away. She was looking full at the second Englishman.

Mr Kendrick took off his sola topi in a brief gesture, and replaced it. He was tall, his thick hair almost white, his grey eyes deep set and always restlessly moving. He was wearing light tan trousers, strong walking shoes, a white shirt and black tie, a thin cotton jacket, and the white topi. He said, 'Ah, Mohan . . . Allow me to introduce Mr Smith. Mr Smith – Mohan Singh Suvala, the only son of the late Rajah of Deori.'

Mr Smith had not removed his topi, because he was not wearing one. His level brown eyes, flecked with green, held Mohan's steadily as he extended his hand. He was shorter than Mr Kendrick, and slightly built, with a thin high-bridged nose and thick brown hair going a little grey at the temples. He wore a khaki shirt, khaki trousers, and sandals. His face and arms were burned almost black but the skin was extraordinarily smooth except for scores of fine wrinkles round his eyes. His voice, as he said, 'It's a privilege to meet you, Suvala-ji,' was high, clear, and soft.

Mohan glanced involuntarily at Mr Kendrick. Mr Kendrick

frowned slightly. It was a strict rule that Mohan should not be addressed in that style until he had been formally chosen to ascend the gaddi. They stood a moment, while an awkward silence developed. Mr Kendrick ignored Rukmini, Mr Smith stared at her with his unwinking, level gaze, and she returned it.

Mr Kendrick said, 'Mr Smith is an archaeologist. He has been excavating the ruined stupa at Elephant Hill.' Mohan nodded. Elephant Hill was the other side of the state. He hadn't known this chap was over there. Mr Kendrick might have told him.

Mr Smith said, 'I just came over to thank Mr Kendrick for giving me permission to dig there, and to tell him that I did not find what I was looking for, nor anything else of value, and that now I must be off.'

'What were you looking for?'

Mohan started. It was Rukmini who had spoken. Mr Kendrick, too, stared at her with unconcealed astonishment. There was not one Indian woman in Deori who spoke English.

Mr Smith did not show surprise. He said, 'Only one question has interested me for a great many years now. That is – why, when, and how did God give man an awareness of Him. Some time ago I came to the conclusion that Brahminism might have the answer.'

'An answer,' Rukmini said. 'I do not think it is the right one, Mr Smith. Did you hear, somewhere, of the Deori mystery?'

Mr Kendrick said, 'What is the Deori mystery? I have been here some eight years now, and I never have.'

Mr Smith said, 'There are rumours in many parts of India, both north and south, particularly among religious men and historians, that a very ancient mystery, connecting art and religion, exists in Deori. The connection is important, because in the beginning art and religion are the same thing. . . . You have heard of the Cave of Altamira, in Spain? It is full of paintings made by cavemen, perhaps thirty thousand years ago. Those paintings were made in the dark – not in a cave where men lived, but in a special one set aside for the purpose. What was that purpose?'

Rukmini answered quickly, 'To speak to God.'

Mr Smith said, 'I think so, madam . . . So, thirty thousand years ago man is already aware of God. But he does not know why he has been given this awareness. The cave paintings do not answer the question, they only ask it . . . Somewhere, surely someone received the answer. Christians believe that they did, on the hill of Calvary. I believe the Brahmins may have, much earlier. The legend of the Deori mystery brought me here, looking for a man-made recording of that revelation.'

'I thought you were an archaeologist,' Mr Kendrick said. His voice was under control, but only just, Mohan knew.

Mr Smith said, 'In a way, yes. I have studied the subject. It is a useful technique – not an end in itself.'

'Oh, you are right!' Rukmini said. 'I wish we could talk more about it.' She spoke English clearly, with a lilting rhythm and a slight misplacing of accent – but very well.

Mr Smith said, as seriously, 'So do I, madam. But tomorrow – I am spending the night at the Rest House with Mr Foster – I must be on my way.'

'Where to?' Rukmini asked.

Mohan stirred, embarrassed, and Mr Kendrick said, 'I fear we must go down to the dam now, Smith, if you are to see anything before work ends for the day. Good day, Mohan.'

Mr Smith smiled, but said nothing, and followed the Resident down the ridge path. Mohan and Rukmini walked on, very slowly, and in a moment the two Englishmen were out of sight ahead.

'That is an unusual man,' she said.

'Mr Kendrick?'

'Mr Smith. But his name is not Smith. What it is I do not think anyone will learn.'

'You seemed to be making eyes at him all the time, I must say.'

'He is very handsome. He has seen many visions, and you, too, can see them, in his eyes, if you look. He is strong, but gentle. He is brave, but tender. Any woman's flesh would melt if he looked at her, to need her.'

They were near the bungalow now; now crossing the lawn; now climbing the steps. 'I don't like the way you looked at him,' Mohan said angrily. 'It was an open invitation . . . the same you gave me.' His anger, working upon itself, mounted rapidly. 'Do you do that to every man you meet?' Of course, she was a prostitute, a dancing whore, nothing else. 'How many men have you had?' he said, 'A hundred, a thousand?'

She looked at his hand, gripping her bare arm above the elbow. Slowly Mohan released his grip. She said sadly, 'You see, what I said? That there will be unhappiness for both of us.'

'How can I marry you if you're going to make love to every Tom, Dick, and Harry who comes within a mile of you?'

She said, 'Do not feel weak, or insufficient, Suvala, or you will go the way of your ancestors, full of jealousy and hatred.'

She spoke so sadly that he forgot his jealous anger, and took her hand. 'Forgive me . . . I love you, I love you.'

She lifted his hand and pressed it to her lips. 'I know, my lord.'

There was a knock on the door. Mohan called impatiently, 'What is it?'

The major-domo's voice answered, 'Foster Sahib is here, with his foreman, tne Pathan. The sahib says he has something to show you.'

Mohan muttered to Rukmini, 'Foster's the contractor in charge of building the dam and the conduit and all the other irrigation works. I suppose we'll have to see him . . . Very well,' he called through the door. 'Ask him in.'

Chapter Four

The man who entered was of medium height, thickly built, about thirty-five years of age. His freckled face, pigmented with the distinctive tone of the red-headed, would never tan properly, though he spent all his days in the sun. Sweat darkened his shirt, and gleamed on the red hairs of his bare forearms. He was followed by his foreman, a tall, thin Lucknow Pathan in his fifties, who wore a rakish turban and a beard dyed much the same colour as Foster's hair, and carried a big sack. Foster was taking a good look at Rukmini.

Mohan said, 'This is – ah – Rukmini. Mr Foster.'

Rukmini joined her palms. Foster mumbled, 'Pleased-to-meetcha, miss . . . ma'am.' He turned quickly back to Mohan, while the foreman lowered the sack carefully against the wall. Foster said, 'I shouted out to you as you passed the pitch just now . . .'

'I didn't hear,' Mohan said. 'I'm sorry.' He had seen nothing for a week. He'd better wake up.

Foster said, 'We found something interesting. Pull it out, Shahbaz.' The foreman reached into the sack with both hands, lifted out a leg and held it upright on the wooden floor.

Mohan started. 'What on earth . . .?'

He sat down. For a moment the sheen on the leg had made it real and alive. Then he saw the areas of encrusted dirt and the uneven break at the top and recognised that it was made of a dark red stone. It was almost a whole leg, the left, broken high on the thigh. The firm muscles inside the thigh showed clear and the smooth round calf was tensed, the knee bent, and the foot pointed.

Foster said, 'Part of a statue, see.'

Obviously, Mohan thought. Foster was keeping his voice neutral to hide his excitement, but he wasn't a good actor.

Rukmini went slowly forward, the sari swirling between her thighs. 'How beautiful!' she whispered. 'It is a woman's leg. A woman dancing, in the pose Nritya Tandava. It is the pose Siva Nataraja is always shown in. Look.'

22

She stooped, one bare arm sweeping down to the hem of her sari. The movement was long and slow, like the bending of a swan's neck. The hem of the sari rose. The Pathan foreman looked out of the window. Foster's blue eyes bulged in his red face. Mohan did not know whether to laugh or blush. She was impossible. Impossibly natural.

Her voice was low and musical. 'See, Mr Foster.'

Another half inch, Mohan thought, and Foster would go out of his mind. Rukmini stood on her right leg, the left raised and bent forward and across, as was the statue's. 'Like this,' she said. 'Look at this muscle here. And see, a woman's knee is quite different from a man's . . .'

The sunset light swept low and flat through the windows, tingeing her skin a glowing red-bronze. Her hand swept down with the same slow grace, and again the sari hung evenly to her ankles. She faced Mohan. 'I feel as if it were *my* leg . . . We must find the rest of her – of me.' She did not laugh.

Foster said heartily, 'That was what I was going to ask about! Statues aren't much in my line, but this one seemed – well, as though it might be old, and important.'

Mohan said, 'What will happen to the cricket pitch?'

Foster said, 'That depends. It'll be delayed, anyway.'

Rukmini said, 'Cricket! . . . How deep under the surface was it, Mr Foster?'

'About eight feet. I thought you'd want to look for the rest of it. I'll put some extra men on, if you like. There shouldn't be much delay with the pitch.'

Rukmini said slowly, 'We must be careful. If we dig without knowing what we are doing we might do more harm than good. Also, we might waste time. We need an expert . . . We need Mr Smith! He's staying the night at the Rest House, isn't he?'

A silence fell. Mohan, glancing at Foster, caught a sense of chagrin on the other's face. Foster liked the idea as little as he did.

Foster spoke. 'Well, I don't know anything about Smith. I've just said hello to him. My men will be careful, I can promise you that. If you want us to go ahead.'

'*Please*, Mohan,' Rukmini said.

Mohan moved restlessly, and got up, and walked across the room. Rukmini was very eager. So was Foster. If he let them dig, Mr Kendrick would tell him that it was a waste of money, which must come eventually from the state's funds, to allow such a diversion of the contractor's effort. He said, 'Mr Kendrick will have to decide.'

Rukmini stood with pursed lips, staring at him. He could not

23

tell whether she was angry or preoccupied. She said at last, 'We must have a case to present. We must take the leg over to Mr Smith. He will be able to say that it is very old, and very valuable.'

'I can do that,' Foster said quickly, before Mohan had time to open his mouth. 'He's there in the Rest House with me. Let me talk to him tonight, and we'll both come over here first thing in the morning, eh?'

'Very well,' Rukmini said at once, again before Mohan had time to think.

Foster picked up the leg, returned it to the sack, and went out in a hurry. Mohan sat down, a little dazed. Rukmini stared at the spot where the leg had been, as though it were still there.

Mohan tried to speak lightly. 'It's beautiful, I know, but why are you so determined to dig up the rest of it? There are hundreds like it in temples and caves all over India.'

She shook her head, without turning. 'They're nearly all bas-reliefs,' she said. 'This was free-standing. It is part of the statue of a queen – of my race, not yours. Do you remember the shape of the leg, the way the bones lay under the skin. Like mine!'

'You have queens on the brain,' Mohan said. 'This woman was naked. And dancing. It's more likely she was a low-caste dancing girl.'

Rukmini said, 'I think, when we find her, you will learn that a woman can be both.'

Chapter Five

The small fire cast a flickering light on the rock. Five men and three women sat round it, all squatting on their haunches. All were old or middle-aged. Three of the men wore bulky white loin-cloths tucked round their waists, and heavy untidy turbans. The other two, smaller and blacker, wore single cords round their waists and small bags for their sexual parts, and wore no turbans. The women sat, wrapped in white cloth, among the men.

A man spoke. 'She has returned . . . A part of one leg was found before dusk today.'

A woman sighed, and, much later, said, 'Gold, too.'

A man said, 'Her power over the mind and the flesh is stronger than gold. By that she will lead them on. She has already captivated them.'

A sickle-shaped cloud drifted across the face of the moon and all the people looked up. One of the blacker men made a cabalistic sign with his fingers, pointing at the moon. Every face was sheened with sweat and lined with anxiety. One of the men snapped irritably, 'Put on more wood!'

The little group huddled together until the fire flared up and the darkness, which had been creeping down on them from above, and inward along the rocky gorge, retreated.

'But she . . .' one of them said. 'Is she, then, evil?'

A woman said decisively, 'No. But where she comes from, and must return to – there are the evil powers, which she will release, unknowing.'

'What can we do?' one cried in a kind of agony. 'If the evil is going to come out upon us, after all these years, how can we prevent it? We are mortal.'

'It is our duty,' another said sombrely. 'It is the duty laid upon us, as well as for our own preservation. But you are right, we cannot prevail by strength . . . They have found gold. Gold is the father of greed. Greed makes men blind . . . the more gold, the more blind. They will see fame, and the ambition for fame makes men stupid. *She* can beckon and lead them, but greed, fear,

25

jealousy, and ambition can be stronger. These we can create among them.'

'Time, too, will work secretly against them,' one said.

'Time? Ah, yes. I had almost forgotten. They can do nothing after the rains come. And when the rains end, evil will lie choked to death, final death, under the new water.'

They sat on in silence and though they were eight separate individuals, the fear encircling them, as real and as impalpable as the darkness, welded them and the little fire into a single entity that was at the same time more and less than human.

One of the men, who seemed to be the prime thinker of the single mind, said, 'All that we have, and are, and can be, all that we know and guess and feel – we will use. Let us think, and then speak by turn.'

Chapter Six

On the verandah of the Rest House Mr Smith watched a sickle-shaped cloud pass across the moon. It was past ten o'clock and the Rainbow Fall made a subdued murmur as it fell into Tiger Pool at the foot of the opposite cliffs. This Konpara was a strange and interesting place. At the stupa site he had worked in an aura of peace, the peace of the Buddha. Here sky and rock and water and all living things breathed an older and darker message. The people here were part of the land. The Gonds, the villagers, even the coolies, seemed to fit in grooves in the earth as though they had laboured here, at the same tasks, aeon upon aeon. The intruders stood out like Gulliver among the Houyhnhnms – Kendrick the Resident, an unfulfilled man; his silent, withdrawn wife; Foster the loud-mouthed contractor in the other part of the Rest House here; Mohan, heir to heaven knew how many thousand years of legend, of godhead, of absolute power, and clearly carrying in his awakening personality the fruit of that past, ready to seed; but, at the same time, a twenty-year-old youth just out of Sandhurst, alternately over-shy and over-aggressive, willing but unsure, standing hesitant at the most important crossroads of his life, ready to turn in any direction according as a strong enough force worked upon him. Two such forces approached him at this instant, from opposite points – Kendrick, and the girl Rukmini.

It was late. He would like to stay here, but he could not, for he had not purpose here. Yawning slightly, he turned into his room. Foster's heavy tread approached along the verandah. A moment later the contractor knocked at the door. 'Smith? Mind if I come in a minute?'

'Not a bit,' Smith answered, opening the door.

The contractor came in, carrying a large sack. 'Got something here that ought to interest you,' he said. Smith waited. They had eaten dinner together in the common dining-room. Why had Foster not brought up this matter then? He waited, smiling slightly. Foster pulled a stone leg out of the sack and laid it on the table.

'There. What do you make of that?'

Smith bent to examine the leg. There was no fold of stone at the ankle, the conventional representation of a transparent skirt. The very oldest statues did not show it.

He said, 'The woman was naked, of course. The attitude shows that she was probably not a maithuna, one of the women shown in sexual intercourse, but a dancer. Or just a beautiful woman.'

'A sort of Venus, eh?' Foster said. 'Like that one with no arms – but with only one leg, instead. The Venus of Konpara!' He laughed with boisterous nervousness. 'How old is it?'

Smith said at once, 'That I can't tell. But it is very good.'

Foster said, 'Mohan's pretty keen on digging up the rest of it. That's the young fellow . . .'

'I've met him,' Smith said.

'Met his new piece, too?'

'Yes.'

'Well, she seems to have got him right under her thumb. My God, they've passed me half a dozen times this week, and he's never seen me. Walking on air . . . Between you and me, she's the one who's really anxious to find the rest of this statue. But they've got to get Kendrick's permission, see, because it's state land. Now, I want to find the rest of this woman, too – sort of caught my imagination, she has – but we've got to persuade Kendrick that it's worth it. You know him well?'

Smith shook his head.

'Well, he's a bastard,' Foster said angrily. 'He's always talking of what *he's* going to do, and how he's going to be a great man – then he doesn't *do* anything. He hates everybody, that's why. I don't know how Mrs Kendrick sticks him. He . . .' He cut himself off short.

Smith examined the leg more closely. It was certainly old, and whatever its age it was the work of a great artist. The complete statue might prove to be a masterpiece. But Foster was not thinking of art, and Mohan Singh's strange, wonderful girl was not thinking of art. He had better find out what they *were* thinking of. Foster's coat was heavily weighted on the right side, he noticed.

Foster could not contain himself. He said, 'There's money in it, for both of us.'

Smith kept his face non-committal. Poor Foster, who had obviously struggled up from the English slums, could not know that money had a subjective, not an objective value, which was different for different people.

Foster said gruffly, 'I know you're a sahib, and I know you're broke, see. No clothes, no servants, no nothing. You're a gent, and you've come on hard times. That's right, isn't it?'

'In a way,' Smith said.

Foster grinned expansively. 'I'm not a gent. Contractor, up and down the country, Burma, Ceylon. Well, God damn it, I *do* think that leg's beautiful . . . But here's my real reason for wanting to do some more looking.'

He dipped into his right-hand pocket and lifted out a block of metal, six inches long by four inches wide by two inches deep, and laid it carefully on the table beside the leg. 'That was found under the leg,' he said. 'Twelve inches deeper. That stuff on it is just encrusted dirt. No rust. The rest of it is – gold. I've got another block in my room, just like that. I'm sending filings off – a long way off – for analysis, but there's no doubt about it.'

'It's gold,' Smith agreed, hefting the bar in his hand.

Foster said, 'Do you know what that bar's worth? Two thousand three hundred pounds. Thirty thousand rupees. That's as much as I've saved in my whole life.'

Smith turned the bar this way and that. 'It's stamped,' he said. 'The device of a bow.'

Foster nodded. 'So's the other . . . I'm a businessman, like I told you. When I made the contract with Deori for this irrigation scheme I got a ten-year lease to exploit all the minerals in the Konpara area. I gave them a good price on the contract, to allow for the value of the lease, because some of the land on the upper plateau looked as though it might have coal in it. Well, it hasn't – but there are other minerals besides coal. Silver's a mineral. Diamonds are minerals. Gold's a mineral.' He paused. Smith said nothing.

Foster roughened his voice. 'The rains are due early in June. The Agent to the Governor-General is going to open the dam on May the twenty-seventh. Let's say we can dig till then. Today's April the seventh. Seven weeks. You tell Kendrick it's worth digging for the rest of the statue, and you want to be in charge yourself. I'll get you a dozen coolies, to dig, and give you my foreman or his cousin to help look after them. I'll pay all expenses, and give you 350 rupees for yourself over and above . . . if you take charge of this job until May the twenty seventh. But two things aren't going to show up in any agreement we make. One, you're looking for more of this gold, as much as you're looking for the rest of the Venus. Two, anything you find in that line, anything at all – that's mine. What do you say?'

Smith said, 'I doubt whether Mr Kendrick would regard a treasure from some previous age as "minerals".'

'No, he wouldn't,' Foster said bluntly. 'That's why he's got to hear nothing about it, see. All right. Ten per cent of the value of anything you find in addition to everything else . . . I can't do more than that. I've got to give Shahbaz Khan, that's my foreman, another ten per cent, to keep him straight.'

Smith sighed slightly. 'You've never accepted this kind of responsibility before, I suppose?' he asked.

'Responsibility, what do you mean?' Foster said.

'For the destruction of beauty, of values which can't be translated into money – like the value of history. No, I do not think I can accept your offer.'

Foster jumped up incredulously. 'What? What harm's it going to do to anyone?'

'I don't know,' Smith said gently. 'Perhaps that's why I must refuse.' He saw that Foster's face was turning pale with a mixture of fear and anger. He said, 'I shall not tell anyone of what I have seen or heard tonight, though.'

'You'd better not,' Foster growled. 'It's none of your business.'

'No, it's none of my business,' Smith said. 'Good night.'

Foster pocketed the gold bar, took the leg and the sack, and left the room.

Smith made his preparations for bed and, ten minutes later, blew out the lamp. He lay awhile in bed, his eyes open. It was not his business. None of the affairs of human beings around him should be his business, if he were to find what he was looking for. But his mind and heart always became involved and so his journey, instead of being fast and purposeful, became crooked and slow. Sighing, he closed his eyes and at once went to sleep.

He awoke, hearing the faint sound, long before the door opened. The soft pad of bare feet approached across the room, and he relaxed. A woman. A hand touched his arm and a low, slightly hoarse voice whispered, 'Mr Smith.' From the angle of the moonlight he knew it was about one o'clock.

'Rukmini,' he said.

'Yes. May I close the curtains?'

He got out of bed and, when the curtains were drawn, lit the lamp. She was standing in the middle of the room, wearing a gauzy sari of pale flame colour, with no border. She said, 'I have come about this statue.'

'The Venus of Konpara,' he murmured.

'What? Ah. That is a good name, in English . . . Mr Foster has spoken to you?'

'Yes.'

'What did you decide?'

'That it was no business of mine.'

She glanced quickly at him and he thought, here is a woman who does not know what sexuality is. Her smallest, most careless movement, the texture of her skin, the gloss of her hair – spoke not of sexuality but of sex.

30

She said, as though to herself, 'Mr Foster has secret thoughts about the Venus, secret knowledge, perhaps. You do not want to involve yourself. No, I do not wish to hear more . . . Do you know of the *Suvala-Gita*?'

'I know it well,' he said. 'I studied it carefully before excavating at the stupa site. I have a copy here.' He opened the tin trunk in the corner, which carried all his possessions.

She said, 'You travel twice as lightly as I do. I have two such trunks – one for clothes and one for books.'

Smith produced the smudgily printed copy of the *Gita*. It consisted of a rhymed couplet, in Sanskrit, for every year since 228 before Christ. Each couplet described the most important event of that year, in the history of the Suvalas.

She said, 'Do you know where a fortress is mentioned? An old priest in Deori told me that it is, and he said it was supposed to have been here, near Konpara.'

Smith turned the pages. 'Yes,' he said. 'The couplet for 195 B.C. says, *The sun hiding his face, the king made prayer at the ruined, sun-darkened fortress.* I made enquiries from the State Archivist about this, because I thought the fortress might have been near the stupa site. He told me there was an eclipse of the sun in 195 B.C. Also, that the last total eclipse before that which could have been seen here was in 556 B.C.'

Rukmini said, 'The first eclipse caused the fortress to be abandoned. That's why it says "sun-darkened." I think this leg is from a statue which was in the fortress, or in a temple inside the fortress.'

Smith calculated – 556 plus 1890. The statue, if she was right, must be at least 2,446 years old.

She said, 'It will mean very much to me if we can find the rest of her. I have told Mohan. This statue is of a woman of my race, who danced, and was a queen. I *must* find her. Will you please tell Mr Kendrick it is a worthwhile and important search . . . and will you please take charge of it?'

It was no use repeating, this is none of my business. The woman's spirit had engaged his own in a wordless harmony the moment they had first met on the path this afternoon. He had entered her and she had accepted him as definitely as though the union were a physical one.

He said, 'I will.'

She joined her palms and spoke in Hindi, calling him 'teacher.' 'We shall succeed, guru-ji . . . It must not be for my sake that you undertake the task. Or even seem to be.'

'It is not,' Smith said, smiling. 'I love a lady even more beautiful than you – and sometimes, also, terrible. Truth. As for my apparent motive, I shall accept Foster's offer.'

She said, 'Thank you . . . We must not search as though in a closed room, no one in it but ourselves and the thing we are looking for hidden under a candlestick. Every action that we take affects others, and theirs affect us. I have been here seven days. Mohan hears nothing, sees nothing, but *I* know that already, down in Deori, his uncle spreads rumours that I have bewitched him. There will be trouble soon. And I know that the City Warden has spoken to Mr Kendrick about me.'

'And I know that Mohan does not like me,' Smith said.

'Ah! Yes . . . And Mr Foster has some secret . . .'

'Two,' Smith said, remembering the contractor's emotion when he had spoken of Barbara Kendrick.

She said, 'If we know so much, already, think how much more we do not know! About Mrs Kendrick. About the villagers of Konpara. The Gonds. Our search will not be a simple game of hide-and-seek'

'No,' Smith said. 'There is greed, and jealousy, that we know of. There will be ambition . . .'

'And fear,' Rukmini said. 'I can feel it, but I do not know yet where it is coming from. These are the enemies. Oh, I wish they could be poured out upon me, here, now. Then they would disappear.' Her arms were out again in the embracing, accepting gesture, her legs a little spread and strongly braced.

An old loneliness swept over Smith and he wanted to step into her arms and hold her, and be held. There could be no loneliness there, only love, of a kind that knew no difference between sacred and profane. It was this love which would fight against the greed and jealousy that had already revealed themselves, the fear and ambition that were coming.

He said, 'I shall tell Foster first thing in the morning.'

She said no more, but arranged the sari over her head and moved to the door. He blew out the lamp and walked on to the verandah with her. A minute later she had disappeared among the trees.

The moonlit ribbon of the waterfall stretched down the dark cliffs opposite. That night was hot and still. He began to walk up and down the lawn in his bare feet. Tomorrow the search for the Venus would begin. Kendrick would certainly agree, for he had mentioned only this morning that the Agent to the Governor-General, a keen amateur archaeologist, would be disappointed to hear that nothing had been discovered at the stupa site. Obviously, Kendrick wanted to please his superior, and a great discovery here would shed some glory on both of them.

So Kendrick would be impelled by ambition, Foster by greed,

Rukmini by love . . . and himself? Since Rukmini had mentioned the fortress part of his mind had been pursuing a new line of thought. She had said that the statue was of a Dravidian, and a queen, and that it came out of a fortress which had existed until 556 B.C. There was a possibility, then, that the Dravidians had originally built the fortress. The problem of the nature of Dravidian civilisation was important, not only to his own search but to Rukmini's. For himself, it was something older than Brahminism and perhaps wiser; for her – when she said she was searching for a queen of her own race, she meant that she was searching also for the whole past glory of that race.

The Aryans entered India about 1500 B.C. Shortly afterwards they wrote the oldest works of literature still extant, the three Vedas: the *Rig-Veda*, the *Sama-Veda*, and the *Yajur-Veda*. The Vedas were religious and also epic, in that they gave detailed accounts of the Aryans' battles, led by the god Indra, against the field armies of the Dravidians, and against their walled cities. But no trace of such cities had been found. The Vedas might be mere fables, no more to be trusted as history than the legends of King Arthur, but then the experts thought the same about Homer until Schliemann, following Homer exactly, found Troy where all scientific methods had failed.

If the Vedas were more than fables Rukmini's Dravidian ancestors had built great cities, and presumably not out of nothing, but out of a powerful civilisation and an advanced culture. If that were so, if that could be proved by the finding of the cities and by uncovering the culture, it might be accepted that the caste system, which had generally put the dark Dravidian at the bottom of the pile and the pale Aryan at the top, was not a law of God but a selfish product of conquest. It was important that the Hindi word for caste was 'varna,' which meant 'colour.'

. . . But this is only the surface of the problem, and of the possibilities. In the Vedas the Aryans describe themselves as they are just after they have arrived from Central Asia. They are meat-eaters and herdsmen. They drive, breed, slaughter, and eat cattle. A thousand years later, by 500 B.C., the cow and the bull have become sacred; the caste system has been established; the higher castes are vegetarian; and no one at all eats beef. In the Vedas there is no female god – the gods are masculine, very much the hunter-warrior type; by 500 B.C. some of the principal attributes of godship are worshipped under the form of goddesses, and those are all aspects of the female principle of energy, called 'sakti.' In the Vedas, there is little or no mention of the worship of the reproductive process; by 500 B.C. the phallus is erected in the deepest sanctuary of the temples, and the sexual act is worshipped as a symbol of the necessary union of two of God's powers – the passive ability to be fertile, and the active power to fertilize. Obviously, neither is of use without the other. The Hindu symbol for it happens to be sexual but the principle is universal. A man cannot think of a mathematical equation, for example, unless he has both a receptive capacity able to take the idea of an equation, and an active capacity to fertilize that receptivity – by speculation, for instance – and out of the union grows the equation itself . . .

The vegetarianism, the female god, the sacredness of cows, the worship of the lingam-yoni symbol, the organisation of the caste system, all these are parts of Brahminical Hinduism. Where did those ideas come from? The old Vedic religion is not unique. Its relatives can be recognised in ancient Greece, in Rome, and in many other societies, even in modern Western European. Indra is unmistakably the same portent as Zeus and Jupiter. Brahminical Hinduism *is* unique. It belongs to India only. If its ideas came from outside India, as the Vedic ideas did, we ought to see its relatives elsewhere, for they too would have spread in other directions. But we do not. Therefore, it must have come from inside India. How?

The Brahmins have an explanation, of course. They say that certain holy men, Aryans, devoting their lives century after century to the philosophical contemplation of God, after the conquest of India, discovered the principles of creation. They themselves became the Brahmins, and the religion which they expounded is Brahminical Hinduism.

But there is another possible explanation, far more subtle and more interesting – that these beliefs came from the conquered Dravidians: not caste, certainly, but everything else. A discovery which proved that would cause a revolution in Indian thought. The discoverer would be world-famous . . .

Smith stopped his measured pacing and looked at the broad, yellow face of the gibbous moon. 'No,' he said aloud, in a low voice. 'Not fame, for me. But the truth, yes, give me the truth.' He smiled and raised both arms. 'And give Rukmini her queen, if that is the truth.'

Chapter Seven

Foster and Smith came to Cheltondale at ten. When Smith had explained what excavation might uncover, Mohan knew he must put the proposal to Mr Kendrick, and must seem to be backing it. In one way he was: it had a hint of digging for buried treasure, which was exciting; and, of course, Rukmini wanted it. But it meant that Smith would stay. Both Foster and Rukmini insisted on that. The man made him feel small and young, while Rukmini looked at him as though they had already slept together. Foster was going to pay the expenses of the excavating out of his own pocket.

At eleven Mohan sent a brief note over to Mr Kendrick at Southdown, asking if he and Foster and Smith could come in the evening to discuss an archaeological problem. As soon as he had sent it off he left the bungalow and walked aimlessly down the Dobehari Ridge. For the first time since the coming of Rukmini he wanted to be alone.

When he returned in time for a late lunch, he asked whether any answer had yet come from Mr Kendrick. Rukmini, reading in the window seat, said, 'Yes.' She handed him an envelope. He tore it open and read:

Dear Mohan:

Please come to Southdown at nine p.m. to talk about the archaeological problem. Afterwards I wish to discuss other matters with you, in private.

Yours,

C. Kendrick

Mohan folded it carefully, but Rukmini said, 'May I see it, please?' He gave it to her. She read it in silence and returned it to him. She said, 'I also had a caller.'

They were walking through to the dining-room. The major-domo stood behind Rukmini's chair. She sat down gracefully. Where, how, could she have learned these European customs? Had she been the mistress of some Englishman?

'I had a caller,' Rukmini repeated.

'Who?'

'Mrs Kendrick.'

'Looking for me?'

Rukmini did not speak. He glanced up quickly and began to explain, 'I broke an appointment, for a portrait sitting, after you came, and . . .'

Rukmini smiled slightly. 'She was certainly hoping to see you. But she was calling on me. That is very brave of her.'

Mohan bent over his soup. Brave? Or inquisitive? And what exactly did Rukmini understand by 'calling'? Rukmini said, 'She has invited me to come over to Southdown when you go there this evening.'

Mohan put down his spoon. 'Impossible! It's you Mr Kendrick is going to talk about afterwards.'

'Of course.'

'You can't come,' Mohan cried. 'Not even an Englishwoman would have the . . . the nerve to come at a time like that!'

Rukmini said calmly, 'Mrs Kendrick needs my help just as much as she needs yours, my lord. Mr Kendrick too, perhaps . . . That unhappy woman has had no experience of a man.'

Mohan stared at her, feeling a little cold and frightened. 'What do you mean?'

'She is a virgin.'

'But they've been married eight, nine years! You're saying that Mr Kendrick is . . . How can you know? Do you mean she *told* you?'

'No,' Rukmini said. 'But I know. Poor, unhappy people! The fact is bad enough, but when you think what can have caused it, and still is . . .' She spread her hands, and Mohan saw that she was crying.

He jumped up to go round the table towards her, as the major-domo came in with a note. 'From Kendrick Sahib?' Mohan asked automatically, as he held out his hand.

'From the City Warden,' the major-domo said. 'The messenger is at the front.'

Mohan looked at the envelope. It was addressed to C. Kendrick, Esq., I.C.S.

'This is for the Resident Sahib,' he exclaimed. He hurried along the passage. The messenger stood at the foot of the front steps, holding his horse's reins. He had ridden hard. Long splashes of greenish foam from the horse's mouth were not dry on his tunic, and he was soaked with sweat. As soon as Mohan approached he said, 'The Resident Sahib's not at his bungalow. They told me he had gone out with a gun.'

Mohan opened the envelope. After the usual flowery Hindi greetings, it began:

In the past two hours many persons have been gathering in the Batala quarter of the city. They sing patriotic songs and prevent all movement on streets in that area. The police have arrested five men, who claim they only went to that place to find the cause of the commotion. Several attempts to disperse the crowd have failed, since the people melt away and gather at once in another place near by. One sweet vendor's shop has been burned down in the block called Rajgarh. I hesitate to disturb your honour with this trifling matter, but in obedience to your command to be kept informed I send you these few details, assuring you that the matter is well in hand, and no further trouble is expected.

Then the signature of the City Warden; and then a postscript:

I have just ordered the army to stand to arms in the palace court-yard, to be ready for any eventuality.

Mohan began to reread the note. It was vaguely mysterious. Why all the fuss about people singing patriotic songs, songs of the past glory of Deori?

Damn it, he was an Indian, a prince, and a Suvala. He had read the letter as a straight-riding Gentleman Cadet of the Royal Military College, but it had been addressed to Mr Kendrick, an officer of the Indian Civil Service, who could read Hindi as well as English, both on and between the lines.

Now it became clear. The key was the reference to the burning of the sweetmeat seller's hut. All the buildings in the Rajgarh block belonged to the City Warden, the writer of the note. And he supported Mohan for the gaddi against the claims of his uncle Prithwi. The City Warden was saying that the gathering – one could hardly call it a riot – had been fomented by Prithwi. He put it in an oblique way in case the message fell into the wrong hands; and in case Prithwi did succeed to the gaddi.

Mr Kendrick was out in the jungles. The City Warden had not been to Sandhurst and therefore had not put a time on his message; but the messenger had ridden hard, and it was ten miles and a fraction from Deori, say an hour. The time now was two in the afternoon.

Rukmini's voice close behind him made him start. 'What are you going to do?'

He hesitated. 'I suppose I should send the messenger back to the City Warden with a note to say that Mr Kendrick will see the letter as soon as he gets home.'

She said, 'Why don't you go to Deori yourself?'

The idea had crossed his mind. Any of his fellow cadets at Sandhurst would not have hesitated; but then, they were not princes waiting for their principality. 'What good will that do?' he asked. 'I have no more authority to issue orders than the City Warden. Less.'

He admitted to himself that he was afraid; not much, a little. A mass of men acting, however indirectly, at the behest of his uncle would not be a pleasant crowd to be caught in. The Batala quarter lay on the opposite side of the city, so that he should be able to reach the palace without passing through it, but all the same . . .

He noticed that Rukmini was very pale, and her hand rested on his arm with an almost painful pressure. 'Oh, why can I not ride in by your side, and show them!' she cried.

'Of course you can't,' he said. 'There might be trouble.'

'It is about me,' she said. 'That is why I want to be at your side – and that is why I must not be.'

'About you . . .?'

'You will see,' she said. 'Are you going to take a pistol?'

'No,' he said. 'If my own people are going to shoot me, let them.' He turned to the waiting major-domo. 'Tell the syce to saddle Leander for me, and the waler for himself.'

'And while they're doing that, you must have some more to eat,' Rukmini said, pulling him into the bungalow.

The tunnel of trees ended and Mohan reined in from a gallop to a canter to a walk, and stopped. On this western side of Deori the jungles reached almost to the houses. The backs of the hovels, the thorn zarebas that guarded the chickens and the rooting pigs, faced him like a wall, pierced by the entrance of the narrow road. Straight ahead, half a mile farther into the city, the red battlements of the castle and palace rose high above the other houses and to the left of them he could see the tower of the temple. Listening carefully he heard no sound of shouting. If any buildings had been set on fire the flames had been extinguished. The small, ancient city dozed, shimmering, under the wavering pall of the heat.

Mohan rode forward, at a walk, followed by the syce and the messenger. *Hurry to the scene of action; then move slowly and keep calm*, Mr Kendrick had told him a hundred times.

Between the houses a pair of vultures were ravishing the entrails of a dead dog. The stench of ordure rose in the filth-laden dust and caught in his nostrils. The street ran nearly straight for a hundred yards. In that distance it was quite deserted. Mohan rode on with a slight slackening of inner tension. Not many people would be about at this time, even normally;

now, everyone must be over in the Batala quarter. The street turned a corner. He quailed at the sight before him, and his knees began instinctively to tighten on Leander's flanks, his hand to pull on the rein to turn the horse. Controlling the movement, he rode on at a steady walk. The street was full of people. *Remember, Mohan, never cause a panic by your own actions. A crowd is like a barrel of gunpowder. The results of a senseless panic, an explosion, are usually worse than the results of deliberately rebellious rioting.*

He was among them now. The first glance showed him that they were all men. Many carried staves but he saw no swords or daggers. The faces – there was something strange, something astonished about them. He had expected anger, determination, exaltation: these men were surprised.

Banners rose, haltingly, first here, then there, as though the banner-bearers were doubtful whether the signal to raise them had been correctly given. DOWN WITH THE WHORE, Mohan read. SAVE US FROM THE WHORE. He rode on, anger reaching down from the surface, first reddening and prickling the skin on his face and neck, then forcing down to his chest, his belly. A familiar slurring rasp of metal close behind told him that the messenger had drawn his big cavalry sabre.

BANISH THE GODLESS WHORE, a sign read.

Of course, they were expecting Mr Kendrick! The banners informed the British, through the Resident, that the people would not tolerate Rukmini. But why? Some of his ancestors had kept a hundred dancing girls for their pleasure.

The movements of the crowd began to take on shape. Voices rose, the murmurous awkward silence changed to a hubbub of shouts and cries, mostly meaningless, none informed with real anger. Among them he heard the lower, urgent voices of the organisers. 'Move closer.' 'This way.' 'Down the street.' 'Block them off.'

At his left side the syce gibbered in terror. At his right the messenger said, 'There's a side street just ahead, lord. I can clear the way into it.' He pushed the big sabre more prominently into view. 'These scum won't stop us.'

'No,' Mohan said. 'We will go on to the palace.'

The next moment the crowd surged close and packed in and seemed to double, treble, quadruple in numbers. The horses could not move. Even if the messenger had used his sabre it would have been to no avail, for the crowd was pressed tight and far. Mohan waited for the hands to reach up and drag him out of the saddle. He felt strangely unafraid, and found himself looking down into a thin, dark, peasant face, the man pressed against his horse, his eyes wide in terror of the big thoroughbred's hoofs, unable to move either forward or backward. 'Do not be afraid, my friend,' Mohan said. 'The horse will not kick unless you hurt him.'

Voices from the back of the crowd took on a rhythmic chant: 'Down with the whore. Banish the godless whore.' The pushing increased, the crowd swaying and bending like wind-blown wheat. The horses began to panic and twice Mohan had to fight to control Leander from rearing up on his hind quarters.

The noise and the heat grew. The dust rose in the narrow street until he could hardly see ten yards. The city dissolved into a brown, choking fog full of high-pitched screams. Banners waved half-seen, swirling and dipping in the dust. He heard the sharp crack of a stick against bone, and again. The syce had disappeared. A moment later the messenger faded back into the pall, the weary horse trying to buck and the sabre gone from the man's hand, knocked away by a long staff, but no other hurt done to him.

A small knot of men fought their way to Leander's head and a voice yelled up to him, 'Dismount, lord!' He looked down and recognised one of his supporters, a heavy-set young man who was a relative of the City Warden's wife. He dismounted quickly, and at once felt the unity and purpose of the group immediately surrounding him. Leander went forward, plunging and kicking now, two men at his head; but the phalanx round Mohan turned left and forced through the crowd, shoulders butting and sticks stabbing down on bare feet, yells of pain and anger falling back in the dust pall.

A door opened and he was inside a house, the others behind him. The door slammed. Bolts and bars ground into place. 'Upstairs, lord,' an urgent voice commanded. He stumbled up steep, narrow steps into a small room. The roar of the crowd was close still, but muffled by the thick walls. Outside there, a single voice screamed above all other sounds, 'He's in here, this one!'

'They know you're here,' the chief of his rescuers said. 'I don't think they mean serious damage. They were expecting the Resident. So were we. We, too, have men with banners out there. *Long live Mohan Singh Suvala, our rightful Rajah.*'

He moved to the small back window, the only source of light for the bare, whitewashed room. He said, 'Some of Prithwi's men are coming round the back already.'

Mohan felt the first attack of fear since meeting the crowd. He was trapped in a house in a back street. They could set fire to it. His hands began to shake and he fought to control them, pushing them deep into the pockets of his breeches. *Never show fear, Mohan.*

There were five men in the room, one of them an older man who had been here when they arrived, and whom Mohan now recognised as a priest of the Shivaite temple. Another was an important landowner from the lower valley. The other two he did not recognise.

The priest said, 'We are your friends, Lord Mohan – have no fear.'

'I'm not afraid,' he said curtly.

The man at the window said, 'They're prying a big beam loose from the cowshed to use as a battering ram. I don't think they're under control any more.'

The priest said, 'Lord Mohan, we are your friends. We and many others are risking much by organising support for you – and now by rescuing you from Prithwi's mobs. We will lose our property certainly, and perhaps our lives, if Prithwi does eventually succeed to the gaddi. A week ago there seemed no chance that he would do so. Now, through your attachment to the dancing girl called Rukmini . . .'

'What has she got to do with it?' Mohan snapped.

'It is said that you intend to marry her.'

'It's not true!' Mohan said.

The priest bowed his head slightly, but continued as though Mohan had not spoken. 'This morning early, it was all over the bazaars that you had promised to marry her if a certain statue is found.'

'They've pried the beam out,' the man at the window said.

'But . . . but the leg was only discovered yesterday afternoon!' Mohan said. 'Mr Kendrick hasn't even given permission for the digging yet.'

'And Deori is but ten miles from Konpara,' the priest said. 'The rumour was known in Deori by nine this morning. An hour later Prithwi took action to use it. As it is false, I beg you to announce your intention, now, of banishing this girl from your life and from Deori – or of marrying a suitable lady. Otherwise it will be all but impossible for the Resident to recommend you for the gaddi. It is not the truth that matters, but what people believe to be the truth.'

A heavy crash shook the house. Mohan stared at the men round him. To rule in Deori. That was his birthright, for he was the Suvala, the heir of Indra.

And Rukmini? *Loyalty to your friends, to those who love you, stands above every other duty,* Mr Kendrick had said. Mohan said, 'I will not banish her. But I am a Kshatriya by caste. I can see no way of marrying her.'

The priest sighed. The man at the window said, 'They've dropped the beam. They've been forced to. A lot of our men are round them, shouting and arguing.'

41

Through the walls Mohan heard the new cries, 'Long live Mohan Suvala!'

The man at the window said, 'Five soldiers have arrived.'

They ran to join him. Crowding among them Mohan saw a mob of people, close-packed, struggling round the back door below. Horses had appeared to the left, four troopers led by Captain Manikwal, sabres drawn, carbines still in the buckets.

All the men in the room except the priest rushed to the stairs. As Mohan made to follow, the priest laid a hand on his arm. 'The danger to your person is over, for the moment. The situation is unchanged.' Mohan shook him off impatiently and ran down the stairs. The troopers crowded through the house from back to front, on foot, carbines in their hands. Captain Manikwal, a genial, reckless rake in his early thirties, saluted him with a grin. 'Now we'll show the dogs,' he shouted. 'Come out and see the fun.'

The bolts on the front door ground back, and a heaving mob of men tried to force in. The two leading troopers, shoulder to shoulder in the narrow passage, lifted their carbines and smashed the butts into the foremost faces. The mob fell back and the shoulders pushed after them. Mohan followed. The crowd sound out there had become a continuous caterwauling of fear. Those at the front tried to get away, while from behind the people pressed forward as hard as ever; but slowly a space cleared. The troopers moved out into it, facing both ways.

'Load!' Captain Manikwal bawled.

'They can't get away,' Mohan said. 'They're trying to.'

'They'll move after a volley,' Manikwal shouted cheerfully.

The landowner from the valley hurried to Mohan's side. His hand gripped Mohan's elbows. 'Look!' he said urgently. 'We've got him! Prithwi!'

'What?' the captain said. 'Impossible! He'd never get himself caught in a mob like this.'

'It is, it is,' the landowner grated. 'There, about twenty feet in, under the wall, struggling like a madman to get away . . . his head down, in the old dirty robe.'

'By heaven, I believe it is,' the captain said softly. 'It is! He couldn't keep away, when he heard Mohan had come, and now he's caught.' He rubbed his hands and shouted, 'Left file, aim!' He walked forward and took a carbine from a soldier's hands. 'Fire when I do!'

Mohan watched with a pure deep thrill of excitement. Twice Prithwi had tried to poison him when he was a child, so his nurse had told him. All the time he'd been in England Prithwi had been intriguing against him.

Prithwi, sensing his peril, flung himself to the ground. By stooping, Mohan could see him quite clearly among the flailing legs. But now he could not possibly be shot without wounding others. Mohan almost groaned in despair. 'No,' he cried to Manikwal. 'Don't fire!'

Manikwal said, 'You'll never get another chance like this, my lord, never in a thousand years.' Kneeling, he aimed the carbine.

Mohan pushed down the barrel. 'No!' he shouted. 'I'm not going to start by killing my own people.'

The captain stood up, and after a moment handed the carbine back to its owner. He looked at Mohan and said, 'Suvala-ji, you may not have signed your own death sentence. After all, if you don't succeed to the gaddi, you can go away. But you have certainly signed mine.' He turned his back and bawled, 'Order arms! Stand easy!'

The crowd began to disperse more easily as soon as the immediate threat of firing was removed. *Unless a crowd is really bent on trouble, Mohan, a firm, gentle hand is the answer.* He leaned back against the wall, feeling suddenly weak. He should have allowed Manikwal to shoot Prithwi, who was a murderer. British ideals, Rajput tradition; Rajput blood, British upbringing. His life would be simpler if it had all been one or the other. Even Rukmini.

The 'feel' of the crowd changed again, without warning. At one instant they were dispersing in near-silence; the next – their voices rose to a roar, a shriek, their movements trebled in speed but lost direction. They turned back on themselves, ran together, and formed impenetrable knots which increased the panic.

Mohan ran out into the street, shouting, 'Keep calm! There is nothing to fear.'

But now above their heads he saw the horses, the bright turbans and the flashing sabres. A trumpet began to shrill the 'Charge' over and over again in a hysterical brassy blare. He grabbed Captain Manikwal and yelled, 'Tell those fools to stop! It's all over. *They're* causing the panic.'

Men fell around him, were pushed over and trampled on by the fear-maddened crowd. The trumpet echoed from the houses down the street, and from that direction the people rushed towards the cavalry, while others rushed away. The sabres rose and fell.

Mohan yelled, 'Stop!' and raised his arms and jumped as high as he could above the crowd to attract the cavalrymen's attention. There were about twenty of them. He saw Mr Kendrick riding in the third or fourth row, his riding crop rising and falling, his mouth open.

Slowly Mohan's arms fell. Pushed and jostled, Captain Manikwal's arm guiding him, he returned to the shelter of the doorway and the four troopers who now waited there, in close protective order, guarding the entrance.

The turmoil in the street slowly subsided as the cavalry reached the doorway. Mohan noticed dully that they had mostly been using the flats of the swords. Only a score of people lay dead or maimed or unconscious in the street. Mr Kendrick's face was white, wet, and contorted, his eyes burning as he laid about him with a riding crop, yelling, 'Take that, and that . . .'

Mohan stepped forward, and Mr Kendrick reined in sharply. 'Are you all right?'

'Yes, sir,' Mohan said. 'We have not been in any real danger.'

'Just in time, thank God,' Mr Kendrick said.

The twitching of the right side of his face stopped, and his breathing slowed. Dismounting, he put his arm briefly round Mohan's shoulder. His voice was normal. 'Firm action, taken in time, eh? Captain, recall your men . . . and then, give an account of the events of the day, if you please.'

Mohan stood back. Mr Kendrick was so calm now. He would not have been wearing that coat, or the black tie, or the tight white riding overalls while he was out with a gun; so, after he had been found, he had taken time to change into formal clothes before coming down. He had followed his own advice, the sort of advice he was always giving Mohan – to put on a calm, un-hurried front, to show that nothing out of the ordinary was in prospect. Until the decisive moment. Then he had panicked.

Mohan stirred uneasily. How could he tell what the situation had looked like from Mr Kendrick's position? Who was he, even to think that Mr Kendrick had acted foolishly?

The City Warden arrived riding a fat mare. Mr Kendrick drew him aside and they talked in low tones for several minutes. Then Mr Kendrick replaced his topi and called, 'Mohan? If you are ready, I think we will return to Konpara.'

The syce appeared, leading Leander. Mohan swung up into the saddle, and at Mr Kendrick's side rode out of the city. Nei-ther spoke until they had left the houses behind, and entered the jungle. The syce fell back to his proper position, too far away to overhear his master's conversation.

Mr Kendrick said, 'You know the cause of that riot?'

'Prithwi,' Mohan said. 'He was the instigator.'

'The cause was the young woman now living in Cheltondale, and the rumour . . .'

Mohan said, 'It's not true, sir.'

Mr Kendrick's tone changed. 'Do not misunderstand me,

Mohan. I'm a man of the world and I've – ah – sown my wild oats in my time.' He laughed, a short, forced chuckle. Mohan realised that Mr Kendrick was embarrassed; no – more, he was deeply ashamed. The tic in his cheek had begun again. 'I should have foreseen that something like this was bound to happen. Well, I'm afraid I didn't – but you've seen the consequences. You'll have to send her away.'

Mohan said, 'I can't do that, sir. I love her.' He spoke in a low voice, for he had learned that the words were obscene, when spoken by one Englishman to another.

Mr Kendrick's voice cracked. 'You can't. She's just a prostitute. All she can give you is sex, and sex is . . . vile, animal!'

Mohan did not speak. Mr Kendrick's self-control had always been thin, and behind it there had always been this wild anger. He used to think it was terrifying. Now, its chief characteristic seemed to be impotence.

After a while Mr Kendrick said, in his normal voice, 'Tell me about the archaeological matter. I gather that it concerns the statue which the rumour links with this girl, Rukmini.'

Mohan explained. Mr Kendrick said thoughtfully, 'This is more complex than it seems. You say that Foster is proposing to pay the expenses out of his own pocket? I find that strange.'

Mohan thought it was a little odd. Foster was a reasonably open-handed man, like most of his class; but to spend money on archaeology seemed out of character for him. The discovery of the leg had made everyone act strangely.

Mr Kendrick said, 'And then there is the dam. You realise that several hundred people will face starvation if anything occurs to delay its completion?'

Mohan said, 'Foster said there was no chance of that. Mr Smith asked him this morning.'

'H'm. Of course, we ought to make a search if the results could really be important. The Agent to the Governor-General would be delighted . . . But there is this rumour.'

Mohan said, 'Even if we find the Venus, I do not see how I can marry her.'

Mr Kendrick said, 'Then I think we should proceed. You agree?'

'Yes,' Mohan said.

'And after our meeting, we must have a long talk. Something's got to be done about this – uh – situation with the girl or the consequences to your future will become incalculable. We must talk, man to man.'

'Yes, sir,' Mohan said. He felt very tired, and much older.

Chapter Eight

Charles Kendrick ate his dinner in silence. When guests were present the pretence of an affectionate household had to be maintained, but when he and Barbara were alone he could ignore her existence and turn his mind to important matters.

He thought about the afternoon's riot. It would necessitate a special report to the Agent to the Governor-General. The report must not stress the seriousness of the affair, or the A.G.G. would come down himself, which he must not do until Mohan had got rid of the woman. It was a pity, because in minimising the riot he would also have to minimise his own part in it. Actually, until he led that charge with the few cavalrymen, the situation had been out of hand. Prompt, firm action had saved the day. He frowned. No one there, not Mohan nor the captain nor the City Warden seemed to realise just how close to disaster they had stood. From their manner, an awkward near-embarrassment, most noticeable in Mohan, you would have thought he had done something foolish. Were they too, like the heads of his own service, in the conspiracy to see that he never received the recognition due to him?

He raised the fork to his mouth with deliberate calm. He must not show that these pinpricks wounded him, or his enemies would be on him like a pack of jackals – led by his wife.

He looked at her covertly as she ate, her head slightly bent, her face hidden. He had married because a wife was a necessity to a governor; and then his superiors had made up their minds he would never be a governor. Of the ladies available to him he had married her because she was young and, as he had thought, innocent; and then he had found that the beastly craving for sexuality lay as strong in her as in any woman of the streets.

She looked up suddenly, catching his eye, and said, 'Today I called on Mohan's young woman. Her name is Rukmini.'

Kendrick stared at her. 'You – called on that woman?' he said, hardly believing his ears. '*Called* on her?'

'I didn't leave a card,' Barbara said. 'But I invited her to come here this evening with Mohan.'

Kendrick felt his cheek twitching. To hide it, he dabbed his lips and face with the napkin. His hands trembled and he put them down quickly, holding the napkin in his lap. 'You are trying to destroy my work here with Mohan,' he whispered furiously.

'I wanted to see what kind of a woman she was,' Barbara said. 'I went prepared to find that she was a simple prostitute. But she is a very remarkable woman, and a lady. She is more. She is an aristocrat, far more than you and I are.'

'A lady?' Kendrick snarled. 'You are mad!' The servants were listening, but they had heard such quarrels before, and they knew better than to hint about them outside these walls. He was the Resident and the Administrator, and he had many sources of information, many ways of punishment.

The meal was finished. He prepared his ultimatum and stood up. He was going to say, That woman is not to be permitted inside this house, or socially recognised in any way.

But as soon as he was on his feet a multitude of new thoughts raced into his mind, so that he stood scowling at his wife but saying nothing. If they ignored Rukmini, Mohan would spend more time alone with her. On the other hand, if Mohan saw her in English society he would realise how ludicrous it was to consider her as anything more than a night-time companion of lechery. And he himself would never be able to speak to her, whereas he should probably establish a seemingly friendly relationship; then, when she fully understood the position, and the extent of his power, he could offer her some sort of a bribe to leave Deori and Mohan. She was certainly after money.

Barbara said, 'When I know her a little better, I am going to paint a portrait of her.'

Kendrick leaped quickly at the opportunity she had presented to escape from his dilemma. He said with heavy sarcasm, 'Ah, of course, your art must take precedence over the ordinary customs of society. I hope that, when the portrait is finished, she will think more highly of it than I did of mine, which, if you recall, I *burned*. To ashes.'

He left the room and stalked through to his study. On the wall behind the desk a huge oil painting dominated the room. It showed an Englishman in the pride of manhood, as the centre of a battle scene. He had long fair hair and bestrode a rearing horse with the ease of a centaur. He was wearing a blue frock coat with gold epaulets, and was shown leaning down among a crowd of red-coated Indians, snatching from one of them a large Union Jack.

The man was his father, Dighton Kendrick. The Indians were a mutinied regiment of Bengal Native Infantry that had marched into Deori in 1857, at the invitation of Mohan's grandfather, the then Rajah. Dıghton Kendrick had been bayoneted to death a few moments after the incident depicted. For half a generation copies of that painting had hung in thousands of English homes. 'The Galahad of Deori,' the Queen herself had called the gallant officer.

Kendrick stared at the painting, as he did whenever he entered this room or the study in the Residency, for he took it with him wherever he went. *His strength was as the strength of ten, because his heart was pure.* That had been the popular quotation in the days of Dighton Kendrick's brief, posthumous glory. But it wasn't true. Dighton Kendrick avoided work, drank heavily, and seduced any woman who looked at him twice – which many had, both Indian and English. Everybody worshipped him, including his wife, his superiors, his mistresses, and their husbands.

Kendrick groaned under his breath. Why, why, what was the difference? He recalled, in an ecstasy of self-torture, the details of the portrait that Barbara had painted of himself. He had known she dabbled in art when he married her. Nothing strange about that. For the next eight years she had painted nothing but pretty landscapes and a few portraits. Then, this last cold weather, he had had one of the most unpleasant surprises of his life.

A group of tourists visited Deori. One of them was Sir James Allcard, the baronet, banker, and art collector. Dinner ended, the men sat over their port in the big Residency dining-room. Sir James pointed his cigar. 'Kendrick, you're going to be famous.' He remembered smiling in anticipation. Sir James was rumoured to have the ear of the Prime Minister.

The baronet continued, '. . . as the husband of Barbara Kendrick! I'll give you a thousand pounds for that portrait.'

He sat numbed in his chair, the glass of port half-way to his mouth. A thousand pounds? 'What portrait?' he asked.

'Good heavens, man, the one of you! Do you mean she has others as good as that?' He realised that the baronet was not joking. 'My wife happened to visit her in her workroom, and called to me. She – your good lady – says she has been experimenting with a new style. Well, Kendrick, I may claim to know a little something about these matters, and her technique is nothing short of masterly. A little advanced, some would say. A little reminiscent of Goya, others might think. But there's no doubt about it. She is going to be famous, and don't think I'm doing you a good turn by offering you a thousand. I'm making a sound investment.'

48

Kendrick managed to get through the next half-hour without admitting that he had never seen the painting. Afterwards, when they went to the drawing-room, he took Barbara aside and asked fiercely what she meant by it, where was this portrait – but Sir James and Lady Allcard were there, crying to see it again, and Barbara, very pale, at length said, 'Wait here. I will fetch it.'

She brought it into the drawing-room. Kendrick felt that he would suffocate. It was done in oils. It was a monstrosity, a deliberate insult a – a . . . Even in memory, words failed him. Every angle of his face was distorted, the colours a garish clashing of daubs. Worst, out of it all, out of the distortion and the daubs and the misdrawings – it was himself – himself, as sometimes in dark, lonely nights he saw himself: weak, ineffectual, suspicious.

He managed to pull himself together, find a smile, and refuse the baronet's offer. The portrait was a personal treasure; he could not consider parting with it. The following morning, when the visitors had gone, he burned it before Barbara's eyes, she standing very stiff and upright in the study the other side of his desk, saying nothing.

The insult of the portrait was bad enough. The possible consequences were unthinkable. For *that* she could achieve fame and wealth, while he languished in Deori, a failure. Letters had come from Sir James, also one from a world-famous painter, and one from another art collector. He had destroyed them all. She did not know that she had only to revert to that horrible style to become famous. *A woman!* His wife. He'd sooner see her dead first.

He picked up a pencil. On a sheet of paper he carefully drew the trident sign of Vishnu.

'Rukmini,' he said aloud, in a low voice. He had seen her three times before the meeting with Smith and Mohan. Mohan, blinded by lust, did not know they had twice passed him near Konpara, on their evening walks, but Rukmini did. She had looked at him, met his eye, passed some message, and gone on. But what message? Availability? Invitation? Comfort? Pity? Every line of her body, every fold in the drapery of her sari swept down into the fold between her thighs and drew the beholder's eye and thought.

The third time, seeing them coming, he had hidden himself and watched her through binoculars. She was disgusting. John Knox's 'monstrous regiment of women' in one body. He must study her and find her weaknesses, to turn them against her. Or Mohan's. The boy had looked jealous that time she met Smith. And now, from the rumours that had reached him, Smith was going to stay here in Konpara. There was a possibility in that situation.

They would come soon – Mohan, Foster, and Smith – to talk to him about the leg that had been found at the site of the cricket pitch. It was already rumoured in Deori that the statue to which the leg belonged was a kind of Golden Fleece, able to work magic; and that, if it were found, Mohan would marry Rukmini. So he should not, really, help or encourage the search. Suppose she had secretly placed the leg where it had been found – and, previously, hidden the statue where it *would* be found? But that was to credit her with too much cunning. The statue was probably genuinely old, genuinely important. He might send the A.G.G. a telegram announcing the important discovery . . . No, it would be wiser to wait and see, meanwhile encouraging the excavation.

The butler's voice outside the door announced respectfully, 'Sahib-log a-gye.' Charles Kendrick rose and walked down the passage to the drawing-room.

Half an hour later, having heard the story of the stone leg and its possible meaning in full detail, he pretended to spend a few moments weighing his decision. Then he said, 'Very well. On condition that there is no interference with the work on the irrigation project, you may proceed. When will you begin?'

'Tomorrow,' Smith answered.

Chapter Nine

Nine days later Mohan strode rapidly up the steep zigzags of the cart track from the foot of the dam to the plateau. He had been out since one, after an early lunch, and now it was three. After two hours of aimless, bad-tempered walking he had decided to go to Tiger Pool and have the cool swim he'd suggested to Rukmini in the first place. When she refused, saying she was too interested in the digging, he'd lost his temper and stormed off. They hadn't found anything, and what was there to see except men digging – and Smith?

When he saw Barbara Kendrick at her easel he had just reached the head of the final steep slope. From her position, fifty yards off the cart road, she looked along the length of the Kendrick Dam, slightly curved and now almost completed from cliff to cliff across the mouth of the Konpara pit. The coolies were still pouring the earth into the dam, and the files of women, each one carrying a basket of earth on her head, strode swing-hipped and flat-footed up the path from the fill pit.

Barbara Kendrick leaned forward intently and her hand moved in long firm strokes across the paper stretched on the easel. She was wearing the lilac dress again. After a time she turned her head slowly, and he was near enough to see that her face wore an expression of intense, calm absorption, quite different from its usual nervous instability. As soon as her eyes focused on him her hand began to move, to unpin the cartridge paper. Then she realised who it was, and she stopped. Mohan came close. Red and black charcoal lines slashed the paper. From them the dam sprang forth, and scurrying humanity, and effort, heat, and sweat.

The shock of the drawing's power made him stammer. 'Mrs Kendrick, it's . . . it's tremendous!'

She said quietly, 'Please don't say anything about it. Not to anyone.' She finished unpinning the drawing, rolled it up, and put it away in the long metal cylinder beside her. She faced him. 'When are you coming to let me finish the portrait of you?'

'Whenever you wish,' Mohan said.

'Tomorrow? About ten o'clock?'

'All right.'

Tomorrow Mr Kendrick was going down to Deori early. This was an assignation. But what would he do when the moment came?

'Don't forget, this time,' she said. She laid her hand on his wrist, her fingers closed and moved slowly, caressing the skin.

Leaves crackled behind him, and he turned. Her hand fell away. Jim Foster was walking towards them from the path, a peculiar expression, half grim, half fearful, on his face. He came closer, staring at Mohan. A yard from them he said abruptly, 'They've found a statue.'

Mohan recovered himself – 'At the cricket pitch?'

'No. Beneath the Konpara Cliffs, about half a mile south of the Rainbow Fall.'

That was nearly a mile from the site of the digging, Mohan thought, puzzled. 'The rest of the Venus?' he asked.

'I don't think so. I'm going to see what it's all about. Some villagers found it and came direct to me. Smith doesn't know yet. Or Mr Kendrick. I'll tell them on the way. Coming?'

Twenty minutes later, in a single party, they all approached the site of the new find. Here the Deori River ran in a shallow depression between the Konpara Cliffs on one side and the Konpara Ridge on the other. The Tiger Pool bund blocked the river's course just below the pool, but water was coming over the spillways and would continue to do so until it was ready to be diverted through the conduit into the pit. For half a mile below the pool heavy cultivation made the valley a patchwork quilt, its edges sharply defined by the containing walls of cliff and ridge. The cart track from Konpara wound between low dividing banks, forded the river – but there were also stepping-stones – and died out. Here Huttoo Lall, the headman of Konpara, met them and led them forward. He stopped. 'There.'

They stood at the edge of a small fallow and looked at a field of stubble. It was larger than most of the fields, and was not flat or evenly sloped, but rose to a hump at the far edge under the cliffs. Foster's foreman, Shahbaz Khan, and half a dozen villagers were standing in the middle of the field.

Smith said, 'Wait a minute. I wonder if that could be a man-made tumulus. It's difficult to see, but look, there . . .'

Mohan saw that the hump had a definite limit, being a rough semicircle, the diameter against the cliff and the circumference reaching out into the valley. The radius was about a hundred and twenty feet and the height about six feet above the 'normal' level of the fields.

'It could be,' Foster said. 'Come on.'

They moved forward, and soon stood at the edge of a trench which ran diagonally across the hump from the foot of the cliff towards the river. A stone statue, still half embedded in mud, lay on its back in the trench. Jim Foster walked over to his foreman and the two drew a little apart.

The headman of Konpara was speaking to Smith. 'When the river is blocked, sahib, these fields will be dry. But we will not be moved to the new land in the Deori valley for three years. So the Resident Sahib gave us permission to take water out of the pool, and we made a channel along the foot of the cliffs from the pool to here. From here we are going to lead it by other channels to all the fields below. These men were digging one of the channels when they came upon this . . .' He pointed down.

Smith stepped into the trench. Jim Foster raised his voice. 'Nothing more for you here, Shahbaz. Go to the conduit and make sure they're fairing off the lower lip properly at the exit. That's important.'

The elderly Pathan strode off. Foster rejoined the group. 'Reward,' murmured one of the villagers. 'We are entitled to the promised reward.'

'You'll get it,' Foster said impatiently.

Smith was out of the trench again, taking measurements and writing in his field notebook. Then he said, 'Carefully now, let's get it out.' Many hands reached down to help. Smith wiped off the clotted mud with his hand, and the statue lay bare before them.

It was an image of a standing man, a large plate-like halo rising out of the back of his head. He wore a kind of toga, its sweeping folds carved out of the reddish stone with the utmost delicacy and precision.

Foster knelt and tapped the statue. 'It's made of basaltic traprock,' he said. 'Almost as hard as flint, very hard to work. The man who made this knew how to use his tools.'

'And he was an artist,' Smith said.

The statue was discoloured in patches. Particularly noticeable was a stripe, two inches wide, that began near the hidden navel and curved across the body and under the left arm.

Smith said thoughtfully, 'What, exactly, do we have here?'

'A Buddha,' Mr Kendrick said.

Smith said, 'I agree. Greek influence. Of the Gandhara school. The carving of the toga, the long straight Greek nose, the curled moustache . . .'

'By the same fellow who made the Venus?' Foster interposed.

'Oh, no!' Rukmini cried. 'That is Indian, all Indian, before anything came here from Europe . . . Where is Gandhara, Mr Smith?'

'It is the old name for the Peshawar District, in Northern India. The Gandhara school flourished about the beginning of our era, and a little earlier. Most examples are in the north, but some have been found elsewhere – farther south than this, even.'

Rukmini said, 'Then this is comparatively new, and it is a mile from where the leg of the Venus was found.'

Smith said, 'Yes. We'd better take it to the Rest House. It seems to me that it presents us with more problems than it solves.'

The villagers led up a bullock cart, and carefully the statue was loaded into it. The cart moved off, jolting slowly along the track through the fields, Smith at its tail, the rest following.

Half an hour later the statue lay on one of the rough tables in a spare bedroom of the Rest House, which Smith had set aside as a Find Room. The afternoon light filtering through the dusty windows shone full on the subtle, carved smile.

Mr Kendrick asked Smith the question that was in all their minds – 'What do you propose to do now?'

Smith said slowly, 'I think that we should transfer operations to this new site – the tumulus, the Buddha Tumulus, let us call it. We have found nothing on the Dobehari Ridge, except traces of partition walls – dry stone, apparently. Further search there would be valuable, but it can be done another year, by other hands. It is an important task, but it is too big for us. We are looking for the Venus . . . and we need to make some spectacular find. I regret it, but it's true. With a spectacular find, such as the Venus, you will be in a better position to interest the learned societies and the universities and museums which finance these researches and, of course, do a better job than we can.'

'Does this mean you will need more men?' Mr Kendrick asked.

Smith said, 'Yes. The work at the cricket pitch was going very slowly. Now it seems that we have wasted – or, at least, lost – a week . . .'

Mr Kendrick said, 'Remember, Foster, no delay in the completion of the irrigation works.'

Foster appeared to be calculating, but Mohan thought that he had already made up his mind. At length he said, 'That's all right, sir. I can provide another ten men. They can start work tomorrow.'

The meeting broke up. Mohan and Rukmini walked back to Cheltondale. Mohan was preoccupied. The Buddha worried him. Perhaps it was the calm beauty of the face. Or the unmistakable foreignness of it. Men from Europe had been here two thousand years ago, imposing their ideas on India. Because the ideas were superior?

They were nearly at the bungalow. Rukmini said, 'Mr Smith's

going to swim in Tiger Pool after supper. He says he goes almost every night. It's a wonderful idea. Shall we go too, tonight?'

'No,' Mohan snapped. 'I have work to do.'

'Then I will,' she said. She seemed to be waiting, as they walked up the steps, for him to forbid her. Then she would say, 'Yes, lord,' in her meekest, most obstinate Hindu manner.

'Have a good time,' he said, in the careless drawl the English used when they were angry.

Chapter Ten

It was very dark by the pool. The stars glowed in a deep night, but the moon had not risen. Smith stood under the edge of the fall, wearing only a pair of tattered khaki trousers, and let the water pound down on his chest and upturned face. His forehead was set in a slight frown, for he was perturbed. There had been an aura of doubt, almost anxiety, round the Buddha's grave this afternoon. Why?

He turned his head as a movement in the starlight caught his eye. A silver ghost approached him round the edge of the pool. Only one. He sighed, with a touch of weariness. The most metaphysical problems were always being clouded by the complexities of human relations. This was what the Buddhists meant when they insisted that freedom from the wheel of existence was the first necessity in the search for truth.

She came close, at the edge of the splashing water, and said, 'You are very thin, and hard. You don't eat enough . . . Have you been in swimming yet?'

'No,' he said.

She looked at the water, up at the towering cliffs, and began to unwind the blue and silver sari. Then she took off the bodice, and stood naked, one hand out so that he could help her into the water. They went down side by side over the uneven rocks, and into the water. He swam beside her for half an hour, sometimes floating on his back, her hand touching his. When he could see her face it was very solemn in the moonlight, and calm. They did not speak a word until they reached shore and stood again on dry land.

She looked out at the pool, and said, 'This has been a place for love. The feeling is still here.'

Smith said, 'The pleasure and pride of the senses. Nothing more, here.'

'You recognise it, too?' she said eagerly. 'I see, in my mind, a hundred girls, and men, enjoying each other in the water, under the fall, all smiling, none possessed by jealousy, or any mean thought.'

'Like the carved wall of Mamallapuram.'

'Yes,' she said. 'And I am part of it.'

'One of the girls?' he asked.

'All of them,' she said. She stood a little distance away from him, showing him the beauty of her body. After he had admired it for a time, and the generosity of the full eyes that met his, she dressed unhurriedly, and sat down again beside him, staring out across the pool. She said, 'You are in love.'

He said, 'I have a woman – yes. A wife. And children. They gave me all that a man can need. I left them because I could not give them anything in return.'

'So you do follow the path of yoga,' she said. 'Though you are not a yogi . . . This wife, why did you not try the path of bhoga with her? Perhaps that would have enabled you to take her with you, wherever you are going, instead of going alone. Bhoga is my path.'

Smith smiled, but did not answer. As yoga was the right-hand road, the path of contemplation, and denial of the flesh, bhoga was the left-hand road, the path of action, of acceptance of the flesh. Every Hindu temple showed the choice, and impartially glorified the passivity of those who denied and the activity of those who accepted.

He said, 'Why isn't Mohan here with you?'

She said, 'Because he is jealous. And I love him. I love him as a wife, though I am not his wife. Oh, it is not all his fault. I become angry, and make up my mind to be just what he expects. When he thinks I am a loose woman, I act like one. When he thinks I do not love him, I do not love him. That is what some men – most men – want a woman to be: a mirror to their own thoughts and wishes . . . I have learned many new things since I came to your room that night. Mrs Kendrick desires Mohan. You are wise. What should I do?'

'Nothing,' Smith said.

She said, 'I wish Mohan could talk to me about it, though. He looks so worried, almost frightened, and yet expectant.'

'He is only twenty,' Smith said. 'And he admires Mr Kendrick.'

'I am twenty-one,' she said.

'You are older than the rocks among which you sit,' he said. 'Like the vampire, you have been dead many times, and learned the secrets of the grave; and have been a diver in deep seas, and keep their fallen day about you, and trafficked for strange webs with Eastern merchants: and, as Leda, were the mother of Helen of Troy, and, as St Anne, the mother of Mary; and all this has been to you but as the sound of lyres and flutes, and lives only in the delicacy with which it has moulded the changing lineaments, and tinged the eyelids and the hands. The fancy of perpetual life, sweeping together ten thousand experiences, is an old one . . .'

'I do not recognise that,' she said apologetically, 'I have not read enough in English.'

'Walter Pater, on the Mona Lisa,' he said.

'Oh. Perhaps that explains why I cannot really be jealous of Mrs Kendrick. It seems important, but not to Mohan's love for me, or mine for him. Besides, it is she who has more right to be jealous of me, and yet I know that she is not. She came to the bungalow to see me, full of jealousy. When we had met and looked at each other, there was none – though we both knew everything.'

Smith said slowly, 'I do not think any woman in the world will be jealous of you, Rukmini, whatever you do. You do not take, you give. No woman can know you without feeling pride in being of the same sex. You are the apotheosis of woman.'

'Mr Kendrick thinks so,' she said. 'I feel his eyes on me when he is sure no one notices. I feel the turmoil of his heart, hating me and desiring me at the same time. He is a desperate man. If someone does not help him soon . . .' She did not finish the sentence, and Smith said nothing. Charles Kendrick's tortured impotence was like a miasma hanging over Konpara and all the human relations being formed there. He knew what was in Rukmini's mind – or, rather, in her deep sense of tragedy and her deeper sympathy with every human need; but there was nothing he could say or do.

She stirred and said in a changed, more matter-of-fact tone, 'Have you noticed the names of the places here?'

He nodded. 'Yes. None of them are quite ordinary. The pit's real name is Devi-ka-garbha, "the womb of the goddess." The rock at the end of the Dobehari Ridge is actually called Indra's Rock, but the Rainbow Fall here –' he indicated the splashing water beside them – 'is also connected with Indra, for –'

'Indra-dhanus,' she said, using the Hindi word for 'rainbow.'

'Indra's Bow. And Dobehari means "noon," the time of the height of the sun, Indra's sun.'

Smith said, 'I have tried to work out some connection between them, but have not succeeded yet.'

'Nor I,' she said. 'But I think we should not forget these names. They were not given to the places unless, in the minds of those who named them, they were linked with Indra . . . and so perhaps with Indra's heirs, the Suvalas.'

'I agree,' Smith said. 'We shall go wrong in our search if we try to think of it solely as a scientific problem.'

'Yes,' she said eagerly. 'This statue was not made by a scientist, but by an artist. An Indian artist.'

'Aryan or Dravidian?' he asked, smiling.

She laughed lightly, then became serious. 'You remind me. The Buddha which was discovered this afternoon has nothing to do with Indra, so it cannot belong here in Konpara.'

Smith said, 'That is what I have been thinking, but hardly daring to accept.'

'It is so,' she said decisively. 'We may be able to prove it . . . One day in January my troupe was performing at a little village below Deori. The snake charmer wished to visit a shrine in the jungle, and I went with him. You should go there, at once. Do you know the Gurgaon Steps?'

'On the Deori River, about twenty miles below the city?'

'Yes. Climb the escarpment on the right bank immediately opposite the steps. A footpath runs along the top. Go east and after four or five miles look out for a very overgrown path leading down to the right, away from the river. Another two miles or so and there is a small, deserted shrine in the jungle. That is the place.'

Smith said, 'What am I to look for?'

'You will know.'

He glanced at the sky. He would start at once. And it would be a good idea to take someone with him. Mohan – he was the only one not deeply involved, in a personal way, with the search for the Venus. Perhaps this would draw him in, and so closer to Rukmini.

He told her of his thought, and she said at once, 'Oh, yes!' and leaned forward and kissed him. Then they set out, walking fast, for Cheltondale.

Chapter Eleven

Mohan ran through the jungle at Smith's heels. It was very hot even at this hour, a little after four in the morning. Soon full daylight would begin to spread over the hills across the river.

Smith set a terrific pace. Mohan wished he had not suggested running, confident in his ability to run Smith off his feet, and looking forward to the chance of doing it. Now he would like a rest, but his pride kept his mouth shut, while the breath whistled in his nostrils and his lungs were ready to burst. He kept his eyes fixed on the small of Smith's back. Smith and Rukmini had been alone at the pool together. His grandfather would have invited Smith to a feast and put ground glass in his food. His father would have had Rukmini's nose and breasts cut off. What should *he* do? Institute legal proceeding in a proper English manner? For alienation of affection of a concubine? Challenge Smith to a duel? The sights of an imaginary rifle, aimed at that back in front of him, slowly came into focus. The imaginary trigger was under his finger.

Smith stopped, breathing slow and deep. 'This must be the place where we turn off,' he said.

The dawn was upon them now, and they stood near the edge of the escarpment. To the left the land fell away in a thousand-foot sweep into a broad valley of dense jungle, split by the river. To the right the escarpment curved off into a tangle of gorges, cliffs, and flat-topped kopjes of traprock. The shrine was somewhere down there. Smith said, 'If Rukmini's suspicion is true, there might be a man or two guarding the shrine to discourage investigations. We'd better go carefully, though I'm afraid we'd have to be ghosts to go unseen if it's a Gond on guard.'

'But why should . . .?' Mohan began. He stopped, for Smith had raised a finger to his lip and was staring over his shoulder at something behind him. Mohan turned quickly.

A tiger came up the steep escarpment out of the valley. It was a large male, and carried a full-grown buffalo cow in its mouth, its jaws meeting in the middle of the cow's back. The tiger trotted slowly up the steep slope, its head raised high, so that only the

60

buffalo's head and forelegs trailed along the ground on one side, and its hind legs and tail on the other. Mohan felt a queer tightening in the pit of his stomach. He had seen tiger once or twice, as a child, when he had been taken out in the howdah of an elephant on a formal hunt in the valley. From up there the tigers had looked like no more than big cats that had strayed into the tall tiger grass by mistake.

This was different. He and Smith were strangers and this was no cat but a god who owned the escarpment, the jungle, and the rising dawn. Mohan's muscles ached with a kind of puny exhaustion as the tiger gathered its hind legs and scrambled up a steep rock, the half-ton buffalo cow firm in his jaws. Now he was on the same level as the two humans, and he saw them. A deep rumbling roar grew in his chest and Mohan's legs jerked. He wanted to run, above all he needed to run, hurl himself over the escarpment and down, as fast as muscle and acrid fear could take him, to the hazy blue valley below. Smith's arm was on his and the fingers tightened slightly. The tiger, motionless, the buffalo held steady, stared at them for a long time. The subterranean rumble slowly died away in his throat, and he turned and walked into the jungle, continuing his journey.

Mohan found his whole body shaking. Smith stared after the tiger and, when all sound had died away, said in a low voice, 'We have been lucky.'

Mohan wiped the cold sweat from his forehead. 'If he'd come for us . . .' he began.

Smith shook his head. 'Lucky to see him,' he said. 'In our civilisation it is the most we can hope for. In older ones there can be a closer relation between man and the other animals. The Gonds, for instance . . . they can still understand tigers.'

'But they kill tigers sometimes,' Mohan said. 'And tigers kill them.'

Smith said, 'I do not mean anything against the laws of nature, anything magical. I mean that they can live on that plane of life, like deer or antelope. Tigers kill those, too – but they understand each other.'

He turned down to the right, moving as fast as the overgrown state of the trail would allow. Mohan followed, and in the exertion soon stopped trembling.

Forty minutes later, the sun a line of yellow fire along the crest of the eastern hills, they were working carefully through dense jungle in the bottom of a shallow valley. Twice Smith stopped and bent to examine the ground; but shook his head.

At last he pointed, and Mohan saw the tumbledown shrine. The roof was still in place, broken in one corner. The stone platform beneath had been wrecked by ten generations of neglect, and torn up by the roots of trees. A loose, fallen arm of creeper, two inches thick, that had recently been cut off with an axe at the lower end, lay across the platform. That was all – that and a vaguely man-shaped discoloration of the back wall, and the clear marks where stone feet had stood, heels to the back wall. A statue had stood here.

Smith examined the area for a hundred yards in all directions, and returned, saying, 'Nothing. And I think that no one is here.'

Mohan said, 'What does it mean?'

Smith said, 'It means that some people went to a lot of trouble to move the statue that was here. And they did it in secret. It means, as Rukmini told me at the beginning, that we six who are searching for the Venus of Konpara are not working in a vacuum. Another world is observing us, just as we observed the tiger . . .' He shook his head and said with sudden vehemence, 'And, like the tiger, if we were not so cut off, so isolated in our civilisation, we should do more than see. We would understand . . . We'll rest, down by the river, and then go back.'

Chapter Twelve

At the Buddha Tumulus Charles Kendrick kept a suspicious eye on Rukmini. She must know where Mohan and Smith had gone, but was pretending she didn't. She ought to have told him about their absence before he rode down to Deori this morning. As it was he knew nothing until he had returned half an hour ago.

Kendrick stood in the shadow of the Konpara Cliffs; Rukmini knelt beside the trench out there in the sun. Foster stood in the trench. Beyond them, the bodies of the labourers shone dark and wet as the picks swung.

Kendrick saw Mohan and Smith first. They were walking fast along the cart track. He watched them suspiciously. They had recently washed and changed, but Mohan looked tired. They must have gone a long way. By heaven, suppose Smith were in Prithwi's pay? He had had all the opportunity in the world to kill Mohan . . . Better stop thinking like that, or he'd be suspecting everybody. Why not? How many friends did he have in the world?

Rukmini saw them coming then, and ran to greet them. Kendrick went out to join the group. Before he could ask a question Foster scrambled out of the trench, calling, 'Look here! There's something funny here . . . Oh, Smith, you back? Well, listen. You know you left a note that Shahbaz was to get the men on to digging straight down to find the depth of the soil before we reached bedrock, here at the tumulus?'

'Yes,' Smith said.

Foster was hot, dirty, and excited. 'The villagers' trench was two feet deep. After another three feet we came to debris, pieces of rock of various sizes – that stuff.' He indicated the pile of stones. 'Most of them have got the marks of chisels on them. The marks are worn by age, and by the earth chemicals, but you can't mistake them.'

He showed them a stone in his hand. The stone, red-brown in colour, bore a long broad score on one side. Smith turned it over; the other side was a clean break, the rough grain of the fractured surface clearly showing.

Foster said, 'This is red sandstone. I thought first it came off the cliffs' – he jerked his head, indicating the cliffs – 'but it can't have. Because these cliffs are traprock.'

Smith said, 'Very interesting. We'll discuss it in a minute . . . We too have made a discovery.'

Mohan cut in. 'Somebody put the Buddha in the earth here – recently. It came from a shrine thirty miles away.'

Kendrick's nerves began to tingle. He must control himself, must control himself. 'Are you sure of this, Smith?' he asked in a steady voice.

'Morally, yes,' Smith said. 'The stripe of discoloration on the statue is as near proof as we shall get. It was caused by a creeper that had grown across it, which had to be cut off before the statue could be moved.'

'I *thought* that earth came off easily,' Foster muttered. 'But everything was wet . . .'

Mr Kendrick said, 'You realise that this theory carries wide implications, Smith?'

'I am aware of them,' Smith said.

'Someone's trying to lead us up the garden path,' Foster exploded.

'Or to help us,' Rukmini said. 'That is possible. It has led us to a new discovery here – these chipped stones.'

'How can it help us to attempt to deceive us?' Kendrick said. 'Where's Huttoo Lall?'

'He's here,' Foster said. The headman had suddenly materialised, though no one seemed to have seen him coming.

Kendrick turned on him. 'What's the meaning of this? Where are those men who claimed to have discovered the Buddha here? Bring them at once. They must be the criminals.'

The headman's face showed great distress. 'It is possible, sahib,' he said. 'But – with respect – not certain . . . Originally the trench was dug to one foot. The criminals, whoever they are, could have brought the statue here, dug down a further foot or two in one place, laid the statue in the hole, and replaced the earth to the original depth.'

Foster said, 'They'd have to know that the channel was going to be deepened to two feet, and pretty soon.'

The headman said, 'We were running water through the channel for a few days last week, just after Smith Sahib came, when it was still at one foot.'

Jim said, 'That's why the dampness and looseness of the earth round the statue didn't make me suspicious.'

Mr Kendrick interrupted. 'This is a serious matter, Huttoo Lall. I expect your full co-operation in bringing the culprits to book.'

64

The headman said, 'I will do my best, for this causes shame and disgrace to all of us. But, sahib, it is an act of madmen. The process of reason cannot always catch the mad.'

Mr Kendrick said, 'Return to Konpara and start inquiries at once. I want to see those men who found the Buddha myself – and anyone else who can throw any light on the matter – as soon as you can find them.' He turned to the others, 'If you will be good enough to come to Southdown now. These matters had better be discussed in private.'

He led the way along the track, walking fast with head bent to avoid conversation, his mind racing. Things were happening without his consent, without even his knowledge – Mohan going off in the middle of the night, unknown men bringing the Buddha from far away and planting it under the Konpara Cliffs. He must regain control, or he would be lost.

At Southdown they gathered in the drawing-room. Barbara joined them, unbidden, from her workroom. Charles Kendrick faced Smith. 'Why was the Buddha placed where it was found? That is the first question we must answer.'

'To earn the reward,' Foster said at once.

'The people of these hill villages are very honest about money,' Rukmini said. 'That wasn't the reason. Did they do it to lead us to the tumulus? Because someone thinks we will find more there?'

Smith shook his head. 'Why couldn't they just say so? No, I'm afraid it's the opposite – to lead us away from the cricket pitch.'

'But why?' Mohan asked.

No one answered. Very interesting, Kendrick thought. Somebody knows that there *is* something near Cheltondale, and does not want it to be found. He said, 'The next quesion is – who?'

Smith said, 'That will be almost impossible to answer until we know why, and vice versa. I don't think that Huttoo Lall will learn anything in his investigations. If he does, of course, it will be easy. But supposing he is met by silence, ignorance?'

Barbara Kendrick said suddenly, 'That will be it. Darkness and silence. It will be like night in the jungle, when you know something is moving, but not what, or where, or why.'

Kendrick found a tolerant smile, and said, 'We had better leave that subject until after Huttoo Lall has reported to me.'

Smith said, 'Deceit, with intent – what intent, we don't know – against a person or persons unknown. Remanded for further investigation.'

'Which means,' Rukmini said, 'until something else happens.'

Smith said, 'I would like to make one suggestion, sir – that we walk very gently in our investigations. We don't know what's at the bottom of this mystery, but I have a feeling that our only hope is to gain the confidence of whoever is concerned. If it's fear that's making them act, and I suspect it is, then fear of us won't prevent them, but understanding might.'

'Of course,' Kendrick said coldly. 'I do not need instructions in the handling of natives . . . The next point is, what is the meaning of today's discoveries in the tumulus – the debris, the worked stone?'

Jim Foster said, 'That stuff is red sandstone. If it's from this area at all, it must come from south of the Deori River. The river's the dividing line, pretty near exactly. Basaltic trap on the north side – the tumulus, the Konpara cliffs. Sedimentary overlay of red sandstone on this side, the south – the Konpara and Dobehari ridges, and the pit.'

'How much of this worked stone debris is there?' Smith asked.

Foster said, 'It'll take a lot more digging to be sure, but we can guess. I think the whole tumulus is made of debris, from a depth of five feet on down. The top five feet is soil, deposited by rain and so on.'

'How far down?' Smith asked.

Foster said, 'We don't *know* yet – but suppose the whole place was flat whenever that debris was dumped there. Since then, five feet of soil have been deposited on top of the dump of debris. So there'll also be five feet on top of the original level of the earth *outside* the dump. So the height of the tumulus above the rest of the ground – six feet – is the actual height of the debris that originally made it.'

Smith said, 'Good! The tumulus is a semicircle of radius about a hundred and twenty feet, and depth six feet. The cubic content would be $\frac{1}{2} pir^2h$ . . .'

Foster wrote carefully in his notebook. After a time he looked up. 'One hundred and thirty-five thousand, seven hundred and seventy-one cubic feet.'

Mohan exclaimed, 'It's the ruins of a big building. The old fortress that's supposed to have been on Dobehari! But it wasn't! It was there!'

'Right under the cliffs?' Foster sneered. 'Besides, it's not that kind of cut stone. They're not shaped blocks, but irregular pieces. It looks like the debris of a quarry – but you can see there's never been a quarry on that cliff face. And anyway it's the wrong *kind* of stone, damn it. Pardon.'

Smith said, 'It could have been from a special kind of quarry . . .'

'A tunnel!' Barbara Kendrick said. 'A dark, silent tunnel.'

'My dear . . .' Kendrick began warningly.

Smith said, 'A tunnel? And the debris was removed from the site of the tunnel so that afterwards no one would know where it lay? I think you are right.'

'The men who built it would know,' Mohan said.

'If they survived,' Smith said.

Kendrick drummed his fingers nervously on the occasional table in front of him. 'One hundred and thirty-five thousand cubic feet, Smith!' he exclaimed. 'That represents an enormous excavation – beyond the capacities of Indians even today, let alone in the distant past. You are being over-fanciful.'

Rukmini let out a sudden, small, bubbling scream of excitement. 'Mohan!' she gasped. 'Recite the titles of the Rajah of Deori!'

'What's that got to do with it?' Mohan said. In her excitement Rukmini had laid her hand on Smith's wrist, and was gripping it hard.

'Please!' she cried.

Mohan said, 'Devari ke Raja, Suvalonke Pita, Suraj ke Chote Bhai, Indra ke Uttaradhikari, Khoha ke svami, Devataon ke Priyatama . . .' He broke off, staring at Rukmini, and began again in English. 'The Rajah of Deori's hereditary titles are: Rajah of Deori, Father of the Suvalas, Younger Brother of the Sun, Heir of Indra, Lord of the Cave, Beloved of the Gods . . .'

'Lord of the Cave,' Rukmini repeated.

'And it is not known what cave this title refers to?' Smith said.

Mohan said, 'No.'

A cave, Kendrick thought. A cave or tunnel of the dimensions they had just calculated. He pressed his handkerchief to his cheek. Rukmini was the instigator of the search. Everyone knew that. If such a cave were found the superstitious would be certain that the gods had guided her to it. Even the priests, however much they hated her, would have to bow before the people's adoration. And such a cave might contain carvings. It might contain something which she could claim was the Venus. His suspicion that she had planted the stone leg returned, redoubled. And the Buddha, too? He must think . . .

Smith swept out his hand in a wide gesture. 'We have five and a half weeks to find a cave, whose mouth has been concealed, somewhere this side of the Deori River.'

'It's not as bad as that,' Mohan said. 'Didn't we agree that no one would take the trouble to put us off the track unless they thought we were on it in the first place?'

'The Dobehari Ridge,' Smith said. 'Somewhere near, or under the cricket pitch. I agree.'

'Bats,' Jim Foster said suddenly. 'I heard about a cave being discovered somewhere by people watching all the bats that came out in the evening, and noticing where they came from.'

'Good!' Rukmini said. 'We can start now.'

'Too late,' Smith said, glancing out of the window. Outside, it was almost dark.

'Tomorrow, then,' Rukmini cried.

Smith said, 'I think the two men are here, sir, the ones who found the Buddha, with the headman.'

Kendrick jumped up and hurried out of the room. The two men waited patiently in the twilight near the verandah steps. The headman of Konpara was talking to a servant, a little apart. Kendrick leaned over the verandah railing. 'You,' he said. 'You! Did you find the statue in the trench?'

'Yes, lord,' one of the men answered nervously.

'It was put there!' Kendrick cried. He felt his voice rising. 'You put it there. Confess! You put it there for the reward.' He was almost screaming. He could not help it, though he was conscious of Smith at this side, the others close behind.

'Lord, sahib . . .' the man stammered.

'Don't lie! You put it there for the reward.'

'Sahib . . .' The man fell to his knees. 'I swear we did not.'

Kendrick began to tremble. 'Take them away,' he said to the headman and hurried back into the house, and to his study. His father's sword waved bravely in the gloom, his father's bold eyes flashed. Kendrick slumped into the big chair at his desk, his fists clenched.

The swine were lying. Every one of them was lying – to him. Not to Rukmini or Mohan or Smith. The conspiracy was against *him*.

He must think. Logically . . . There was a cave. It might contain the Venus. To please the A.G.G. he had authorised a search to find it. But now its discovery would improve Rukmini's position, and therefore be disastrous for his own plans. Therefore he did not want it to be found. Nor did the unknowns who placed the Buddha in the tumulus under the cliffs. So, somewhere, he had allies. But who – and why?

Chapter Thirteen

On the second following evening Mohan sat on the bare summit of Indra's Rock, his elbows supported on his knees, staring through his binoculars. It was the first moment of twilight and from his position he had a good view of the southern face of the pit walls. Yesterday, from a point beyond Cheltondale, he had watched the eastern half of that face, which ended at the dam. Today he was to watch the western part, for bats.

He thought he heard a voice and looked round, but saw no one. Then he heard it again, more faintly. It was a woman's. He went to the edge of the cliff and peered over. A file of men and women, all coolies, were wending away through the dense scrub, heading for the dam at the far end of the pit. Directly below him, where they had been working, it appeared that earth had been turned over under the trees. He could make out a pair of shallow trenches, twenty yards long and about the same distance apart.

That was odd. He did not know anyone had been working at this end of the pit, nor what their purpose could be. He must ask Foster some time. He returned to his post on the summit of the rock. The light was still strong enough to show the far cliff clearly in the beautiful German glasses, a present to him from Mr Kendrick on his eighteenth birthday.

Again he heard a woman's voice; but closer this time. It could not be the coolie woman again. It was calling his name. He lowered the glasses, and Barbara Kendrick walked quickly up the final slope and sat down beside him.

'No one gave me a task,' she said, 'but I have nothing to do – so I've come out to help you.'

'Thank you,' Mohan said, a little nervously.

He remembered that he had again broken an appointment with her. Instead of being alone in Southdown with her, he had been running to the shrine with Smith. She had said nothing about it, nor had he.

Mohan held the glasses to his eyes, but the light was dimming fast. Even the fine lenses could not draw in enough of it. He put them down. Barbara Kendrick sat close beside him, facing the opposite direction, as in a conversation chair.

She said, 'I don't think this is the way to find the cave. We must use our imagination. But there are many kinds of imagination. Which are we to use?'

Mohan thought a moment and said, 'If the cave is as big as we think, the men in charge must have been good engineers. Perhaps we should think as an engineer would, if someone told him, now, to build such a tunnel and cave.'

'Perhaps,' she said.

Several bats swooped and turned along the walls of the pit to right and left, but there was no concentration of them, and Mohan could not tell where they had come from.

Barbara Kendrick said, 'The smoke of the supper fires is rising from Konpara. It just creeps out through the walls and under the eaves. It hides the whole village in a blue haze that doesn't have any source. It softens it, so that you don't notice the poverty . . . I can just see the bullocks grazing on the thin grass near the village. The children are going out to drive them back into shelter for the night – shelter against wild animals and demons of night . . . These are the people who built the cave. They're not engineers.'

Fast now the ocean of darkness welled up out of the pit. It washed at their feet, and soon would engulf them. Her hand groped for his, found it, and held tight. He turned his head slowly, unwillingly.

She was crying, without a sound, her face turned to him and the wide eyes wet, the tears forming slowly in the corners and slowly trickling down her cheeks. The hand moved continuously, up his arm, gripping, kneading, down to his wrist again, for a moment on to his thigh, a touch, and flew up, back to his elbow.

She moved suddenly, enveloping him in both arms, leaning into him, and pulling his body towards her. She pressed her lips, open and wet, against his. Her body began to move in a jerking, painful rhythm. She relaxed backwards, and he felt the frenzied pull of her hands on his shoulders. For a moment longer he struggled against her, but the animal nature of the assault and the virility of his own youth were too much. Her legs spread wide and her skirt fell back to her waist. His male lust noticed she had come prepared; she had nothing on underneath. Her nails bit into his shoulders and her thighs grasped him. He felt a strong resistance in her secret parts, but only a moment for he would not be checked now. She shrieked once, and then moaned and writhed under him until it was done.

For a time she lay on the hard rock, her body shaking with slow, deep, almost soundless sobs. Then she sat up and arranged her skirt carefully over her legs.

'Don't be sorry,' she muttered.

'I am,' he groaned. 'I meant to say no. How can I face him?'

'The same way I have, for nearly ten years,' she said. 'By pretending. You have only done one thing wrong, and that in a moment. My crime is taking place every minute of every day. I am a woman, and now – worse – I could be famous.'

A vivid sensual memory of a minute ago sprang into his mind. Rukmini was right. Barbara Kendrick, until this hour, had been a virgin. The light which the knowledge threw on Mr Kendrick was too harsh, too painful to be borne.

'He is impotent,' Barbara Kendrick said flatly. 'For three years I tried to help him, but he rebuffed me coldly. For three years I begged him to see a doctor – but he flew into blind rages. You know. You saw one yesterday, not half an hour after he had agreed with Mr Smith that we must gain the confidence of whoever is concerned in this extraordinary business . . . For the next two years, I was numb, prepared to live like this the rest of my life. Since he burned my painting, when he learned that it was good, I have hated. I am sorry, but it is true.'

Impotent. Mohan found that he was not thinking of sexual impotence. In every facet of life – except the killing of big game – Mr Kendrick made good plans, and came to the point of crisis in good order, knowing the right words and the right actions. And then he failed. He, Mohan, had tried, in loyalty, to pretend that it was not so. Now he had to admit the truth.

He rose miserably to his feet. 'We'd better go back,' he mumbled. 'There's a conference.'

She stood up beside him. 'Don't be sad,' she said. 'Please. You've saved my reason. For over a year I've been thinking that I couldn't be made like other women. That there must be something repulsive . . .' They had come down from the bare top of the rock and were crossing the valley towards the Konpara Ridge and the lights of Southdown. She said, 'Worse . . . I felt that it would be a physical impossibility for a man to make love to me even if he overcame his repulsion. Then, when I met Rukmini, I knew it was not true. She made me feel that I was as truly and as wholly a woman as she is . . .'

'Sex,' Mohan muttered. 'She makes everyone think of sex.'

Barbara Kendrick gripped his arm. 'Oh, Mohan, *please*! Try to understand what a wonderful, unique woman you have, who loves you. Jealousy isn't . . .' She groped for words and her voice, close to him, was hoarse with earnestness. 'Jealousy doesn't exist in her nature, in the world she lives in. Let me tell her about this evening. Let me thank her. I could do it and she would understand. I think she knows already.'

'No,' Mohan said at once; then wished that he had not; but it was too late.

'I'm going straight into my bathroom by the back door,' she said. She stepped forward and kissed him on the lips. For a moment her body pressed against his, then she turned up a diagonal path behind the servants' quarters and disappeared into the darkness. He knew she would never come to him again. She had broken free.

Smith said, 'At a point in the cliff wall about forty feet above the floor of the pit, in front of Cheltondale, there must be a small crack or fissure in the rock, though the configuration of the cliff makes it invisible from below – certainly in that light.'

They were gathered in the study of Southdown. Barbara Kendrick had not appeared. Rukmini, coming in alone a few moments after his own entry, gave Mohan a keen look when she sat down beside him, but said nothing.

Smith continued: 'I saw nearly fifty bats emerge over a period of five minutes. Other bats came out from all along the wall, but in most cases I had seen them hanging from the roofs of small overhangs before they flew out. I mean, there is no other fissure that definitely enters the rock . . . Now we have to find a way of getting up to the crevice. Or down from the top, perhaps.'

Mohan watched Charles Kendrick. The Resident sat silent at his desk, biting his lip and saying nothing, his eyes always moving.

Foster said, 'That crevice can't be the main entrance to the cave. We've got to search the surface, and do it methodically. We've got to divide the whole area into squares, and search each one.'

'With the men we have available,' Smith said slowly, 'we can hardly cover the area in the time. We don't know where to begin.'

'We've got to begin somewhere,' Foster said. 'Begin at Cheltondale. I'll give you some more men.'

Smith said, 'Thank you, Jim . . . I think that's all we can decide now. Jim and I will have to work out how we can get at that crevice, but we won't waste your time here.'

Mr Kendrick nodded silently. The meeting broke up, and they went their ways to their own places.

Chapter Fourteen

Far away, a man squatted under an overhang of rock on top of a hill. He was old, bent, and totally naked. In his clasped hands he carried an axe, the handle long and light, the blade small.

The old man squatted, motionless, and stared through half-closed eyes at the sweep of rock and tree, and the rolling hills, and the shimmering heat. The sun swung slowly across the zenith and dipped into the western ranges. At noon the jungles were silent. In the worst of the afternoon they became possessed by something more positive than the absence of sound, a physical menace of silence that oppressed the whole earth. Towards evening the trees stirred, the grass moved. Birds flew across the leaden sky and monkeys chattered. In the reed grass of the dried marsh two miles behind the old man a pair of sarus cranes sang a harsh duet. Once, immeasurably far, a hunting leopard measured the silence into five-second lengths, each one clean-cut by the rhythmic coughing saw. The old man did not move hand or foot or eye.

In the last dusk four other men came to the overhang from different directions, one by one. They were all small, and black, with long thick black hair, heavily greased, and flattened aboriginal faces. All were naked except for a short bow in the hand, and a crossbelt of woven grass, which carried a quiverful of small arrows. They were all younger than the man who had waited under the overhang.

They squatted around him in a semicircle. One of the new arrivals said, 'He is to the west, ten miles. He ate the night before last – a sambur doe.' Their language was guttural and blunt, full of strange-sounding clicks and glottal stops.

'He can hunt?' the old man asked.

'Well. He kills men because he has lost fear. After killing the doe he crossed the river. He is asleep now . . . There are three others not far – one very close.'

'And his mate?'

Another man spoke. 'I found two females twenty-five miles to the south. I have not learned yet which is his mate.'

'The mate will move tomorrow, to meet him.'

'I think so, grandfather.'

The old man stared into the darkness with the same flat, unwinking intensity with which he had stared into the day. After ten minutes he said, 'They must be brought north separately. Have you heard both the females call?'

'Yes.'

'Make both calls for him, then. You – note which he follows and take him north with it. Keep to the far side of the western-most hills . . . You – bring her north, with his call, in the same way, but keep well to the east of the river. Neither must hear the true call or they will become puzzled.'

'And if they will not follow, grandfather?'

'Drive. Do not let them kill. If they kill, do not let them eat. Do not hurry them. Two or three days it will take.'

He rolled over, the first movement he had made for nine hours, and lay down on his side. The earth was friable there, where the rock had sheltered it for a million years. In a minute he was asleep. The younger men spoke among themselves for a few moments in low voices; then one by one they lay down beside the old man and went to sleep.

Near midnight a leopard passed along the ridge close by. His gliding passage through the jungle stopped, and slowly he turned his head, until he placed the scent. The five sleeping men lay twenty paces above him and to his left, up the slight wind. He padded up to them, and stopped a yard away to examine them. Stooping forward he sniffed the old man's naked toes. The old man's eyes were open and for a moment the two examined each other. The leopard went on his way and the old man closed his eyes.

The four younger men left three hours before dawn. Just before first light the old man went out of the overhang and walked silently among the rocks along the ridge crest, pausing now and then to turn his head slowly, his big ears trembling and his nostrils sniffing the air. The jungle stirred with a thousand small sounds, as its people prepared to end the night of hunting.

The old man pounced, leaping up and forward like a cat and landing on all fours beyond a round rock. A heavy lizard, two feet long, struggled momentarily in the old man's black claws, then the neck snapped with a short crack and the old man carried the lizard back to the overhang. A quarter of an hour later he placed the lizard's bare and bloody bones in a corner, wiped his mouth with a tuft of grass, and took up his position.

Towards evening he heard the deep rumbling roar of a tiger in the west. Half an hour later it was repeated. The old man gathered handfuls of red ants off the lizard bones, ate them, and, when the sun set, lay down and went to sleep.

Chapter Fifteen

Mohan stood on the edge of the pit cliffs, above the eastern end of the dam, and wondered what he could do. Mr Kendrick was in Southdown, working on revenue papers. Foster was somewhere in the coolie camp below the dam there, wrestling with the forces of water, stone, and earth. Smith and two labourers were on the scaffold, sweating with mallet and crowbar. They had made a respectable hole in the cliff face.

From here he could see the scaffold clearly, though it was nearly three-quarters of a mile away. If he had had his binoculars with him he could have seen the faces of the men at work on the platform. The scaffold had taken three days to build, three days when every time he looked out of the southern windows of Cheltondale he saw Foster, waving his arms and striding to and fro, working in a continuous frenzy of impatience. This was the scaffold's fourth day of operation. It was in two sections. The lower section was built up from the ground. Foster had placed fifty-foot logs against the cliff and buttressed them in place with other logs, as long, that leaned at an angle against the cliff face. Forty feet up from the pit floor a working platform four feet wide by twelve feet long was cantilevered out from the uprights. Strong wooden rungs climbed the cliff between the uprights, forming a wide ladder. The upper section of the structure consisted of two massive beams on the cliff top, anchored into the soil well back from the edge. The last six feet of the beams projected over the cliff. From them a light bamboo ladder reached down to the working platform. A sheer-legs stood a little to one side, where it could be used to lower heavier equipment, cut stones, and roof props down to the working platform, when they were needed.

As he stared, Mohan saw one of the three figures on the platform begin to ascend the ladder. At the top a point of red colour joined the figure, and the two went up the path towards Cheltondale, soon disappearing in the trees, reappearing on the verandah of the bungalow, disappearing once more into the shadow – Smith and Rukmini. Directly behind and above the point where he had last seen them the gold mohur tree that hung over the thatched roof was bursting into a brilliant orange and gold flower.

Mohan turned and strode down the steep slope towards the coolie camp. What should he do? Hurry back to Cheltondale and order Smith out of the house? That would be acting like an oriental potentate. Ignore it? There were a hundred reasons why Rukmini might have asked him in – for a cup of tea, to bandage a cut. The place was full of servants. It was broad daylight. Mr Kendrick kept hinting that once a woman had been a prostitute she would never be faithful. But had Rukmini ever been one? And what was Mr Kendrick's view of any woman worth?

He climbed the dam and stood on top, gloomily surveying the pit while the coolies passed and repassed him at their labour.

'Mohan!'

He turned quickly. Barbara Kendrick was sitting at the end of the dam, her back against the cliff, the drawing-board on her knees. She was only twenty feet from him. She said, 'I have been making a sketch of you. No, you can't see it yet.' She unpinned the paper, rolled it up, and put it away in the familiar metal cylinder. She stood up. 'Time to go back for tiffin. I want to go through the pit, but it's so eerie, somehow. Will you take me?'

There was no coquetry in her manner. He thought, I can talk to her now. I'll ask her about Rukmini and Smith; she'll make me see how mean and degrading my jealousy is.

'Come on, then,' he said gently. 'Let me carry your drawing-board.'

'Going back for tiffin now, Mrs Kendrick?' The voice behind him was rough and determined. Mohan turned and found Jim Foster close at his elbow.

'Yes,' Mohan answered for her. 'We're going back through the pit.'

'Fine,' Foster said. 'I'll come along too. Pretty nasty for a lady, getting up that scaffold and the ladder.'

Barbara Kendrick hesitated a moment, her eye meeting Mohan's. He knew that she had sensed his desire to talk to her. But there was no help for it. They followed Foster along the top of the dam. Foster talked volubly, pointing out various wonders of the work. At the head of the steps leading down the inner face, into the pit, he said, 'Careful now, Mrs Kendrick. They're a bit slippery.'

Slowly they descended the steps. From the foot a narrow path plunged into the scrub jungle, leading to the foot of the scaffold. As they entered it the leaves and twined tendrils roofed them in, and Mohan could no longer see the spindly scaffolding ahead, or the foreshortened mouth of the conduit beyond, or even the bare, stark jut of Indra's Rock beyond that.

'Look where you're putting your feet,' Foster called back over his shoulder.

They passed slowly on, stooping under the clutching arms of the scrub. The path was clearly marked, for the carpenters had come in and out this way when working on the scaffold.

Barbara Kendrick stopped. 'This place is wonderful! I'd like to be here at night, when there's a moon. Look at those creepers . . . and the arms of that tree, reaching out towards us, like a prisoner's.'

The tree stood high above the scrub, its trunk twisted, its arms bare. It reminded Mohan of Laocoön and his sons wrestling with the giant python. There was a patch of colour beside the path twenty or thirty yards farther on. Beyond that he heard voices. The colour was yellow. It moved.

He was looking at a tiger crouched beside the path, the body facing away from him but the head turned, the yellow eyes staring into his. Beyond, the voices grew louder, and he heard the chink of metal.

People, coming along the path. The tiger, lying in wait for them. Himself, frozen with fear.

His arm came up slowly, pointing. Barbara saw it first, then Foster. The tiger did not move. It was waiting for the other people. Foster was frozen, like himself. Barbara stood between them, staring at the tiger.

He'd got to do something to warn the people. Anything he did would bring the tiger upon him. Mr Kendrick would run at it. Mr Kendrick was not afraid of animals, only of women.

He jerked himself into motion, but Foster had moved a fraction of a second earlier, shouting a warning and running forward. Mohan ran, a pace behind him. He found he had something in his hands, and hurled it at the tiger. The drawing-board flew through the air.

The tiger roared and leaped away from them. A moment later a moaning shriek towered slowly out of the jungle, cut off short under a deep cough. Twigs cracked, the bush creaked. Barbara Kendrick was here. Foster flung his arm across her chest, forcing her back and down. No revolver, no gun, no knife, nothing. Voices still yelled in front, but dwindling.

Fifteen feet ahead a black and gold shape sprang over a thicket, a man in its mouth. A tigress, not a tiger. She had the man by the middle of the back, so that his body hung down on either side, just like the buffalo cow. He was a coolie, his bare head towards them, the neck twisted and a trickle of blood

77

running from the corner of the mouth, the wide eyes staring straight at Mohan. The tigress saw them, but took no notice and trotted off into the dense scrub, forcing a passage through it, with the man, as though it had been grass. The rustling and breaking of bushes continued for a few moments, then stopped.

For a long time there was no sound at all in the pit. The distant cries had died, and the midday wind stirred the heat, but in silence. She's close, Mohan thought. Barbara was pressed close against Foster, not shivering, her eyes tremendous and her face utterly concentrated, looking the way the tigress had gone.

No sound there. She'd be licking her paw, perhaps, like a cat, sniffing the man, tapping him to see if he'd move again.

A loud crunch, the unmistakable sound of jaws champing on flesh. Mohan's back hairs crawled. A decisive *crack*, like a dry stick breaking – the spine.

The low singsong whining purr rolled through the jungle, coming from there . . . no, there. She was moving. Mohan sank lower to the ground; Foster's arm pressed Barbara down. She was moving, purring. His own tongue and lower lip dripped blood. She was not moving. He'd heard about the terror of that particular sound. It seemed to have no source. How long must they wait here, listening to this?

Foster pointed forward. The tigress had gone to the left and then a little back, towards the dam. Mohan rose, crouched low, took a careful step, placed his foot down. A twig snapped. The purr dropped to a thunderous growl. Mohan dropped, hardly breathing. After a minute the purr began again.

A new sound came from the west, ahead. The purring stopped; again the tigress gave her warning growl. Staring along the path under the overhanging scrub Mohan saw a pair of legs, moving, wearing khaki trousers and strong canvas-topped boots, the tip of a gun barrel . . . another pair of legs behind.

The tigress snarled once more. Bushes rustled, the sound fading rapidly towards the north.

'She's gone,' he called shakily. 'Here, here . . .'

Mr Kendrick appeared, Smith behind him. Smith carried a stick, Mr Kendrick a double-barrelled shotgun, and binoculars slung across his chest.

'Mohan!' he cried. He broke into a run. 'What are you doing here? Haven't I told you to take care of yourself? Don't you realise . . .' His voice rose, broke.

'I'm all right,' Mohan stammered. Kendrick's outburst enabled him to regain his own nerve. He said, 'She took the man in there and started to eat him, and then went off towards the dam.'

Mr Kendrick's tic had ceased. 'Not worth following her,' he said. 'She'll be going fast. She knows the danger as well as we do. She has to get back over the dam, which must be the way she came in. There's no other. She won't hurt anyone there, unless they shoot at her.'

'No one there's got a gun,' Foster said.

Kendrick said, 'We'll pick up her trail at the dam, Smith. But first we've got to go back to Southdown and get proper rifles.' He turned and strode fast back along the path, Smith following.

Foster, Mohan, and Barbara Kendrick looked at one another, in silence. Foster shook his head at last and they went on, in silence.

At the top of the scaffold they found a few coolies and Ahmed, the foreman's cousin. Rukmini was not there. Surely she might have come, Mohan thought.

Foster spoke to Ahmed. 'Who was it?'

'One of the Nagpur coolies, sahib,' Ahmed said. He was still trembling, his mouth working uncontrollably. 'We were coming back from our work, and heard someone shout, "Careful, tiger!" – so we ran, scattering into the jungle, but it was no use. The tigress had already chosen him. She came and took him, *aiiih*, right in front of me! I could have touched her as she stood up and bit his neck, so that it broke, the neck broke, then she seized him, and was gone, all in a second, two seconds . . .'

Mr Kendrick galloped up on a horse. Now he had a heavy rifle slung across the saddle. 'Has Smith Sahib gone to the dam?' he called. Ahmed said, 'Yes, sahib.'

Kendrick said, 'Mohan, did you say she'd started to eat him, there in the pit?'

Mohan said, 'Yes. She . . .'

'She must be very hungry. She won't go far. Get everyone inside their houses. No more outside work today.' He galloped off.

Ahmed and the coolies vanished, hurrying towards the coolie camp. Mohan turned to Barbara. 'I'll pick up my rifle from the house and escort you back to Southdown.'

'No, you won't,' Foster snapped. 'I will.'

Mohan blinked. He saw that Foster had worked himself into a towering rage.

'Please, please!' Barbara Kendrick's voice was soft between them. An unwilling triumph illuminated her face, her colour had returned, and she was almost smiling. 'I'm not going to Southdown just yet,' she said. 'I'm going back into the pit.'

'What?' both men cried together.

'I've left the cylinder there.'

'We can fetch it later,' Mohan said. He realised she was determined that her husband should not get at it; but, all the same, this was sheer folly.

She was obstinate. 'I'm afraid I must go now.'

Mohan said, 'Then I'll go with you.'

Foster turned on him. 'I just told you to keep out of this. Step this way a minute.' He grabbed Mohan's arm, and pulled him away. Mohan allowed himself to be dragged off, for he had begun to think Foster had gone mad. Foster pushed his face close, dropped his voice, and grated, 'You keep your hands off Mrs Kendrick, see? You don't mean her any good and she's too much of a lady to know it. Leave her alone. Got it?'

Foster let go with a final shake, turned, and stalked back towards Mrs Kendrick. Mohan took a step after him, anger rising at the way he had been spoken to. Then he thought, by God, Foster thinks he's protecting a white woman against a dirty nigger. Blind with rage, he broke into a run.

Rukmini ran out from the trees on his left. She threw herself into Mohan's arms. 'Are you all right? My dearest, my dearest, are you . . .?'

'Yes,' he growled. 'Get out of my way.'

She held him fast, and he could not move. 'The tigress!' she said. 'I was with one of the parties searching for the entrance to the cave, and only just heard. I've run all the way.'

'I'm all right,' he said. Her tears were warm and wet against his neck. He stared over her head at the top of the scaffold, where Foster and Mrs Kendrick had just disappeared. 'I'm going to see that that fellow is dismissed,' he said.

Rukmini stood away from him. 'Let's go up to the house,' she said. She took his arm. He went slowly with her, frowning.

Rukmini said gently, 'My dear lord, you can't give *her* anything, except what any man can give any woman. Foster can.'

He muttered, 'He thinks I'm a nigger.'

'Did he say so?' she asked.

'No, but . . .'

She interrupted him. 'That's not it at all. He's in love with her. He'd pick a fight with Mr Smith if Mr Smith meant the same to her that you do.'

Mohan felt an enormous relief. He didn't want to hate anyone with the intensity of hate he had just felt towards Jim Foster. They reached the drawing-room and he sank down on the sofa, Rukmini curled up beside him, her head on his chest. 'I don't see what they are ever going to have in common,' he said thoughtfully.

'Love, trust, affection, admiration,' she said. 'Four things she's never had . . . I heard that Mr Foster tried to warn the coolies, though the tigress must have been very close.'

'I tried, too,' Mohan said. He added, 'He moved first, and I think he was more frightened than I was.'

Rukmini said, 'He wanted to show Mrs Kendrick, and himself, that he was as good a man as you.'

Mohan nodded. He had found the strength to move in the same manner – determination to stand on a level with Kendrick.

Rukmini said, 'Let her go, my dear lord. Let her go to Mr Foster.'

She seemed to become depressed. After a while she slid to her feet and walked across the room. She stood, wringing her hands slowly together, looking out of the window. He asked her, 'What is it?'

She burst out, 'I cannot bear to think of Mr Kendrick's unhappiness. Does he fail everywhere because he is impotent, or is he impotent because he has always failed? Thank God, it is something a woman cannot know – to be absolutely unable to give. It must drive a man to despair, to hatred . . .'

Mohan said, 'She hates him as much.'

She said, 'Something must be done. No man should suffer that.' She ran back, and threw herself into his arms. 'I love you, only you. Will you remember? Always? Promise.'

'I'll remember,' he said.

'Until the first time you doubt!' she said. 'Was it love that made you give Mrs Kendrick what she needed?'

'No!' he said, jumping up. 'Of course it wasn't.'

'Why did you do it then?'

'She . . . she needed me!' he cried. 'I couldn't resist it. You don't know what a man feels like, Rukmini, when . . .'

'Yes, I do,' she said. 'You must remember that a woman sometimes feels the same.'

In the evening Charles Kendrick came to Cheltondale, with Smith. They were both grimed with dirt and the stains of the jungle. Kendrick said, 'She left the body three miles beyond the coolie camp. She'd eaten half of it while she was travelling. She won't come back.'

Smith said, 'Foster and the headman of Konpara met us at the camp on our way back. They've been having trouble. At first all the coolies refused to work, anywhere, until the tigress is killed. Finally, they did agree to go back tomorrow, but only on the dam and the conduit. There'll be no more archaeological work until she's killed.'

'I shall devote all my time to tracking her down,' Kendrick

said. 'But don't expect results too quickly. It will be a slow job.'

'No work at all?' Rukmini said in dismay.

Smith said, 'The headman offered to work, with his brothers, but I couldn't accept that.'

'He has too much to do in the village,' Kendrick said.

'Then I shall,' Rukmini cried. 'I won't let the tigress stop the search! I can hold the crowbar for you to hit, at least.'

Smith smiled at her, the flecked eyes dancing with admiration and an intimate knowledge. Mohan turned away, gripped by the familiar, hated ogre of jealousy. He had imagined, for one mad moment, that Rukmini was telling him, earlier, that she felt a helpless passion for Kendrick, and would not be able to resist him if he made an advance. But it was Smith, of course, whom she had meant.

Smith said, 'I'll come down early tomorrow, and we'll see what the three of us can do on the platform.'

'I shall go out after the tigress,' Mr Kendrick said. A thought seemed to strike him suddenly. 'Ah, we must all put off work, even tiger hunting, until the day after tomorrow. I had almost forgotten. Tomorrow is the day of the cricket match, Mohan Singh's XI against the Gentlemen of Saugor, down in Deori.'

Mohan said shortly, 'I cancelled it a week ago. We have more important things to do than play cricket.'

'You should have told me,' Mr Kendrick said angrily.

'I'm sorry,' Mohan said. 'I forgot.'

Chapter Sixteen

The following day Smith reached the bungalow at eight in the morning. Rukmini flew out to the verandah to greet him. When they came in Mohan saw that Smith had already been at work, probably since dawn.

Smith sat down and accepted a cup of tea. After drinking, he looked at Mohan, and said, 'Have you thought to wonder who was killed yesterday?'

'It was a coolie,' Mohan said, puzzled. 'Not a Konpara man. One of the Nagpur coolies Foster brought in – the ones who live in the coolie camp.'

Rukmini said, 'Ah, what a fool I am! What were they doing up there?'

Smith nodded. 'That's it. Those people, under Ahmed, were returning to the coolie camp from work at the west end of the pit – somewhere west of the scaffolding. I'm as slow-witted as any, because I've seen them going back nearly every evening, passing under the scaffold, and I've never thought to wonder what they were doing, until now.'

'I know!' Mohan said suddenly. 'They've been digging trenches in the floor of the pit, directly under Indra's Rock. I saw them, the second evening we were looking for the bats. A week ago.' He remembered well. He had heard a coolie woman's voice; and, a little later, Barbara Kendrick had come to him.

Rukmini said, 'I think we shall have to ask Mr Foster.'

Smith said, 'I took the liberty of inviting him to come here at half-past eight. I think he's here now.'

The major-domo announced, 'Foster Sahib.' The contractor clumped in, his brows set, the red hairs thick and wet on his forearms. He too had been at work.

'You wanted to talk to me?' he asked Mohan, with barely controlled belligerence.

Smith said, 'It was my idea, Jim. I wondered whether the excavations your people are doing under Indra's Rock might have anything to do with our search.'

'I thought that was it,' Foster said. 'Some busybody been

telling you about it, eh? Well, it's my mineral rights. I've got a right to look for minerals, haven't I, under the contract?'

'Yes, of course,' Mohan said hastily. He wanted to make the fool understand that there was no quarrel between them.

'I was looking for iron ore,' Foster said. 'Thought there might be a trace. There isn't . . .' He searched in the breast pocket of his shirt and drew out two small flat objects. 'But they did find these. Two, three days ago.'

Mohan turned the objects over carefully in his hand, while Smith and Rukmini bent to examine them. They were about three inches square, greenish in colour, and bore a design in high relief. The design on one included, across the top, some marks that might have been writing, and, below, the figure of a naked woman. She had a wasp waist, heavy hips, huge round breasts, and an exaggerated sexual cleft. The second object, otherwise similar, carried the device of a tree, a three-headed semi-human being under it, and an unmistakable hump-backed Indian bull.

'They're soapstone,' Foster said. 'No value.'

Smith felt the pieces carefully between his fingers. 'A form of soapstone,' he said. 'Steatite. See the holes in each end? These were brooches. I've seen something like them before – Assyrian seals of 3000 B.C.'

Foster said, 'The only other thing we've found is bones. Thousands of bones. So old that most of them turn to powder when they're exposed to the air.'

Mohan leaned forward. Why on earth had Foster said nothing about that? Rukmini's eyes warned him to hold his tongue.

Smith said, 'I think we'd better have a look at the site, if you can spare the time to show us.'

'Of course I can,' Foster said. 'Would have shown you before if I hadn't thought it was a waste of your time.'

Fifteen minutes later, having climbed down the scaffolding to the floor of the pit, they were winding in single file along a narrow trail through dense scrub. Soon Foster stopped and they gathered round him. 'Here we are,' he said. 'I always wondered whether this reddish soil might be iron ore. So finally I put some fellows on to find out. The coolies have been digging trenches across this hump, and bringing me samples of the soil. Nothing doing, and they didn't like finding the bones. I was going to stop today, anyway.'

None of the scrub had been cleared. There were a few small random holes and two trenches running under the trees at the base of the pit wall. Mohan noticed that all the work lay in the semicircular area of a flat-topped hump, where the level of the pit floor stood several feet higher than elsewhere.

'Smith,' he said with sudden excitement, 'this is another tumulus!'

'Very like,' Smith said. 'A little smaller, not quite so high.' He glanced into a trench, Mohan beside him. Near the bottom, above five feet down, the colour of the soil changed sharply from reddish to pale grey. Here and there the shape of bones was visible, but not the substance, in the manner that burned ash holds its shape on the end of a cigar.

Smith said, 'The bones are about the same distance down from the present surface as the stone debris is in the Buddha Tumulus. We don't know that the rate of soil deposit would be the same in both places, but the conditions are similar. They're both under the north wall of a cliff, and each cliff is about a hundred feet high – the Konpara Cliffs there, the pit wall here.' He bent back his head and stared up the face of the wall. 'The centre of the tumulus appears to be directly under Indra's Rock.'

Rukmini said, 'The bones, Mr Foster – do they cover the whole of the tumulus, at that level?'

Foster nodded, 'As far as we can tell. In both trenches, at five feet, there are bones. I thought it might be a cemetery of some kind. To tell you the truth, that's why I haven't said anything about it, in case Mr Kendrick told me I wasn't to dig any more.'

Smith said, 'Hindus have always burned their dead . . . since Brahminism began, at any rate. These could be enemies, slain in battle. Or, just possibly, a pre-Brahminical cemetery.'

Rukmini whispered, 'Look at the bones piled one on top of another. Think what it must have looked like when the flesh was on them.' Her voice was low and bitter. 'Thrown down, spread out like so much manure . . .'

'Thrown down,' Smith said quickly. 'That's it! You remember my saying that there would be no point in moving the debris from the cave, to preserve the secret of it, unless the men who made it were also silenced?' He looked up again at Indra's Rock. 'That is where they were thrown from. This is their tomb. It's only a guess, but I think it's true.'

'They'd all land in one place,' Foster objected. 'The bodies would be piled up directly under the rock, not spread out as far as this.'

Smith said, 'There would have been executioners below, to drag the bodies away, and to ensure that all were dead. A few would survive, by a freak of their manner of falling, among numbers as large as this.'

Rukmini turned. 'I can't stay here another moment,' she muttered. She began to hurry along the path. Mohan ran after her. She broke into a run when he came close, and ran ahead of him, the low branches whipping her face and catching at her sari, until they reached the foot of the scaffold.

'Rukmini,' he said, 'what's the matter?'

'Don't touch me,' she whispered fiercely. 'Don't touch me!' She hurried up the scaffold and the ladder. When Mohan reached the top, she was gone.

He ran up to Cheltondale. She was in the drawing-room, looking out across the roll of the low valley at the Rainbow Fall and the hanging arch of the rainbow. He went close to her and said anxiously, 'Rukmini . . . dearest . . .'

She said, 'We must get some of the bones out whole. And send them to Calcutta, or Bombay – to find out whose bones they were. What kind of people. They can tell. Especially if we find a whole skull. They – you – can't have smashed every head quite to pieces – every man's, every woman's, every child's. You're blood-thirsty enough, but not efficient enough.'

'Me? We?' Mohan said. 'What are you talking about?'

'Yes, you,' she flared. 'You, the splendid Suvala Aryans – murderers. Oh, I wish I'd been born English. What a joy, to order you about, treat you like scum. I'd like to have been the sergeant who pulled the cord and blew your grandfather from a cannon, there on the walls of his own palace!'

Mohan cried, 'I don't know what you're talking about!'

She said fiercely, 'Those bones are the bones of the slaves who made the cave. The cave is a pride of the Suvalas – Guardian of the Cave is your title, isn't it? Who do you think it was who suffered, slaved, and died? *My* people.'

'You are being silly,' he snapped. 'Even Smith says it's only a guess, and even he didn't say the bones were of your people. And it was a long time ago.'

Her anger left her suddenly. She said wearily, 'I am sorry. I was angry because, although it is a long time ago, that spirit still lives.'

Chapter Seventeen

Ahmed, the foreman's cousin, was thirty years of age, a tall, handsome man with a weak mouth. It was shortly after dark on April 29, a few days after the tigress took the coolie from the pit. Ahmed, hurrying through the jungle, not on a path, a bundle under his arm, wore a very different expression from the terror he had shown then.

As he hurried along his mind raced. His eyes shone with a peculiar glow, and the focus of them kept slipping in and out, for sometimes he saw the ground under his skipping feet, and sometimes the trees and the rocks vanished and a vast glittering plain spread out before him, gold from end to end, and fine silks flowed like water through his hands, and women with flesh like silk beckoned from golden cushions. His lips moved all the time, though the small noises that escaped them made no sense. His face and forehead were damp, his stomach tightly contracted, and his hands trembling.

He wore his Pathan clothes, of baggy white pyjamas, a long coat, and turban wrapped round a tall kullah. Under one arm he carried a bundle containing a loin-cloth, a pair of Bundelkhand-slippers, and material to make one of the untidy turbans the infidels of this part of India wore. He could not afford to be seen here in the local clothes, for everyone here knew him; once he passed over the hills, he could not afford to be seen in the Pathan clothes. They made him too conspicuous.

He came to the edge of the fields bordering the Deori River below Tiger Pool and paused a moment to listen. Now it was full dark. He heard nothing and hurried across the fields towards the Buddha Tumulus. When he was very close he saw the man waiting with the cart, and the two bullocks.

What a fool! All these black Konpara infidels were fools. This was the man who had taken a few minutes off from his work in the fields to look into the open trenches of the Buddha Tumulus; and had found, just under the surface, twenty bars of metal; and had come to tell him; and had told no one else; and who, by sheer chance, was normally the driver of one of the contractor's bullock carts. What an idiot!

Ahmed had told him to ask no questions, give no information, and take the bullock cart to the tumulus one hour after dusk. And here he was. The golden light shone brighter in an effulgence that almost dazzled Ahmed.

The man rose and made a humble salaam. 'Quiet!' Ahmed whispered fiercely. 'Let me have a look at these beasts. We have a long way to go.' He examined the cart, feeling the wheels and the axle with his hands, ran his hands over the backs and down the legs of the bullocks. 'Good, good. We'll load it now,' he muttered. 'Get down and pass them up.'

The man stepped down into the trench with a spade and for a few moments worked steadily, throwing earth out from the trench on to the land. Ahmed looked round . . . no sound, no light except from the Rest House on its ridge. Red Hair would be having his bath. The other, Smith Sahib, was probably over at Cheltondale with the young Rajah.

The man in the trench passed up a heavy bar of metal. Carefully, Ahmed took it, loaded it into the bullock cart, and returned. His breath came unevenly as though he were in the arms of a woman, as he knelt at the edge of the trench, where another bar waited. And another. And another.

He counted twenty. At twenty the man below said, 'That is all, master.' Ahmed jumped down and checked. It was true.

Twenty bars, at thirty thousand rupees each. He had done the sum a hundred times already: six hundred thousand rupees. Rs.600,000. Six lakhs.

The man was throwing straw over the gold in the back of the cart. Could anyone be such an idiot? Was it really possible even for a black Hindu to see nothing beyond the end of his nose, to do this without thinking why?

'Ready?' he asked. His bundle was in the cart now, on top of the gold. He felt his waist. The knife was there, ready.

A small sharp pain pricked the middle of his neck and he jerked his head impatiently. Biting flies, at this time of night! The voice of his elder cousin Shahbaz Khan whispered venomously, 'Ahmed, my beloved cousin.' The pain returned, but harder, and he fell to his knees.

His cousin spoke to the villager. 'Wait here. We must speak together, my cousin and I.'

'Yes, master,' the man said.

The knife point pricked hard and Ahmed felt the blood flow down his neck. 'Up!'

He struggled up and stumbled ahead of the other, past the limit of the Buddha Tumulus, to the edge of a cornfield a hundred yards away.

'Now, my beloved cousin,' Shahbaz Khan said.

Ahmed whined, 'My noble cousin . . .' turned, dropped to one knee, drew his own knife, and struck with the upthrusting Pathan stroke, blade up, thumb up. The knife slashed soundlessly through the edge of his cousin's coat. The other's knife flashed up and cut his ear. Shahbaz Khan's slippered foot kicked him under the wrist and his knife flew from his hand. Shahbaz Khan stabbed again. Ahmed writhed away, leaped back, and threw the older man down. Now he was half kneeling, half lying on top of Shahbaz Khan's knife arm. They pressed face to face, snarling and spitting. Ahmed could not pry loose his cousin's grip on the knife. Shahbaz Khan could not free his arm. For a minute they lay, panting and hating.

'How much . . . is it?' Shahbaz Khan gasped at last.

'Six lakhs,' Ahmed said.

They lay silent, the sum bursting over them afresh in its hugeness, all lit by gold. 'Enough for both,' the older man said. Ahmed hesitated. Three lakhs was not the same as six. 'I have the knife,' his cousin said.

'Throw it away,' he said. Shahbaz Khan jerked his wrist and the knife flew a little distance off. They climbed to their feet, and both went to pick up their knives, and came close, but not too close. Shahbaz Khan said, 'Do you think I am a fool, to believe you were going to Deori, wearing that expression? What was your plan?'

'Go by the old jungle road over the hills to Vishnuswara,' Ahmed said. 'Bury most of the gold in the jungle. Take one or two bars to the Marwaris in Bombay. Come back for the rest when it was safe.'

Shahbaz Khan stood thinking. 'Red Hair will suspect at once,' he said. 'Should we not hide the gold near here, and wait till the end of the contract? Then we can leave, taking the gold, and no one the wiser.'

'The man with the cart,' Ahmed said.

'He would not have reached Vishnuswara, in any case – would he?'

'No.'

'Then the same here. He can vanish. The cart will be found, abandoned. The tigress ate him.'

'Yes. But I do not like to stay here. Too much can happen in the next four weeks. Red Hair can dismiss us. The gold can be discovered. Let us go to Vishnuswara.'

Shahbaz Khan thought. It was the best course. The black man would disappear. Ahmed, too, perhaps. Perhaps not. Not at once, anyway. First bury the gold. Then lull him into security.

The young were impatient. The gold . . . hundreds of thousands of rupees? A golden brilliance illumined the darkness. Power, young girls, great feasts, a mansion in Lucknow.

'Come,' he said. 'We must move fast.'

They returned to the cart, and told the man, 'Move now. On the old road to Vishnuswara.'

'Very well, master,' the man mumbled. The bullocks leaned into the yoke and the cart began to move. Shahbaz Khan noticed that the axle was well greased, and made no sound. The two men climbed on to the moving cart, and the cart rolled slowly west and then north-west, climbing gradually into the trees that marked the limit of the cultivated land.

In the Rest House, Jim Foster finished tying his tie and brushing his hair, and surveyed himself briefly in the mirror. He didn't wear a dinner jacket at night, because he wasn't a pukka sahib, but he could make himself clean and put on a coat and tie. He poured himself a whisky, went out on to the verandah, sat down in one of the long-armed cane chairs, and sat staring moodily at the darkness.

He thought of Barbara Kendrick. She was a lady, and he was not a gentleman. He was an ex-private of the Royal Engineers, who'd made himself what he was. She was married – to Kendrick. She was miserably unhappy. She liked him.

He repeated that to himself. 'She likes me. She likes me more than Mohan.' Well, he'd shown Mohan where he got off, and the young fellow didn't seem to bear a grudge. And now what?

Barbara Kendrick was a lady . . . not just a la-di-da lady, but someone you wanted to take your hat off to, to protect and look after, and speak gently to. She was a lady, and he was not much different from a thief. Those three gold bars in the trunk under the bed didn't rightly belong to him. A crooked contractor could say so, a lying private could say so, but not a man whom a lady could . . . say it, damn it . . . could love.

He swore, finished the whisky, and poured another. He saw Huttoo Lall, The headman of Konpara, approaching across the lawn. The man made a salaam at the foot of the verandah, directly below Foster. Jim greeted him with a wave of the arm. Huttoo Lall was a good fellow. Didn't look like much but everyone knew who was the boss in his village. 'What is it?' he asked in Hindi. He spoke with a bad accent and a limited vocabulary, but he could make himself understood.

The headman said, 'I have come to ask whether you wish me to strike those two men off the work lists from my village. The ones who were fighting in the conduit this morning.'

Foster waved his hand. 'No,' he said. 'You punish them with words. Swear at them.'

The headman said, 'Thank you, sahib. They are not bad men.'

Foster said, 'Your men work well . . . except for the drunk.'

The headman said, 'Work had not started then, sahib.'

'No, it hadn't,' Jim agreed. 'The drunk' was a strange occasion, soon after the irrigation scheme had been agreed on and explained to the headman, when the whole village and all the Gonds on the upper plateau were drunk for five days and nights on end. Since then their work and sobriety had been exemplary. They had worked much better, in fact, than his imported Nagpur coolies, which was unusual. Well, when it was finished, and good land in the valley was ready for them, the whole village would be moved down there; so they had something to work for. That must be the reason.

The headman said, 'That is all, sahib. I am on my way back to Konpara. Oh! I hesitate to mention it, but perhaps . . . there are no tigers in the Pathan country, you see, and perhaps the foreman does not know how great a risk he runs . . .'

Jim frowned, 'What are you talking about?'

The headman said, 'Kendrick Sahib has not yet succeeded in slaying the man-eater. To move about at night, away from the village, is dangerous. As one of my people returned from wood-cutting in the jungle, he saw Shahbaz Khan and Ahmed driving a bullock cart along the old jungle road. It may be, of course, that . . .'

'When?' Jim asked.

'Just now, not more than a quarter of an hour ago. It would . . .'

'That's all right,' Jim said. 'I'll see to it.'

The headman bowed and drifted away into the darkness, heading along the path that led past Southdown to Konpara.

As soon as he had gone Jim jumped to his feet. Shahbaz Khan and Ahmed, with a bullock cart. On the old jungle road to Vishnuswara. What the hell were they doing, at this time of night? Moving earth? Going to fetch something? He stiffened. The blood flowed from his face and neck, leaving the skin a mottled red and white. Something had been found! And ten per cent wasn't enough for the thieving swine. He ran into his room, found a pistol, made sure it was loaded, fastened on his belt and holster, and hurried out.

In a moment he was in the darkness, but he had been walking these trails for over two years now, and he moved fast. The thought of the tigress made his skin creep, but then he thought of

91

gold. How much had they got? He broke into a heavy purposeful run.

Charles Kendrick, dressed for dinner in white duck trousers, black tie, black waistcoat and dinner jacket, sat reading a government paper on the verandah of Southdown. His wife, in evening dress, sat a few feet farther along, staring out at the darkness, doing nothing, saying nothing.

Kendrick could not hold his attention on the paper. Who had moved the Buddha? He wanted to see him, talk to him, privately. Mohan and Smith, working together, with Rukmini as assistant, had considerably enlarged the crevice in the pit wall, and the air current still flowed in. The systematic search of the ground had stopped, and would remain stopped until the man-eater was killed, but some new clue might be unearthed at any minute . . . would be, if Rukmini was 'planting' them.

The headman of Konpara drifted up out of the darkness, crossing the lawn on his way to the servants' quarters. Kendrick watched him. He was going to tell the butler to announce him. Kendrick put down the paper and called, 'Huttoo Lall!'

The headman changed direction, came to the foot of the verandah, and made salaam. 'What is it?' Kendrick asked.

'I came to ask, sahib, whether you needed another buffalo or cow to use as bait for the tigress tomorrow.'

Kendrick said, 'Not yet. The Gonds have lost track of her. She's somewhere on the far side of the upper plateau, but Aitu can't tell where with sufficient exactness to make it worth while putting our bait. But have one ready – a buffalo calf.'

The headman said, 'Yes, sahib.' A frown creased his face and he spoke hesitantly. 'If she is on the upper plateau . . . I wonder whether Foster Sahib knows.'

'Foster Sahib?' Kendrick said. 'What do you mean?'

The headman said, 'I have just come from the Rest House, sahib, where I mentioned to Foster Sahib that the Pathans were putting themselves in some danger by going in a bullock cart on the old Vishnuswara road, in the dark. A little later I went back, having dropped something, and saw Foster Sahib run out with a pistol. He went in the direction of the old jungle road, which, of course, crosses the upper plateau.'

Kendrick said, 'H'm. Very foolish. I'll speak to the sahib.' He nodded in dismissal.

When the headman had disappeared in the darkness down the path to Konpara, Kendrick sat up, his hands moving convulsively. Something was going on. The two Pathans, with a bullock cart, heading north-west, at this time of night. Foster rushing off after them, with a pistol, the pursuit more important than the danger from the man-eater. Foster had found the steatite seals in Indra's Rock Tumulus, and said nothing about them – or about the bones – until circumstances forced him to. Foster had provided money for the excavation.

He jumped up, went into the bungalow and to the gun-room, drew out a rifle from the rack, found the key of the safe on his key chain, opened the safe, drew out the bolt for that rifle, fitted it in, relocked the safe, seized a loaded cartridge belt off a numbered hook, loaded both barrels of the rifle, and walked out of the bungalow by the back way. He moved at a steady walk, not fast, not slow, the rifle cocked and held ready. He, at any rate, would not forget that the tigress could take a hand in this criminal enterprise – for that, surely, it must be. Treachery; he smelled it heavy and rancid in the air. An intrigue against him. Money also, he smelled. The darkness down the ridge swallowed him.

A minute after he had disappeared, his wife rose, walked into the bungalow, went to her room, and quickly changed out of her evening slippers into strong walking shoes. Then she left the bungalow by the front door, strolled slowly across the lawn, and, as soon as she was out of range of the verandah lights, lifted her skirts and broke into a breakneck run, running as fast as she could, stumbling sometimes, the boughs of the trees reaching out in vain to slow her.

Jim Foster strode up the old jungle road, the pistol now in his hand. He did not think the two Pathans would attack him, but it was possible. It depended on how much gold they had found – and stolen. One more bar? Two? It was very dark, and the jungle very silent. He walked fast for a hundred paces, and then stopped for a second to listen. The bullock cart could not travel faster than two miles an hour.

There must be at least six bars of gold, or they would have fled on horseback. A hundred and eighty thousand rupees. He licked his lips, paused, listened. Not a sound. The hoofs of the bullocks would make more noise than his own feet on the dead leaves. But Ahmed might be walking a couple of hundred yards behind the cart, just to catch someone following. He gripped the revolver more tightly. The swine would get a bullet if he tried anything.

He stopped again. Not a sound. Yes, there was though. Breathing. Jim pressed himself behind a tree, his own breath coming shallow and uneven. The other breathing was steady, deep, slow. Very loud for a man's. A tiger's. His knees shook with uncontrollable terror.

A ruffling, blowing snort sent a convulsive jerk down both arms, so that he all but fired the revolver. In the same instant he recognised the sound – a bullock blowing through its nostrils. He raised his voice. 'Shahbaz Khan, I can see you.' No answer. 'Shahbaz Khan, Ahmed, don't try anything. Several people know I've come out after you.'

No answer.

He waited, pressed against the tree. The bullocks steadily breathed. One of them blew again through his nostrils. Jim took a step forward. The cart couldn't be more than fifteen paces off. He crept up the side of the track towards it. At ten paces he saw the white bulk of the bullocks and the vague shape of the cart. Two more and he saw a pattern of blackness in the track beside the near wheel of the cart. One more, and he saw another shape spread over the front of the cart.

The bullocks snorted and jerked the cart into motion. He ran forward and caught them, and after a moment they stood again, patient. Jim knelt beside the shape in the road and saw that it was Shahbaz Khan. He put out his left hand, nervously, and touched the face. Warm. 'Shahbaz Khan,' he muttered, trembling. The open mouth did not answer. Jim jumped up and looked at the other, the body sprawled over the front of the cart. Ahmed. Ahmed did not answer, either. Jim stumbled to the front of the cart. A hurricane lantern was hanging from the usual place on the shaft. He unhooked it, found a match in his pocket, and lit it. The light spread, and he lifted it to Ahmed. The face was contorted, the body bent like a jack-knife. No wound. Yes, there was: a cut in the back of the neck and a deep gouge in his right heel, just above the tops of the battered European shoes he always wore. Neither could have killed him, but he was dead.

He took the lamp again and knelt beside Shahbaz Khan. Again no wound. He felt very cold and frightened, with a kind of terror that he had not known to exist, not fear of a definite thing like a tiger, not fear of the unknown, but fear that was breathed into the lungs like air, and that entered through the skin like heat. Every second it possessed him more strongly.

He seized the lantern and leaned in over the back of the cart. He threw aside some straw and a bundle, and saw the bars. A row of five. And another. And another . . . The straw hid the front of the cart. There might be another row. A hundred and fifty thousand a row. Four hundred and fifty thousand rupees there before his eyes. His mind leaped up and away, fear vanished. Gold, gold, gold, the jungle shining under a brilliant golden light, and himself the centre of it. He scrambled up into the cart and pushed the forward straw aside.

The flat snake head rose, swaying, rising just beyond his hand, higher and higher, level now with his knee, a foot away. The forked tongue flickered ceaselessly; the sharp eyes held his own. The hood began to spread, the strong neck to arch back. The cobra reached its full height, the heavy coils moving a little under the straw, on top of the gold. Jim's right hand jerked. The pistol fired.

The cobra's raised body sagged, blood spurting from the torn pulp at the top. Jim hurled himself out of the cart, and fell, rolling over and over among the leaves and tree roots.

For a minute he lay retching, holding the earth with his hands. The lantern still burned inside the cart. Jim climbed to his feet. Now he knew what had killed the two Pathans. The gold remained. The nausea left him. He had twenty bars of gold. Six lakhs of rupees. The golden light came back into the world. Six bloody lakhs! A country house in England, more suits of clothes than he would know what to do with, servants to boss about the way he'd been bossed about, pictures in golden frames. Barbara Kendrick's pictures, they'd be.

His mind began to race. He wouldn't have one rupee if Kendrick got to hear of this. Or Mohan. The Pathans were dead. No one else knew gold had been found, or, if so, how much. Must leave some in the cart to explain why the Pathans were running away. Enough to need a cart. Say four bars. Take the other sixteen into the jungle here, cover them with leaves, come back tomorrow.

He jumped up into the cart, picked up the slowly writhing body of the cobra and heaved it over the side. He picked up a gold bar.

He heard a swish of leaves and a patter of feet down the road, in the direction from which he had come. He put down the gold bar and drew the pistol from its holster. No one was going to take it. Not this much. Not when he was so close to . . .

'Jim,' a voice called close. 'Jim, is that you?'

He stood, dumbfounded. Barbara Kendrick came out of the darkness. A meaningless tangle of thoughts whirled through his head. One stayed, made sense. He jumped down. 'What are you doing here?' He held her arm. 'The tigress! You might have been killed!'

She was out of breath, and leaned forward, drawing the air into her lungs with slow, painful gasps. After a few moments she stood up shakily. 'My husband's coming. With a rifle. He thinks he's going to catch you doing something wrong. I know his face, every expression, every thought.'

Jim's shoulders slumped. 'Yes,' he said heavily, 'I was doing something wrong.'

'I didn't want him to catch you,' she said.

Staring at her, he saw that she meant it. She didn't want him to do wrong, either, but saving him came first. He saw her eyes on the dead Pathans and said quickly, 'I didn't kill them. A cobra did. Now quick . . . get into the jungle here, out of sight, and when he comes I'll delay . . .'

'I'll make my way back,' she interrupted. 'Don't worry about me.'

'But the tigress –' he began.

'I'm not afraid,' she repeated, and slipped into the jungle. He followed her for a few paces and then stopped, listening to the fading fall of her feet, and, afterwards, silence. He stood among the trees, motionless, thinking. She had come from Southdown through the jungle. Something stronger than liking made her do that. She had come several times during the week, to sketch where he was working. They had spoken more together in this week than in all last year.

He heard a faint sound and saw Charles Kendrick coming slowly up the track, his rifle in his hand. Jim made a small instinctive move, and all but a corner of his face was then hidden behind a tree, and that sheltered by leaves, and the tree in the darkness outside the circle of light thrown by the lantern in the cart. Kendrick advanced steadily. If the light wasn't burning, Jim thought, I would think those stealthy steady sounds were the tigress stalking me. I would raise the pistol. He raised it. Take careful aim at the sound. And wait. It would come on. I would swear it was the tigress. And afterwards, when I lighted the lantern, I would see my mistake, because I would see that I had shot Mr Charles Kendrick through the head and chest, with two or three shots fired in succession at ten-feet range. Then Mrs Kendrick would not have a husband, and Jim Foster would have several lakhs of rupees.

The pistol held very steady in his hand. He noticed how steady it was, the barrel lined exactly with Kendrick's right temple.

And I would be further from her than ever. A thief. I can stop myself being that. A murderer – she would like to kill him, but she doesn't. It will have to come some other way. A force squeezed his finger against the trigger, and he pushed back against it. It was very strong, a force of the jungle, as strong and definite as the fear he had known before finding the cobra.

Sweating, he won the silent battle. Kendrick passed, reached the cart. Jim put the pistol carefully into the holster and called, 'Mr Kendrick.'

Kendrick swung round slowly. Jim walked out of the jungle. 'This is bad business,' he said.

Kendrick looked at him suspiciously. 'What were you doing in there? What's happened?' He indicated the corpses with the barrel of the rifle. 'Did you kill them?'

Jim said, 'I was looking to see whether they had hidden anything in the jungle. They were running off with twenty bars of gold. A cobra killed them.'

Kendrick walked round the cart, examining the bodies and the gold. At length he said, 'We will take everything back to the Rest House now.' The two of them loaded the corpses into the cart. 'The cobra, too,' Kendrick said. 'And its head.' Jim had to hunt for several minutes before he found the shattered head and neck ten yards up the track.

They turned the bullocks and headed back down the slope. Before they moved Kendrick broke off a sapling and stuck it into the centre of the path. He said, 'That will mark the spot, to enable us to search the area carefully by daylight, in case some of the gold has been removed from the cart and hidden.' They set off, walking beside the cart.

The bastard's always suspicious, Jim thought, and always on the wrong track. None of the gold was concealed in the jungle; but the back of Kendrick's head was there a few feet in front of him, and the pistol was still in his holster . . . No, that was over, too. A whole way of life was over.

The jungles were full of strange noises now, like birds stirring on their perches, or the slither of something, or a leaf falling. Barbara Kendrick had run through these jungles, over these rocks, to warn him. He acknowledged to himself, firmly, that he loved her. Encompassed in the same thought, without words, he acknowledged that a thief was not fit to love her.

When, after another hour, they reached the Rest House, they found Mohan, Rukmini, and Barbara Kendrick there, all clothed for the jungle. Barbara Kendrick said, 'You didn't come back. I sent a messenger to Cheltondale . . .'

'We were coming out to look for you,' Smith said.

Barbara Kendrick met Jim's eye with a question. He nodded, and said aloud, 'It's all right,' unable to contain his happiness or his new sense of determination.

'What's all right?' Kendrick snapped. 'It looks very wrong to me.'

Foster mumbled something, but Kendrick had already turned to the others. Servants bustled about carrying the gold bars into the bungalow. Smith was examining the bodies, and the two parts of the cobra, and untying the bundle.

Kendrick said, 'There are no other Mohammedans up here. You'll have to send a message down to the mullah in Deori first thing in the morning, Foster.' With Smith's help he carried the bodies into a spare room. Jim noticed that Barbara did not flinch from them as they were taken past her. Rather, she bent to look more closely into their faces. By God, he thought with a sudden flash of intuition, I'm glad I'm not an artist. Barbara was. She had to understand and feel everything, including death.

It was late and no one had eaten. The servants brought tea and scrambled eggs, and Jim signalled to his bearer to pass round the whisky. He took a good large glass himself. A little whisky would help him say what he was going to say.

Kendrick said, 'The main outline of what has happened tonight seems clear enough. The foreman and his cousin discovered the gold bars, and decided to make off with them. The cart, I notice, is one of yours' – he looked at Foster – 'it will have a driver in charge of it?'

'Yes,' Jim said. 'But –'

'But he will only have been told that the foreman wanted it left at a certain place. Of course. The two men then fled. But a cobra had secreted itself in the cart, as they sometimes do, and later it attacked them, perhaps when they were moving the straw to shift the load.'

'The bundle contains local Bundelkhand clothes,' Smith said. 'Only one set. It is possible that the robbery was planned by only one of them, and the other came upon him and forced himself into the enterprise. There is a fairly deep knife mark in the back of Ahmed's neck, and a cut on his ear. They might have been caused by fighting. The gouge in his heel is, I presume, the place where the cobra bit him, and where he had tried to cut out the poison.'

'Three lakhs each wasn't enough,' Rukmini said sadly. Jim flushed, remembering the madness, the magnificent glow of power that had come with the golden light when he realised how much gold lay to his hand.

Smith said, 'Where did they find the gold?'

A long silence followed. Jim took a deep breath. He said, 'I don't know for certain. But I can make a guess. It came from the Buddha Tumulus. Wait.' He slipped out of the central dining-room where they were gathered, and returned a moment later dragging the tin trunk that lived under his own bed. He unlocked it in the same silence and lifted out three bars of gold. Two were partly encrusted with earth. He pointed at them. 'These were found under the cricket pitch, right at the beginning.' The other bar was clean. 'This was found under the Buddha,' he said.

Kendrick's voice was harsh. 'And why has nothing been said about any of this until now?'

Jim said, 'Because . . .'

Smith interrupted. 'Jim told me about them, Mr Kendrick. I advised that their existence should be kept secret until proper assay should tell us for certain what they were.'

Jim bent his head. He had been about to tell them of his determination to use his contract to keep any precious metals that were found. Smith knew about the first two bars, but not about the one found under the Buddha. Now he was assuming responsibility for all of them. An unaccustomed pricking behind his eyes made him turn away. By God, he was on the point of crying.

Kendrick snapped, 'An unjustified, and unjustifiable decision, Smith. I am the Administrator here! I have a right to know! There will be no more secrets from me. Do you understand?'

'Yes, sir,' Smith said politely. 'I apologise. The assay report should be received in a day or two. But I think we must assume, now, that it is all gold.'

He carried to the table one of the gold bars that had been taken from the cart. It was a little dirty, but a light brushing with a handkerchief removed the dirt easily, leaving it clean and dully shining.

Smith said, 'You see, the Buddha bar, and all the twenty from the cart, are clean. All bear the stamp of a trident, a bull's head, and four bows, very small. The original two are earth-encrusted, are not so well finished, and bear the stamp of only a single bow. I think the State Archivist in Deori may be able to decipher the meaning of these marks for us. I will go and see him as soon as I have time . . . Jim Foster suggests that since the twenty bars from the cart look and are stamped like the one Buddha bar, they came from the same place – the Buddha Tumulus.'

'That's right,' Jim muttered.

Smith said, 'I agree. But, as we know that the Buddha was planted in the trench, it is probable that all twenty-one gold bars were, also.'

Jim shook his head dully. 'But,' he said, 'the gold is a thousand times more valuable than what we were going to give for finding new objects. We thought someone put the Buddha there to get a reward . . .'

'I did not,' Rukmini interposed.

'But what's the point of getting a reward of twenty rupees and giving away half a million?'

Rukmini said, 'That is not the right way to look at it, Mr Foster. The Buddha would attract some of us away from the Dobehari Ridge, and the gold would attract others. So much gold as this could do more. It could destroy us. Suppose the cobra had not killed those two poor men. You would have come upon them in the jungle, in the night. They would have attacked you. All three of you, and perhaps Mr Kendrick too, might have been killed in a fight caused by fear and greed . . . born of gold.'

Jim looked down at the bars on the table. Rukmini did not know how truly she spoke. A hair's width of love – his love for Barbara – had stood between Kendrick and death. And then – he saw it clearly now – the search for the Venus must have stopped, for the A.G.G. would have come, and agents of the C.I.D., and there would have been courts of inquiry, investigations, trials. Whoever planted that gold had a horrible knowledge of human nature.

Kendrick said angrily, 'Someone else must have known about the discovery of the gold. Some of the labourers.'

Jim said, 'Only Shahbaz and Ahmed – that they ever told me.'

'And the villagers are not going to tell us,' Smith said.

Mohan said, 'Someone in the village *must* know *something*. The headman can learn nothing. We shall have to distrust all of them.'

Smith said, 'Not exactly that. Whoever these people are, it's wrong to look on them as our enemies. They are not. They are involved with us in the same problem, only they have a different viewpoint from ours. We've already learned more from their actions, although those actions were intended to throw us off the scent, than if they'd done nothing. If we feel pressure we should give with it – but keep our thinking minds unaffected, so that we can recognise the pressure for what it is, and try to understand the true motive for it . . . For the moment, I think we should recognise that the expenditure of half a million rupees was designed to bring into existence a greed, a hatred, which would have stopped our search. It so happens that the tigress is already slowing down work on the crevice and totally preventing the methodical search of the ground for the cave entrance, but Mr Kendrick may succeed in killing the beast at any moment. I think, therefore, since the gold has not caused hatred among us, that another attempt will be made to stop our search.'

Rukmini muttered, 'I wish I could think why. It is not what they do, but *why*. It is not greed, it is not ambition, it is not love . . . It is fear, but fear of what? *I* ought to be able to guess.'

Smith said slowly, 'There is one other point which I must make. In my opinion, it is unlikely that Shahbaz Khan and Ahmed were killed by the cobra.'

The silence was heavy again, with something of the atmosphere of terror that had been so powerful in the jungle.

Smith said, 'All of us here know that two methods of committing murder are particularly hard to solve, and both are common in India. The victim is bludgeoned unconscious, and then killed by men armed with steel talons and padded clubs resembling a tiger's claws. Or he is held helpless and venom collected from a poisonous snake is injected by a home-made double syringe that duplicates the marks of a snake's fangs. Afterwards it is easy enough to make any other marks, such as the hole in Ahmed's heel. I think the two Pathans were probably murdered in that manner, and the cobra then put into the cart to kill the next man. If we could examine this cobra's poison sac we could learn something. If the sac were empty it would prove nothing. The snake might have been milked of its venom for use in the murder – or it might have used up its venom in killing the two Pathans, without any human intervention. But if the poison sac were full, we would know that murder had been committed – because, if it had bitten the two men, its sac would be empty.'

'Let's look!' Mohan cried, taking half a step towards the corner where the cobra lay.

Smith said, 'Jim's shot destroyed the poison sacs.'

'They call upon the old gods to aid them,' Rukmini said, 'and the old gods have the power even to aim a Christian's bullet.'

'Nonsense,' Kendrick said loudly. 'We must now kill the tigress, and then the search for the Venus can continue. This will be the end of their interference, you mark my words.'

Chapter Eighteen

Charles Kendrick carefully wiped his mouth with the corner of the white napkin. The bearer eased back his chair and he stood up. He said, 'Today I shall stay at home and deal with paperwork.'

'Very well, Charles,' his wife said.

'You, I presume, will pursue your artistic genius?'

'Yes, Charles,' she said.

As he entered his study he looked at the painting of his father. The Galahad of Bundelkhand. How would Sir Galahad have solved *his* problems? By smiling at the harlot Rukmini and, half an hour later, lustfully mounting her? Charles Kendrick glared at his father with real hatred, turned his back, and sat down at the desk.

It was two days since the two Pathans had died, or been murdered. No more evidence, either way. Ahmed had told the driver of the bullock cart to leave it below the Tiger Pool bund at seven o'clock, and he had. Two men had gone with him. They had thought that a tiger might get the bullocks, leaving them there alone, but that was none of their business. They were Foster's bullocks.

Damned idiots. This plot, and there was one, was far too deep for men of their stupidity to be involved in. No one knew anything about gold, snakes, or the Buddha. The gold bars were safe in the Deori Treasury.

The harlot had said, during that meeting in the Rest House, that the motive mattered. She was wrong. Only the fact mattered, and the fact was that Rukmini needed to find the Venus and the cave, while he, Charles Kendrick, and the unknown plotters, needed to ensure that she did not. His whole future depended on it. If that woman stayed, Mohan would not succeed to the gaddi. Or if he did, her influence, not his own, would govern Mohan. She would see that he never even became Prime Minister. But he would be! He must be! His father had been the Galahad of Deori; *he* was going to be the Gladstone, the Disraeli, the Great Administrator. When they'd forgotten his father, they'd remember him. The bright dream began to shatter in his mind as he thought of it. He'd got to do something about Rukmini, and soon.

Meanwhile, it would not be safe to find any more excuses to delay action against the tigress. The next time she gave him an opportunity he would have to kill her. It would not do to lose his reputation as a hunter, as the man who protected the poor from the wild animals that preyed upon them. Besides, he liked it. Animals were strong and straightforward, and the tracking of them gave power that achieved a climax in the explosion of the cartridge, the ruthless penetration of the bullet.

Someone was knocking at the door. 'Sahib, sahib!' It was the butler's voice. He called, 'What is it?'

'The lady Rukmini is here, sahib. The tigress . . .'

Kendrick got up slowly. Rukmini – tigress. Now she was interfering there too. He went along the passage.

Rukmini waited on the verandah, her sari falling in a clean sweep down the side of her head and on to her shoulders. Barbara was there. Rukmini spoke quickly. 'I was in Konpara visiting a sick woman. She is dying . . . A man rushed in to tell me that the tigress has been seen . . . Mohan's in bed with a light fever.'

Her sari was pale green, of the thinnest cotton, with no border, and under it the choli was almost transparent.

She said, 'The tigress was near the path between Konpara and the Gond village an hour ago.'

North-east, about half a mile away, Kendrick thought. Rukmini said, 'The headman has sent out to order all who were working in the fields to return at once to the village. The men working in the conduit are safe. He has also sent to tell Mr Foster, so that the coolies on the dam can go back to the coolie camp.'

A man burst out of the trees, crossed the lawn, ran up the verandah steps, and hurled himself to his knees at Mr Kendrick's feet. 'Sahib, the tiger – a woman – a woman – the wife of . . .'

Kendrick pulled him to his feet. 'Tell me! Don't stutter, man!'

'A *tiger*, sahib, not a tigress. In the grass beyond the village –' The man flung out his arm. 'The woman was cutting leaves at the edge of the jungle, not a hundred paces from the houses, with another woman. The order to return to the village reached them, but they did not hurry. They were so close, and the tigress was to the north-east. When they started back, the tiger was there, it must have been there all the time! It took one, left the other. That other ran screaming to the village. Huttoo Lall sent me at once to you'.

Fifteen minutes ago. A tiger. The tiger and tigress must work as a couple, one frightening the people into the arms of the other. The butler was waiting. Kendrick began to rap out orders. 'Joseph, fetch Aitu! Bring number four rifle, with its cartridge belt. All work is to stop. Everyone inside their houses. Barbara, tell Foster to come here and keep watch over you. Lend him a rifle.'

She said quietly, 'Very well, Charles.'

'Everyone must keep out of my way. That is the reason for these precautions, not safety. I cannot guess what the animals will do if people are moving about.'

Aitu, the Gond tracker who had been living in the caretaker's hut since the first coming of the tigress, soon appeared and crouched ready, black, simian, and silent at the foot of the verandah, the short bow in his hand and the quiver across his shoulders. Joseph handed Kendrick the double-barrelled rifle and cartridge belt. He checked them carefully, loaded the rifle, and set off down the cart track. A slight south wind blew straight across the ridges and up the face of the Konpara Cliffs, but it was not yet strong enough to form the spray and the rainbow.

The headman met him at the outskirts of Konpara, together with two or three other men. Kendrick said, 'I am going on with Aitu. Watch carefully, from the top of the village. But first point out the place.' They hurried down the street among the piles of dust and offal, through the black pools of cow urine. At the last house the headman stopped and pointed. 'There, sahib, by the lone fig tree.'

Kendrick said, 'I see it. Now get up on to your roof. I must know what the tiger does if I cause it to move.'

He waited impatiently while the headman and the others hurried up a narrow lane to the right. A few moments later they appeared on the flat roof of a house, and Kendrick made a sign to his tracker.

Together they walked out on to the village common. It was an irregular-shaped piece of land, about four hundred yards by two hundred in extent, from which the jungle had been excluded over the centuries by the feeding of goats and a few cattle, but there were small patches of dense scrub on it, such as covered the floor of the pit. In the open areas the grass was thin and the ground broken up by dried hoof-prints and wheel ruts. The herd boys often lay in the shade of a scrub patch, and played on their pipes. Once, through the binoculars, he had seen a girl come out from the village to one of those places where a boy lay on his back with his reed pipe, and, after a little play, the boy had had carnal knowledge of her. Neither of them could have been more than twelve years old. That one, it was: the patch he was now approaching on his left. He felt again the sharp, bitter hatred he had known while watching them, again every detail of the spectacle recreated itself before his eyes, as it had in the circle of the binoculars – the girl standing, kneeling, lying back, pulling up her skirt.

He motioned Aitu farther to the right, and himself stood at the edge of a thorn patch, the rifle held before him, loaded and cocked, his finger on the trigger. Aitu trusted him and went forward quickly, making no sound. The Gonds were little removed from animals themselves. Aitu and one or two others in the village on the upper plateau had even retained a sense of scent, like a hunting dog's . . .

Aitu reached the fig tree and looked carefully round in all directions. Then he crouched and sniffed the air, turning his head slowly from side to side. At last he beckoned, and Kendrick went forward.

Aitu pointed at the ground. A large splash of blood stained the grass near the foot of the tree. Aitu walked slowly northward, pointing here and there at the grass. Kendrick peered closely, but could see nothing to show that a heavy body had recently passed over it; but, as Aitu trusted him, so he trusted Aitu. This was the way the animal had gone . . . north-east now, as he had expected.

A little farther on, when the village had fallen from sight behind them, Aitu stopped in light jungle, and knelt. The ground here was softened by the welling-up of some underground moisture, and Kendrick thought he could almost make out the shape of a tiger's pug mark.

Aitu said, 'Male tiger. Left forepaw, one toenail does not pull back. Very large paw.'

Very large paw. Kendrick thought hard. Last year, about this time, he had been in the Saugor club. Some men were talking about two man-eaters that had been ravaging the district. A pair, male and female, who worked as a team. Nothing about a damaged toenail, but some mention of the male's very large pug marks. Disproportionately large, they said – the animal had been seen and was big but not exceptional. They had killed a woman near Saugor only two weeks ago. The Saugor District adjoined Deori to the south-west. He must telegraph the Deputy Commissioner there as soon as he got back, find out whether the pair had left the district, and all that was known about their careers, habits, and attempts that had been made to kill them. He must know, for his own safety, even though he delayed killing them. Good! He could kill one now, and the other would still hold up the search for the Venus.

The silent, sunny jungle crept past and round them as they went on. The Konpara Cliffs fell back and ended on the left, and they climbed towards the upper plateau. The wind hung steady over Kendrick's right shoulder, making the back of his neck damp and cold on that side, where it evaporated the sweat. A peacock rose in a clatter of green and purple, burst up into the sunlight, and slanted downhill above the tree-tops. Aitu, walking twenty feet ahead and to his left, made no sound as he glided over the earth. Under Kendrick's own boots, though he was a hunter, the twigs cracked and the leaves crunched.

Aitu stopped, his movements congealing to a halt without any suddenness. He pointed with his chin, and gave the sign – careful! Staring ahead, Kendrick at first saw nothing. Gradually a point of red grew larger in the scene . . . a sheen of something smoother among the rough tree boles and the corroded stones. He walked slowly forward. The dwarf teak trees stood many feet apart, and between the trunks there was no scrub. It was impossible to believe that a huge animal, brilliantly striped in black and gold, could be waiting there in full view, but he knew that it was possible, and that not even Aitu could say whether the tiger was there or not.

The sunlight streamed through the thin branches in black and gold. The bare earth and the scattered leaves were red-brown and barred with the shadows of the tree trunks. The red spot grew like an orchid against a fallen limb of teak. Keeping it carefully in the exact centre of view, and exactly downwind, Kendrick looked slowly from half right to half left.

Aitu moved. Kendrick stopped. He caught the Gond's eye, and Aitu motioned with his hand – nothing.

The red spot was a corner of a coolie woman's pleated shirt, sticking out from under her body. She lay on her back, naked, the skirt underneath her and the ripped choli ten feet away. Her left knee was raised and fallen sideways, and one arm was stretched out above her head. A raw patch marred the sheen of her right thigh, where the tiger had licked off her salt sweat with his rasping tongue.

Aitu, crouching to peer below her, pointed under the exposed groin and said, 'He has eaten. All of one buttock. Then he turned her over and licked her . . . Then he pulled this dead bough to her. It was lying over there.' He traced with his toe a faint trail of bruised grass and overturned pebbles.

Kendrick turned his back. Ten o'clock. The wind would stay steady in the south until late afternoon now. There was a strong tree fifty feet from the corpse and in the right direction. The tiger would come back from the north or north-east downhill and upwind, quartering the hillside. At the moment he was resting, or perhaps watching from a hiding-place close by.

'Aitu,' he said, 'go back to the village and tell the headman to bring men here at once, to make a machan.'

As soon as the Gond had gone Kendrick turned to the dead woman. Young and lovely she had been. A bar of sunlight shone on her belly and raised, spread knee – the very gesture of lust, even in death.

Kendrick began to pace slowly up and down in the forest, his ears alert, his head turned downwind. The machan should be ready in three hours at the most. He must get up into it as soon as it was ready, send the people away, arrange a system of signals. One of the beasts he *must* kill tonight. Two man-eaters that worked together were at least four times as dangerous as one. Nearly eleven o'clock. They were taking an unconscionable time. He was hungry and thirsty, and would be more so before the night came.

He stiffened, hearing the crack of twigs. It was the people coming from the village, the headman in the van, half a dozen men in his wake, carrying planks and tools; and Aitu; and Rukmini. Kendrick glowered furiously.

Behind the headman rose a frantic shriek, and a slight young man in a loin-cloth stumbled past, his arms outstretched.

Kendrick seized him. 'Stop, fool! Quiet!'

'My wife,' the man wailed. 'My love . . .' Tears streamed down his cheeks and his jaw shook in an ugly paroxysm of grief.

He wiped his brown arm across his face, dashing the tears to the ground. He said, 'My wife and the mother of my child shall not lie there, thus. I have come to take her back. No one can stop me.'

Kendrick's cheek twitched. Now this young man was about to spoil everything. Kendrick shouted, 'I know about your feelings! What about the others whom the man-eaters may kill? The body must stay!'

The headman said, 'I have told him, lord. He will not listen.'

The young man said, 'I must take her home.'

Kendrick yelled, 'No!' He raised his hand to strike, but the young man jerked free and ran towards the corpse of his wife. Kendrick threw him to the ground with a flying tackle. Rising winded and angry, the man struggling in his arms, he shouted, 'This fellow is under arrest.'

The headman beckoned to two or three villagers. 'Come. Seize him.' They shuffled their feet uneasily in the high Bundelkhand slippers and looked from one to another, at the shaking young man, never at Kendrick.

Rukmini spoke, softly, but all turned to face her. 'What is your name, father of a child?'

'Buddhoo,' he muttered.

'And your wife, who lies before us in her beauty, was the mother of . . . a daughter?'

'Praise be – a son,' the young man said, raising his head.

'How old?'

'One year old.'

'And he is healthy and strong, like his father?'

'He is strong and fat. Her milk was full in her breasts, and though she and I went short of food, our son never did.'

'He is beautiful?' Rukmini asked, her hand now caressing the young man's arm.

'He is a son,' he said. 'A son for a man to be proud of, a son for my field, for my old age, for my death.'

Rukmini said quietly, 'From that womb he came, father of a son. Next week he may lie where she lies, as beautiful as she, and as dead, if the sahib may not kill the beast that took her.'

The young man began to tremble again. Again the tears started in his eyes. Kendrick watched, his cheek jerking.

The young man cried, 'Leave her then!' He ran back down the hill, through the jungle, and away.

Kendrick turned away with an angry grunt. Deori was governed by Hindu law, and if the fellow had insisted he would have been forced to let him take the woman – the bait – away.

He said, 'Build the machan there. Work fast, but with care.' He turned to Rukmini. 'You should not have come here. But I must thank you.' He bowed brusquely.

Rukmini said, 'These are my lord's people.'

Kendrick grunted again. The villagers didn't share the Deori priests' suspicion of her. They obviously respected her. Of course, they were all low caste in Konpara, like her.

The villagers set to work, directed by Aitu and the headman. Rukmini was at his elbow. 'Mr Kendrick . . . I shall go back to Southdown now to collect a lantern and the food and drink that I told your khansamah to prepare for you. I think you will need a coat, too, with long sleeves against the mosquitoes. There are often red ants in these trees, so I shall also bring some oil which I have. It has no scent, but it keeps off all insects. Is there anything else?'

He thought slowly. She was a whore, but competent. 'Ten more rounds of ammunition,' he said. 'In case both tigers come, and for signalling. This sort of ammunition.' – He gave her a round from his cartridge belt. 'Joseph will show you, in the gun room, but don't trust him to match the cartridges. Nor my wife. Do it yourself.'

'Thank you,' she said, smiling. 'I shall be back in an hour.'

108

She walked away. Kendrick waited for her to signal one of the men to accompany her; but she walked on, and in a moment was alone, going down the hill at her usual slow, lithe pace, her buttocks swaying. He ought to call to her to stop, and send Aitu with her. But every man was needed here, and . . . Would he be sorry if she lay, her secret parts revealed, like the woman's behind him, and dead?

He turned to work and began to help the men. He noticed at once that the machan would be too small to seat two people in comfort. Aitu would have to return with the villagers, then.

An hour and a half later Rukmini returned, as casually as she had gone. An hour after that the machan was ready – several rough planks nailed together and laid across a fork of the tree, and another fastened crosswise to a lower bough. He would have to sit on the platform, and rest his back against the tree; or he could half turn, sit forward, and rest his feet on the lower plank.

Aitu swung easily up to the machan and the villagers passed up the lantern and the food hamper to him. It was nearly three o'clock and the jungle shuddered in the heat. The afternoon would be almost intolerable – but now was the time to take post, especially with a man-eater. Helped by Aitu from above, and the headman from below, Kendrick struggled up into the machan. It was about twelve feet above the ground, and seemed a good deal lower once he was up there. A tiger standing up on its hind legs would almost be able to touch it, without jumping. Aitu scrambled down.

Rukmini gathered the villagers. He watched her sourly as she pointed out a small saw that had been overlooked, and made another man pick up a pile of fresh-cut chips. At last she bowed in silence towards the corpse, and turned to the villagers. 'Now, to Konpara, and let us leave the Resident Sahib to kill the tiger for us.' She made a low namasti towards him, her eyes warm as she looked up at him over the joined palms. 'We shall pray for your success.'

'Go on,' Kendrick called impatiently.

They went, and he was alone. He checked that the rifle was loaded, rested it across his knees, reached for the hamper, drank some cold tea, and ate a mutton sandwich. The tiger would not come for at least three hours. He leaned back.

Far to the south-east, through the upper branches of trees lower down the slope, he could see the drab green wash of the cultivated land in the plain. In the opposite direction, north-west, he was looking up the rocky hill. Twenty feet beyond the corpse the roots of the trees were level with his eyes, and the spreading foliage of his own tree obscured the view. The air moved like a slow furnace draft across the slope, leaves rustled, boughs creaked. His eyes kept wandering to the corpse. The woman lay spread-eagled, stripped of her clothes by the tiger's eagerness to get at the succulent flesh. The tiger was strong and bold, a male. The woman might be the same girl who had lain under the bush with the herd boy. He raised the rifle slowly. When the tiger came he would wait until it was engrossed in feeding, crouched over the belly, over the swelling breasts. He held the sights steady on her body, moving them slowly over her, here, there, his tongue caught between his lips. His breathing shortened. *There* was desire, and failure. He should squeeze slowly on the trigger, squeeze, squeeze, until the butt plate struck back against his shoulder and the blued steel barrel jumped slightly and a thin wisp of smoke curled from the end. And fire again and again until the cold barrel was hot and the scornful, twisted smile smashed to pulp.

He closed his eyes, sweating and shaking.

He heard a strange sound and quickly looked up. Soon he located the source of the sound as being in the north-west, up the slope. The wind had almost died, but such as there was blew towards the sound . . . the disturbance, rather, for it was not a clean-cut sound of any kind, but a thudding, a jerky unrhythmical disturbance of the heat.

He listened to it with all his attention. It came from the direction of the Gond village, on the upper plateau, but closer than that. It could be men, clearing an open space at the limit of hearing; but no men would be abroad, against his orders and with the tigers near by. Or it could be a heavy animal, moving jerkily. Not a tiger, that was certain – and no other carnivorous or hunting animal. A cow or buffalo, though. He strained his ears. Yes, that was it. Probably a buffalo, tethered, stamping its feet.

His first feeling was of anger. What fool had left a buffalo tethered up the slope, to spoil all his plans? The tiger would come downhill, right past it. The chances were strong that the tiger would be suspicious of the activity that had taken place round the corpse, and would take the buffalo instead of coming on down to the kill.

His anger increased. The act was deliberate! The villagers had been here until three o'clock. The headman's first order to them, to return at once to the shelter of the houses, bringing in all grazing cattle and goats, had gone out long before that. If the owner of the buffalo was too frightened to go and bring it back at the first order, he could have come out with the headman's party, knowing that Kendrick himself would escort him up to the

110

buffalo. But he had not come. A buffalo represented a great deal of wealth to the villagers of Konpara – to any of them, including the headman. Now he remembered that there was no grass on the slope above his present level. Therefore, no reason to tether a buffalo there in the first place.

His mind slowed, caught hold. The buffalo had been put there deliberately. The purpose of such an action must be to prevent the tiger coming to its kill. If the tiger did not come to the kill, it would not be shot. Someone, or some people, wanted the tiger to remain alive. That had been his own wish, until the danger of trying to hunt a pair of man-eaters, and other reasons, had decided him he must shoot one of them immediately. Again, he felt the presence of allies.

The momentary warmth vanished as soon as it had come. These two man-eaters had been in the Saugor District two weeks ago. Why had they come north? Someone did not want them killed, because their presence delayed the search for the Venus; but that someone could not have known they were coming. Or could he? Some of the greatest shikaris among the primitive peoples, even an occasional Englishman who devoted his life to the hunt, were able to move tigers large distances at will, by imitating their calls and playing upon their sexual instincts. The idea was not impossible; but it was chilling. For these were man-eaters. They had already claimed two victims here. How could the someone, or the people – it would take more than one – know that they themselves would not be among the victims? Or their wives or children?

Money meant nothing to these people. Nor life. He sat hunched and cold for a long time, while the shadows lengthened, and the sun set, and twilight came. At last he sat up. One thing was certain. He could no longer allow himself to be a pawn in their intrigue. He must control it. They must be made to understand that a pair of man-eaters was too dangerous – to himself, who must pretend to stalk them; to Mohan, who might walk into them.

Meanwhile, he could relax. The tiger would not come tonight.

A heavy thudding and cracking of twigs approached down the slope. Without hurry; he raised the rifle. Whatever this was, it was not the tiger. A dirty grey buffalo cow cantered into view, crashed past the foot of his tree, and hurried on down the hill, her udder swinging, her tail streaming out, and a short length of rope trailing from one hind leg.

Kendrick thought, she's broken her tether. Now the tiger might come after all. He grinned without mirth. Other people's plans, as well as his own, sometimes went astray.

111

Something else was coming down now, slow and subtle among the boles of the trees. He aimed carefully along the gleam of the rifle barrel. The monkeys began to chatter farther up the hill. The sights steadied and held on the moving blur in the dusk . . . a dull blue, a point of red near the top. Rukmini's face floated over the foresight.

Kendrick lowered the rifle and pulled back the safety catch. She was wearing a red-jewelled brooch at the shoulder of her sari. She had reached the foot of his tree.

He bent forward. 'What are you doing here?' His voice rose and cracked. 'I said no one was to come out! What do you mean by it?'

The light was failing fast, the darkness riding down the slope, the jungle settling into the special quiet of nightfall. She turned up her face. 'Did you see the buffalo cow go by?'

'Yes,' he said. 'What has . . .?'

She said, 'May I come up, please? We can speak more softly.'

'There's nothing else to be done now,' he snapped. Dimly he saw her lift her sari, the sheen of her leg, a hand grasping a bough. Another reach, a lithe step, and a pull, and she sat beside him.

She said, 'The buffalo was tied to a peg up the hill. I cut the rope and she ran home.'

Kendrick muttered, 'Oh.' He boiled with rage. The woman was intolerable. 'You came out just to do that? How did you know?'

Rukmini's voice was very soft. 'I was in Konpara, visiting the sick woman again. It was against your orders, but I had to do it. She died in my arms. On my way out of the village I saw a buffalo in a stall, with a yoke hanging on the wall, and a place for another buffalo beside the first. I was curious. I spoke to the man, who seemed very nervous. At last he said that the other buffalo was up here. He brought it up early in the morning, he said, and tethered it to eat the jungle grass. Then he went away and was working the other side of the village when the tiger took the woman. He said nothing. He was afraid the headman would make him go up and get the buffalo. But there is not any grass up there, where she was tethered.'

'I shall speak to the headman about it,' he said curtly.

'Or shall I?' she asked.

'No,' he snapped.

He settled back against the tree. He'd sent Aitu away because there was hardly room for two on the machan – and now she'd come.

Sharp stars swelled out of the darkness. The moon, three days before full, blazed above the latticed trees. The wind had died, not a leaf stirred. She smelled faintly of her strange, Hindu perfume – but very faint, no stronger than the animal tang of his own sweat. Her hips touched his on the narrow machan. Her breathing was light, slow, and even, and the rise and fall of her breasts caused the material of her sari to hiss with a sound so small that he had to strain his ears to hear it. The corpse was a paler blur under the trees. Cold and stiff she would be now. The thigh lay warm against his, and he could not move away, for he was already pressed against the tree.

An hour passed. Another. Kendrick's thoughts kept returning to her thigh, her breasts, the hollow of her loins.

Her fingers crept out and lay along his arm. The pulse at his temple began to beat painfully. His grip tightened on the rifle. The hand crept up his sleeve, to his shoulder, to his neck. The faint odours of musk and sandalwood and female dilated his nostrils. Her hand crept round his neck and lay flat along his farther cheek, the soft wrist pulsing against the back of his neck. Power was risen and straining, and his finger on the trigger.

Her hand pressed steadily, turning his head towards her. The pressure held him, facing to the north. The fingers stretched down and under his chin, and raised it, till he was looking a little up, above his own level.

A pattern moved steadily down the slope, coming down among the striped and mottled moonshadow without sound or colour or size, only motion. Her hand fell away as he raised the rifle.

Not yet, too far yet. The motion continued – fifty yards, twenty, the corpse a little to the right. The rifle butt fitted into his shoulder. Eyes reflected yellow and the shadow stopped. Gold tinged with green of moonlight, black softened to grey, the woman pale and shining under the eyes. The sights held fast and his right hand squeezed.

The explosion thundered away through the forest; in the boom of it the tiger leaped into the air, clawed at the top of the low tree above him with both huge forearms at full stretch, and somersaulted out of sight. After a time Kendrick saw him, lying on his side thirty feet from the woman. He aimed carefully at the exposed heart under the elbow of the forearm, fired the other barrel, and at once reloaded.

After two minutes of total silence the acrid tang of cordite left his nostrils. Gradually musk and sandalwood and female replaced it. His mouth was dry. Rukmini handed him the bottle. He uncorked it and drank, and after a hesitation passed it to her.

She said, 'That was a beautiful shot.'

113

'Not bad,' he said. He ought to thank her for drawing his attention to the tiger. How did she know it was coming? Were her eyes better than his? Or was she in league with the devil, as he had begun to suspect? He dared not speak of the incident, for the memory of her hand on his neck had returned, and his strength was rising again. It was always the same after a kill. Several times, on these occasions, he had come to the very point of making advances to Barbara; but each time the certainty of failure had overcome him, and, a moment later, hate for the mocking temptation.

The machan creaked as Rukmini moved her buttocks. 'It is hard here,' she said, the laughter liquid in her voice. 'And I am softer than you, where I sit. You must be very sore.'

He gritted his teeth. Soft she was, soft and full. Her hand crept out again, reaching towards him. In the starlight her eyes shone and a trick of the shadows emphasized the roundness of her breasts. The hand was close.

'Would you like a sandwich?' she said.

It was in the hand, offered to him. He pushed her hand away. 'No . . . I'm not hungry.'

With Rukmini the moment of panic would not come. But while the strength was with him he always thought that. He could count the occasions when the temporary confidence had led him on to disaster – a barmaid in Oxford, a prostitute in London, two more in Calcutta, a widow in Simla – five. It always ended the same, a moment of panic, of insufficiency . . . He had been the man of the family since he was eight. He remembered his mother giving him the money to buy the railway tickets, tip the waiters, a hundred duties, playing the charade that he really was a man, his mother and sisters waiting with folded hands for him to do the job, the bowings and 'yes, sirs,' . . . But he couldn't see over the counter and his voice was treble – everyone laughing and pretending not to, then in that moment the panic, always dropping the money on the floor, always disaster, fumbling, impotence, and afterwards loathing, uncontrollable revulsion, the tic in his cheek.

With Rukmini that could not come. She had no morals. She was ashamed of nothing. The certainty was too hard this time to fail again. His hand crept out and lay along her thigh.

She slid one arm around his neck in a firm unhesitating movement, voluptuous but full of affection. Her breast pressed, yielding, against him, and her other hand closed gently on the pride of his body. She said, 'Here, I am here.' His hand glided over satin skin, over the full curve. It found. 'Forget everything, see nothing,' she whispered. 'Here. You are very strong.' For a single tremendous moment he was erect, and free, and upon her. A frantic hope surged up. He had entered the very vestibule and in a moment would achieve the unknown.

At the first enfolding yield of her lips, the panic sprang upon him. Her arms pulled him down, her body tried to hold him, and the tears spurted from her eyes. He heard her groan, 'Aaah, you're hurting me!' And, 'Go on!' she cried.

It was not true. It would never be true. He rolled slowly over on the narrow machan. She sat up and took his hands. 'We have all night. For tonight, I am yours.' Gently she guided his hands back to the warmth.

He pulled away, and scrambled down from the machan, leaping the last six feet in a great bound and falling forward to his knees, the rifle in his hand. He picked it up and broke into a stumbling run, but her voice recalled him. 'Mr Kendrick – please – the hamper.' She leaned down and handed it to him, and the lantern. Then slid down herself, landing easily beside him.

'Go on,' he said harshly.

She walked steadily ahead of him through the moonlit jungle. She had offered herself to him. Was it possible, as he had believed for a moment, that she was trying to help him? Absolutely impossible! How could she know he needed help? He didn't need help! She offered herself because she was a bitch, a whore, a harlot, because if he succumbed she would have a hold over him, for ever. His finger itched to touch the trigger of the rifle.

Too dangerous. No need, not when he had allies to whom money and life were of no value. But the urge to destroy her with an expanding bullet was becoming intolerable. He stopped, unloaded the rifle, and threw the two cartridges far into the jungle.

Chapter Nineteen

Mohan and the headman and a dozen villagers met them at the entrance to Konpara, Mohan carrying a light rifle. 'Did you get it, sir?' he asked anxiously. He looked pale, but had apparently shaken off the fever.

'Yes,' Kendrick said briefly, 'only the male.' Rukmini stood close beside Mohan, her eyes averted from all of them.

Mohan said, 'Word's just come in that the tigress killed at Gharial. She attacked a herdboy, but his buffaloes drove her off. She took a calf later.'

Kendrick said, 'Send out for the tiger at first light. Have it skinned. Let the husband take his wife's body.'

The headman said, 'Very good, sahib.'

Kendrick said, 'I shall sleep for a few hours, then I shall go to Gharial after the tigress.' Gharial was a village in the flat jungles, ten miles north of the dam.

Mohan said, 'Can I come too, sir? I'm feeling quite all right now.'

'No,' Kendrick said curtly. 'It's too dangerous.'

'But . . .' Mohan began, an obstinate look settling in his face.

Rukmini touched his arm. 'You have to go to Deori tomorrow, for the rite.'

Mohan muttered, 'Oh, yes, so I have. After that, though, I really think I ought . . .'

'We can discuss it later,' Kendrick said. 'Headman, I have a few matters to discuss with you, and we had better do it now . . .' With his eyes on the headman's, he said, '. . . as you are going over to Vishnuswara in the morning – aren't you?'

He waited, his heart pounding. The headman had said nothing about such a visit.

The headman said, 'Yes, sahib.'

Kendrick turned away, trying to keep his excitement out of his face. The headman understood, or he would have told the truth.

'Come along then,' he said. 'Good night.'

'Good night, sir,' Mohan replied.

'Good night, Mr Kendrick,' Rukmini said. Her voice sounded

116

very small and tired. Well, she'd failed, and the days of her power were numbered.

With the headman walking five paces behind him Kendrick strode up to Southdown. The lights in the drawing-room blazed across the lawn as he approached. Why wasn't Barbara in bed? Usually she went very soon after dinner.

Foster rose as he entered the drawing-room. Kendrick stared at him in astonishment. Foster stared back. Then Kendrick remembered that Foster was there to guard Barbara. 'I killed the male,' he said. 'Thank you, Foster.'

Foster left. Barbara said, 'I shall retire now.' Kendrick hardly heard, but walked out of the room, calling to the headman to follow. When he had lighted the lamp in the study, he sat down behind his desk. The headman stood opposite.

Kendrick said nothing for a long time. He must go carefully, though he was certain. At last he said, 'The Buddha was placed where we found it – by men of Konpara.'

'I fear so, sahib,' the headman said. His hands were joined in front of his waist, the left uppermost, showing the stump of the missing thumb.

Kendrick said, 'There was a bar of gold worth thirty thousand rupees under the Buddha.'

'So I have heard. It was not told to us at the time.'

'Twenty more such bars were placed where the Pathans would find them.'

The headman did not speak.

'A buffalo cow was tethered on the hillside above the machan tonight.'

'It returned to the village at dusk.'

'You are a good headman, Huttoo Lall. Nothing happens in your village that you do not know.'

'Your honour is gracious to his servant.'

'So you knew that the buffalo cow was there. In fact, you ordered it to be taken there, while the machan was being built.'

He expected that he would have to wait, to overcome denials; but the headman said, 'Yes, sahib.'

'And the man-eaters – they were brought here from Saugor.'

'Yes, sahib.'

'Why?'

'Your honour can read the hearts of such simple men as ourselves more easily than a book.'

'Where is the cave?'

'The gods will lead your honour to it, if that is their intention.'

Kendrick's voice rose. 'You aren't going to tell me? I shall not

117

reveal the secret. I do not wish it known. You know why . . . But tell me.'

'The knowledge would be dangerous to your honour.'

Kendrick sat back and controlled himself. 'There must be no more guiding of tigers. Leave the female. I shall deal with her – at the proper time.'

'Very good, sahib.'

Kendrick picked up a pencil and idly drew the trident sign. 'What else? We are of one mind, but it is very dangerous if the right hand does not know what the left hand is doing. I must know.'

'Your honour shall know . . . It is proper and needful to make a sacrifice at this time.'

'Who?'

'One, above all, threatens us.'

'Threatens us all,' Kendrick said. He looked up. 'A thousand rupees for you.'

The headman's eyes flickered and Kendrick knew he had made a mistake. Money did not matter to these people. The headman said, 'Two bars of gold for your honour, to temper justice if anyone is caught.'

Sixty thousand rupees, Kendrick thought. Carefully he erased the trident. 'Remember, I must appear to use all my powers against whatever, or whoever is discovered.'

'It is understood, sahib.'

Kendrick rose abruptly. 'That is all. These words that we have spoken have not been spoken.'

'I have heard nothing, lord . . . I shall punish the man responsible for leaving the buffalo cow on the hillside.'

'Punish him severely,' Kendrick said, as he walked down the passage at the headman's side. 'He nearly prevented me getting the tiger.'

Chapter Twenty

The five men and three women sat in a loose circle in the shade of a tree. The hookah in the centre of the circle gurgled gently as one of the men drew the long pipe to him and, holding the mouthpiece in his loosely clenched fist so that his lips should not touch it, began to suck the acrid fumes into his lungs.

Another spoke. 'Now, with only the female left, it will not take long.'

Another said, 'He is cunning and skilful in the jungle. A week, at the most.'

There was a long pause. The man with the hookah passed the mouthpiece to his clockwise neighbour. 'Not enough,' he said.

Another long pause. 'The sacrifice must be made, then,' one said.

Silence. Silence was acquiescence, here.

'Who?'

'The leader.'

'Who leads? Not he who came, and will go?'

'She.'

The hookah tube passed again. One of the dark, naked men was using the blade of his long-handled axe to shape a small piece of wood into a flat plate, about three inches square. He spoke without looking up from his task. 'It is right. She leads. She will not rest. She has no fear. Did she not free the buffalo cow?'

'I do not like it. She is of us.'

'By blood, a part. She has left us.'

'The blood is thick. She knows. I have seen it in her eyes.'

'So be it.'

The hookah bubbled. A long-tailed grey monkey peered down at the men from a lower branch of the tree, his eyes darting from man to man, his shoulders hunched.

'Who then will act? We appoint by lot?'

'I have the marked stones.'

'No. We appoint by choice. They must be strong. Young, but not foolish. Knowing the land.'

'How many?'

'Two.'

The monkey crept out along the branch and dropped to the ground a few yards beyond the outskirts of the gathering. There he paused a moment, crouched for flight, momentarily frightened by the sudden movement and the small sound of his own fall. Reassured, he squatted on his haunches, his head bent forward, the ninth of the council.

The men and women began to speak in turn, a single word at a time. Each word was a name. The others listened, digested, and shook their heads. At last a name was accepted and, thirty minutes later, another.

Everyone smoked from the hookah. The monkey watched. One of the men said, 'It is wrong that the Impotent One should raise his hand secretly against *her*, without cause and without sorrow.'

'It is a sin. He is a fool, and will not understand.'

Silence.

The whittler finished the wooden square, gave it to one of the others, and started on a second. One by one they stood up and drifted away in different directions, until only one man was left, with the hookah. Below, in a small clearing, three tethered buffaloes grazed on the sere grass. His back against the tree, the last man watched them as they grazed. The monkey, which had hurried back into the tree when the first man made a move, became bored and swung away, chattering, to join his friends in a distant part of the jungle. After a time an old woman came through the trees and the man picked up his hookah and axe and strode away, while the old woman untied the buffaloes' tethers and drove them after him, beating their backs with a long stick and calling them names in a cracked, high voice.

Chapter Twenty-One

Stripped to the waist, his body glistening, Mohan huddled against Smith in the narrow tunnel of the crevice. A few feet ahead Foster placed the last of the present batch of charges into position. Behind them the tunnel now extended fifteen feet towards the irregular oval of the entrance.

'All right. Out now,' Foster muttered.

They crawled out, Foster uncoiling the fuse behind him. Near the mouth of the excavation they set to work to re-erect the rough, low wall of big stones which they built across the entrance before blasting every charge, to prevent accidents and protect the structure of the platform. Then, from the foot of the scaffold, Mohan and Smith watched Foster light the fuse and hurry down to join them in shelter under the cliff. Seconds later a heavy boom shook the pit wall and a cloud of dust shot out of the tunnel entrance.

The three of them climbed back up the scaffolding. The dust was settling, and they crept through a thinning reddish haze to the farther end. Mohan saw that another two feet of shaft had been forced in, very rough and small now. Foster moved the lantern carefully over the newly exposed stone, and tapped the rock with his hammer. Mohan could detect no hollowness in the sound, no sign that there was anything but more rock ahead. The fissure that they were following continued its path into the rock, faintly discoloured at the edges where exposure to the air currents had caused a continuing chemical process.

They crawled back in silence, and in silence climbed the ladder to the top of the cliff. Foster said, 'That lot of debris will bloody well have to stay there for now. I haven't got time to clear it.'

'I'll clear it tomorrow,' Smith said.

'I'll help,' Mohan said.

'No,' Foster said roughly. 'You've got a more important job. Help Kendrick with the man-eater.'

'He won't let me,' Mohan said.

Foster said, 'Make him! I wish I knew that this tunnel was leading us somewhere, with all the time and trouble it's taking, and now no coolies on the job.'

Smith said mildly, 'We know the crevice has another exit.'

Early in the morning Foster had burned a bundle of kerosene-soaked wet grass inside the shaft. Nearly all the smoke had been sucked into the crevice, but although Smith and Mohan himself, with binoculars, had watched from the verandah of Cheltondale, they had not seen the smoke emerge on the ground above.

Foster shrugged. He looked at Mohan. 'Why don't *you* have a try at getting some villagers to come back to work? They're safe enough on the platform, at least.'

'I'll try,' Mohan said. 'When I come back from Deori. The headman's doing his best, too, but – they're frightened, and this search doesn't mean anything to them. The dam does.'

'Well, have a try,' Foster said. 'They'll listen to you in the way they won't to anyone else.'

Mohan acknowledged the compliment with a smile. Foster's manner to him had altered greatly. The outward roughness was still there, but there was no venom beneath it, nor contempt. He seemed to know that Mohan's relations with Mrs Kendrick had changed, and to realise, at the same time, that the change was not due to his own threats. In his awkward manner he had made an effort to establish a new relationship, of curt familiarity on his side, and neutral acceptance on Mohan's. He had changed in other ways, too, unconnected with the personal relations between them. He spoke less and his red, open face was sometimes marked with the lines of unaccustomed emotions, of decisions whose weight he was finding unexpectedly heavy. At other times he stood looking at nothing, and then his face was completely calm, with a confidence that had never been there before.

Smith turned to Mohan. 'In about an hour?'

Mohan nodded, and walked up to Cheltondale, called for his servant, and ordered a bath. He would ride to Deori in English clothes. The clothes he needed for the ceremony tomorrow were in the palace, in charge of the Chamberlain.

Where was Rukmini? He climbed out of the tub and called to her. No answer. The servant spoke respectfully through the door. 'The lady went out an hour ago.'

He began to dress, frowning. What had made her insist on going out to Kendrick that night, the night before last? There was the mysterious business of the buffalo cow, of course, but . . . And her determination that the search for the Venus should be resumed, but . . . He was heading for madness if he started suspecting her of having an affair with Mr Kendrick, knowing what he knew about him, but . . .

It couldn't be Kendrick – but, when they returned here after the killing of the male man-eater, he had found that he was not as

122

fully recovered from his fever as he had thought. Exhausted by the walk across to Konpara and back, and by the excitement, he had fallen into bed and at once to sleep. A little before dawn Rukmini's moaning and muttering on the other side of the big European bed awakened him. Drowsily resentful, he put out his hand to push her, and mumbled, 'Rukmini.' As his hand touched her she said, 'Aaah, you are hurting me. Go on, go on,' and her body writhed rhythmically as though in a sensual transport. She spoke some more, but unintelligibly.

She spoke in English. Her endearments to him were always in Hindi. He had lain stiff and a little afraid under the sheet, staring up at the ceiling. Her words, her actions, pointed to a sensual dream, the re-creation of a memory – but the tone of the voice did not. He had never heard that tone from her, asleep or awake. It was flat and hopeless, utterly despairing, the contrast with the words so great that he had felt deeply troubled for her, rather than jealous.

He finished dressing. God knew what she had been thinking of. She was full of affection when she awoke, and he told her nothing of what he had heard in the night.

Now he saw her coming up the path along the edge of the ruined cricket pitch, Smith behind her. He stiffened and put his hands in his pockets. They entered the room. Rukmini said, 'Leander's ready. And the mare. Mr Smith's riding her, isn't he?'

He said, 'Yes. Where have you been?' He tried to speak nonchalantly, but there was an edge to his voice.

'Having a cup of tea with Mrs Kendrick,' she said. 'She's alone, you know. And then I came back by the Rest House.'

Mohan picked up his white topi. 'We'd better be going,' he said to Smith.

Smith nodded, and followed him from the room. Rukmini came out to the verandah. 'I wish I were coming with you,' she called down as the servants held the horses' stirrups for them. 'The two most handsome men in Deori. In all India!' She laughed happily. Mohan did not answer, and a moment later rode off, without looking back, Smith placidly silent at his side on the borrowed mare. A syce followed twenty paces behind them on a third horse.

Soon after they had passed the coolie camp and entered the long stretch of jungle Smith said, 'Tell me more about this ceremony you are going to perform.'

'We throw a man off the battlements,' Mohan said shortly, and waited for Smith to laugh.

Smith said, 'Not a live man, these days, I suppose?'

Mohan said, 'No. Not since 1858.'

Smith said, 'It sounds un-Hindu to me. Very old, I imagine.'

Mohan said, 'It is.' The other's interest made him forget his sulks. 'It's older than the Brahmins, I think. They don't approve of it, and never have, but they knew they'd never suppress it, so they took it over. The Suvala himself is supposed to carry it out, with Brahmins to advise and assist. That's why I'm going down. If I weren't there, my uncle would go, as the next nearest in blood. He did all the time I was in England – and each time that happens, more people think he is or ought to be the Suvala.'

'Perhaps they're right,' Smith said.

Mohan stiffened. 'What do you mean?'

'It is the exercise of duties and rights that make a king, as much as birth.'

Mohan said, 'But the eldest son *is* the Suvala. He can't do anything about it, any more than he can about his caste.'

Smith said, 'In one way, I agree. But I also think that if a hereditary monarch doesn't inherit a sense of duty towards the position, as well as the position itself, the people usually have a right to choose another . . . What are the details of the ceremony?'

'Guards go out from the palace before dawn, seize the first person they find in the streets, and drag him up to the battlements. After some ceremonies his hands and feet are bound, and he is thrown off, at dawn. A dummy is thrown off nowadays. The man hides in the palace the rest of that day and the next dawn he gets twenty rupees and goes back to his home, but he has to change his name.'

'To preserve the fiction of his death,' Smith said thoughtfully, 'which used to be a reality . . . Do you know what the purpose of it is?'

Mohan said, 'Not exactly. The priests say it is to make homage to Indra, others that it is to avert evil from the state. It's called the Rite of the Labourers. No one knows why. Hundreds of people come into Deori for the day, and there's a big fair – but no one's allowed to watch the ceremony itself.'

'Very interesting,' Smith said, 'and very unusual.'

There was little more conversation between them until they reached the outskirts of the city. As the three horses forced a passage through the crowded streets Mohan carefully examined the people's expressions. He had been into Deori two or three times since the riot, and never without a qualm of anxiety as to what awaited him. But today the people had come for the fair, and those who recognised him greeted him with profound respect. Amid the same respect he rode into the palace court-yard, and walked between salaaming servants into the palace itself.

Later he joined Smith in the great reception room and together they went to the museum-like room allotted to the Archivist. The old gentleman greeted them with a long flowery speech and ceremonial cups of tea. An hour later he was still showing them through the relics, statues, and manuscripts he had collected in the past forty years, and the subject of their visit had not yet been mentioned.

Smith's patience and interest never flagged, but Mohan at last could stand it no longer. He interrupted a learned lecture. 'You have seen the gold bars in the treasury, guru-ji. Can you tell us anything about the stamp marks on them?'

The old man said, 'I fear there is nothing about such marks in the *Suvala-Gita*,' He shook his head sadly.

Smith caught Mohan's eye. They waited.

The old man said, 'But *elsewhere*, yes, there are records. You see, each Suvala sovereign had a personal mark. One of the marks – that of the trident, the bull's head, and the four small bows – was used by three different Suvalas; that is, by your grandfather, my lord, and by a ruler of the twelfth century A.D. . . . and by the Suvala who was defeated and driven out of Deori in 147 B.C.'

'Not as recent as your grandfather, surely,' Smith said. 'One of the other two. But which?'

'The other mark,' the Archivist said, 'the plain bow. I can't tell you whose mark that is because once it was used by all Suvalas. It is the mark of the god Indra, as you know. In the earliest times the Suvalas were believed to be actual reincarnations of Indra, so they used his mark without further identification. A better, and nobler concept than the later one, if I may say so.'

'What was the latest period in which the bow was used thus, alone?' Smith asked.

The Archivist said, 'The fifth century B.C.'

Mohan whistled. So the gold bars found by the Venus's leg were stamped some time earlier than 400 B.C., perhaps centuries earlier. He tried to remember more of the history which Rukmini kept urging him to study. He had rather resented her efforts. It was one thing for her to improve herself; he *was* the Suvala, whether he knew everything or nothing about the past. But Smith's remarks during the ride, and now a growing interest in what the old Archivist was telling them, made him wish he knew more about the sources of his own pride.

Smith said quietly, 'Four hundred B.C. is a long, long time ago, guru-ji. Can you tell us anything about that age? A date means so little.'

The Archivist pushed his spectacles up to his forehead. 'The Prince Gautama Siddhartha, later called the Buddha, lived from 560 to 480 B.C.,' he said. 'The sacred Brahmins at about the same time gave its final form to our religion. Brahminism and Buddhism began a long struggle for the souls of men here in India. It was the Golden Age, for as men sought in their souls to find the truth, their spirits flowered. But I have said, of that bow mark, only that it was used earlier than 400 B.C. How much earlier, I cannot tell you.'

'Later than 1500 B.C.,' Smith said.

'Certainly,' the Archivist agreed quickly. 'We accept that in that century Indra led the Aryans into this land . . . I sit here alone, my lords, all day, every day. I have done so for forty years. I do not have visions, but – sitting and thinking, hours on end, in silence, alone – I see the past. However far back I go, I cannot see the jungles without the Gonds, just as they are now. But later I see others coming here, the remnants of the defeated Dravidians, men, women, and children, and babes in arms, fleeing before Indra. They have fled from their ruined and burning cities, as described in the Vedas. Those cities must have been of the plains, my lord – where else can subsistence come for the populations of such cities? I see the Dravidians reaching this valley. It is much smaller than the great plains where the cities stood – but there are many fewer Dravidians. Here they make a new beginning. They till the land, perhaps building a walled town. Time passes. How much time, who knows? A score of years, a hundred, three hundred – they are nothing in the sight of the One. But soon Indra's sons, your fathers, march again. They come here. Again the defeated are defeated; again the land is taken from them. What did they do? What would you do, lord? I see some staying as slaves, some going up into the hills, to begin once more. Their bands are very small now, for the land they can find to till is small and poor . . . Konpara is such a place, a few acres tucked among great cliffs. But back here in Deori I see the leader of the invaders, astride his horse, looking round this valley. He is not the greatest of Indra's sons, nor yet the least. I see his army gathered round him, and black corpses lying in the lanes, the survivors crouching in chains, waiting. The Suvala speaks – "This shall be my kingdom." To his yeomen he gives land in the plain, and authority under him, and slaves to till the land. Thus he rules.'

'Like the Normans in England,' Mohan said. 'After the Battle of Hastings.'

'I have heard of that event,' the Archivist said.

Mohan said, 'But later the Normans and the Saxons became one people.'

'It was a long time, I think,' Smith interposed, 'before Sir Roger de Montmorency really felt that he and Hal Bloggs the cultivator were both Englishmen. Until recently de Montmorency had much more in common with Sir Bertrand de Prévert over the Channel in France.'

The Archivist said, 'It would be the same still, sahib – if the original difference had been fixed by caste.'

'But there *was* an original difference,' Mohan said obstinately. 'The Normans were superior to the Saxons, and the Aryans to the Dravidians.'

'They won,' Smith said.

'They were more civilised,' Mohan said.

'Certainly, certainly,' the Archivist said soothingly. 'We were discussing the time, not later than 1000 B.C., when your ancestors established themselves in Deori . . . The armies of Indra were many, my lord. The Suvala was here, but another son of Indra was over in Saugor, another in Nowgong, another – there were many, and they were all warriors, and all hungry for land and glory. The Suvala builds a fortress. It must have been here in Deori, for his herds and flocks and fields were here. But there would have been another – built upon a rock, in an impregnable position, not to guard the whole region, but as a last keep for the soldiers and the royal household only. A strong place, able to be defended against any attack. As long as it held, no enemy could rule in Deori.'

'Konpara,' Mohan said.

The Archivist nodded. 'I have long thought so, lord.'

'And the cave?' Mohan said. 'Do you think it is something to do with the fortress?'

The Archivist said, 'No one knows where the cave of the Suvala title is. I have a feeling that it, too, must be at Konpara. The sahib's letter about the stone debris and the bones has convinced me.'

'But what *was* it?'

'It exists still,' the Archivist said quietly.

'What is it, then?'

'If we knew that, we might be able to find it tomorrow.'

'A shrine of some sort,' Smith said.

'I agree, sahib.'

'A shrine, but not a universal shrine – otherwise there would be no need to keep it secret.'

'I agree, sahib.'

'A shrine in which only certain people were permitted. That

applies to the fort, too. Only Brahmins and Kshatriyas?'

'Perhaps – But I believe it is older than the acceptance of those caste divisions.'

'Only for the Suvalas?'

'And their men – the knights, courtiers, picked soldiers. All Aryans.'

'And it was finished some time between about 1000 and 400 B.C.? That is a long spread, guru-ji.'

The old man said eagerly, 'It is! But the execution of the workmen by throwing them off Indra's Rock . . . that seems to me to be a deed which would not, could not have been done in the Golden Age, or anywhere near it. The slaughter of enemies in battle, of prisoners, of whole populations – yes. I fear such deeds have been done in my own lifetime. But the slaughter of workmen, to keep a secret . . . there is something primitive about that deed, sahib. It is an act of superstition, not of vengeance or reason, nor done in hot blood. So I think the cave was made very early . . . Well, perhaps I shall know before my eyes take their last look at these relics that have surrounded me for so long.'

Smith said, 'Have you thought of anything that could give us an idea as to where the mouth of the cave might be, guru-ji? We are exploring a crevice in the pit cliffs, and we are searching the ground above, but there is so little time.'

'Time?' the Archivist said. 'Men die, but learning does not.'

'The dam,' Smith said.

'Ah. The dam, which will fill the pit. I see . . .' He stood up and hobbled across the room. 'Sit down, my lords. Here.' He produced a large tome, hand-written, and clothbound in the Western manner. 'This is my own copy of the *Suvala-Gita*, made with my own hand. In the original Sanskrit, of course. I might mention that I am now composing a couplet which I hope will be suitable for this year. It links the opening of the Kendrick Dam and your ascent, my lord, to the gaddi – in a single couplet. Not ill-turned either, if I may say so. The scansion is extraordinarily difficult, you know, and . . . Ah, yes, the cave. Here is the couplet for the year 265 B.C. Do you see?'

Smith read the couplet aloud. He knows Sanskrit, too, Mohan thought. Smith said, 'It seems to have nothing to do with the matter.'

The Archivist said, 'It doesn't! Because that is not the original couplet. On three occasions the original couplet was so false – or so true, eh? that a successor succeeded in having it expunged and replaced by another. These three occasions were A.D. 1858, A.D. 810 – and 265 B.C. The expunged couplet officially ceased to have had any existence . . . but those of us responsible for the past, sahib, have a higher duty.'

The old man looked cautiously round the room, and then opened a locked drawer. Pulling out a single sheet of rolled cream parchment, he unfastened the yellow tapes binding it and spread it on the table. His voice sank to a whisper. 'This is the true verse for 265 B.C. Do you see?'

Smith read aloud, and then translated into Hindi. '*From ridge to ridge the impious son his evil battle raged, Nor stayed the king his hand inside the holy place.*'

The Archivist beamed. 'A scholar, sahib! It is strange. When we first met, I had a notion that I smelled about you gunpowder, battle, stratagem, and, h'm, rape – but for an English gentleman to have acquired your mastery of Sanskrit and Hindi points in an entirely different direction. It was surely midnight oil that I should have smelled. Parchment, ink?'

'What do you infer?' Smith interrupted politely, but firmly.

'Ah. The new couplet states merely that the King bought twenty elephants and made a pilgrimage to the Ganges. The next year he died, and his son succeeded him – and expunged the original record that he had tried to overthrow his father and had been defeated, but not, apparently, executed. You see?'

Smith said, 'You think the holy place referred to is the cave?'

The Archivist said, 'It might be. There are no ridges down here in the valley.'

'*From ridge to ridge,*' Mohan said. 'From the Dobehari to the Konpara.'

The Archivist nodded. 'I agree, my lord . . . Suppose the ridges marked the limits of the fighting, as stated. The last stand of the insurgents would have been made at one limit, rather than in the middle. And at the site of that final stand was the mouth of the cave, so that the last survivors could enter it, and continue the fight. You agree?'

'It seems logical,' Smith said. 'Unless the rebel prince was surrounded. But in which direction was the king attacking?'

The Archivist spread his hands and sighed. 'I am not a military man. I had hoped that you . . .'

'I have no idea,' Smith said.

A little later they left the old gentleman, bowing profoundly outside his narrow door, and walked back to the main part of the palace. To Mohan the cave had taken on a reality, during their talk, that it had never had before. He found his mind running over with thoughts and ideas about it. *From ridge to ridge* . . . Until the man-eaters came, a large party had been systematically searching the ground between the ridges. Perhaps it would be best, with time so short, to concentrate on the ridges themselves, if the battle had ended on one of them and immediately continued into the cave. That must mean that some of the defeated party had fought on in there – or taken refuge in it. But the Konpara Ridge at least was dotted with human habitation – the village itself, Southdown and the Rest House with their servants' quarters and caretakers' huts, and the cart track, numerous footpaths. Surely if the mouth of the cave lay there it would have been discovered long ago? The Dobehari was more likely.

'We must talk this over with Rukmini,' Smith said. 'Jim Foster's an excellent chap, but he thinks in cubic yards. I think in logic, though I try to make it flexible. But Rukmini does not think, she feels.'

On an impulse Mohan asked Smith to stay for dinner. Smith agreed, and they separated, Smith to walk in the city and Mohan to discuss palace affairs with the Chamberlain. After bathing and changing into his full Suvala costume, he went eagerly to the small drawing-room and found Smith waiting for him. For the first time he felt himself at ease with Smith. At first they discussed the Archivist's theories, but soon they had exhausted the little concrete information they possessed, and the conversation widened.

Mohan was reminded of something which Smith's gentle manner had never before forced upon him – that the Englishman was nearly twenty years older than he, and had spent those years as much inside as outside the mind, producing an outlook of extraordinary depth and flexibility. Mohan began by listening to his guest's far-reaching speculations, and thinking that the quiet, almost hesitant tone in which he put them forward was more convincing than Mr Kendrick's flat statements had ever been. Soon he found himself joining in, advancing suggestions, discussing with a warm eagerness the life and beliefs of the past.

Every few minutes he would catch a glimpse of himself in one of the long, ornate mirrors on the walls, and think, Is this I? How long ago did I leave Sandhurst, trying to grow a thin moustache on the upper lip and dreaming of cricket matches? He felt a certain pride that he could say something of value . . . or was it only the other's courteous manner that gave his words value? . . . but, more and more dominantly as the evening progressed, he felt that these hours with Smith marked the end of his youth, as definitely, in its sphere, as the coming of Rukmini had marked another end, another beginning. I am a man, he thought wonderingly. Smith had helped, Rukmini had helped . . . but, more than all, the Venus had done it, and the search for her, and the sense of peril, of unity, of great unexplored depths which the search had revealed and the realisation that however long he lived he would never live long enough, in one life. Only a month ago the years had stretched in endless boredom before him to the burning ghat. Now those years seemed few and short, for he was a man.

Almost without interruption of their talk they had eaten, slowly, and Mohan had taken a couple of glasses of liqueur brandy – Smith drank only water. Now Mohan wanted to talk to Smith about more personal matters. He wanted to talk of himself and Rukmini, of Mrs Kendrick and Foster, of Kendrick himself, of the web of relationships into which the search for the Venus had drawn them.

He poured himself a third brandy and prepared to introduce the subject.

Smith rose to his feet with a smile. 'And now, my most excellent host, I must be getting back.'

'Now?' Mohan exclaimed. 'I had hoped . . . it must be nearly ten o'clock.'

'I like riding at night,' Smith said.

Mohan felt a sudden strong resentment. Even as he acknowledged it, and tried to suppress it, he knew it was totally unworthy of him, now; but it would not be denied, and when he was alone he sat on, swirling the brandy round in his glass.

What drew Smith back to Konpara at this time of night? If he'd waited till after breakfast tomorrow they could have gone back together. Was his show of interest in him, Mohan, merely a pretence? The debris from the last blasting had to be cleared out of the shaft, but there was no need to start on it at dawn. 'We must talk it over with Rukmini,' Smith had said. 'Rukmini doesn't think, she feels,' Smith had said.

A deputation from the Chamberlain's department was announced, and Mohan stood up, still thinking of Smith. The Chamberlain himself came in, knelt at his feet, and handed him a small square of wood, punched with a hole in each corner, and a long loop of light cord threaded through the holes. Mohan tucked it impatiently into an upper pocket. The Chamberlain's chief assistant then handed him a white cloth, heavy with silver. He put that in the other pocket. The deputation left, and Mohan sat down, his train of thought hardly interrupted.

The thoughts came fast and disjointed . . . Rukmini's hint that if a man needed her as desperately as Barbara Kendrick had needed him she too would give what was asked. Smith hurrying off as though he had an appointment. Rukmini in her sleep, moaning *Go on, go on*. The Suvala's chosen favourite, whoring with casteless, English upstarts! Degrading him, and herself.

131

The English thought they had the right to sleep with any Indian girl, just because they had conquered the country. Didn't she have any personal pride, even if she didn't care a damn about his?

He poured another brandy. His thoughts circled: the cave, the Venus; Rukmini and Smith, embracing; the cave – who had the Venus been? Rukmini and Smith, talking, sharing an intimacy she wouldn't share with him. Marriage. No, that's what he wouldn't share with her.

He felt miserable. Was this, too, being a man, suffering this horrible, degrading jealousy?

Near eleven o'clock he staggered to his feet and called the servant. 'Prepare my horse.'

'Yes, lord. At once.'

'Tell the Chamberlain I have gone back to Konpara. Let him perform the ceremony in the morning.'

The servant stood thunderstruck. 'Back to Konpara, lord? But, but . . .'

'Yes, back to Konpara,' Mohan snarled. 'Hasten now, or I will have you beaten.'

The servant ran from the room. Ten minutes later, with the half-dressed Chamberlain wailing that now he would have to send for Mohan's uncle, it was his duty, Mohan galloped out of the gates.

The Chamberlain waddled after him, shouting, 'Lord, lord, the sacrificial brooch! We do not have another prepared . . .'

But Mohan did not hear, for by then he was galloping through the crowded streets and the blaring music of the fair, the sleepy syce rolling farther and farther behind.

Chapter Twenty-Two

Lights burned in Cheltondale when he reached it, near one o'clock. That was strange. He dismounted and walked up the verandah steps, leaving the blown horse with dropped head and dangling reins. The major-domo met him on the verandah, running out of the front door as he walked in.

'Lord . . .' the man stammered.

'Out of the way,' he said wearily. So she had bribed the servants.

He walked into the house, the major-domo hurrying after him. He opened the bedroom door. The lamp burned low on the dressing-table but the bed was empty and had not been lain in. An enormous gush of relief swept away his weariness.

The major-domo's stammering words reached him. 'The lady Rukmini . . . has disappeared . . . They are over at Southdown, the sahibs, getting ready to search for her. A groom is preparing even now to ride into Deori to tell you . . .'

'Disappeared,' Mohan repeated. He didn't understand.

The major-domo said, 'She went to the Rest House . . .'

Mohan aroused himself. 'They are at Southdown?'

'Yes, lord.'

He ran out of the house. Now he had wits to notice that lights also blazed from Southdown across the shallow valley between the ridges. A few minutes later he dismounted on the lawn there, one of Kendrick's syces running to the horse's head. The light from two hurricane lanterns shone on the gathering – Kendrick, a rifle under his arm; Foster, a revolver strapped to his waist; Aitu, the Gond tracker; two syces in the background with horses; the headman and several villagers with long-handled axes. He searched the group quickly. Where was Smith?

Smith stepped forward from the shadows and Mohan's heart missed a beat. His suspicion – half hope, half fear – vanished. Rukmini was really missing.

Smith said, 'I got back from Deori at about half-past eleven. I didn't hurry. Foster was awake. Rukmini had passed by the Rest House a little earlier, and told him she wanted to see me as soon

133

as I came back. I went down to Tiger Pool, and –'

'Why?'

'I knew that that was where she meant.' Smith's steady look never faltered. 'But she was not there. After twenty minutes I went back to Cheltondale, but she had not returned.'

'She must have fallen down . . .'

Kendrick interrupted, 'No, Mohan. I fear not. We have already searched the path between Cheltondale, the Rest House, and the Pool.'

Smith said, 'She may be safe, but we cannot take the risk. We are just starting out to trail her.'

'The tigress,' Mohan gasped.

Kendrick said slowly, 'I cannot deny that it is just possible. But it is very unlikely. When I left Gharial the tigress had just been heard ten miles away – in the opposite direction . . . Aitu, are you ready?'

Aitu handed back a piece of red cloth that he had been fondling and carefully sniffing. Mohan saw that it was one of Rukmini's cholis.

Kendrick quickly gave Mohan the instructions. While Aitu was tracking, no one must come closer than ten paces from him – downwind if there was any. On no account could anyone smoke. The horses, under the headman's control, were to be kept at least twenty paces back.

'Do we need horses?' Mohan asked. 'They'll make so much noise.'

Kendrick said, 'She may be hurt.'

They set off for Tiger Pool. Where the path from the Rest House reached it, Aitu walked round in a circle, came back into the light of the hurricane lanterns, and raised one finger, then two. Kendrick muttered, 'Two men.'

He stared over Mohan's shoulder. 'What are you doing here?' he snapped. Mohan turned and saw Barbara Kendrick. She had not been among the group on the lawn, but she was here now, bareheaded, dressed in a long skirt and blouse. 'I told you . . .' Kendrick began. She interrupted him, her voice polite but strained. 'I was afraid to stay there alone.' She turned to Mohan. 'And I am the only other woman here. Rukmini may need me.'

Kendrick turned away. 'Go on,' he told Aitu. Over his shoulder he flung at his wife, 'Keep back with the horses.'

The tracker headed west round the pool, crossed the bund, and continued west again on the left bank of the Deori River. Close at Kendrick's side Mohan kept his ten paces from the tracker, a villager with a lantern a step behind. His anxiety grew steadily. The idea that Rukmini had actually vanished slowly

134

forced itself deeper into his heart.

They came to a cart track. A long delay followed, but eventually Aitu led on again, heading south-west now through thin jungle. Progress became very slow. At one of the innumerable checks Mohan could not contain his impatience. 'We ought to have got some dogs from the village.'

Kendrick said, 'I'm afraid not, old chap. There are ways of putting a dog off the scent, or of killing it. Poisoned bait. A trained hound would ignore them – but there aren't any here. Try not to worry.'

'But what's *happened* to her?' Mohan cried. No one answered.

After three o'clock now. Aitu could not find the trail. Suppose Kendrick didn't want him to? He hated Rukmini. Suppose Aitu wasn't even trying? The Gonds might have kidnapped her to rape her, or keep her as a goddess, or use her in a blood sacrifice. He was sweating heavily in the magnificent costume. Aitu was a Gond. He might be deliberately leading them astray. No one would know.

Movement began again, continued for half an hour, then stopped. Began again. Barbara Kendrick walked just behind the villager with the lantern. She was paler than ever and her face shone, the hair raised and thick round it like an aureole in the glow of the lantern. She kept staring at him, Mohan.

Movement stopped. Mohan hurried forward. Kendrick was speaking to Aitu. 'Cast again.'

'I am sure, sahib,' the Gond said. 'At first, there seemed to be two trails, but now I am sure.'

'Cast again,' Kendrick said, his voice shaking slightly.

'If he's sure . . .' Mohan whispered in agony. 'Let's get on.'

The Gond began to make another cast. Kendrick gripped Mohan's arm. 'Get back. I know what I'm doing . . . One mistake through trying to hurry and we will lose the trail altogether.'

At last movement started again. Stopped.

Mohan put his head in his hands and tried to think of nothing. But the jungle intruded, then the whole land. No, it was he who intruded here. He was a visitor from another planet, another time. The dark figures crouched around him were carrying out some rite familiar to them. They belonged here. They had done this a thousand times before. Rocks and snakes, the swinging monkeys, the crackling heat of the jungle were not strange to them, but were parts of life and shareholders in the land, even in the village.

He opened his eyes. Aitu was making a wider cast. Was there almost a trace of light? The horses back there had become some-

135

thing more than a sound of creaking leather and jingling bits.

Barbara Kendrick said, 'Please, Mohan. It's been driving me mad. Why are you dressed like that?'

Why *was* he dressed like this? Deori. Something to do with a sacrifice. Ah, he remembered. 'The Rite of the Labourers,' he muttered.

They'd been heading south-west, then west, then due north, south-west again, and now . . . south-east.

It wasn't the land that had taken Rukmini. She knew it too well. It was people, then. What people? Why, why? Darkness and moonlight surrounded them, separately and together. Forces emanated from the silence. Not the forces of mechanics, but the forces that made a tiger take one man instead of another. That caused drought. That sent death. There was no counter-force in reason, only in fact, and in the response to fact. Fear. Caution. Silence. Sacrifice.

His hand touched a hardness in his upper pocket. It was the sacrificial brooch which, in a few minutes now, he should have been fastening round the neck of the ritual victim in Deori. It was the same shape as the steatite brooches found among the bones under Indra's Rock.

For a moment he sat, blinded. Then he jumped to his feet, ran to Kendrick's side, and cried, 'Give me the rifle. Quick. Indra's Rock!'

He wrenched the rifle from Kendrick's hand, ran back, and leaped into the saddle of one of the horses.

Kendrick stood dumbfounded, but Smith had understood. He was already mounted on the other horse. 'Due east,' he called. Then they were off, at full gallop.

The dawn spread fast through the scattered trees. Mohan rode as fast as the horse would go, the rifle across the saddle bow, the thin branches whipping his face.

Smith touched his bridle hand. They dismounted. Smith held the horses. 'Two hundred yards to the edge of the pit,' he muttered. 'Four or five hundred west of Indra's Rock. Don't let them hear you.'

Mohan ran, slowed to a walk. The depths of the pit spread out suddenly below, close through the trees ahead. He dropped to his stomach and crawled the last five yards. He lay down on the very edge of the pit and looked along the line of cliffs to the east. Indra's Rock rose on his left, four hundred yards away, its sides striped with the decay of ages. Behind it the yellow day rolled along the dark crestline of the Dobehari Ridge. He pushed forward the safety catch, and set the sights.

Doubt attacked him. Why had he come here? Perhaps she had

fallen and broken her leg going back from the pool . . . had a cramp swimming, drowned. No one had thought of that.

The sun burst over the horizon, and a woman hobbled slowly out on to Indra's Rock, alone, her arms and legs loosely bound. She stood there a moment, looking east and west along the cliff line. Then she turned and he thought that she was speaking, but he could hear nothing. She must be telling her captors she would not jump; they would have to throw her. No, that they were *supposed* to throw her. That was the ritual. They ought do the thing that was supposed to be done – that must be done. It would be wrong to hate them.

Two men came out on the rock, both grey-coloured, naked, and carrying axes. Mohan aimed. They approached Rukmini, and put down the axes. Mohan fired. One of the men dropped, the other hesitated, then went forward again. Mohan fired again. The man reeled, hobbled on one leg, and fell. He sat up, holding his leg, and rocking from side to side. Rukmini turned slowly, looked in the direction of the shots, and stood still. 'Lie down!' Mohan shouted. There might be other men. They couldn't see her if she lay down on the outer step. But she did not move. He struggled to his feet and ran along the cliff edge. Circling carefully round Indra's Rock, he searched the jungle. No one was there. He climbed the rock. One man lay on his face in a lake of blood, a big red hole in the middle of his back. The other, his knee shattered, looked up at him without expression.

He untied Rukmini's bonds of jungle lantana. She rubbed her wrists slowly. 'Thank you, my lord,' she whispered. She took his hand, raised it to her lips, and touched it with them. Then she walked quickly over to the wounded man and knelt beside him. 'Ah, my poor man,' she cried. 'But you will walk again. Do not fear.' As she leaned forward a flat wooden object dangled from her neck on its loose cord. Mohan saw that the wounded man was also wearing one. And the corpse – he could see the cord, though the plate was hidden under the body.

Smith came, riding one horse and leading the other. As he dismounted Rukmini ran to him and gripped him by the elbow. 'Are you unhurt? I was afraid, when they took me, that they would take you, too.'

Mohan stared out across the pit. His eyes hurt. It was certain now, laid like a sentence upon him, that only one woman could share his life; and she was Rukmini, without a father, who loved Smith.

Half an hour later Aitu came, with Kendrick, the headman, and the rest of the party. The headman looked down at the wounded man. 'It is not a Gond, as I had thought – and hoped,' he said sadly. 'It is a man from Konpara, Ram Rattan.' He turned the corpse over with his foot. 'And this is his cousin, Ghulloo.' He turned sharply on the wounded man. 'Who else?'

'None,' Ram Rattan answered indifferently.

Kendrick stood over him. 'Why did you do this thing?' he asked sternly.

The prisoner was a slight, short man in early middle age. Smith knelt by him, probing his wound. The man must have been in agony, but his face showed nothing. He answered Kendrick's question. 'For Konpara, sahib, we did it.'

'Explain yourself,' Kendrick snapped. 'Remember, you have committed an act for which you can be transported across the Black Water for life.'

Ram Rattan spoke slowly, long pauses between each sentence. The climbing sun burned hotter on Mohan's back. 'Konpara lives each for all, all for each. When a man's house falls down in the rains, all must work to restore it. The upper forest is common land. All must work in it, to cut the bushes, to put out fires . . . One night my cousin Ghulloo dreamed a dream. The god Indra came to him in all majesty, armed with the lightning and the rainbow. He commanded Ghulloo that he must make sacrifice in the ancient manner if disaster was to be averted from Konpara. My cousin was much frightened. He told me of the dream. I told him that he had eaten too much dal the night before. Twice again the dream returned to him. The third night, to me also. Then we knew that we must do it. We debated long whether we should tell the headman, for if it concerned the village he should know. He should lead us, even. But my cousin said, No. He said, "Huttoo Lall has not had the dreams. He will tell us to wait. He will prevent us." Even so, to make sure, I asked Huttoo Lall whether he had had any dreams –'

'Did he?' Kendrick interrupted.

'He did,' the headman said. 'Yesterday. I told him to mind his own affairs, for I slept well.'

'Go on,' Kendrick said.

'So we did it,' Ram Rattan said.

'But why her?' Kendrick said, 'Why not Smith Sahib, Foster Sahib? Why not me?'

Ram Rattan said, 'In our dreams, Indra commanded us – a woman.' Almost as an afterthought he added, 'Afterwards, we were going to sacrifice ourselves.'

'I don't believe it,' Kendrick said.

Ram Rattan pointed to the wooden plate at his neck. Rukmini showed hers, and said, 'It is true.'

Mohan produced the brooch from his pocket. All were very

138

similar, except that his own, the one prepared for the ritual in Deori, carried no mark. He knew that when a Rajah had been appointed, it would carry his personal mark. The others bore, burned into them with a fine point, the device of a bow.

Kendrick stared down at Ram Rattan for a long time, then said, 'What was the nature of the disaster which would come to Konpara?'

The man said, 'How should we know, lord?'

Kendrick turned to the headman. 'Have him carried to Deori, under escort. To the jail hospital. He will be tried in the high court next month.'

The headman stooped and hit the man savagely across the head with the handle of his axe. 'Fool, idiot, criminal!' he said. 'Instead of saving the village, you would have destroyed it.'

'Stop!' Rukmini cried.

Mohan started forward, shocked by the sudden outburst of violence. Until now the whole affair, from the beginning through Ram Rattan's explanations, had been carried out in a dignified, almost ritual manner.

Ram Rattan said, 'I have deserved it . . . It was Ghulloo and I who brought the Buddha statue and buried it. Let me be punished for that, too.'

Rukmini cried, '*You* did?'

Ram Rattan said, 'We brought it in a bullock cart, pretending we had gone to Deori for two days. We did it for the reward.'

'And the gold?' Kendrick shouted. 'You placed the gold bars there too – just for a reward of a few rupees?'

The man said, 'Of the gold we knew nothing. How could we?'

The headman raised his hand again, but Smith said, 'Enough! Send now for men to carry him, and a stretcher. It is a bad wound.'

The headman said, 'I have already done so, sahib. I will wait here till they come.'

'Don't touch him again,' Rukmini said.

The headman said, 'I will not – though he deserves to die.'

Mohan helped Rukmini into the saddle of one of the horses. 'I'm taking her home now,' he said briefly to the others.

Smith stood by her saddlebow, looking up. 'Rest, sleep,' he told her. 'Think of nothing.' She nodded, smiling down into his eyes.

A thin loin-clothed young man ran up the side of the rock, and stopped, panting slightly, in front of Kendrick. He made a deep salaam. 'In the middle of the night the tigress returned to Gharial, sahib, and broke into a house. The house was empty. We had her trapped, and set fire to the house. She escaped through the roof and away, breaking one man's shoulder.'

Kendrick ran a hand through his hair. As though speaking to himself, he muttered, 'She is too clever for us. She has learned too much. I shall have to go to Saugor and learn all that I can about her. I fear it will take me some days, and meanwhile you will not get anyone to work for you in your search.'

'We must kill the poor tigress first,' Rukmini said. 'It is her fate – her part.'

Kendrick said, 'I will start out tomorrow. There's work to be done before I can go – and I am . . . tired. I have ridden twenty miles, walked twenty, and slept only two hours, and those in a tree, since killing the male.'

Mohan and Rukmini rode away from them all, down the slope, along the ridge crest. Rukmini said, 'Who understood that they would take me to Indra's Rock?'

Mohan said, 'I did . . . No, I think Barbara Kendrick did. She said something that made me understand . . . that made me feel, first, and then I understood.'

'That is why she is an artist,' Rukmini said. 'And I am alive, and we have learned much.'

'Don't think about it any more,' he said. 'It's all over.'

'I want to,' she said earnestly. 'The Rite of the Labourers in Deori, and the attempt with me, are both continuations of the sacrifice of the workmen who made the cave, and for the same purpose – to keep the secret of the cave. The people down in Deori, you and the Chamberlain and the Archivist – the Aryans – do not know why you want to keep it secret. You do not even know that that is the purpose of the rite. But the people here – the Dravidians – do know.'

They entered Cheltondale and servants scurried about with fruit juice and warm milk and food, while Rukmini sank back on the couch, drawing her feet under her and still talking. Mohan watched her with a deep pang of love and despair. The events of the night, the hours in the jungle under threat of death, the lack of sleep had only served to put a film of languor on her vitality.

'By what right do we try to wrest the secret from them, then?' she asked, looking at him but speaking to herself. 'If they are willing to die, to kill, to give up lakhs of rupees – who are we to force them to such lengths? It is the Venus, Mohan. I cannot believe that evil lies in wait for them where that statue, that woman, stands and dances. They are afraid, but I believe there is no reason for fear. We must go on until we can lift this fear from them . . . with which they have lived for a long time.'

'What can we do?' Mohan said. 'No one will work until the tigress is killed.'

She said, 'Our servants here. Why should they not help?'

'If they can be persuaded . . .' Mohan began doubtfully.

'I will ask them to,' she said, leaping to her feet. 'Time is becoming short.'

'You must lie down, get some sleep,' Mohan cried.

'Later,' she said.

Chapter Twenty-Three

Mohan paced carefully through the thin jungle, his head bent. Every five paces he glanced up to make sure he was heading straight for the white stick stuck into the ground a hundred and fifty feet ahead of him. Two grooms, a water carrier, and the dishwasher walked spread in a line to his right. Mohan glanced at the dishwasher and called, 'Don't keep looking around you. Don't look anywhere except on the ground. After all these years the mouth of the cave may be so small that a dog can hardly enter.'

The youth said, 'Very good, lord.' He was visibly shaking with nervousness.

Mohan said, 'The tigress is not here. She is beyond Gharial.'

'Very good, lord,' the youth whimpered. 'But she is a devil.'

They continued their slow pacing. They reached the white stick and Mohan carefully moved it ten paces to the north, and turned. Now the other white stick, at the east end of this line, was dead ahead of him. The search continued.

The afternoon sun poured down almost without check through the scrub teak. The ground was covered with brown spear grass up to a foot and a half high, rocks large and small, tiny fissures and larger ones, gnarled roots of trees curving under split rocks. Hardly a quarter of the area in which it was geologically possible for the cave to be had been searched.

As Mohan moved his white sticks for the twelfth time, one of the grooms said, 'Lord, two men are coming.'

Mohan straightened his back and wiped his forehead. Two men were walking fast towards them over the shoulder of the Konpara Ridge, apparently having come from the village. The groom said, 'One is Huttoo Lall, the headman.'

Mohan waited in the stifling heat. Soon the two men arrived. The second was the young messenger from Gharial, he who had brought news of the tigress yesterday morning. His face was twisted in pain, and his left arm hung across his body in a loop of grass rope.

'Lord,' he said, knelt, and rose again. 'Lord – she has killed.

A woman of our village. At an hour before noon today. She has taken the body into the jungle, but not far. She has been growling and roaring since then. Our lambardar thinks she has not started to eat yet.' He swayed on his thin, whipcord legs. 'It was the Resident Sahib's order that the news should be brought at once, day or night.'

'Your arm?'

'I fell, lord, running over the rocks in the dry bed of the Hariganga.'

Mohan said, 'Huttoo Lall, please send him down to Deori at once, to the hospital. I'll see what we can do about the tigress.'

He hurried up the gentle incline towards Cheltondale with long strides, his servants at his heels. Mr Kendrick had left at dawn this morning for Saugor. By now he would be twenty or thirty miles beyond Deori. He turned to the dishwasher. 'Run to the scaffold, and tell Smith Sahib what has happened. Ask him to come to Cheltondale at once.'

The youth dashed away, grinning, his nervousness evaporated. Mohan slowed his pace. His heart beat fast and his belly felt empty.

Smith arrived. Mohan said, 'Did the boy tell you?'

'Yes.' He said nothing more.

Well, Mohan thought, what am I to do? Why don't you say something? Say 'Of course you can't go after it yourself, that would be suicide. You don't have enough jungle knowledge.' Accompanying Mr Kendrick was one thing. Going by himself was another. Smith said nothing.

Mohan said, 'What do you think we ought to do?'

Smith said, 'Someone should go to Gharial at once. It might be possible to surprise her on the kill. She's acting strangely, almost as though she's challenging them to go out and get the body away from her.'

'Where's Rukmini?' Mohan asked suddenly. 'Wasn't she with you?'

'For a time, soon after tiffin. Then she went to Southdown.'

Mohan wished Smith would give him an order. Now he had to say it. 'I suppose I could go myself . . .'

Smith said, 'Yes. They seem to have some good men in Gharial. I'm sure if you picked a couple of their best shikaris you'd be in much less danger.'

'Why don't you come with me?' Mohan asked suddenly.

Smith said, 'I have given up killing – anything – with my own hands. I wouldn't be much protection for you. Besides, I think I should stay here.'

'Why?' Mohan asked him bluntly.

Smith looked at him with his deep head-on stare. He said, 'I don't believe that those two men, Ghulloo and Ram Rattan, were responsible for bringing the Buddha here from the shrine.'

'What does it matter?' Mohan muttered, not disbelievingly, but because he wanted to know.

Smith said, 'It means that the conspiracy is not broken up. It means that we do not know who is involved, but we do know that they will kill. Rukmini was their objective last time – why not again? Someone ought to be here to guard her.'

Mohan paced rapidly up and down the floor. 'Foster,' he said, 'why shouldn't Foster come with me?'

'He'd like to,' Smith said. 'But if I were you, I wouldn't take him. He's eager to show that he's as good a man as – anyone – but he's too clumsy in the jungle. You might be signing his death warrant.'

'His?' Mohan said bitterly. 'What about mine?' He faced Smith suddenly, 'Look here! I'm not going unless you come too.'

He met Smith's eye. Let him think what he liked. He would not leave the man here with the self-appointed task of guarding Rukmini, while he himself went away, perhaps to be killed.

Smith seemed to be thinking. Rukmini slipped into the room. 'What's this about the tigress, Mohan?'

The men rose. Mohan told her briefly. When he had finished, Smith said, 'We're going to Gharial.'

She said, 'But you don't take life.'

'I don't,' he said, smiling, 'but I will help others. Illogical, I know. Also, I shall carry a long stick. Giving a tigress a poke in the eye is permissible. Even tigers have to be taught good manners. May I order your grooms to get the horses ready, Mohan? And have some food prepared?'

'Of course,' he said. Smith left the room.

Mohan faced Rukmini. 'Mr Smith is worried about your safety. He thinks another attempt may be made. I want you to go down to Deori at once, and stay in the palace, in the women's quarters, until I come back. Don't leave them for any reason at all. Go at once.'

Rukmini said slowly, 'I think I must stay here, my lord.'

'Go to Deori,' he repeated. He wanted to tell her he could not bear to think of her in danger, but if she loved Smith he must not reveal to her the new, overwhelming depth of his love for her.

She said, 'I don't want to leave Mrs Kendrick alone here.'

'Ask her to go to Deori with you.'

'She won't go,' Rukmini said. 'Not with Mr Kendrick away for three days – and two nights.' She met Mohan's eye.

Mohan said, 'Oh. I see.'

'It's her first chance to talk, to find out how much it really matters, apart from the sex.'

'Has she told you all this?'

'A little. But that's not the only reason, Mohan. We will never learn anything unless we bend with these people. Don't you remember? If others besides Ghulloo and Ram Rattan are involved, we must give them a chance to show themselves.'

Smith returned. 'They'll be ready in five minutes. What rifle are you taking?'

'I only have one here,' Mohan said. 'A '300 magazine Zago.'

'Rather light,' Smith said. 'And a double-barrelled rifle would be better for this. What about borrowing one of Kendrick's?'

'We can't,' Mohan said. 'He keeps the bolts in a safe in his study with his confidential papers – and he has the key. The '300 will have to do.'

Smith said, 'It will do all right, if you hit the right spot. Are you going to send Mr Kendrick a telegram?'

'I'd better.' Mohan went to the desk, found a pencil, and scribbled the telegram. Rukmini said she'd have it sent down to Deori after they'd gone. The major-domo announced that the horses were ready, the wallets loaded with sandwiches and cold tea. As they left the room Smith took Rukmini's hand. 'Be careful,' he said. 'Keep close to the bungalow. Tell Jim Foster we've gone.'

A few moments later Mohan rode at Smith's side down the steep zigzags to the foot of the dam, and past the coolie camp. There, instead of following the cart track in its right-handed curve round the base of the hills towards Deori, they took a narrow path that led due east, straight into the shallow roll of the jungle. Mohan forced ahead and urged his horse into a canter.

The shadows stretched long ahead. The sun would set in less than half an hour. It would be full dark in another forty minutes or so after that – say an hour and a quarter from now. Ten miles to go – about an hour, on this path. They would reach Gharial just in time, and then they'd have to wait until the morning. Stalking the tigress in the dark would be suicide. In the morning he would be afraid again. Now, the horse moved powerfully under him and he felt only an excited determination.

Near half-way he saw ahead the streaked red and black rocks that formed the dry bed of the Hariganga, a hundred yards wide between low cliffs. At this time of year there was only a trickle of water in the centre of it, linking a few scattered black pools. Here the messenger from Gharial had broken his arm.

They reached it and descended the cliff at a place where the feet of generations had worn a steep slope into the rock. In the stream bed Smith came up alongside him. 'I would carry the rifle ready if I were you, Mohan.'

'We're miles away yet,' he said. The sun had just sunk in a brilliant spread of scarlet and purple.

'She's behaving strangely,' Smith said.

Mohan began to unstrap the rifle, which was slung across his back. The horse, picking its way carefully, left the river bed and with a powerful surge of its hindquarters forced up the narrow exit on the far bank.

The horse saw the tigress coming a fraction of a second before Mohan did, the same fraction of a second before her bellowing roar struck him a physical blow in the face. The horse bounded forward and upward, his hind legs on the firm rock, and arched twenty feet forward and five feet into the air in a single tremendous convulsion of terror. Bounding horse and leaping tigress met in mid air. The shock slammed Mohan out of the saddle and the rifle flew from his hand. As he tumbled he saw the black and yellow stripes rolling over, and the horse already twenty feet beyond, bounding away at full gallop. Then his shoulder hit the ground; he rolled like a shot rabbit, fighting to get to his feet, trying always to keep the yellow and black stripes in view. Smith's mare had panicked, and followed the other horse at a bucking gallop. Mohan rolled to a stop in a kneeling position against a tree, the breath knocked out of his body. Groaning for air he saw that Smith sat firm in the mare's saddle, his long stick held down. The mare leaped over the tigress and in her frantic plunging her hoofs caught the tigress full in the chest. The tigress coughed once with a deep, rasping grunt. Smith could get away, Mohan thought. The rifle, where was the rifle? He saw it close to his hand and crawled towards it, one eye on the tigress. She was up again, apparently unhurt. Ten yards behind her, Smith slid off the mare. The mare stumbled, fell. Smith came steadily back towards the tigress, the long staff in his hand.

'Ohe baghini!' he cried.

The tigress's ears flicked back, but she watched Mohan, and crouched lower, her tail lashing slowly. The rifle lay three feet beyond his reach. He made up his mind. The tigress's tail stiffened like a bar, he lunged for the rifle, and Smith, directly behind her, broke into a run at her, the staff held like a spear. Mohan loaded the rifle with a convulsive jerk of the wrist, and whipped it into the aim. The tigress bounded sideways with another huge roar. He fired and she vanished into the scrub. He held the rifle in the shoulder, following the crash and creak of the bushes in the jungle.

They ceased. Smith said, 'You hurt?'

'Bruised,' Mohan muttered. He moved his shoulder carefully, then his fingers, his legs. 'I'm all right.'

'The mare's broken her leg,' Smith said.

'On the tigress?'

'No. Kicked the rock wall in the cut just afterwards.'

The mare stood head down, panting, her coat staring and flecked with foam, the soft eyes huge in her fine head, her near hind leg hanging twisted, the big white bone showing splintered through. Mohan walked carefully to her, put the rifle to her head, and shot her. At once he reloaded, and at once the roar of the shot was echoed by the tigress from the jungle, close to the east. The light evening breeze came from the west. It was becoming dark, fast.

They stood back to back under a large tree at the head of the path up from the river. The whining singsong purr rolled through the jungle, now near, now far, just as he had heard it in the pit, but this time it was a personal message to him.

'She means to have us,' Smith said softly.

'Was she lying in wait for us?' Mohan said.

Smith said, 'Every time she was seen near Gharial someone came or went along this path, in a hurry, not thinking of precautions. She knew.'

'Should we try to get on to Gharial? Or back to the coolie camp?'

'Too late,' Smith said. 'It'll be dark long before we can reach either of them. There's plenty of dry wood lying round here. This is as good a place as any. We'll build a fire and wait here.'

'Up the tree?' Mohan asked.

Smith shook his head. 'Too low, and you couldn't fire accurately from it. No, at the foot, with the tree trunk behind us.'

He picked up a dead twig and placed it in position a few feet from the base of the tree; then another. The purring snarl droned on. Mohan could have sworn it went round and round them, but Smith muttered, 'She's downwind. Always has been. Watch that way . . . unless the wind dies completely.'

The snarl closed in, and Mohan started up, every nerve tense. Smith dropped the big log he was dragging, and waited. The snarl suddenly ceased. They waited a long time.

Smith said, 'Trying to make us panic. She won't attack until it's dark. Match, please.'

Mohan handed him the matches and he stooped to light the fire.

Mohan said suddenly, 'Why don't we set fire to the jungle? Especially as she's downwind.'

'I'd thought of it,' Smith said. 'We might drive her away if we did – but we'd stand a very good chance of burning ourselves to death. Feel the wind now.'

Mohan raised his head. The coolness of moving air touched his left cheek, then his right. 'Going every way,' Smith said, 'as the heat leaves the soil. We'll have to protect this fire.'

Deliberately he set fire to the brown grass round the fire, and stood ready with his shirt off and bunched in his hand. As the grass caught fire and advanced outward, before it could get out of control he smothered the flames. As darkness fell a ten-foot belt of burned grass surrounded their fire. Several big branches lay ready to hand. The glow of the fire reached fifty feet into the scattered trees ahead. Mohan twisted his head to look past the tree trunk against which his back rested. Smith said, 'Don't look round. She's watching you, because you've got the rifle. She only needs a second's start. I'm looking behind, but I don't think she'll come that way.'

Mohan nodded. The tree stood only six feet from the lip of the low cliff above the river bed. To attack from that angle the tigress would first have to leap up the cliff.

The fire crackled. Mohan wished it would burn silently. Straining his ears to hear the slightest sound beyond the circle of light, the noises distracted him.

He saw eyes, huge and yellow, burning in the jungle at the edge of the firelight and jerked the rifle into his shoulder with a gasp. The eyes vanished before he could fire. He held the rifle, trembling, in the aim.

The tigress's roar, coming from the side, shook the tree trunk against his back. He swung that way. Nothing. Smoke drifted suddenly into his eyes. They began to water, and smart. Everything blurred.

'Close your eyes,' Smith said. 'I'll hold the rifle.'

Mohan close his eyes and rubbed them desperately. He wondered, for a moment of insane fear, whether the tigress knew that Smith had vowed not to kill. His eyes felt a little better and he opened them. They watered freely and the fire was a yellow blur at his feet, all beyond invisible. After a time vision returned, and he took the rifle. The singsong purr moved slowly closer.

'I can't stand much of this,' he muttered.

His hands shook so much that if she attacked now he would not be able to aim. The smoke from the fire wavered towards him and he ducked with pure terror . . . Another minute of blindness and he'd run screaming into the jungle, firing blindly until the magazine was empty. Then she would leap on his back.

The tigress roared from close, directly behind them, the sound hollow and echoing. Mohan swung round convulsively. 'She's under the cliff,' Smith said.

Mohan struggled to his feet, 'I'll get her,' he cried. 'Shoot straight down . . .'

The tigress roared again, a long low deep thundering murmur – from the left. Mohan sank to his knees. All sounds died.

An hour passed, his eyes aching, his skin crawling, and the smell of fear so heavy that it made him retch. No sound from the jungle, the fire burning low. Smith pushed the log a little farther into the red heart of the fire.

A breath of fetid air drifted into his nostrils. 'To the right,' Smith murmured. 'Close . . . Now follow round, left.'

Mohan stared, his eyes burning. 'Can you see her?'

'No. The wind changed . . . I think she meant us to get the scent – but only for a moment.'

The eyes suddenly glowed like strong lamps to the left, and Mohan jerked up the rifle and fired. The eyes vanished. 'I got her, I got her!' he cried, leaping to his feet.

There was no sound. 'Think,' Smith said, his hand tight on Mohan's arm. 'Think. Where were the sights? On the eyes?'

Mohan tried to concentrate. The eyes had hung there, yellow and huge, and the black sights there, coming up, and then the jerk of his finger – nowhere near, the black V had been well below the eyes. Sick with despair he sank back. The singsong purr began again.

After ten minutes it stopped. A moment later Smith touched his arm and muttered, 'Listen.'

Mohan could hear nothing. 'Can't hear,' he moaned at last. 'Where is she?'

'Voices,' Smith said. 'Listen.'

Mohan shook his head. He had been trying to hear the pad of her huge paws, the sound of her breathing. Now the other was quite clear – the distant voices of men, raised in continual shouts, somewhere in the darkness ahead. A point of light appeared, then another, and another . . . Lanterns, flaring torches.

Smith muttered, 'The men of Gharial.'

Smith's grip was hard on his arm. 'I don't think she's here,' he said. 'She's gone, after them. Come on.'

'But . . .' Mohan rose unwillingly, and nearly fell. He held the tree for support, and slowly strength flowed back into his legs.

Smith waited. Mohan hated him with all his heart. They'd been through enough.

He groaned. These men of Gharial were his people and they were risking their lives for him.

'Come on,' he said. He broke into a fast walk, but Smith

sprang ahead of him, throwing over his shoulder: 'If I see her I'll stand aside, or lie down. Shoot over me.'

They moved fast along the path. Mohan kept stumbling and tripping. How could Smith see where to put his feet in this nothingness? The lantern lights ahead had disappeared. He remembered dimly that there was a low rise in the jungle a mile beyond the river bed. The men must have been coming over that when they first saw and heard them. Now the jungle hid them.

The lights appeared again, at their own level. Only a hundred yards of jungle separated them. Long, faint shafts of light illuminated the path. Smith broke into a run and Mohan ran at his heels, his heart pounding. The leading man of the party saw them and stopped, raising his lantern. The rhythmic shouts of the men behind him stopped. The leader shouted 'Sahib?'

The tigress broke from the jungle to the right, well short of the leading villager, and charged straight at him. A moment later and he'd have reached her, with no hope. Smith cried, 'Now!' and stepped aside. Mohan raised the rifle. The tigress was at full stretch – just beginning her leap. The man waited, his axe raised. Mohan fired. The tigress somersaulted in the air, rolled over and past her intended victim, knocking him flat, and bounding away into the darkness.

Mohan ran forward. The men of Gharial were gathered in a tight knot now, facing the direction the tigress had gone, sticks and axes and a few spears pointed, torches flaring. Smith knelt over the man lying on the ground. He rose. 'One or two broken ribs. She didn't use claw or tooth.' He helped the man to his feet. 'Back to Gharial now.'

Mohan found that his fear had gone. He stood, breathing deeply, looking at the men of Gharial. He said, 'You are brave men. I shall not forget.'

The leader said, 'If the Suvala risks his life for such black men as us, how can we be backward?' There were about a dozen men in the group – just villagers, fear and determination mixed on their dark, thin faces. 'The horse arrived, cut and bleeding at the village just before dark . . .'

'On now,' Mohan said. 'We can discuss it there. I'll lead. Keep close.'

'One moment,' Smith said. 'Bring a lantern here, *bhai*.'

He bent low over the ground and pointed. 'A little fur, and blood . . .' He followed the path the tigress had taken in her somersault and escape. 'More. You hit her.'

'Not badly,' Mohan said briefly.

Smith said, 'In the right forearm, I thought, when she bounded away. She'll bleed from it every time she moves.'

'We ought to follow her now then,' Mohan said.

'I wouldn't,' Smith said gently. 'We'll get her tomorrow. No one is going to use this path now.'

It took them three hours to cover the five miles to Gharial, and when they reached it Mohan's head was swimming with the strain of long-continued utter concentration. The tigress had roared twice on the flank of the party in the first half-hour. After that, they had seen or heard nothing, and that had been worse.

Gharial consisted of twenty houses huddled together in a jungle clearing. Every entrance was blocked by a dense zareba of thorns, and thin yellow bars of light showed below every door. The lambardar, he with the broken ribs, took them into his own house. His wife hurried forward with warm milk in a brass pot. Mohan drank, swaying on his feet. Smith said, 'Sleep now, Mohan. I'll wake you in good time.'

Mohan lay down, waves of sleep rolling over him like an irresistible ocean swell, each one carrying him farther out towards the deep of extinction. 'You didn't run away,' he mumbled. 'You could have.'

Smith's voice reached him from the ever-more-distant shore. 'Don't forget the mare had a broken leg . . . And what would Rukmini say to me?'

What would Rukmini say? Something full of trust and understanding. And love. He fell asleep.

Chapter Twenty-Four

Foster lay awake, Barbara Kendrick beside him, her head on his shoulder, one arm across him, holding him tightly, one leg flung across his loins. After the passion, after the ecstasy that seemed more like pain, after the fitful twitchings of the first hour of sleep, she slept soundly against him, her breath slow and even.

It must be nearly two o'clock. He had come in by the side door after dark, but probably the servants knew he was here. In India servants knew everything. Kendrick might return in a hurry, hearing of the tigress, though he was supposed to be away for two more days at least. He was a jumpy, unstable man, and it would be just his luck to come back all prepared to deal with one situation and find another, and then lose his head.

He kissed her, and whispered, 'Time I went, love.'

She stirred, yawned, and sat up. 'Are you going to marry me?'

'Of course, love,' he said softly. 'If you'll have me.'

'You aren't worried about what you told me in the evening? About my being a lady and you, what you are. It doesn't worry me, but it worried you.'

'It does worry me,' he said. 'But not enough . . . We'll find it a bit awkward at first, I expect. India's like a small village, and not many people of your sort are going to have much to do with us. Even without the divorce.'

'I don't care,' she said. 'I only want to be loved. No, I want something else. I must show you.'

She slid out of the bed, and he followed her carefully across the room and down the dark passage. She opened the door of her workroom and went to the windows, carefully checking the curtains. Then she lighted the lamp on the table. 'You oughtn't to be going about barefoot,' he said reprovingly. 'There are scorpions and snakes and heaven knows what.'

She turned quickly and flung her arms round his neck. 'Oh, God, Jim, that's the first time I've ever heard that – that tenderness, someone caring what happens, thinking of me, not what I can do for him. I love you, I love you.'

She broke away and bent over a tin box in the corner, found a

152

key hidden behind the bookshelf and opened the box. From it she drew out three or four large sheets of cartridge paper and spread them on the table beside the lamp.

A few strong lines in red and black charcoal were scrawled on the paper. At first he could see no form to them, and then the head of an Indian boy jumped out at him. He caught his breath sharply. The drawing wasn't right. Nobody really looked like that. A kid could have done it better. But the boy's hunger sprang out of the paper, and the glare of the sun, and a cringing terror before the world, where the boy had found no kindness.

Barbara drew the picture away. The next was of the dam, and the coolies at work on it. The same distortions – and the same power.

The next was of Rukmini, naked, in an Indian dance pose, every curve of her body speaking sex, and the pride of a queen in the carriage of her small head.

'Did – did she pose for this?' Jim asked.

Barbara said, 'Yes. Here.' She leaned back against the table, her head up. 'These drawings, and my paintings, are going to make me famous Jim. If not these, others. Really famous, and rich . . . Do you mind?'

'Mind?' he said slowly. 'I don't know what you mean, exactly. How can I mind?'

She said, 'You will be known as Barbara Foster's husband. Not to me – to the world. You'll never have to work again, unless you want to.'

'Now look,' he said firmly. 'I do want to work, but how can I be jealous when I'm proud? You paint just what you want to, and I'll see to the rest.'

She had locked the box and hidden the key. She faced him, hands outstretched. 'When shall we go?'

'Wait a minute,' he said. 'You showed me this, which you've been keeping secret from everyone except Rukmini . . .'

'Mohan knows,' she said. She waited, her eyes on him.

'Now I've got to tell you something,' he said. 'That story about the gold bars being sent off for an assay wasn't true. I meant to keep them. And I was going to steal the others when you came to warn me.'

'I know,' she said. 'In those days you were that kind of person. That was why it took me so long to acknowledge what I really knew all the time – that you loved me . . . Let us not talk about it any more. We'll have years and years to talk about each other. When are we going?'

'Right after the dam's opened,' Jim said.

She nodded. 'Very well. I shall make ready . . . I've tried and tried, Jim. Ten years. I can't face it any more. I know Charles needs help, but it will have to come from someone else. I thought that my hate would give me strength to last him out – but soon after we came up here and the search for the Venus began, I knew I couldn't.'

'What do you think he'll do?' Jim asked. 'I'm not afraid, mind. I don't care what he does.'

She didn't answer for a time. Then she said, 'I think he might try to kill me. Everyone in India would be saying, in a week, that Charles Kendrick can't even keep a wife. It will be too much for him.'

Jim said, 'Why don't you go now? That's it! Go and hide somewhere until I can get away. After what happened to Rukmini we'd all spend days searching the jungles here for you. That would give you time to get anywhere. Out of India, even . . . I must finish the job here.'

'Finish the job,' she repeated. 'Yes, that's the way an artist feels, too. There's nothing more important, not even living. I must stay, Jim . . . If only he'd shown that he needed me, just once . . .'

'That's enough,' he said. He took her in his arms. 'I've got to get my clothes on and go back to the Rest House.'

'Not just yet,' she said, holding him tight. She blew out the lamp and led him slowly back to the bedroom and the bed.

Chapter Twenty-Five

Charles Kendrick awoke quickly and called, 'Who's there?'

The voice answered in Hindustani, 'A telegram, sahib.'

Kendrick slipped out of bed and turned up the lamp that burned dimly in a corner. The servant put his hand round the door, handed him the flimsy envelope from the Post and Telegraph Department, and murmured, 'The peon is waiting, sahib.'

Kendrick tore open the envelope.

KENDRICK, CARE D.C. SAUGOR TIGRESS KILLED WOMAN GHARIAL THIS MORNING STOP SMITH AND I GOING THERE IMMEDIATELY MOHAN

Handed in at the Deori Telegraph Office at ten p.m. They must have left Konpara before then.

'No answer,' he called.

'Very good, sahib.' The servant's bare feet padded away down the corridor.

Kendrick sat on the edge of his bed. Two o'clock in the morning. He had arrived here at nine p.m., and sat up till midnight talking about the Saugor man-eaters with Johnson, the Deputy Commissioner, and his wife. Tomorrow – today – he was due to meet three or four other men and a famous local shikari to get more information.

Now Mohan's impetuosity would spoil everything. Besides, he was walking into real danger by attempting to kill the tigress, ignorant as he was of the jungle. Smith should have prevented him; but Smith had no authority, except that of being English, and he did not attach enough weight even to that . . . Suppose Mohan were killed? Then what would happen to the plans? But surely the men who had moved the man-eaters north would protect Mohan, knowing that of all the 'outsiders' at Konpara neither Mohan nor himself must come to any harm?

He did not *know*. It was intolerable. He must go back. At once. Pray that Mohan had not yet had an encounter with the tigress. Meanwhile, send word, through the headman, that the man-eater must be led back, at once, to Saugor. Then he and

Mohan could safely spend a week in the Konpara jungles looking for her.

He put on his light dressing-gown and went along the passage. At his host's door he knocked. Johnson's sleepy voice answered, '*Kaun hai?*'

'Kendrick here, Johnson. I've just had a telegram.'

'Hold on. I'll be right out.'

The Deputy Commissioner came out a moment later, rubbing his eyes. Kendrick had a momentary glimpse of another shape in the wide bed. Johnson was ten years younger than himself, and already marked for advancement.

Kendrick said, 'It's about the tigress. She's killed again. I'm afraid I shall have to go back.'

Johnson blinked. 'But you've only just arrived . . .'

'You've told me a great deal about her. I must go.'

Johnson said, 'Your horse will be foundered. You'd better take one of mine.'

Now he was fully awake, and there was a hint of quiet amusement in his voice. Kendrick knew why: he was living up to his reputation, of dashing hither and thither, of making a great commotion and achieving nothing. Let the young puppy grin. He'd be laughing on the other side of his face in a year or two's time. He found no difficulty in controlling his voice as he answered, 'Thank you. I'd be most grateful. My syce can follow more slowly with my animal, and return yours in a day or two.'

'Fine . . . Here, I'll get the bearer to make some tea, and something for you to eat.'

Kendrick returned to his room and began to dress. Twenty minutes later the bearer, in full livery, announced that the sahib's breakfast was ready. In the dining-room he bolted down scrambled eggs and tea, filled his wallets with chicken sandwiches, and set off. It was the night of the full moon, and the light was very bright. In the west low, dark clouds, forerunners of the monsoon, hid the shape of the horizon.

For three hours he rode at a steady, fast pace down the road towards Deori. Then the dawn came, and he rested himself and his horse beside a stream. At eight he swung again into the saddle, and at nine turned off the road, to head into the tangled hills on the old jungle road that led through Vishnuswara.

Less then six miles from Konpara he was trotting along a narrow valley in the glare of noon when he saw Huttoo Lall seated under a tree beside the path ahead of him. The man rose to his feet as he approached, and made a profound obeisance. Kendrick slid to the ground and tethered the horse loosely to the tree. Glancing anxiously about him he noticed that the ground rose to left and right, and curves in the path prevented a long view in any direction. No one could see them unless he was already concealed in the area.

'You came out here to meet me?' he said abruptly. 'Why?' He fought to control the nervous exasperation that was becoming increasingly common, increasingly near the surface.

The headman said respectfully, 'I heard that a telegram had been sent to Deori for dispatch to your honour.'

'You know what was in it,' Kendrick said. These people always knew. Knew more than he did.

Huttoo Lall inclined his head. 'I considered it likely that your honour would make haste to return to Konpara, and came out to inform you that our friends are trying to lead the tigress back to the Saugor jungles.'

Kendrick nodded. 'How are you doing it?' he asked.

'As before,' the headman said. 'It will be easier now, I think, because she has not heard the voice of her mate for several days. She will follow the call eagerly.'

Kendrick pulled a sandwich from his wallet and began to munch it hungrily. 'Now what?' he asked. 'Mohan Singh Sahib said he would use his servants to search the ground for the cave mouth. Is he likely to find it in time? Why don't you tell me where it is? Then it would be easy for me to manoeuvre them away from it.'

The headman ignored the last question, and said only, 'The cave can be found in a moment by anyone who reaches a true understanding of why it was built, and by whom . . . We may have been too late in our decision about the tigress. To protect the cave, we intend to take further action.'

'What?' Kendrick asked.

'It will be – final,' the headman said.

Kendrick glowered at him. 'When, then?' he snapped.

'It will take four days to put into effect, Sahib. The preparations are already in hand. But it is a dangerous plan that will cause much harm to many. It would be better if the search could be prevented by other means.'

'We've tried everything,' Kendrick muttered.

The headman said, 'The cave will never be discovered by the means now being used. It is a matter of inspiration, as I told your honour. Two people among you have the capacity to receive that inspiration, at any moment.'

'Who?'

'The lady Rukmini, and your honour's mem-sahib.'

'My wife?' Kendrick cried. 'What does she know about it? What inspiration can she get, moping about with her paints and her pencils all day long? She's not interested, and if she were she doesn't have a brain in her . . .' He stopped, breathing hard.

The headman said soothingly, 'Your honour knows her much better than any. As your honour doubtless has some reason for permitting her to defile your bed with Foster Sahib.'

Kendrick's mouth went dry, his heart thudded painfully, and for a moment he thought he would faint. '*Who?*' he whispered.

'Foster Sahib.'

For a moment he understood. For a moment he acknowledged the years when she had tried to reach him with her love. For a moment he saw himself, at last, giving her something of value – a warm and generous release. Then the fear closed down. The future opened like a lividly coloured landscape. She would run away with Foster. The story would spread like lightning, and with it the scorn and laughter. Rukmini had engineered it all, to destroy him.

The headman said, 'I was saying, lord, that our plan was dangerous. Should the two ladies suffer harm – it would not be necessary to put it into effect.' Kendrick waited, licking his lips. The headman said, 'In the corner of your study I have left a package containing a Gond bow and two poisoned arrows. If the ladies should be found with the mark of the arrows in them, the Gond village will be willing to take the punishment.'

Kendrick felt his cheek begin to twitch. He put his hand up to it. 'You want . . . expect me to commit murder?' he stammered.

The headman looked at him with a deep, long, cold stare. 'Your honour knew that we intended to sacrifice the lady Rukmini, though we love her. What difference is there, to your soul, if it is your hand that strikes, not ours?'

Kendrick said, 'Why don't the Gonds do it themselves, if they are to be blamed in any case?'

The headman said, 'They will not be able to approach close enough, now that suspicions have been aroused. Your honour will . . . Since no individual Gond will be found on whom to fasten the guilt, it will be a collective punishment that your honour will be forced to impose. A heavy punishment, doubtless. Crippling fines, forced labour. The Gonds will accept it.'

Kendrick cried, 'I haven't said I am going to do it!'

The headman said patiently, 'I am trying to save life, sahib. Our own action will involve everyone in Konpara. If your honour can remove the women, only two will die instead of many, and those two . . .'

'They deserve to,' Kendrick muttered, but he was cold, and now his hand trembled too.

The headman said, 'Today is the first day after the full moon.

We act on the fourth day. Your honour must make plans to be away from Konpara at that time.'

'I can go with Mohan Singh Sahib to Nowgong the day after tomorrow,' Kendrick said. 'We can tell the A.G.G. about the Venus. There are other problems I can discuss with him.'

'Very good, your honour,' the headman said respectfully. 'Unless you succeed before then.'

Kendrick swung into the saddle. 'We have not met,' he said. The headman bowed. Kendrick dug his heels into the horse's flank and cantered away from him.

Had the headman smiled faintly? The swine did not believe that he could do anything on his own, when it came to the point. Murder. Perhaps he couldn't. Before, he had seemed to be a spectator of a drama, a tragedy, that would run its course without him. He was required only to hold his tongue. Now they were dragging him on to the stage, pushing weapons into his hand, and telling him to act his part. But he did not know what his part was.

Cuckold, and laughing-stock, and total failure. That was his part. His flesh began to crawl with the strength of his hatred for the two women. He would try. He would take the arrows and the bow and see if opportunity offered, and, if it did, two arrows would finish everything. If only they could share one body, so that a single arrow would kill two treacherous lustful women in one; and, in that one, all women.

Chapter Twenty-Six

Mohan awoke with a cry and a start, his hand flying to the rifle beside him. A lantern burned dimly in the corner. Smith and the lambardar of Gharial stood there, talking in low voices. The lambardar's wife crouched near him. On the floor stood a brass bowl of milk, and a broad leaf heaped with vegetable curry and cold rice. Her voice was humble. 'Poor fare, Suvala, for tiger hunters.'

He roused himself and spoke without looking at her, as etiquette demanded. 'No king could eat more nobly, or in nobler company.'

He began to eat. Smith said, 'Half an hour to dawn. I expect Kendrick has had the telegram, and is on his way.'

'He can't reach here until this afternoon,' Mohan said. 'We'll have her by then.'

He was not frightened. He must kill the man-eater before Kendrick came. 'What was done about the woman whom the tigress killed yesterday?' he asked.

'The remains were brought into the village, and will be burned today,' the lambardar said. 'I was sure that she would not return to them.'

Mohan nodded. It was nearly time to go.

As they left the house the lambardar pushed the thorn zareba out of the way with a long spade. The first pale green-grey light tinged the sky above the jungles in the east. Mohan loaded the rifle carefully, and walked out of the village, Smith at his side. Here and there a face watched from a half-shuttered window, a half-barred doorway. A woman's voice called, 'God be with you, lords,' and then they went at a steady, careful pace into the dim, shadowless tunnel of the jungle at dawn. A ground mist hung under the trees and there was no wind.

Just over two hours after leaving Gharial they reached the scene of the tigress's last attack, the sun now bright and hot. A dozen vultures rose heavily from the river bank ahead, and flapped up into the trees. Mohan fingered the rifle.

'The mare,' Smith said briefly.

160

Mohan carefully examined the country. The jungle was featureless for haif a mile, then rose gradually eastward to the crest line where they had first seen the torches and heard the cries of the men from Gharial. A spur of the upper Konpara plateau swept down from the main hills to form that gentle crest. Otherwise – nothing; and everything – rock and tree, grass and thorn, and the sun throwing hard shadows athwart the winding path.

Smith rose from his knees. 'Arterial blood,' he said. 'You must have hit her a bit higher than I thought.' He moved across the path in the direction the tigress had taken. 'Here it is again . . . I'll track her, as best I can. I suggest we do it in bounds – first I'll go forward, then you come up to me.'

He licked his finger and held it up. A breeze had risen with the sun, out of the east, but it was still very slight. 'Watch the breeze all the time,' he said, 'and remember she'll only attack from downwind. Ready?'

He moved off parallel with the path and about a hundred yards from it, on the left. After a few moments he stopped and pointed down. Obviously another blood splash. Mohan had counted his paces – twenty-seven from the previous blood marks. He went forward to join him. Smith moved on.

Mohan waited under a tree, his head turned downwind. Smith covered thirty paces, stopped, and signalled briefly with his big staff. Mohan went forward, and again took up position.

Now they did not speak any more. The rhythm of the stalking took possession of them. Smith stepped slowly, staff in hand, examining the ground. Mohan waited, his back to tree or rock, his eyes downwind. Smith stopped. Mohan moved.

Sometimes Smith found the blood streak directly under his feet. Sometimes, after taking thirty-five paces, he had seen nothing. Then he pushed a twig into the ground and walked in careful arcs round it. Usually, within five minutes, he found more blood.

An hour passed. Two. Three. Four . . . Mohan's throat was clogged with mucus. Smith moved steadily forward through the blinding yellow glare of sun and jungle grass. Mohan's bloodshot eyes began to falter, so that, when Smith moved into a patch of shadow, he totally disappeared, and Mohan broke into a run, only to have him spring into view as his weary eyes jerked back into focus.

They had long since left the path. The tigress had followed them for a little less than a mile last night. Then she had lain down and made a long attempt to staunch the slow jet of blood from her wound. Long streaks of blood marked the hard earth, the grass was flattened over a small compact area, and they found many white and yellow hairs, some still wet with spittle. From that point the trail had led a little north of west, generally back towards the upper plateau above Konpara.

It was noon, and they rested in the most open place they could find, where there was no cover for the tigress they stalked – or who stalked them – and no shelter from the fury of the sun. Mohan drank greedily from the bottle in his haversack, and passed it to Smith. Smith wetted his lips and handed it back. 'Go on,' Mohan said. 'That's not enough.'

'That's all I need,' Smith said.

'You didn't take any,' Mohan said, almost angrily.

'No,' Smith admitted, 'I didn't. I have learned a great many peculiar accomplishments in recent years. Once I went thirty days without water –'

'In the hot weather?' Mohan interjected.

'In the hot weather, near Bareilly,' Smith said. 'I can do without water. I was supposed, at the same time, to learn impassivity – imperviousness to human problems. There, I failed. Or I wouldn't be here.'

He rolled over and went sound asleep. Then it was Mohan's turn. He tried to sleep but could not. After ten minutes he got up. 'Let's get on.'

Smith said, 'We're seven miles from Gharial now, and getting farther away at about one mile an hour, as long as she keeps going in this direction. But we're approaching the Gond village on the upper plateau at the same rate. By sunset we won't be more than two miles from it.'

'We'll get her before then,' Mohan said.

'We must,' Smith said. 'An hour before sunset I'm going back to Konpara.'

'Why?' Mohan asked.

'I told you. I think Rukmini is in danger.' He loves her, Mohan thought. And she loves him. He felt very tired.

They had rested near a blood streak. Smith took up his unwearying, careful search. Soon he gave the signal, and Mohan moved forward across the small rocky clearing to join him. Heavy jungle began again on the far side of the clearing.

Just before he reached Smith he heard a distinct distant roar. He turned his head quickly in the direction he thought it had come from. A minute later, he heard it again. He asked Smith, 'Did you hear that?' He noticed that Smith had not turned his head at the distraction, but was steadily scanning the rocks and the grass downwind. He answered now, still without breaking his concentration, 'Yes. It's not the tigress.'

'Another tiger?' Mohan whispered. 'My God, what's happening? There have never been so many tigers in this district at the same time. Is it another male? Can you tell?'

'I can tell,' Smith said. 'It's the voice of a male tiger, yes. We've heard this particular one before – all of us.'

A roar, slightly higher pitched and noticeably less thunderous in volume, sounded from nearly the same direction as the others, but apparently closer. Smith relaxed. 'That *is* her,' he said. 'A couple of miles in front of us.'

Mohan rested on his rifle and wiped his streaming forehead. 'What did you mean about the other, the male?'

Smith said, 'That voice is quite distinctive. It is the voice of the male man-eater – her mate.'

'But he's dead!' Mohan cried. 'Kendrick shot him.'

Smith nodded. 'Yes, he's dead. A man made that roar.'

Mohan looked fearfully at the jungle wall close ahead. Smith said, 'I have been almost sure for some time that the man-eaters were guided up here from Saugor. Now, the same people – and I don't know of anyone except the Gonds, in this area, capable of doing it – are moving the tigers back to Saugor – or at least, out of this district.'

'But why?' Mohan asked.

Smith said, 'If she is shot, our search for the Venus will begin again. If she is merely not heard of, it will not. Not for some days.'

'But . . . is everyone against us?' Mohan said. 'What are we going to do?'

'Nothing,' Smith said, 'except continue as we are. We decided a long time ago. We must bend with the wind, but notice where it is taking us . . . Come on now. We can move fast for an hour or so. She is not stalking us, but trying to reach her mate, who keeps moving on ahead of her. See, everything they do helps us – if we know.'

They entered the jungle again. At two o'clock they were slowly climbing the Konpara Hills, some five miles north of the dam site. At three o'clock they heard her calling less than a mile ahead. By four o'clock she had changed direction slightly to the south. They climbed more steeply now, and behind them the forested plain stretched farther towards the blurred horizons. The character of the jungle changed, for there was more water in the sub-surface soil here. The trees became bigger, greener, and more widely spaced. Here and there clumps of bamboo stood like feathery plumes among the sal and teak.

They struggled through an abandoned field, dense with undergrowth, waded a stream that ran sluggish over a muddy bottom towards a small, distant lake, and faced another slope, dotted with bamboo clumps.

On that slope, very close, the tigress roared – once, a pause, twice.

Mohan crouched in the bushes on the stream bank. Smith muttered, 'No answer. The caller knows we're here.' He indicated some large bamboo clusters, each twenty feet by twenty, on the slope about a hundred yards ahead. 'She's in one of those.'

Mohan held the rifle ready, his forefinger along the trigger guard. The clumps were all of thorny bamboo, the spikes six inches long and hard as steel, the ten or twenty stems of each clump so close-packed that a rat could hardly squeeze between them. The clumps stood a foot or two apart – room for a tigress, crouched low, to lie in wait; but anyone who wanted to enter must wriggle in on his belly.

Mohan said, 'First, we have to make sure which one she's in. 'I'll go forward, and . . .'

Smith interrupted. 'Wait!'.

A wild sow with five piglets at her heels came down the far slope, browsing and rooting. Mohan understood at once. The wind blew from left to right across the slope. The sow would come down among the bamboo clusters, and her forward progress would 'clear' each cluster upwind of her as she passed it: for if the tigress were inside any one of those clusters the scent would reach the sow, and her actions would show it.

She came on down, lean, reddish, long-snouted, razor-backed. She passed all the farther clusters, downwind of them. Clear, clear, clear, Mohan muttered. The stream made small liquid noises behind him, and his nerves quivered at full stretch. Now only three bamboo clusters remained. The piglets wandered far from her heels and she grunted angrily at them to keep closer. She passed the left hand of the three clumps. 'Left, clear,' Smith muttered. She was going to pass by the centre clump, but on the upwind side of it.

The tigress must be in the centre or right-hand cluster – but which? The sow would pass upwind of both of them, and so would give no sign. Quickly Mohan raised the rifle, and, aiming carefully at the ground a yard to the left of the sow, pulled the trigger, and at once reloaded. As the bullet kicked up the dirt beside her, the sow spun and dashed for the nearest cover – the centre cluster of bamboos – the piglets hard on her heels. She crashed in between two clumps, head down under the reach of the thorns. Mohan waited, the rifle in his shoulder. Something moved inside the bamboo, a blur of yellow among the dense green. The five piglets tore out of the cluster and raced away across the slope. The sow did not come out.

She was in the centre cluster. He thought at once of setting fire to it – but this area was quite damp and bamboo was hard to set fire to under any circumstances. Here, where they could not even approach the cluster, it was impossible.

Smith said, 'I think we must provoke a charge.'

'She knows where we are now,' Mohan muttered.

'Yes. We'll have to do it quickly, or she may creep away out of the back of the cluster . . . I'll go past her on the downwind side. Believing that I must have her scent, I think she'll charge.'

'No!' Mohan whispered. 'I'm not a good enough shot and now . . . look!' He held out his left hand, and watched it trembling.

'You will be good enough,' Smith said, smiling.

Mohan looked down. The man's courage was impossible to emulate, and, with it, he was so gentle. How worthless he himself must seem to Rukmini, in the balance against this man, who was both brave and compassionate. He felt inadequacy like a physical suffering, and, knowing the cause and despising himself for it, the moment of inadequacy brought to flower a full, despairing hatred of Smith.

Smith put down his long staff, and, searching around in the undergrowth, found a shorter piece of wood. Tearing two buttons from his shirt he fastened them to the stick with small thorns. 'There – that will look enough like the gleam of metal.'

Mohan could hardly bear to listen to the soft voice as it continued: 'I want her to think that I am armed. Therefore, that she must charge. I think she will attack about five paces before I could get her scent. Or – remembering that you are not accounted for, she might try to escape by the back way. So, if she doesn't charge me by the time I'm level with the middle of the cluster, run like hell out to the side – there – where you can see the open ground behind.'

Mohan opened the breech of his rifle, noted the brassy gleam of the cartridge case in the chamber, and snapped the bolt forward. Smith walked into the open, the short stick carried close to his right side, the side away from the bamboo. He walked in a peculiarly cautious and purposeful manner. He's going to shoot her himself, Mohan thought, he's going to shoot her . . . but he had no rifle. It was for the watching tigress that he played the charade. The perspiration burst out on Mohan's palms, and he could get no firm grip on the rifle. Smith went forward. He was fifteen paces from the bamboo cluster, and ten to the right. Fourteen. Thirteen.

The sights wavered and blurred along the barrel. One fraction of a second's delay and the tigress would bear Smith to the ground. She would die, but so would Smith. Rukmini would never see him again. The spasm of impotent hatred returned, and with it the memory of another moment like this, when he had run through the jungles at Smith's back on their way to the shrine. At that time, too, a knowledge of incompetence had made him think of murder. The blued barrel shivered and the sights danced like madmen. There would be no need for jealous intent. Sheer incompetence would kill Smith. In desperation he screamed at himself, 'No!' and the tigress came running fast from under the bamboos.

Smith turned – she was a quarter left from him – and raised the stick, not hurrying. The tigress gathered her hindquarters under her and roared. On the rifle the sights steadied, and Mohan fired. The shot hit her behind the shoulder, but her spring was already launched. She passed over Smith's shoulder, and landed on her nose ten feet behind him. He turned, as slowly as he had made all his movements, and looked at her. Mohan's finger trembled on the trigger for a second shot. Smith called, 'She's dead.'

Mohan struggled to his feet and broke into a stumbling run. As he reached Smith he threw down the rifle and embraced him. 'Smith, Smith . . . oh, my God, my God.' Tears streamed down his face and his body shook violently. Smith put his arm round his shoulders. 'Sit down. Here. It's over.'

He had to get it out. He cried, 'I wanted to fire too late.'

'All right,' Smith said.

'But . . .'

'But you didn't. You killed the man-eater, and now you know that the only dangerous man-eaters don't have stripes or spots or four legs, and you don't kill them with a rifle. And look, my friend, let's speak a moment about what is in your heart, and then never speak about it again. Rukmini and I love, admire, and understand each other in a different dimension from that in which she loves you. From you she asks – she must have – total acceptance, and then you will be linked, for ever, to the finest woman I've ever known – a universal woman.'

But she wants to be my wife and my queen, and it's impossible, Mohan thought. Should he ask Smith what to do? No. He must find the solution to the insoluble himself.

Smith said, 'Now we must go back to Konpara as fast as we can. Wait a minute, I'll just make sure the sow is dead.'

He walked to the bamboo cluster and crawled inside. Mohan picked up the rifle. The last man-eater was dead and he had located one certainty: Rukmini mattered more to him than position or power. He'd marry her, leave the state, and go to live in England or America on a small pension. Perhaps some great Maharajah would give him a post in his army. No Hindu would accept them, though, so it would have to be a Muslim. The Nizam of Hyderabad, perhaps. Then he and Rukmini would have to turn Muslim – and she would not do it. The plains of Deori stretched out to the east and the sun was low. No man or woman or child was in sight, only rock and tree and sky, his country.

Smith joined him. 'She broke the sow's neck,' he said. 'Now . . . lead, Mohan, as fast as you can.'

'How far is it?'

'About three miles.'

Mohan began to walk, going very stiffly. Gradually he was able to increase the pace. Always he felt Smith hard at his heels. They dropped down from the upper plateau on game trails and jungle footpaths, passing close below the Gond village. The sun set in a blaze of violet and orange under high clouds. The village of Konpara crouched on the end of its ridge in a haze of blue smoke that drifted northward towards the great cliffs and the silver line of the Rainbow Fall. Skirting the lower side of the village they crossed the valley towards Cheltondale in the rapid dusk.

Mohan stopped slowly, his hand out in warning. Someone, or something, was crouched under a tree ahead. Twenty yards beyond it he could see the profiles of two people sitting in deck chairs on the Cheltondale lawn. The sound of their voices reached him – Rukmini and Barbara Kendrick. Smith stood motionless at his side. Mohan raised the rifle. The thing under the tree moved with infinite caution, a pace forward, making no sound . . . then another.

Smith coughed. The thing stopped moving, and a pale blur of face turned. Then there was a double snap, like two twigs breaking one after the other, and the figure below the face jerked, and sprang into focus.

Mohan lowered the rifle, and walked forward. It was Mr Kendrick. He was carrying a small bow, and in the other hand the broken-off heads of two arrows, and in the look on his face was fright, overlaid with pure relief. To break the long silence Mohan said, 'We killed the tigress, sir.'

Kendrick said, 'What? Oh, the tigress. You killed her?'

The two women had heard, and risen from their deck chairs. They were coming down. Kendrick said, 'Foolhardy of you to go out after her.' The sweat poured down his face. 'You're old enough to know better, Smith. Still, all's well that ends well, eh?'

The women had come. Kendrick turned to them. 'I was coming over to tell you to be on your guard. I found these on the verandah steps at Southdown just now.' He held out the bow and the broken arrowheads. 'I think they must have been put there as a warning . . . I will take you back now, Barbara, if you are ready.'

'Yes, Charles,' his wife said.

Kendrick said, 'Oh, by the way, Mohan – you and I have to go to Nowgong. We'll leave the day after tomorrow in the afternoon.' He strode down the hill, his wife a few paces behind him. Neither looked round.

Rukmini ran into Mohan's arms. 'Oh, Mohan, you did it!' She put out a hand and touched Smith's cheek. 'And you . . . thank you, thank you!'

Smith smiled. 'I was there.' He waved his hand and left them alone at the edge of the rough lawn.

Chapter Twenty-Seven

Mohan glanced at the sun. Half an hour to sunset and the men had just completed the search of another block. 'Very well,' he told the headman beside him. 'That's enough for today.'

The headman raised his arm and called. The thirty close-spaced men who had been searching this lower slope of the Konpara Ridge broke away and began to straggle off towards the village. Mohan watched them go with a peculiar feeling. Some of those men, who had been searching diligently for the mouth of the cave, did not want it to be found; and would go to any lengths to ensure that it was not found. One of them might have passed over it during the day and said nothing. Did they know he knew that much? Everyone here was involved in a secret drama, but who was audience and who were actors?

He set off across the valley towards Cheltondale. This was the first day after his return from killing the tigress, and – as far as he could tell – a good day's work had been completed. Tomorrow, an hour after dawn, the same men would come, under the headman, and continue the methodical search. He himself would have to leave at two o'clock in the afternoon to go to Nowgong with Kendrick, but Rukmini would take charge for the rest of the day, and while he was away.

Trudging up the slope of the Dobehari Ridge he glanced towards Indra's Rock, which he could see clearly about a quarter of a mile off. Rukmini was still on it. She had started the day with him, but about noon had left suddenly, with no word of explanation, and gone straight to Indra's Rock. He had found her sitting silent and preoccupied in Cheltondale when he returned there, a little later, for tiffin. After eating, he had returned to his task – and she to Indra's Rock.

The rock, and the pale blue figure – she was wearing a blue and white sari today – disappeared from view as he came under the steeper section on the ridge below Cheltondale. He was ready to look for her again when he reached the lawn, but he found Kendrick there, and a foam-flecked horse, the trooper standing at attention at its head. Smith and Foster were there, too.

Kendrick was reading a note. He looked up as Mohan approached.

'Ah, Mohan . . . some Gonds have raided Purankhola.'

'Purankhola?' Mohan echoed stupidly. He remembered it. A dozen huts and a couple of stone-built houses, beside a small stream. A poor village. A small Gond tribe lived in the jungles behind it, near the state boundary on that side. It was nearly thirty miles from Konpara.

He took the message and saw that it was signed by Captain Manikwal. It reported that a party of Gonds had raided Purankhola early in the morning, wounded a couple of villagers, not seriously, and driven off half a dozen head of livestock. 'They're mad,' Mohan said slowly. 'What on earth do they want with livestock?' He read on. Manikwal had taken the cavalry – the whole army, that meant – out to deal with them. He smiled slightly. That was just what Manikwal would do. But Gonds, stealing cattle? 'I don't understand this,' he said.

'Nor do I,' Kendrick said. 'We can leave it to Manikwal. I would go myself, but we must go to Nowgong.'

'We could put that off,' Mohan began, but Kendrick said, 'No, we must go,' rather loudly, and Mohan held his tongue. Kendrick turned to Smith. 'I came over to ask how your work progressed.'

'Very well,' Smith said. 'It has made all the difference having expert blasters, and men to clear the shaft afterwards. We'll be at it again the same time tomorrow.'

He and Foster walked away along the ridge. Kendrick strode off towards Southdown, with a word of good-bye. Mohan noticed that he was carrying the same haversack he had worn yesterday evening, and into which he had carelessly dropped the poisoned arrowheads just before leaving. He wondered whether they were still in there.

Mohan went up into Cheltondale. He was in his bath when Rukmini returned at dusk, but he hardly noticed. The events of the past two days pursued themselves through his mind.

He found that he was at the dinner table. His mouth fell open and he looked at Rukmini; her thoughts were as far removed as his own, but in some other direction. He bent his head again to his plate. Yesterday Kendrick had been creeping towards the two women. There was no other word for it. He would have noticed it at the time if his relief at finding that the mysterious shape *was* Kendrick, and not another man-eater or a Gond, had not overcome every other thought. And the snapping noises. Suppose they had been made by Kendrick breaking off the arrowheads? That would mean that Kendrick had been carrying a bow, and full-length arrows, which could be shot from it.

Tomorrow, at dawn, he would go out and search for those arrow shafts. If he found them . . . He sat back, wiping his lips with his napkin. Kendrick's taut, twitching face stared up at him from his empty plate.

He found himself in bed, lying on his side, staring at the wall. Rukmini spoke. 'I saw your face at dinner. What were you thinking of?'

'Kendrick.'

'Yes,' she said. 'I think we have reached the truth about him.'

'I shall know tomorrow, soon after dawn.'

'Foster and Mrs Kendrick,' she said. 'The truth about them came while you were away. They are not a beefy contractor and a neurotic woman who paints. They are lovers, that's all. That's the truth about them. They found it, too . . . Mr Smith – I have always known, and you found out on the hunt, didn't you?'

'Yes,' Mohan said. 'He's a pilgrim.'

'But he'll never find his shrine. He knows it . . . I once said to him, or he to me, that until we saw the people here as they really are, we would never find the Venus. Now I think there are only three whom we do not *know*. One is the leader of those who want to preserve the secret of the cave. The others are – you and I . . . Look at me, Mohan.' He turned and faced her. 'Suppose we found the cave tomorrow,' she said very carefully, 'and the Venus was in it, and she was low caste, and a queen – what would you do?'

He said, 'There is no chance of my becoming Rajah of Deori if I marry you. But yesterday, while we were hunting the tigress, I learned something, at least. I love you more than I love Deori. We shall be married at once. To prevent rioting and bloodshed, we will first leave the state, and I will renounce all claims to the succession on behalf of myself and my descendants. I will tell the A.G.G. when we see him in Nowgong.'

She did not answer, but lay, looking at him.

After a time he muttered, 'I thought you wanted to marry me.'

She said, 'So – we are to be the lovers, those who find themselves just in that discovery. But Mr Foster and Mrs Kendrick are the lovers.' She seemed to be speaking to herself. 'There are not two pairs of lovers in the group – I know there aren't! No, no, Mohan, the truth about us is beyond that. We are lovers already. We are also the king and queen.'

He bunched his fist and cried, 'It can't be, Rukmini! You know it can't.'

She said, 'Then, O Suvala, it is better that you never see the cave, or the Venus-Queen.'

She lay on her back, and though he tried three times more to make her speak to him she did not answer.

Let the morning come. Perhaps there was some way out of the impasse, though he could see only the walls of custom and tradition, and the British and his uncle and the chief Brahmin standing armed to defend them. It would need Indra's Bow and Indra's Thunderbolt to overcome them. Wearily, he fell into a deep sleep.

He awoke in a strong dawn light and rolled over, yawning, determined to sleep another ten minutes.

The arrow shafts! He must look for them. He opened his eyes. Rukmini was not in the bed.

'Rukmini,' he called.

He slipped out of bed and went into the bathroom. He looked into every room. As he ran out of the drawing-room he met the major-domo hurrying in. The man was panting with excitement. 'The headman,' he gasped. 'The headman . . . the cave has been discovered . . . by the lady Rukmini!'

Chapter Twenty-Eight

Mohan ran out to the verandah. Huttoo Lall, the headman of Konpara, waited at the foot of the steps, his usually expressionless face transformed by a warm smile.

'What's happened?' Mohan cried.

The headman said, 'Success! One of my people saw the lady Rukmini in the pit below him, just at dawn, as he passed over Indra's Rock on his way to cut twigs. She called up that she had found the cave, and that you were all to come at once. The man told the Resident Sahib on his way back to the village to tell me. I believe the Resident Sahib has already gone down. I sent word to Smith Sahib and Foster Sahib on my way here – and Kendrick Mem-sahib, who had not been informed, since the Resident left in such haste.'

Looking down the slope Mohan saw Foster and Barbara Kendrick at the head of the scaffolding. The headman broke in respectfully, 'Your honour will need a lantern, perhaps?'

'Yes, of course,' Mohan said. 'Get one. Full.' The major-domo hurried off.

He waited impatiently. The servant came out in a minute, a puzzled frown on his face and a hurricane lantern in his hand. 'They are all empty, lord,' he said. 'And the one in the spare bedroom, where I went first, is not there. I filled them all only yesterday, and . . .'

'It doesn't matter,' Mohan cried. 'Fill it now!'

The man hurried away. When he returned Mohan made sure that he had matches and then ran down the short path to the head of the scaffolding, followed by the headman.

As they reached it Foster cried, 'Hello there! We seem to have done it, just in time . . . I can't understand it, though. I've been right round the pit, on foot. I'm sure I didn't miss anything that could have been a cave mouth.'

'You must have,' Mohan said.

Smith arrived, carrying a rifle. He held it out to Foster, with a handful of cartridges. 'I thought you'd better have this,' he said. 'There are quite a few snakes in the pit.'

Foster indicated the pistol strapped to his waist. 'But I've got this . . .'

Smith said, 'Sorry.' He handed the rifle and cartridges to Mohan, taking the lantern from him. 'Perhaps you'd better carry it, then . . . The magazine's loaded. It's a Mannlicher, isn't it, Foster – normal bolt action?'

'Yes,' Foster said. 'Let's get a move on.'

Smith said, 'I saw Rukmini, by the way, or someone who looks like her. She was over to the west, past the Indra's Rock Tumulus.'

'Why didn't she tell me she was going?' Mohan muttered, so that only Smith could hear.

Smith did not reply, but said, 'There are a couple of villagers with her. She waved, and then disappeared. I never saw her clearly.'

Foster stepped out on to the ladder. Barbara followed, then Mohan. He heard Smith, behind him, call to the headman, 'Are you coming down now?'

'In a moment sahib. I am waiting for my cousins.'

Then Smith came too. Mohan hurried down the ladder, a new thought boiling with all the rest in his mind. If the cave mouth was in the pit, the filling of the dam would flood it. Perhaps it could be blocked off and another entrance made from above. That would cost hundreds of thousands of rupees. It would depend on the importance of what was inside the cave.

He reached the foot of the scaffold. The heads bobbed and wound on ahead of him, now directly under the towering cliffs, now passing into the dense brush. At those times the cliffs disappeared and they were in a dark tunnel, hurrying along the narrow track the coolies had made during the excavation of the Indra's Rock Tumulus.

They passed the tumulus and Foster commented that someone had filled in the excavations. 'Not on my orders,' he said. After five more minutes Smith said, 'This is about where I saw her.' They all stopped.

Mohan cupped his hands and shouted, 'Rukmini!' The others joined in; then they shouted again, to right, to left, listening between each call. There was no answer.

Smith said, 'There is someone in the bushes ahead.'

Mohan saw the movement too, and shouted, 'Rukmini . . .' He broke into a run, but it was almost impossible to run in that tangle. After a few moments, though, he recognised the back of the struggling figure ahead of him, and shouted, 'Mr Kendrick! Mr Kendrick!'

The Resident turned. He was dressed for the jungle, the haversack slung across his shoulder.

'Have you seen her?' Mohan called urgently.

Kendrick looked bewildered and a little mad. 'What are you doing here?' he asked slowly. His gaze passed over Mohan's shoulder and he saw the others. 'All of us,' he mumbled. 'Barbara, Foster, Smith . . . except Rukmini. He told me she was here alone.'

'Have you seen her?' Mohan shouted.

'What's the day?' Kendrick said suddenly. He grabbed Mohan by the arm. 'What day after the full moon?'

Mohan nervously shook off the clutching hand. Kendrick had lost his mind. Smith said, 'This is the morning of the third day after the full moon.'

'*This* is the day we are going to Nowgong, isn't it?' Kendrick whispered.

'Yes,' Mohan began, 'but . . .'

Smith said, loudly but calmly, 'Look back, towards the scaffold.'

Mohan swung round. A huge tongue of flame climbed slowly out of the jungle and up the cliff face back there, a quarter of a mile to the east and almost directly below Cheltondale. As he stared, a thin black smoke rose above and around the flames. The sun burst over the rim of the pit behind, and instantly it was hot.

'I'm not sure,' Barbara Kendrick said softly, 'but I think the scaffolding has gone.'

For a moment they stood, while the flames grew into long yellow and red tongues and the smoke thickened.

Kendrick began to scream oaths at the top of his voice. 'Oh, the swine! The filthy murderous swine! They said . . .' He broke into a run, mouthing incoherently.

They followed, but none reached the scaffolding, for a hundred yards from it the jungle had become a wall of flame, and beyond it, above the slowly marching spears of the fire, they saw the bare cliff, and the mouth of the excavation forty feet up, but no signs of scaffolding or ladder. The fire also blocked the path towards the dam. A breeze had risen, stirring the brush.

'Rukmini!' Mohan cried. 'Where is she?'

Kendrick stood waving his clenched fists above his head. 'Back to the tumulus,' Foster said sharply. 'Barbara, stay close to me. Mohan, keep an eye on the cliff tops as we pass under them. Shoot at sight.'

They ran back, and soon reached the tumulus. Mohan looked round hurriedly. Now he understood why the trenches had been filled in. No chance of sheltering in them, even though they would have given little enough protection against such a fire as this. It was coming slowly, for the heat sucked in the air and the fire had to advance against the wind which it itself had created.

They were gathered in a tight group under the cliff, facing the fire. Kendrick licked his lips. Foster spoke in a soft voice to Barbara. Smith watched the fire with detached admiration.

'Rukmini, Rukmini,' Mohan whispered, 'where are you?' He turned to Smith. 'Did you actually recognise her from the cliff top?'

'No,' Smith said.

Mohan gritted his teeth. Then she probably was not in the pit at all, nor ever had been. His chances of seeing her again, if she were still alive, depended on his escaping from here. Smith could take control of the group, and was the natural person to do it, but, as in the hunt for the tigress, he was deliberately standing back.

Mohan put Rukmini out of his mind. In a loud voice he said, 'We must try to reach the dam. I don't know whether we can force our way through this scrub, past the fire, in time, but we've got to try.'

Barbara said almost conversationally, 'I'm afraid that won't do now, Mohan. They've started another fire.'

Mohan looked where she pointed and saw more smoke, more fire, in the distance to the east – where the dam lay.

Foster said, 'We'll have to set light to the jungle here. Burn a patch.'

Not safe, Mohan thought. The wind swirled every way now. The new fire had upset the pattern.

Smith said, 'There's nothing else for it, though.'

Kendrick shouted, 'Murderers!' and shook his fist at the blank cliff. Mohan looked at the sky, at the cliffs, at the fires, and produced his box of matches. He called, 'Along here. Are we far enough from the cliff? Farther in. Here. Light a line a hundred feet long, starting here. Here, everyone take some matches.'

The fires flickered, flamed, and burst into small crackling furies. When Mohan ran back from the far end of the line, the near end was a mass of flame.

'Coats off,' he cried. 'Break off branches. Keep our fire from spreading in *this* direction; let it go in the other!' Barbara Kendrick took off her skirt and hoisted her petticoat in a tight wad round her waist. They all began to beat, with coat and skirt and shirt, at the flames that crept back towards them from the line of fire that they had lighted.

Mohan watched anxiously as he worked. 'The wind's changing over there,' he shouted to Smith. 'If it turns right round our fire will die, and the burned area isn't big enough for us yet.'

Smith nodded. But there was nothing any of them could do about it. To the east, towards the dam, the flames of the biggest of the three fires now spread across the whole pit from cliff to cliff. The smoke dimmed the sun, and the flames luridly lit the underside of it. Mohan could not tell how far away it was, nor how fast it was coming. But coming it was, and so strong now that the wind whisked up great arms of trees and whirled them around, burning fiercely in the base of the smoke, before allowing them to fall again. And dead trees exploded from the violent assault of the heat, and sent rockets of golden sparks towering up to drift and wheel like fiery birds in the smoke.

Foster yelled, 'We've got to be a hundred feet clear of that when it comes or we'll bloody well fry just the same . . . two hundred feet of burned land we need!'

Mohan coughed and retched, caught by a low swirl of smoke. The air currents were forcing most of it high, thank God. The original fire at the scaffolding seemed lower. In half an hour it might burn itself out, or reach to their blackened area here; but by then it would be too late, for the great fire from the dam would come first.

'Wind's changed,' Smith called. Mohan saw the flames lean out to the north, and cursed helplessly.

'We'll have to let it go, get behind it, and hope for the best,' he shouted. The roar of the great fire deafened him.

Smith said, 'I think the wind must settle towards the big one soon. Look there!'

Even as he spoke, it happened. The flames leaned again to the east. Their own fire marched more rapidly away from them. A huge lizard ran across Foster's feet, going north. Then another, in the opposite direction. More animals came – nothing large, for the dam had long since turned the pit into a trap for them – but more lizards, snakes, a wildcat, a mongoose, several rats . . . A jackal ran out of the scrub and headlong through the thickest part of the flames along the line that they had set. A moment later it burst out again, screaming, its coat afire. Mohan spun, lifted the rifle, and whipped off a shot as the jackal disappeared. The scurrying, howling ball of flame sank down. Mohan ran heavily to it crashing through the brush. With his hands he beat out the flames that had already started to spread from the corpse into the area where they were sheltering.

Now the great fire was a hundred and fifty yards away, and coming on more slowly against the hurricane of wind that it had created.

Foster said, 'My God, the jungle on top's caught, too.' He pointed up, and Mohan saw trees and scrub burning below Cheltondale and above the dam.

'That may help us later,' Smith said. 'It can't have been intended.'

Mohan slung his charred jacket over his shoulders and called to the rest of them to join him. Kendrick had recovered some of his poise, but the twitch was very noticeable. Mohan said, 'There's nothing more we can do now. The wind has settled in towards the big fire. In a few minutes it will reach the land that we have burned. We must go out on to it now –' He motioned towards the charred, sparkling desert in front of them. 'As the big fire passes round the edge, we must move into the middle of our burned patch.'

'Good plan!' Kendrick exclaimed. 'We shall escape, after all! And then . . .'

To the east the advancing fire spread from wall to wall of the pit in a reverse crescent, the wings edged back against the cliffs, the out-thrust centre soon to meet the tiny, advancing flames of their own line. The blackened area which was to be their refuge was neither flat nor unobstructed. It was not grass or heather that had burned, but dense jungle, mainly of brush and creepers from four to twelve feet high, with larger trees scattered about in it. The larger trees still stood, like soldiers burning alive, each surrounded by an almost visible belt of heat that prevented sanctuary close to it. Some of the burned brush had fallen to the ground to form a shallow carpet of grey and black and white, the red glow of fire shining through from below. Some stood in brittle caricature of the shape they had held in life, here and there the arms sprouting buds of flame, mostly black and dead, but all hot.

A foot at a time they walked out across the burned and burning floor of the pit, faces barred and blackened, clothes wrecked, hands scorched. The giant centre wall of the great fire met the small, leaning spires of their own. The wings of the crescent moved on along the cliffs.

The heat began to come through the soles of Mohan's boots. To his right he saw Barbara Kendrick biting her lip in agony. He moved towards her, but Foster was quicker, sweeping her up and carrying her in his arms. The heat poured directly at them from three sides, and from the fourth the cliffs radiated heat. Three mongoose and a pair of jackals had followed them on to the burned ground, and now danced around and among them, howling and grimacing after their fashion of pain, but keeping close. Low and high the smoke rolled in dense billows.

Mohan found that the handkerchief tied across his mouth was having no effect. He felt himself losing his senses, slipping to his knees, the black earth close to his eyes, and living red flame under it . . .

He came to, coughing violently, and found he was on Kendrick's back, Smith supporting him. 'Let me down,' he croaked.

'In a minute. We'll get through,' Kendrick cried. 'You and I!'

Mohan struggled down, retching painfully. The ground was still agonisingly hot, the drifting smoke still choked him, but while he had been unconscious some crisis had passed, as in an illness, and he knew they were going to survive. All their faces were lighter under the filth.

Kendrick croaked, 'In half an hour . . . we'll start, towards the dam.'

In that direction the flames were dying fast, and they looked out over a blackened desert, the bigger trees burning and writhing, and everywhere sparks towering into the wind.

'When we go,' Kendrick gasped, 'keep to the centre of the pit.'

'Safe enough that side,' Smith said, pointing north. All the forest there, along the Dobehari Ridge, seemed to be on fire. Cheltondale burned furiously, sending up a thick, oily column of black smoke.

Kendrick said, 'Must conduct our progress as an operation of war . . . decide at the dam, what next.'

An hour passed. They began to move forward. The first quarter of a mile was the worst – a vivid agony. After that, it was a slow, plodding numbness of horror. At last the dam took shape in the drifting smoke, and Kendrick stopped.

'Foster, up the steps. Shoot any armed man you see. Smith – with him. Mohan, you cover them. Go, go!'

'No, I'm going first,' Mohan muttered. He stumbled forward. Each one of the hundred and eighty steps up the centre of the face was pain. For the last fifty he could feel Smith bodily pushing him. When he reached the top he fell down. Dimly he heard Smith say, 'No one here. The spread of the fire has upset their plans.'

Mohan crawled to his knees and looked round. The coolie camp was a tangle of burned and burning huts, some black, some red, some orange. The whole of the Dobehari Ridge was burning. To the south and east the jungles towards Deori had not caught. He looked again. They had. Eight or nine miles away, on the outskirts of the city, a line of black smoke lined the horizon. Not a human being was in sight.

Kendrick, Barbara, and Foster joined them. One of the jackals had survived, and now crawled past and down the outer face.

'Rukmini, Rukmini,' Mohan groaned, and knelt, hunched, his eyes closed. He forced himself to his feet. 'Now – ' he said.

Chapter Twenty-Nine

An arrow sighed past his head and fell, clattering, on the stone. Too exhausted to duck, Mohan scanned the cliffs at the southern end of the dam, whence the arrow had been fired, but saw nothing. Smith urged them all down the outer steps and off the dam. As they went another arrow hit the stone behind them.

In the ruins of the coolie camp they stopped. 'That arrow went over a hundred and fifty yards,' Jim Foster said resentfully.

'He was above us, and the wind was with him,' Smith said. 'We're safe here. We're safe anywhere as long as no one can hide within a hundred yards of us. Until nightfall.'

'Until nightfall?' Kendrick croaked. 'Here? No. Go to Deori.'

Mohan said, 'There's a fire that way, too. We'll never get there through the jungles, with the Gonds waiting for us.'

'This fire must have been seen from Deori,' Kendrick said.

'They have their own fires to worry about,' Smith said.

'The cavalry . . .'

'Are at Purankhola.'

Mohan tried to recall what they had taught him at Sandhurst. They must have water, if possible. And an open place to defend themselves. No help from Deori would reach them until tomorrow morning. It was about eleven o'clock now. Nearly twenty-four hours.

Smith said, 'We won't have to worry about water, soon.' He nodded towards the east. Over there the sky had turned a deep purple-blue. Under the purple a bar of primrose yellow ran across a forty-degree arc of the horizon, leaving a thinner band of angry green between it and the blurred blue of the distant hills.

'A mango shower,' Kendrick muttered.

Foster laughed, without mirth. Mohan smiled with him. Sometimes those 'mango showers' were like tornadoes – a dust storm, cyclonic wind, rain in buckets.

'Where can we go?' Mohan asked. Several places were suggested and discarded. At length Smith said, 'I think Indra's Rock is our best chance. No one can be above us, it's bare, and we'll be protected on one side, at least, by the cliff.'

They moved off in a small diamond-shaped formation –
Mohan at the point with the rifle, Foster at the right with the
pistol, Smith at the rear, Kendrick and his wife at the left, where
they would be moving along the edge of the pit.

On the slope leading up from the coolie camp, as in the pit, the
scrub had burned out, but the bigger trees were still on fire. They
moved very slowly over the charred land and among the burning
trees, and, seeing no one, came after twenty minutes to the
beginning of the Dobehari Ridge. As they reached the spine of it
the desolation spread out plainly around them. Cheltondale was
a smoking pile of twisted beams in their path. Across the valley
the village of Konpara still burned furiously. Southdown and
the Rest House had gone. The Konpara Ridge stood devastated
from end to end, the fire still raging along the western flank.
Smoke and flames boiling up from beyond it showed that the
woods round Tiger Pool were burning, but to the north, above
the Konpara Cliffs, the jungles had not caught.

The wind had died. There must be a local wind round those
farther fires, but here there was nothing, and Mohan found the
silence more terrifying than the noise to which he had become
accustomed. Smith called, 'That's the storm coming. The wind
always dies first.'

Mohan's tongue felt thick and painful in his mouth. There
would be no water at Cheltondale. The bhistis had always
brought it by hand from Tiger Pool.

It was lucky Smith had brought the rifle. But obviously Smith
had suspected a trap. Another thought struck him. He stopped.
'The other rifles,' he cried. 'They must have got them. We're
sitting ducks for anyone with a gun!'

Smith said, 'I think not. Mr Kendrick's bolts are in his safe.
That only leaves yours, and Huttoo Lall would not risk arousing
the servants' suspicions by trying to get it. This was going to look
like an accident.'

Mohan led on. They passed Cheltondale. A little later he
became aware of a low, continuous noise which he could not
identify. It grew louder as he advanced, and sounded like a
distant train, then like a waterfall. Everyone had heard it, and
Kendrick was looking round with renewed bewilderment.

Foster recognised it first. From his position at the right of the
diamond he hobbled across to the edge of the pit and looked
over, Mohan following. Directly below them a thick column of
pure green water leaped out of the mouth of the conduit and
arched down to burst in a low thunder of white spray among the
blackened devastation of the pit floor. It was an impressive sight,
though it made Mohan's tongue swell painfully.

'I suppose they've jammed open the inlet gate in Tiger Pool,' he said. 'But why? To drown us, if we'd still been down there?'

'That would take days,' Smith said. 'I think it's to prevent us using the conduit as a shelter. We might have been able to lower ourselves into it. That means this has been done since we left the coolie camp. We're being watched.'

Five minutes later they reached Indra's Rock. A short search showed that no one was hiding within two hundred yards of the flat summit. They all looked at Mohan. He realised that they were waiting for his leadership. But why do you look at me, he thought angrily. You are all older than I, and more experienced. Any one of you should be able to say what must be done – except perhaps poor Kendrick, whose attention wanders so that I am not sure that he always realises where he is, or what has happened . . . and I am thinking of Rukmini, and looking across the blackened hills, and crying out, Where are you, let me come to you.

He was the Suvala, and they were acknowledging it. If he was the Suvala these people who were trying to kill them were his own people. He should be able to think as they thought, and so guard this little party of strangers until help came.

He said, 'They have been watching us, and they are watching now. But the spread of the fire was not planned, and they are disorganised. No attempt will be made on us until dark. Or during the storm. It will be dark and confused for two or three hours then.'

'What's happened to all our servants?' Foster asked. 'The coolies. My new foreman. Are they all in it? Or have they all been killed?'

Mohan said, 'They've been sent away. The headman could give orders as from us, as soon as the fires began – to collect valuables, go to some appointed place. There must have been great confusion. One man speaking with authority would be believed . . . We must get to work.' He eyed Kendrick doubtfully; but he'd have to be trusted now. Mohan handed him the rifle, and said, 'Will you sit on top here, sir, and keep watch?'

Kendrick took the rifle and turned it over in his hands. His expression brightened. 'Yes. I'll keep watch. And if I see any of them . . .' He laughed loudly.

Mohan led the others down the north face of the rock. The ground was covered with isolated tangles of thorn scrub that had burned to black charcoal without crumbling to the ground. Each made a patch of cover which would certainly hide a man in dusk or storm. Mohan said, 'We'd better start pulling these down.'

Barbara Kendrick said suddenly, 'Wait! Will the wind reach us before the rain, before the clouds?'

Mohan answered impatiently, 'Probably. It usually does.'

She said, 'It's coming! What's the time?'

'About noon, a little earlier.'

'That's near enough.'

Foster said, 'We'd better get to work.'

'Wait,' Barbara insisted. 'Watch!'

The light turned a sickly yellow and the wind came, at first in short, sharp gusts from the south, then more steadily. To the east the Deori Plain vanished under a brown-yellow pall, and overhead the sky sank slowly upon them. The wind caught the waterfall, the familiar mist formed, a rainbow began to take shape, then vanished as that gust died.

The wind set in steady and hard from the south, increasing every moment in force. Barbara Kendrick called, 'Now look!' She was on her feet, her grimed face ugly in its concentration. 'The rainbow!' The rainbow took full and perfect shape under the strong wind, spanning the Konpara Cliffs in an arc of violet, red, orange, yellow, and blue.

Foster said, 'We ought to . . .'

Barbara Kendrick cried, 'Where are we standing?'

Smith said, 'Indra's Rock.'

'And this ridge is called Dobehari, meaning . . .'

'Noon.'

'It is noon now. And who was the ancestor of the Suvalas?'

'The Lord Indra.'

'His weapon?'

'The bow. Indradhanus,' Smith said. 'Indra's Bow. The rainbow.'

'It is four days after the Rite of the Labourers,' Barbara said, 'but that's close enough. Look!'

The smoke from the fires flowed flat and fast towards the north now, making the atmosphere extraordinarily dark but shot through with a yellow glow from the sun, like a London station on a foggy day with bright lamps trying to burn through from a high roof. The rainbow, its colours slowly becoming more lurid, stretched across the sky, the left end seeming to rise from the valley of the Deori River near the Buddha Tumulus, the right end falling to earth on the Konpara Ridge, a little to the right of the ruins of Southdown.

Barbara said, 'Standing on the Noon Ridge, at noon, in Indra's country, Indra's bow seems to rest there.' She pointed. 'At the right hand – the left is the unclean side. The cave was made by artists and priests, not by engineers. There is the mouth of the cave – there, *there*! Where the caretaker's hut of Southdown stood.'

Kendrick had joined them. 'What's happening?' he asked anxiously. 'What are you all pointing at?'

His wife turned on him. 'When we first built Southdown, what stood there, where the caretaker's hut was?'

Kendrick said, 'What? What's that got . . .?'

'Tell me!'

'There was a big pile of wood,' Kendrick said, 'ready to be burned for charcoal. When I planned the bungalow, the headman said we'd need a caretaker's hut. I agreed. They took the wood away and had the hut built before work began on Southdown.'

'The mouth of the cave is there,' Barbara Kendrick cried. The wind howled across the rock, and the air was full of black and grey ash. The sun had vanished. She said, 'Rukmini's there. She understood, yesterday, because she is – Rukmini. Oh, why didn't I see it sooner!'

Kendrick shouted, 'There's nothing there! Right in our own compound, all these years! You've got art on the brain, rainbows, waterfalls . . .'

Barbara said, 'The people who built the cave didn't know what caused the rainbow. It wasn't something pretty and harmless to them. It was the Bow of God!'

Mohan stared hungrily across at the Konpara Ridge. Southdown had stood near the point where the level top of the ridge began to slope gently down towards the village. A few yards beyond the edge of the back lawn, where the servants' quarters had been, a rock spine worked its way out of the soil, rose to ten or twelve feet in height, and sloped on down with the ridge. Near the beginning of that outcrop, not more than thirty yards from the servants' quarters, the caretaker's hut had stood against the rock. He had never been in it, but he remembered asking the headman once, perfunctorily, whether the quarters and the hut had any cave or hole opening out of them, and the headman assuring him with a sad smile that there was nothing of the kind.

'The caretaker was the headman's brother,' Smith said.

Kendrick said, 'He was, but . . .'

Mohan said, 'That settles it. I'm going.'

Barbara said, 'And I, with you.'

Charles Kendrick tried to seize her, but she wriggled out of his grip and ran away down the slope, Mohan close behind. He remembered that Kendrick had the rifle and, feeling cold in the small of the back, turned quickly.

Kendrick held the rifle half raised, but Smith stood beside him, very close. Smith called, 'I'll stay here with Mr Kendrick. We'll hold Indra's Rock in case you're wrong and have to come back. Jim, you go with them, and keep that pistol up where it can be seen.'

Jim Foster ran down the slope to join them. Smith and Kendrick stood silhouetted against a dark, oncoming mass of dust, earth, ash, and smoke.

Then with Barbara on his left and Foster beyond her Mohan began to run. The wind smoked among the standing army of dead trees. Here and there it found a bough split like a reed, and made a droning roar. The sun had gone from the sky and the rainbow from the fall. They crossed the shallow valley and began to climb the Konpara Ridge. Foster shouted, 'If it is the place, and if Rukmini's inside – alive – someone will be on guard.'

Mohan said, 'Only to prevent her getting away. One, two men . . . Split here – I'll go right, you and Barbara left.'

They approached the rock spine from different angles. Mohan reached the top first, and cautiously looked over. A dark, naked man sat half asleep against the other side of the rock almost directly below him, a long-handled hatchet in his hand. Jim's head appeared thirty feet to the left. The pistol glinted a moment as he aimed. He fired. The sitting man jumped where he sat and did not move again, blood and brains leaking out of his smashed face. Mohan scrambled down the rock face and met Jim and Barbara.

Ten paces to their left the burned-out planks and timbers of the caretaker's hut lay in an orderly pile against the foot of the rock spine, crosswise and endwise as they had burned and fallen.

Mohan said, 'Keep watch. 'I'm going to have a look.'

Jim muttered, 'Be quick. Visibility's getting very bad.'

Mohan stepped cautiously into the wreckage. Near what had been the right corner of the back wall of the hut the rock turned sharply in a sort of buttress before continuing its northward course down the ridge. The face of the buttress had been cut into to form a doorway, three and a half feet wide and five feet high. Mohan drew a deep breath and, crouching, entered the doorway.

The entrance ran straight in, at the same dimensions as the doorway, for five feet, then turned sharply to the left. The sound of the wind was louder there, roaring and bellowing in the confined space. The floating ash particles made his eyes smart. He turned the corner, and found total silence, almost total darkness.

He waited, his heart pounding steadily and loudly. He'd got to know what was here. He'd had some matches in his trouser pocket. When he put his hand down he remembered that they had exploded during the fire, and burned his thigh.

He reached up. The roof was over six feet here, and he could stand. He began to walk forward. The floor sloped sharply downward, but was cut and smooth-paved under his feet. The walls had fallen back. His reaching fingers told him that the passage was five feet wide here.

At forty paces the gradient lessened and he came to another right-angled turn. He stopped. Forty paces between right-angles, and no one in that length, unless they were crouching low against the wall. A rifle and a pistol could defend that as long as the ammunition lasted. More enemies might be hiding farther down the passage . . . but he was sure there were none; the place smelled of the emptiness of centuries. 'Rukmini!' he whispered, but there was no answer.

He hurried back, and crawled out. 'We must get the others here,' he said briefly, and explained what he had found. Jim said, 'I'll go,' and clambered up the rock spine. At the top he sank to his knees, but slowly, his eyes turned to the north. He said, 'Three men are coming up the side of the ridge towards us, from the direction of Tiger Pool.'

'After us?' Mohan asked.

'I don't think so. They're moving carelessly. No one saw us come over the ridge.'

'They must have! Or heard the shot!'

'Smoke, wind,' Jim said. 'Lie down!'

Mohan and Barbara lay down among the burned timbers and waited. After a long anxious wait the pistol roared above them. Mohan jumped to his feet. Two villagers stood transfixed beside a blackened bush ten paces off, staring over his head at Jim. A third man lay twisted at their feet. Jim fired again, but missed. The two men turned and fled like madmen down the slope.

Mohan went out to the fallen man. It was Huttoo Lall. Barbara knelt and put her hand on his heart. 'Unconscious but not dead,' she muttered. The bullet had gouged a trough along the side of his face, and he bled heavily. Mohan said, 'We'll take him in with us. Perhaps we can make him tell us why they're trying to kill us.'

They bent to the wounded man, struggled with him to the mouth of the cave, and left him there. Then they scrambled up the rock to Jim's side. 'We must get Smith and Kendrick,' Mohan said. 'Can they see a signal?'

'Don't think so,' Jim said. 'I'll go.'

'Wait.'

Indra's Rock, a quarter of a mile away, showed but dimly through the murk, and then only for seconds at a time. The wind had sucked the debris of the fire out of the pit and a huge black column, hundreds of feet thick, rose and writhed into the sky before the upper wind caught it and brought it rushing across the valley towards the Konpara Cliffs. Mohan waved his coat frantically, but the wind hung it out like a board in his hands, and it was so dirty that it blended in with the background of sooty sky and cliff.

Barbara, looking down the ridge, said calmly, 'A lot of men are gathering on the common grazing land beyond the village.'

'They've lost their leader,' Mohan said. 'We've got a few minutes before another takes his place.'

'They've started from the rock,' Jim cried. 'They're coming!'

Now Mohan saw two hurrying figures for a moment. Then the storm hid them. A moment later he saw them again, running down into the valley. He watched carefully to see whether they were being followed in the rear or on the flanks, although he did not think it likely. The attack on the rock was to have come from this ridge. The villagers were gathering for it now. The headman had come up to reconnoitre.

Smith and Kendrick were much closer. Thousands of tons of topsoil from the Deori Valley flew past in solid carpets, ten feet thick. The wind tore at his grip and it was hard to breathe – but Rukmini was in the cave, and alive. Otherwise, why would they have put a man on guard outside it?

Smith and Kendrick reached the ridge. Heavy drops of rain began to fall. Jim yelled exultantly, 'It doesn't make a bit of difference now, except that we can have a drink. There're a couple of old kerosene tins in the wreck, Mohan. Put 'em out to collect water.'

They hurried to the cave mouth. 'Get the headman in!' Mohan shouted.

'I'll stand watch at the entrance,' Smith said.

The rain turned from drops to a thunderous torrent, like the breaking of a dam. Behind Barbara, and Kendrick, and Jim Foster, and the inert body of the headman, Mohan crawled into the tunnel. As he passed Smith, the latter murmured, 'See that no harm comes to Huttoo Lall.'

Chapter Thirty

Kendrick had some matches, which had not exploded during the fire. Mohan waited impatiently in the black tunnel, the shallow, irregular breathing of the wounded man loud beside him. A match scraped, and its tiny light burst out in overpowering brilliance. He had to close his eyes for a moment. When he opened them the hurricane lantern had been lighted. Its glass was cracked in two places. Who had had the sense to carry that through the fire? Smith, of course.

Kendrick seemed to have reached some understanding with his inner confusion. His voice was firm, though a little too loud in the confined space. 'How long is this stretch? Forty paces? This is where we shall hold them, then, if they come. Everyone move round the next corner. The lantern will have to be at the corner, where it can shine down this stretch. Foster, tell Smith to stay at the entrance until he is actually driven in. When that happens, he is to come back as fast as possible until he is past the light. Mohan, help me move Huttoo Lall.'

'I'm going to look for Rukmini,' Mohan said.

'In a minute,' the Resident snapped.

Barbara picked up the lantern. Mohan and Kendrick raised the wounded man. Their shadows slanted grotesquely across the ceiling, and fled slowly ahead of them down the long slope of the passage.

Kendrick said, 'What's that?'

They set the wounded man down. Mohan knelt. A neat stack of yellowish blocks lay ranged against the tunnel wall in six rows of five, except that the top block of the row on the extreme right was missing. Twenty-nine bars of gold. Nearly a million rupees. Mohan lifted a bar. It bore the mark of the trident, the bull's head, and the four small bows – the same device as on the bar found under the 'planted' Buddha, and the bars the Pathans had tried to steal. The Archivist said that was the mark of the Suvala who'd been defeated and exiled in 147 B.C. Obviously all the bars bearing that mark had come from this sheltered hiding-place.

They bent again to the headman. The light showed that the floor was smooth, with a slightly curved indentation in the centre, such as might have been made by thousands of feet, over many years. At the corner the tunnel turned right, and, after five paces, left again, then continued its original course. In that short angle they set the headman down.

Kendrick said, 'Sit down. We have a long time to wait. I shall turn the light out in fifteen minutes, and thereafter only use it if we are attacked.'

Foster came down the passage carrying a heavy kerosene can. He set it down and Mohan saw that it was full of water, the water black with ash and dirt. 'It's raining like blazes,' Foster said. 'Running off the rock ridge like a stream, so the tin filled quickly. Smith doesn't think we should try to fill it again. You can't see even three yards outside now.'

Kendrick nodded. 'You've drunk? And Smith? Very well. Now the rest of us.'

They drank, in turn. Mohan said, 'Now, I'm going to find Rukmini.'

Kendrick said quickly, 'You can't take the lantern. Or the rifle.'

'I'm not taking anything,' Mohan said, 'but I'd like to see round the next corner. Bring the lantern that far with me, Jim.'

Foster picked up the lantern at once. Kendrick hesitated. 'Hurry then.'

Mohan set off, Foster beside him. As soon as they passed the corner Mohan whispered, 'See that no harm comes to the headman, Smith said.'

'Oh,' Foster muttered. 'Why . . . who? Does Smith think he'll help us?'

'I don't know. Just stay close to him . . . All right, turn back now.'

'Good luck.'

Total blackness enfolded him. Mohan walked slowly on, and down, one arm outstretched in front, one touching the side wall. Three times he came to right-angled corners, but each was always followed at once by another to the left, so that the direction remained constant. From the position of the doorway and the original turn to the left, he thought he was heading towards the Dobehari Ridge somewhere near Cheltondale – but under it, for already he must be a hundred feet lower than the entrance.

Two hundred paces. The air current blew steadily and gently into his face, cool but thick with a smell of wood smoke.

Three hundred paces.

Three hundred and twenty-seven. Three hundred and twenty-eight.

He stopped. 'Light,' he whispered, then remembered he was

alone. He crept forward, round two corners. The light grew strong in his eyes, a yellow glow illuminating everything as clearly as the sun. The floor in front of him ran level for ten paces, and there a huge stone plinth across the ceiling marked the point where the tunnel entered something much larger.

A woman lay against the wall under the plinth. Her legs were towards him, wearing Rukmini's familiar slippers. The pale blue sari was raised a little over the carelessly flung legs, showing a length of calf. A big square can, which Mohan recognised as his reserve can of gun oil, stood at her head, and beyond that a hurricane lantern, its wick low, burned steadily.

She was breathing evenly. Mohan walked very carefully down towards her. Beyond the plinth the ceiling was higher. Many pillars cast long shadows, and in the further darkness pillars and walls and ceiling seemed to join. He knelt beside her. She looked extraordinarily clean, her face shining like a golden moon. Of course, she had disappeared before the fire.

'Rukmini,' he said softly.

She stirred, opened her eyes, and sat up. She looked at him as though she did not know him, and said, 'Am I alive? Is it you, Suvala?'

He held her tightly. 'Are you hurt? Did they bring you here?'

She said, 'Yesterday, because the tigress had attacked you and I felt real, helpless fear, I *saw* the rainbow, for the first time, as my ancestors saw it. I knew at once, then, where the cave was. Last night I spoke to you. You know what you said. This morning – how long ago was it? – I expected to die here. If I found nothing here, I could not face you or the world again. If I found the Venus-Queen here, I would take my rightful place beside her, and join her, soon, in death. It would be better than the half-truths of life . . . Mohan, have you seen the caves?'

'No,' he said.

She stood up slowly, holding on to his shoulder for support. 'You shall see them, now.'

He said, 'We must go back and tell the others you're safe first. Can you walk?'

'Yes . . . Why are you so dirty?'

Mohan told her quickly about the fire, the continuing attempt on their lives. She listened intently and, when he had ended, said, 'Huttoo Lall is in the tunnel, too, then? Good.' She picked up the lantern. 'I emptied out your rifle oil and filled the tin from the lanterns in the house. Leave it there. We shall be coming back.'

They started up the sloping tunnel. At a hundred paces the yellow light shone on the white skeleton of a large snake; and forty paces farther, upon the skeleton of a tiger. 'Those, too, I would have joined,' Rukmini murmured. 'They have been here a long time.'

The light from the other lantern shone dimly round a corner ahead. Something must be happening. Kendrick had intended not to use it except in emergency. Mohan quickened his pace. They turned the corner.

Barbara Kendrick's face lit up with joy, and she rushed past him. Rukmini, smiling, received her in her arms. Kendrick and Smith and Foster were on their feet. Huttoo Lall lay on his back, his eyes open.

'Is it safe farther down?' Kendrick asked at once. 'Is anyone there?'

'It's safe. No one there.' Now Rukmini was clinging to Smith, and his arm was round her shoulders. Mohan heard a heavy sound of thudding from ahead, but Rukmini was embracing Foster and the tunnel was full of love, all but one smiling, and Mohan felt light in the head and wanted to sing.

Kendrick said, 'They're doing something on top, near the entrance. Digging, and using crowbars. I think they're going to blow the tunnel in, about thirty feet back from the entrance. I brought Foster back. We don't know what's happened to the dynamite in Foster's explosive store.'

'The store was burned down,' Foster said. 'I saw that when we passed the coolie camp.'

Smith said, 'We must assume they took the dynamite first. Several of them know how to use it. They intend to wall us in. Then, when a party comes out from Deori they'll say that we must have been burned in the pit, which is filling with water and will be impossible to search.'

Mohan said, 'We have a few days. They can't flood us out quickly. They have no means of making poisonous gases. Fire can't affect us, nor smoke, even if they could make sufficient.'

Kendrick said, 'We'll go farther in. That digging is too close.'

Mohan stooped to pick up the headman's legs. The dark eyes flickered momentarily across his face, and then reverted to their frozen, upward stare. 'He's conscious,' Mohan said. 'He knows what's happening.'

Kendrick said angrily, 'I've tried to make him talk, but he will not.'

The slow return down the tunnel began. At last they stopped under the plinth where Mohan had found Rukmini.

'What's that?' Kendrick asked suddenly, pointing to the rifle-oil can. Rukmini told him and he muttered, 'Is it full? If we use only one lamp, that ought to give us nearly forty hours of light. Turn the other lantern out. We may need the wick.'

'Not yet, please,' Rukmini said. 'I am going to show you the caves.'

'I don't want to see them,' Kendrick said violently. 'I wish we'd never started this senseless search. It was your idea . . . How did you get in here?' he finished suspiciously.

She said, 'I went to the caretaker's hut. I knew he had no woman. It was about one o'clock in the morning. I imitated the voice of the headman's wife – it is easy; she has a hoarse voice and uses a strong dialect – and whispered at the door that Huttoo Lall wanted to see him at once. He came out soon, and I called to him from a little way down the path to hurry. Then I crouched in the bushes till he had passed – and went into the hut. The cave mouth was hidden behind a charpoy upended against the back wall, in the corner. Of course, I knew he would find out someone had been there, and guess it was I, when he learned that Huttoo Lall had not sent for him.'

Kendrick said, 'If you'd told us, instead, none of this would have happened.'

'Yes, it would,' she said calmly. 'The plan of the fire was ready, and they only had to make a few changes to use my disappearance. Perhaps they would have said it was you who were in the pit, Mr Kendrick, and had discovered the cave . . . You were down there before the others, weren't you?' Kendrick did not answer. Rukmini said, 'Will you come and see the caves now?'

'No!' Kendrick shouted. 'I don't want to, and I warn you, whatever is in them will make no difference to your position.' He subsided. 'The rest of you go. I'll keep watch here, and look after the headman.'

Rukmini said, 'We must take him with us.'

'Why?' Kendrick snapped. 'What good will that do?'

'Much, perhaps.'

Kendrick turned his back and stalked away from them a little distance up the tunnel, the rifle under his arm. Again, Mohan wished he could get hold of that rifle. The Resident's bursts of temper were becoming more unreasonable every hour. Kendrick turned again, glowering. 'Go on, then,' he said. 'I shall wait here, on guard.'

Rukmini bent over the headman and spoke in a low voice, in Hindi. 'My friend, you must walk between us. We are going to enter the caves that you and your people have guarded so faithfully.'

A small moan escaped the headman's bloodless lips.

'Lift him,' Rukmini ordered. They raised him carefully to his feet and put one of his arms round Barbara Kendrick's neck, the other round Jim Foster's. His feet moved slowly, dragging, between theirs. Smith carried the lantern. At Rukmini's side Mohan passed under the great plinth.

Chapter Thirty-One

A giant figure sprang slowly at him out of the opposite wall. Human, it had four arms, each brandishing a mighty weapon. Its advance was supported by an army of beast-men with the heads of elephants, tigers, and bulls. Rukmini said softly, 'Indra's army . . . the fathers of your fathers, Suvala.'

Mohan saw then that the giant figure was not really large, but perhaps only five feet tall, and the others much smaller. In the distance, hewn without perspective and larger than the rest, the whole group was commanded by a tall, handsome figure wielding a huge bow.

They moved slowly into the great hall proper, which Indra and his army guarded. Scores of pillars marched away into the darkness, and every wall, every pillar moved and pulsed with a living creation of stone. The figures leaned out of the stone over them. Here a long-haired naked woman died under the trampling hoofs of advancing horsemen. Here again, the same scene, and again, and again. Again and again the woman died, from decapitation, from a sword thrust in the belly, from arrows, from being cast off a high place. Here white bulls, sacred bulls, died under the axe, and there horses and elephants. Death stretched fifty feet along one wall, where countless captive men and women knelt, and the arrows flew into them. Here Indra strode in triumph through clouds, the great bow in his hand and skulls below his feet. The stone pillars were carved and shaped as though they had been made of wood, and on them proliferated the tortured images of slaughter and sacrifice. Blood dripped from the cold stone, and, most horrible of all, the expressions of the warriors were calm and lovely as they killed and burned – for there were houses burning, and great temple-like buildings on fire.

'See – your fathers, and mine,' Rukmini whispered.

Everywhere the sculptors had shown an essential difference between the killers and the killed. The defeated masses were small and squat, their faces sometimes exaggeratedly simian, sometimes beautiful, but always different, with their broad cheekbones and square shapes, from the tall, straight-nosed, lank-haired heroes who destroyed them and their works.

They moved on. In a far, dark corner the light shone on the broken-off point of a sword, lying under a pillar. The metal was dull, but not rusted. Near by a stone warrior's nose had been broken off – the only damage they had so far found to the sculptures – and several square feet of the stone floor were darkly stained.

'Here the impious sons rose against their father. *Nor stayed the king his hand inside the holy place*,' Rukmini said. 'Two hundred and sixty-five years before Christ. Perhaps they were the last people to come here.'

Barbara Kendrick said, 'This is a hall of death, like Chaucer's Temple of Mars. "There saw I first the dark imagining of felony, and the compassing." '

'It is not death that is terrible,' Rukmini said. 'It is cruelty – human felony, as your poet said. The Hall of Human Felony . . .' She turned quickly to the headman. His breath was coming in short, ugly gasps, and the eyes were bolting from his head. 'This is only the first hall, father. There are two more, which tell a different, better story.'

The lantern light shone on another doorway, marked like the first by a heavy plinth. They passed through.

In shape this hall was a duplicate of the first: the same size – sixty feet square; the same forest of pillars; the same vivid creation of life in the stone. Mohan braced himself for further pain. The ancestors of whom he had been so proud were brutal murderers, rapists, and pillagers.

Gradually he relaxed. The world of this hall was a world of peace. The scenes were fewer and larger, giving an impression of immense space and even height, as though the sky were the ceiling of the cave. The carved figures stood or lay or moved amid a deep, surrounding calm. The women were naked or wore slight, ornamental draperies, which twined gracefully from slender waists about their long legs. Always the round breasts were uncovered. The effect was not religious in a priestly sense, but as though the peace of God informed each moment of the lives of the people. And this God had sent emanations of himself, that could be comprehended because they were in human or half-animal shape, who brooded, smiling slightly, over the various scenes. The smaller people were here again, not suffering death now, but at work in menial positions. Mohan noticed a tall lady completing her toilet, standing by a carved tree. Three women of the defeated race knelt at her feet, washing them, and adoring her; and a nurse held the tall woman's child on her hip, the child shown as large as the nurse.

Mohan looked at his companions and saw that they were all smiling, even the headman. He was smiling himself.

'The Hall of Contemplation,' Rukmini said.

'Or of Peace,' Barbara Kendrick said.

'Much later than the first,' Smith said. 'Centuries later. The technique of the carving is quite different, more sophisticated.'

They came to a third plinth, leading into a third hall. Mohan heard Barbara Kendrick's short gasp . . . The man on the wall waited for a woman, a subtle smile on his face, knees braced and eyes wide, the phallus enormous against the smooth skin of his belly. On the opposite wall the woman smiled at the man, breasts raised, mouth loose, arms spread, hips thrust forward, legs wide, knees slightly bent.

Rukmini's arm gently enfolded his waist, her head caressed his shoulders. Walking thus, they moved forward. A hundred lovers made pause in their proud coupling as they passed. Pyramids of male and female united over them, standing, sitting, kneeling, lying. Here, unmistakable, was the Rainbow Fall, with Indra's Bow arched above it and the arrested spears of water falling on the upturned faces of a score of young men and women. Hands wandered lovingly over breast and nipple and thigh and phallus. The heat of a thousand ecstasies possessed him. Rukmini's flesh trembled where he touched it. The headman stood alone, his thin, thumbless left hand supporting him against a pillar. Jim Foster and Barbara Kendrick stood with arms round each other's waists.

Smith raised the lantern. The light showed that they were almost at the far end of the hall. The colour changed, and Mohan saw that inside a small area, enclosed by three pillars and a length of the back wall, the carved stone had been coated with gold – everything, the pillars, and the walls, and the ceiling, and all that had been carved upon them.

Freestanding – not carved in relief, but a full statue – stood a tall gold man, naked and erect, his smile half proud, half voluptuous. To right and left, on the other pillars and on the back wall, stood or knelt many men and women, all naked, all in attitudes of adoration, all carved in relief, and all smaller than the golden hero.

'The Suvala!' Rukmini cried in a loud voice.

All – the hero and the adorers – were gazing at the centre of the back wall. Here a huge cobra, delicately carved and plated with gold, writhed up the wall and, a little below the ceiling, spread out its hood to form a canopy four feet in extent. On the floor directly below the canopy there was a low, round platform of the same size. The platform was unoccupied.

195

Mohan looked about. Rukmini had slipped away from him into the darkness but he hardly noticed. Something was missing. Surely all these men and women were not adoring the golden cobra? He started violently . . . There was a man standing close beside the cobra, almost invisible in the subtle shadow, but when you looked he was there, right arm outstretched in the action of giving. He was a man in middle age, his expression fatherly and proud. His left arm lay against his thigh, and the hand had no thumb.

For a moment Mohan, thinking he was dreaming, struggled to find some fact that would prove to him, one way or the other, whether he waked or slept. His mind tried to move logically forward from one observed, tangible event to another; but the realisation that there was now no absolute difference between dream and reality, between flesh and stone, between past and present, came upon him unseen from behind, overtaking and absorbing the halting process of logic. His astonishment that the stone elder should have no thumb faded into acceptance of a single reality that could not be divided by dimension, substance, or time.

Thus he saw, beyond the man with the outstretched hand – Gonds, half a score of them, unmistakable, with bows and quivers of poisoned arrows. The jungle trees twined about them; their dark, aboriginal faces peered out in wonder and friendship at the empty platform, and mingled with them in the leafy shadow were a leopard, a wild pig, a mongoose, two monkeys, a jackal, and two tigers.

Now certain of what he would see, and his understanding released from the bondage of time, Mohan looked to the other side of the cobra. There stood villagers with axes in their hands, babies on the women's hips, a silent anonymous multitude, and their cattle under yoke among them. Nearest to the cobra stood a pair of lovers, naked, arms twined round each other, the woman's head lolling blissfully on the man's strong shoulder. Beyond the villagers, alone, a lean ascetic figure watched, long staff and begging bowl and antelope skin in hand. He stood on one leg, naked like all the rest, the other leg twined round his staff, every rib showing stark against the thinness of his body, the deep-set eyes gazing, like the rest, at the empty platform.

Mohan searched everywhere with his eyes. Where was he, the last one? He must be here! 'Behind you,' Smith said in a deep, strange voice. Mohan turned.

The pillar against which he stood, the one closest to the golden hero, was carved with a terrible scene. On top of a great cliff a three-headed, six-legged, six-armed monster wrestled with itself.

One head was that of a man, one of a snake, one of a jackal. The arms ended variously in talons, paws, and hands. It was Indra's Rock on which they fought. He recognised the shape, seen from below, as though he were looking up at it now from the fiery pit. He saw that there could only be one end to the struggle taking place on the bare summit. Whichever part of the monster won, in its hate and triumph it would hurl the others into the pit; but all three were irrevocably joined together.

'No,' Smith said in the same strange voice. 'It is no one man. It is the demon that had to die before the scenes in the first hall could become the scenes in the second and third – the three-headed demon of hate, pride, and fear. It is the demon that cannot be conquered. It can only be recognised – and then it destroys itself.' Mohan remembered that Kendrick was carrying the haversack, where he had put the poisoned arrowheads. Later, later! Let the fears and doubts resolve themselves later. He stared hungrily at the empty platform under the cobra hood. 'What was there?' he cried. 'What are they adoring?' Without sound Rukmini glided out of the darkness, across the floor, one light step on to the platform, naked.

Thus she moves also across the grass, dancing, and the triumphal mating of the lingam and the yoni is stated in her walk, without possibility of knowing whether it has happened, is happening, or will happen, and three weeks are the same as three thousand years, and three thousand years as an instant, this instant.

Turning to face them she raises her arms. Her elbows bend subtly one way, her wrists another. Each finger, one by one, takes attitude, and stays. Balanced firmly on one square-planted foot, the other knee rises, the foreleg bends down and across, the toes stiffen. Her head tilts, her eyes open wide. Her breasts rise, swell to perfect roundness, and still. A patina of non-motion, of arrest of living, spreads over her, and she does not breathe. Dancing, immovable, she hangs between the golden cobra hood and the red floor.

No one moves. Flesh and stone stand together, without knowledge of difference in substance between them, time flowing in one direction for some, for some in another, for others, motionless. The headman's arm is outstretched, and behind the Venus of Konpara her father, hand outstretched, gives his daughter to the king in marriage. Smith stands, hands spread, and the wandering beggar stands, one leg twined about his staff. Jim and Barbara stand close, and the loving couple. The villagers watch, with the Gonds, and the beasts of the jungle and field. The giant golden figure of Indra sweeps across the ceiling above them all, one hand raised in blessing, the huge bow fast in the other. All are focused on, all emanate from the magnificent naked generosity of the dancing woman.

Mohan, and each one there, came to a swooning crisis of love as overpowering as a sexual ecstasy, but total, releasing the tension of spirit, flesh, and soul in a single spasm, like the release of a full-stretched bow. In the long-drawn, shuddering harmonies of the aftermath Rukmini glided off the platform.

Mohan waited, head erect, while she stooped low before him, touched her right hand in turn to her forehead and to the inside of each of his calves. Gently he raised her, and she stood a moment looking at him. Then, making the deep namasti once more, she passed into the darkness.

The headman broke the silence. 'We did not steal the gold, Suvala. We had authority from the Suvala to use it for the guarding of the cave.' His voice was weak but firm.

Mohan shook his head, recalling himself from the timeless ecstasy of understanding to the less real realities of the moment. 'What Suvala?' he asked.

'That, I do not know,' Huttoo Lall said.

Smith said, 'The one who reigned in 147 B.C. It is his mark on the gold near the mouth of the tunnel.'

'The others, the bars found under the leg of the statue,' the headman said, 'of those we knew nothing – neither of the gold nor of the leg. We have done wrong, Suvala, and will gladly accept punishment. If any of us had known what was here . . . None of us has ever entered the tunnel past the corner beyond the gold.' He spread his hands, palms upward.

Rukmini appeared, clothed, and touched him. 'Sit down, lambardar-ji. There.' She helped him and he sat back against a pillar, his eyes closed.

'But why?' Jim Foster broke out. 'Why did you guard the cave so . . . so desperately? *Why* didn't you go into it?'

The headman whispered, 'Death, sahib. Death, for us of the old race.' He sighed, and looked at Smith. 'Tell them, sahib. You know the past.'

Smith said, 'The villagers of Konpara are Dravidians. It was their ancestors who fled to Deori before the Aryans, and then to Konpara. It was their ancient civilisation which the Aryans destroyed. They were the slaves who were forced to hew out the tunnel, and make the first cave, the Hall of Human Felony. When? 1000 B.C. – not later. It was their ancestors who were thrown off Indra's Rock to preserve the secret of the cave. No one of their race, who once entered here, ever returned alive. For nearly three thousand years the men of Konpara – and the

Gonds – have known that what lay concealed here was evil, and *only evil*, and that its evil worked against them. When the dam was to be built they knew that the cave would be flooded, destroying that evil. Then the leg was found, and we began our search. The vital point, which we could not guess at until now, is that they were determined to preserve the secret *in order that the caves be destroyed*.'

'And the rest of the Venus never was down here,' Barbara Kendrick said slowly. 'I wonder where she is?'

'I don't suppose we shall ever know,' Smith said. 'For myself, I shall search no more. I do not want to see any other Venus of Konpara.'

The headman nodded at the carved figure beside the cobra, and held out his thumbless left hand. 'My ancestors have ruled here as long as yours, Suvala.'

'And from a time before caste,' Mohan said humbly. 'Will you give me, again, a daughter of your people for my queen?'

The headman stretched out his hand. 'Take her, Suvala. Treat her as a queen, for we were kings here when your fathers herded cattle beyond the mountains. Have no fear. There will be rejoicing among us all over your kingdom. As for the Brahmins . . . did she not discover the cave, through a miracle of their gods?' He smiled faintly, with a shrewd cynicism that spoke of five thousand years of civilisation. '*Our* gods were conquered, as were our people. But our gods live . . .' His hand swept the room, where the goddess of the first hall, there dying a thousand deaths, now ruled her conquerors. 'And so do our people.'

A heavy, dull hammering reverberated through the hall. Foster started and held up his hand for silence. The sound continued, paused, and began again. Foster hurried along the back wall, past the golden group. 'Bring the lantern,' he called. Smith took the lantern to him and held it high. Foster pointed to a thin crevice in the stone, which began half-way up the wall and continued back for a short distance along the ceiling. It had been there when the cave was made, for two members of an intertwined group were holding the edges for support.

'That's the crevice we have been blasting into,' Foster said. He listened carefully. 'Hard to tell . . . I suppose we were about fifteen feet off.'

The headman called weakly. 'It is my people, sahib. They are preparing to blow in the crevice.'

'They're doing the same at the far end, near the mouth of the cave,' Foster cried. 'We'd better get back, quick.'

They lifted the headman between them and hurried back through the three halls. At the entrance to the tunnel Kendrick swung round sharply as they appeared. 'It's all right,' Mohan said briefly. 'We must get up to the entrance before they blow it in.'

'What . . . what has the headman said?' Kendrick said.

'Nothing,' Smith said. 'He is going to call the villagers off, and accept punishment. He said nothing more, nor will he, ever.'

'There will be no punishment,' Mohan said.

They hurried on up the passage, Kendrick now in the rear.

Chapter Thirty-Two

The afternoon smelled of water and earth and damped fires.
Rivulets gurgled down the ridge, but it had stopped raining. The
villagers stood huddled over their picks and shovels and
crowbars. Behind them boxes of dynamite stood in an ordered
row, and, on one side, the detonators and the fuses. The black
Gonds stood in another group, bows in their hands. All their
faces were informed by fear, not the old time fear that could be
appeased by rites and actions, but modern fear, of courts, of
laws, of hangmen and ships that would transport them to imprison-
ment on distant islands. The headman had spoken to them
from the mouth of the cave, and the little party had been given a
hesitant permission to emerge. The Gonds had arrows fitted to
their bows.

Now Mohan stepped forward. 'It is all over,' he said gently.
'Let none speak again of this time. I am the Suvala, and this is my
promise. Your queen, too, greets you, with peace.'

Rukmini, at his side, made a namasti towards them all, turning slowly with palms joined. One by one every man and woman
returned the salutation. An extraordinary lightening of the
atmosphere took place on the instant. Fear vanished, and relief
came, to be followed immediately by joy. Someone shouted a
wild greeting – 'Hail to the Suvala, Heir of Indra!'

Rukmini raised her hand. 'Go now to your own places, in
peace,' she said, smiling. 'The time to celebrate will come . . .
The cave will be preserved, and the dam built. After three years,
as promised, you of Konpara shall go to new land in the valley
which once was yours.'

Aitu, standing in front of the Gonds, said. 'And *we* shall
remain in our own home.' His slow hand swept over the
unburned jungles on the upper plateau. 'Let the fields of
Konpara return to jungle, also. Let not the jungle be cut. It is our
home.'

Gradually they began to disperse. The group outside the cave
mouth stood watching them. Mohan began to think of the present. All the bungalows had burned down. It was about four

o'clock. He'd better tell Huttoo Lall to get some horses back, and then everyone could go to Deori. He turned towards the headman, who was leaning against the rock near the cave mouth, weak but transfigured with happiness.

Kendrick suddenly shouted, 'Look out! Cobra! There!'

Mohan swung round. Rukmini stood still, looking at the ground near her feet, where Kendrick had pointed. Smith broke into a run, but towards Kendrick.

'Where?' Mohan cried. 'Keep still, everyone!'

A heavy thud and a gasp behind him made him turn. Smith was still a pace or two away from Kendrick, but Foster had reached him, and they were wrestling on the ground, Foster's hand grasping Kendrick's near the wrist, twisting and turning furiously. 'You bastard,' Foster shouted. 'You . . .'

The rifle fell from Kendrick's hand. His struggles ceased. Foster picked up the rifle. 'He was aiming at the headman,' he said. 'It would have been an accident.'

Smith groaned aloud. 'I told you, sir, everyone has told you – there will be no more talking, and no punishment!' he cried in a tortured voice. 'You could have started again!'

Kendrick stood up, panting, his cheek twitching violently. 'Do you expect me to believe that?' he cried. 'Do you think I don't know you were just waiting to get his evidence down in writing, trying to make me feel safe in the meantime?' He raised a shaking hand and pointed it. 'It won't do you any good! His word against mine! Every one of you is against me, and always have been. Every single one. All my life.'

Barbara Kendrick threw one long horror-struck look at Jim Foster and then took a step forward. 'Charles,' she said. Her voice was low and husky. She took another step. 'Charles . . . I'm not against you.'

'Barbara!' Jim cried.

'Whore!' Kendrick screamed. 'You're going to leave me, too. Do you think I don't know?'

Mohan thought Barbara would faint. 'I shall not leave you,' she said. 'I will stay with you, and stand with you, for ever, whatever you do.' Jim Foster, his eyes closed, his face white, leaned against the rock spine.

Kendrick said, 'Do you think I'm going to believe that?' He turned on Rukmini. 'You started it. You planned it. You set Mohan against me, turned Barbara into a whore . . .'

He leaped suddenly at her; one hand fumbling in the haversack at his side. The hand came out, the broken shaft and dull head of a Gond arrow in it. Foster raised the rifle. The headman of Konpara moved half a pace forward and put out his foot.

Kendrick tripped, and fell heavily. He climbed slowly to his feet, bleeding from the right hand. Foster held the rifle aimed at his heart. Kendrick opened his hand, the poisoned arrowhead fell to the ground.

He looked at his palm, and muttered, 'Of course.' Barbara stood stiff, watching him, unable to move.

It was Rukmini who ran to him, and held him fast as he sagged slowly back against the rock, close to the cave mouth. He turned his face up to her and she held the glazing eyes on her own, so that they seemed to be lovers, her arms wrapped around him, until, very soon, he gave a deep, shuddering groan, and died.

Rukmini stayed a long minute with him, then she folded his hands carefully on his chest and rose, weeping, and went to the shelter of the Suvala's arms.

Postscript

Those readers who would like to learn more about the inner history of *The Venus of Konpara* may be interested in the following report, which was prepared in A.D. 1930:

(Author's Note: *All references in this postscript, as in the story, to events that took place in Deori or Konpara are imaginary, but in accordance with archaeological theory. Other references, such as those to the Harappa discoveries, are actual fact.*)

Mohan Singh Suvala, Rajah of Deori, in the fortieth year of his reign, has ordered this report prepared on the Caves of Konpara, and the circumstances of their rediscovery. No eyes but those of the Ruler and the State Archivist may be permitted to see it until A.D. 1960, when, seventy years having elapsed since the events described, all those who had a part in them may be expected to have passed beyond the reach of earthly reward and punishment.

The report falls into two parts. First, that relating to the building of the caves and the earliest history of Deori; secondly, that relating to the events of A.D. 1890.

PART ONE

Supposing the Aryan invaders of India to have reached Deori about 1400 B.C., the fortress of Konpara would have been built about 1300 B.C. Traces of the wall of this fortress were found on the Dobehari and Konpara Ridges by Rajah Mohan Singh's excavations in A.D. 1892 and 1893. The dividing walls first uncovered by Mr Smith at the cricket pitch site proved to have been part of the dwelling quarters allotted to the royal household.

Soon after the fortress was completed the Aryans built, inside it, the shrine and memorial of their great conquest. This was the Hall of Human Felony and the tunnel leading to it. The date of completion of these works is unlikely to be later than 1200 B.C.; but, whatever the absolute chronology, it was certainly made soon after the great wars of the conquest. Indeed, the conquest may still have been continuing in other parts of India, for the atmosphere here is one of triumphant war, of recent victory over enemies whose evil gods are still powerful. The Dravidian cities and monuments which the Aryans are shown destroying were not necessarily in Deori. A great victory five hundred miles away and fifty years back might be shown, for the men who took part in it were still alive, and had come to Deori.

These two works, the tunnel and the first hall, were the products of Dravidian slave labour, working under a few Aryans who had a greater artistic genius than any Dravidian – the Vedas prove that – but no technical ability to transform their vision into stone. The Aryans were cattle herders, only recently come from the Asian steppes, while the Dravidians had built great cities.

Since this was an Aryan shrine its efficacy had to be preserved from the enmity of the subtle Dravidian gods and goddesses (particularly the latter). Those gods could be expected to find entry, for hostile purposes, through their devotees; therefore no Dravidian must be permitted to enter the cave, or indeed to know the exact whereabouts of its entrance inside the great fortress. To this end the slaves were forced to carry the debris from the construction to a considerable distance – to what is now known as the Buddha Tumulus. When their useful work was finished they were murdered by being thrown from Indra's Rock in the rite which has been perpetuated under the name of the Rite of the Labourers.

The wooden brooch used in the modern rite is the counterpart of the original tally issued to each slave, marked on one side with his name, symbol, or number, and on the other with the device of the Suvala who owned him. Three of these wooden tallies were recovered intact during the careful excavation of the Indra's Rock Tumulus which took place in A.D. 1890, causing a six months' delay in the opening of the Kendrick Dam. (No hardship resulted to the people of Deori from this delay, as a part of the gold recovered during that year was used to buy wheat, food grains, and seed for the people.) The steatite brooches, of which thirty-seven were found during the same excavation, were the private property of certain of the Dravidian slaves, perhaps of important men or women, nobles, priests, or the like. The similarity in design between the wooden tallies and the steatite brooch/seals is probably due to the fact that the Aryans copied the steatite seals they found the Dravidians wearing – and indeed were perhaps taught by the latter how to use numbers to identify and differentiate their captives.

The other two halls, of Peace and Love, show such an advance in technique that they must be much later. Even more important is the change of theme, and the settling down of relations between the races. The people were still divided in a class or colour pattern, but the division was not based solely on fear, nor was it immutable. Indeed, the central scene of the Hall of Love shows the Aryan king accepting in marriage the daughter of a Dravidian aristocrat, and, we may assume, thereby elevating her to his own level in the newly formed caste system. Both halls were probably made under the driving impulse of a single ruler of genius – the golden hero of the Hall of Love – who desired to show the spiritual and social progress that had been achieved in Deori since the original usurpation. The time was the fifth century B.C. This may be stated with certainty because the gold used to plate the statues bears the simple bow mark only used until the fifth century B.C., while detailed studies of the Hall of Peace reveal an unmistakable bodhisattva in the background of one of the scenes, and the Buddha lived from 560 to 480 B.C.

To summarise: The caves show the newly arrived Aryans destroying the Dravidian civilisation in about 1250 B.C.; and they show how, eight hundred years later in about 450 B.C., a social and religious system had been built under which both parties could live in peace. They show how the conquered Dravidians yet imposed their dominance on the invaders, for the very goddesses who were being attacked in the first hall have become triumphant in the second and third. The caves have thus shown that the elements of Brahminism which are so much at variance with the classical Vedic religion of the Aryans came from nowhere else but the rites and beliefs of the conquered Dravidians, after a lapse of several centuries.

The opening of the caves to the public, in A.D. 1891, caused sensation and controversy which were to last for thirty years. The problem was essentially no different from that posed by the Vedas – if the Dravidians had indeed built such great cities as those shown being burned and destroyed, where were the relics of them? Argument and accusation flew back and forth among the learned men with regrettable venom, and doubts were even cast upon the genuineness of the caves, until 1922 of the Christian era.

In that year Indian archaeologists discovered, at Harappa in the northern Punjab, and at Mohenjo-Daro on the west bank of the Indus River two hundred miles north of Karachi, the relics of a pre-Aryan culture – the missing Dravidian civilisation. This Indus civilisation, as it was named after the location of the discovered sites, flourished from about 3000 to 1500 B.C. It was a riverine culture, depending for its food upon the rich, flat, alluvial plain of the Indus. Its people were intensely organised, and it contained great cities. These cities were planned in an extraordinarily 'modern' manner, not excluding an ugly and uniform monotony for their low-income housing developments. They had running water, drainage, and sewage systems, and show evidence of a way of life far superior, in terms of what the world has agreed to call material civilisation, to anything else found in India until the late nineteenth century A.D. The art objects found, principally steatite seals, with some statuettes, show a high level of craftsmanship and decorative ability but little genius or creative vision. The religion of the Indus civilisation seems to have been diffuse, composed more of a blend of local and family cults than of a single state religion; but certain ideas were common to all these cults. They are: the worship of the cow and bull, and of a male figure associated with the bull; the worship of a female figure, perhaps a goddess, perhaps a generalised idea of fertility; and worship of the lingam-yoni.

These discoveries have proved the existence of a material Dravidian civilisation. Perhaps there was more than one, though so far only that settled in the Indus Valley has been located. This civilisation was destroyed by the Aryan invaders, who did not know how to live in that manner and would not then have wanted to if they did. It has been 'lost' because its sites in the alluvial plains would quickly be buried by the deposit from annual floods once the bunds, the dams, and irrigation works were allowed to fall into disrepair.

Neither Konpara nor Deori was the original site of the Dravidian civilisation – the country is not alluvial nor riverine – but both were places where Dravidian refugees, perhaps from Harappa, sought to hide from the savage, persistent invaders.

To return to the caves – the chief problem outstanding is that of the so-called Venus. (Reference here is to the original statue of which only a leg has been found, not to the present statue, carved by the famous English artist Barbara Foster in A.D. 1900, and placed under the cobra head by the Suvala in that year.) Detailed study of the central group in the Hall of Love shows that the golden hero-king's ears are of different sizes. He also has a striking but unhandsome and untypical setting of the eyes. The statue was therefore not a stylisation, but an actual portrait. It must be assumed that the Venus was also to be a portrait. Both were free-standing statues, not carved in relief out of the living rock. The work could therefore have been done elsewhere than in the caves. If so, it certainly must have been, for we cannot imagine the royal couple being able or willing to spend weeks in the depths of the caves when it was much more convenient for all concerned for the sculptor to work in a studio above ground.

It is suggested that the Venus statue, the last work of all, was nearly ready when the fortress was thrown into confusion by one of those rebellions or *coups d' état* which are so common whenever a multiplicity of wives and concubines produce many rival heirs to the throne. The rebel would most likely have been a son of the king by a wife who had lost pre-eminence, both for herself and her son, when the king decided to marry 'the Venus.' We may suppose the rebel son to have been victorious. He would not have damaged the statue of his father – which was already set up – for that would be unthinkable sacrilege. But his mother would certainly have caused the execution of the Venus and the destruction of her statue. This statue would still have been in the sculptor's studio above ground – at the cricket pitch site. Probably the pieces of the statue were further broken up, or removed as souvenirs. The sculptor, we may assume, was executed.

The gilding of the central group in the Hall of Love was carried out by a process still in use. The sculptors were given gold bars, which they melted, poured into shallow pans, and cut into pieces the size of small coins. These were then placed, individually, between sheets of parchment or papyrus and pounded until the gold became extremely thin. The gold leaf was then applied to the statues or surfaces with a siccative of egg and milk curd. When the latter had dried, the gold was burnished with pieces of ivory.

The chief sculptor of Konpara therefore had gold in his studio, and, although some accounting of it would certainly have been demanded, it is possible that he managed to cheat his employer, and hide the gold bar which was found by the leg (but lower down, it will be recalled – i.e., under the floor of his studio). It is also possible to suppose that the sculptor, being so near the completion of his work, had been paid in gold. It is of interest here to note that one of the gold bars found under the original leg, and which we now suppose to have been the wages of the original sculptor, formed the recompense given by the Suvala to Barbara Foster for the new Venus.

The fortress had been dismantled, as a fortress, about a century earlier, if we are to accept that the eclipse of 556 B.C. is the 'sun-darkening' which ruined it. (*Suvala-Gita*, couplet for 195 B.C.). What remained were the dwelling places and studios on the Dobehari Ridge – that is, a sort of summer residence; and the mouth of the cave on the Konpara Ridge across the valley. Although the relationships between Aryan and Dravidian had settled down, the cave would still only have been open to rulers, aristocrats, and priests – that is, to people who, under the growing caste system, could only have been of fairly pure Aryan descent. For the Gonds and the low-caste peasants it was a taboo. They would know that in the distant past numerous people of their race had been taken inside the fortress and had never reappeared until they were cast off Indra's Rock into the pit. They would know that the cave contained the power of the gods that had destroyed them. They would never enter it.

The years passed. In 265 B.C. another rebel set up his standard in the summer palace, and the ensuing battle spread to the caves. In 195 B.C., on the occasion of another eclipse, the Suvala made a special pilgrimage to Konpara, and offered prayers, presumably for the preservation of the state's prosperity.

The prayers were not answered, for in 147 B.C. the Suvala king of Deori was defeated *in his capital*, by evil demons, and forced to flee. (We may assume that the demons were the army of a hostile king.) It is important that the decisive battle took place at Deori, not in Konpara. There is thus reason to think that the new conquerors of Deori never learned of the existence of the Cave of Konpara. The Suvala would certainly have done everything possible to preserve that secret, for it was the shrine of his power. Destruction or possession of it would have ruined him and his race, for ever.

He preserved the secret by appointing guards. The nearest people were the villagers of Konpara, and there might have been some memory of the ancient union between a Suvala king and the daughter of the chief Dravidian of Konpara. The defeated Suvala may have passed through Konpara on his flight, or the orders may have reached the village by some other channel – but it is likely that at this point the village of Konpara became, collectively, the 'official' guardian of the caves. A wise ruler, besides reminding them of the fate which awaited anyone who desecrated the cave, would also have promised the village a payment for their duty – and this would have removed any inducement to betray their trust to the new rulers. Such must have been the purpose of the gold bars placed just inside the cave mouth – some for use by the village, some perhaps a portion of the king's private fortune, to be stored for safe keeping. The headman of Konpara has confirmed that from time immemorial one of his first duties, after his appointment or succession, has been to enter the tunnel to count and weigh the gold bars.

Neither the defeated king nor the villagers can have guessed that the Suvala family's exile from Deori was to last 478 years, until A.D. 331. The date, it may be noted, indicates that the Suvalas returned to power under the protection of the Emperor Chandragupta I.

In the course of those 478 years the Suvala family lost all

knowledge of the whereabouts and meaning of the cave that they still carried in the royal title, 'Lord of the Cave.' It would not be strange to find that in the same period the villagers of Konpara had lost the knowledge of exactly why they were guarding the cave mouth, and to whom they were authorised to reveal the secret. Alternatively, since the cave was known to be a shrine of evil meaning for Dravidians, the villagers may have lain low on the return of the Suvalas, in the hope that the supernatural powers which had caused their poverty and their subjection might become extinct through neglect. This closed system, of secrecy on one side and ignorance on all others, was broken by the discovery of the stone leg and the two gold bars on April 7, 1890.

PART TWO

The entrance to the cave had been hidden for a long time, probably since 147 B.C., by the device of placing over it a large stack of wood. The wood was burned to charcoal every year, and immediately replaced by a fresh stack. Mr Charles Kendrick's decision, in 1883, to build a bungalow on the ridge near by caused consternation, because it was obvious that Mr Kendrick would not permit wood to be burned so close to his bungalow. The then headman, Huttoo Lall, acted fast. He built the caretaker's hut before work on the bungalow had started. It was then easy to conceal the cave entrance behind beds, clothes, or other furnishings. The caretaker, of course, was always to be a village elder.

Next, in 1886-7, came the surveying for the irrigation works, and the decision to build them, which was taken on March 11, 1887, when the Resident called the headman into Deori and explained the whole project to him. The next day Mr Kendrick and Mr Foster, contractor, went out to Konpara with him and explained the layout of the work on the ground. The elders knew the approximate path of the tunnel and the caves. They also knew that there was a crevice in the pit cliffs, which might give entry to the caves, for the bats had been noticed centuries earlier. To make sure, a young man was lowered over the cliff, and the current of air verified, at this period. The elders were now sure that the filling of the Kendrick Reservoir would flood the cave.

From their point of view, salvation was at hand. After long ages the evil forces that had cast and held them down were to be destroyed by drowning. It was probably significant that this would come about through the instrumentality of a British Resident and a British contractor, for the British invaders were now going to do to the tutelary spirit of the Aryans precisely what the Aryans had done to them. And the completion of the irrigation works would give them rich land, of the sort from which they had been dispossessed three thousand years earlier.

The headman gathered the whole village, and the chief men among the Gonds, and told them what was to happen. A regrettable but perhaps natural debauch took place. Everyone was drunk for five days. Three men and a woman died, and two houses burned down. Then work began, and the people of Konpara laboured hard and well to ensure that their hopes came true.

Success seemed very near when the headman learned that part of an ancient statue had been discovered on the Dobehari Ridge. Next he learned that Mr Smith, an English gentleman of considerable archaeological learning, was taking charge of the excavation. The search for the Venus began. But the headman was sure that the Venus would be in the cave. He knew that once the cave was found it would be preserved, together with its power for evil; the reservoir would not be filled; the good land would not be given. It was pure chance that the cricket pitch where the leg was found happens to lie almost immediately above the caves, but the headman, knowing the general course of the tunnel, presumed that the searchers would merely go on digging and blasting downward, and would soon come upon the caves.

It was decided that the searchers must be put on the wrong track. A delay until the break of the monsoon would be enough. Someone knew of the deserted jungle shrine. The Buddha there would not be missed. A party set out at once and brought the Buddha back. The problem of where to 'plant' the false evidence caused considerable discussion. But since it was known that the Buddha Tumulus contained debris from the caves, that site was chosen. The tumulus, being of genuine antiquity, would keep the searchers busy and interested, yet it was a long way from the real point of danger. The joint Konpara-Gond council (of which women were always members – itself indicative of a distinctly pre-Aryan outlook) decided that the emergency justified the use of some of the gold from inside the cave entrance, in order that the well-known European cupidity might help in their salvation.

The stratagem failed, by a very narrow margin, and it was agreed that the Gonds should call their still more ancient jungle gods into the battle. The Gonds did, and for a long period the man-eating tigers delayed the search for the Venus.

After Mr Kendrick had killed one of the tigers it was decided that the Lady Rukmini, who was regarded as a reincarnation of the Venus and who was believed to be guiding the searchers to her own shrine, must be sacrificed in the same rite, for the same purpose, and on the same date, as the original labourers had died.

This attempt also failed, and with regret the council decided that all the searchers must die. The plan involved diversion of the

Deori army, the setting of huge fires that would prevent movement for at least twenty-four hours, and the inveigling of the
whole party into the pit. If the victims had escaped from the pit,
execution was to have been carried out by the Gonds, and the
bodies subsequently charred and put in the pit. The Lady
Rukmini's entry into the cave caused a few changes to be made,
since the headman decided to use her as the bait, and she had to
be impersonated, and the impersonator had to escape before the
scaffolding was burned – but the real cause of the plan's failure
was the unexpected spread of the fire.

After the party's final escape the Resident and Administrator,
Mr Charles Kendrick, I.C.S., died as the result of an unhappy
accident. The caves could not have been discovered without his
active intervention. For the rest of his soul and in memory of all
those who had been concerned, from the beginning, with the
caves, the Rajah decreed the erection of a large pillar on the
summit of Indra's rock. On clear days this pillar can be seen
from nearly all points in the state, and is known as the Kendrick
Memorial (or, in the vernacular, *Indra-ke-lingam*). On its base is
inscribed in Sanskrit, Tamil, and English –

*May the One hold in mercy Charles Kendrick and all who died
here in order that the caves of Konpara might pass their message
to man –*

> *In fear, hate; in hate, death.*
> *In death, love; in love, life.*

By the Green of the Spring

JOHN MASTERS

1918 dawns desolate over the fields of Flanders. Decimated by the worst war the world has ever seen, neither British nor German troops can break the deadlock of the trenches. After four years of murderous stalemate, peace seems buried for ever. But finally, one by one, the guns fall silent . . .

BY THE GREEN OF THE SPRING
relives the last terrible months of the Great War and the uneasy, exhausted peace which followed it.

BY THE GREEN OF THE SPRING
from the North-West Frontier to the war in France and the civil war in Ireland, John Masters follows the fortunes of four Kent families – the Cates, the Rowlands, the Strattons and the Gorses – through the cataclysm that ended the golden Edwardian dream for ever.

BY THE GREEN OF THE SPRING
is the third, self-contained volume of the **LOSS OF EDEN** trilogy, a magnificent conclusion to an enthralling epic of war and peace by a major contemporary novelist.

GENERAL FICTION   0 7221 0468 5   £2.50

A selection of bestsellers from SPHERE

FICTION

TOUGH GUYS DON'T DANCE	Norman Mailer	£2.50 ☐
FIRE IN THE ICE	Alan Scholefield	£2.25 ☐
SOUVENIR	David Kaufelt	£2.50 ☐
WHAT NIALL SAW	Brian Cullen	£1.25 ☐
POSSESSIONS	Judith Michael	£2.95 ☐

FILM & TV TIE-INS

MOG	Peter Tinniswood	£1.95 ☐
LADY JANE	A. C. H. Smith	£1.95 ☐
IF I WERE KING OF THE UNIVERSE	Danny Abelson	£1.50 ☐
BEST FRIENDS	Jocelyn Stevenson	£1.50 ☐

NON-FICTION

WEEK ENDING: THE CABINET LEAKS	Ian Brown and James Hendrie	£2.95 ☐
THE POLITICS OF CONSENT	Francis Pym	£2.95 ☐
THE SPHERE ILLUSTRATED HISTORY OF BRITAIN VOLUMES 1, 2 AND 3		£3.95 each
	Ed. Kenneth O. Morgan	☐

All Sphere books are available at your local bookshop or newsagent, or can be ordered direct from the publisher. Just tick the titles you want and fill in the form below.

Name _____

Address _____

_____

Write to Sphere Books, Cash Sales Department, P.O. Box 11, Falmouth, Cornwall TR10 9EN.

Please enclose a cheque or postal order to the value of the cover price plus:

UK: 55p for the first book, 22p for the second book and 14p for each additional book ordered to a maximum charge of £1.75.

OVERSEAS: £1.00 for the first book plus 25p per copy for each additional book.

BFPO & EIRE: 55p for the first book, 22p for the second book plus 14p per copy for the next 7 books, thereafter 8p per book.

Sphere Books reserve the right to show new retail prices on covers which may differ from those previously advertised in the text or elsewhere, and to increase postal rates in accordance with the PO.